About the author

Kath Kincaid was born in Liverpool and now lives in Essex with her husband. She has three grown-up sons. She has written a variety of short stories and plays before MRS MURPHY HIRES A CLEANER, her comic debut.

Mrs Murphy Hires a Cleaner

Kath Kincaid

CORONET BOOKS

Hodder & Stoughton

First published in Great Britain in 2000
by Hodder and Stoughton
First published in paperback in 2000
by Hodder and Stoughton
A division of Hodder Headline

A Coronet Paperback

10 9 8 7 6 5 4 3 2

A CIP catalogue record for this title
is available from the British Library.

ISBN 0 340 76880 0

Typeset by Hewer Text Ltd, Edinburgh
Printed and bound in Great Britain by
Clays Ltd, St Ives plc

Hodder and Stoughton
A division of Hodder Headline
338 Euston Road
London NW1 3BH

For Juliet Burton

CHAPTER ONE

There was a colour photo around somewhere that
Alexander Murphy had taken of his wife, Emily, in the
garden of their semi-detached house in Formby. It was on
the occasion of their daughter Mary's first birthday, and
showed a lusty, beautifully built young woman grinning
teasingly at the camera, a fresh-faced Juno, with thick
brown wavy hair half-way down her back, creamy skin and
a wide, strawberry red mouth, though Emily had never
used makeup. Mary was mounted saddlewise on her
mother's jutting hip, held safely in place by a large,
perfectly curved arm. The other arm tucked Gareth, then
three, against her leg. Emily wore a loose, filmy blouse over
a flowered dirndl skirt and a straw hat with a frayed brim.
Like the photo, the hat was still around, probably in the
attic with the children's old toys.

'You look like an earth mother in this,' Alex remarked, when he collected the film from the chemist. He had the negative enlarged and framed to stand on his desk at the laboratory where he worked. It made him feel particularly blessed. He was married to the only girl he'd ever wanted, and had two lovely children. They had a perfect house with a perfect garden. He was a perfectly happy man, and a glance at the photo on his desk showed that Emily shared his feeling of Arcadian bliss.

That was before Alex discovered Money.

More than two decades later, a bewildered Emily Murphy still hadn't grasped that things had changed. She still thought of herself as an earth mother, even though she was forty-five and it was seven years since Gareth had left home. Mary had followed two years later. Emily's greying hair, the same length, hung down her thickening back, usually plaited into something resembling an elderly rat's tail. The once creamy skin had become a dreary grey, scattered with spots around the chin, largely due to Emily's diet of chip butties and sugary things. She still didn't use makeup. She still wore loose blouses and long dirndl skirts. In her awkward, desperate way, she was trying to pretend she was the woman Alex had bedded and wedded, the woman in the photo, who had once been the most important person in the world to her husband and children.

There were times when Emily felt unable to hold on to this pretence, and she would wonder if she was dead. She saw herself as a branch that had snapped off a comfortably rounded tree and been left hanging by a few shreds of bark that the sap no longer reached. These doubts about her mortality, or lack of it, did little for Emily's confidence and sense of well-being.

Emily woke up one fine sunny morning in May to an empty house silent except for the creaking of the three-centuries-old structure as the spirits of a thousand souls shifted restlessly in its multitude of nooks and crannies and dark corners. The Murphys, gleaming spokes in the wheel of the Thatcherite revolution, had moved from the Formby semi twelve years ago to this seventeenth-century cottage nestling within a small copse in Ince Blundell. The children had sulked at leaving their friends behind and at having to be driven to school and their various clubs and parties.

'People will think we've gone dead posh.' Mary pouted.

Gareth and Mary had had the siren songs of socialism

sung to them since before they could walk and talk, and found confusing the sudden switch to the hip-hop beat of capitalism.

'You're a class traitor, Dad,' Gareth said accusingly.

'Yeah, yeah,' yawned Alex, as he read his bank statements.

Thorntons had been the country home of Robert Eldwell Thornton, a Victorian novelist of little esteem and small output, but nevertheless a name of sorts to be reckoned with in the annals of English literature. Set in two acres of grounds, the tiled-roof cottage was heavily beamed, with mullioned windows, two winding staircases leading down from each end of a small gallery, and a real well containing dirty, poisonous water in the glorious vintage garden. The house was haunted. Or perhaps Emily was. Despite the central heating, the annual cost of which would have kept a small family in relative comfort, the place was difficult to keep warm, impossible in the depths of winter. 'Cottage' was something of a misnomer, as Thorntons had five bedrooms, four reception rooms and two bathrooms, plus numerous little dens and snuggeries that nowadays the Murphys could find no purpose for.

'I am not dead,' Emily said aloud, to the black-beamed yellowing ceiling that loomed threateningly overhead, seeming low enough to touch, and the sound of her own voice half convinced her of the truth of this statement. She was at least half alive. She glanced at the clock: nearly half past eight.

The pillow beside her own was as smooth as it had been when she'd got into bed, alone, the night before, which meant that Alex had slept in his study again. She tried to remember the last time they had shared the bed, but couldn't. A memory skipped its way through her lethargic brain, of two youthful, sweaty bodies slipping and squelching against each other in healthy, lustful passion to the sound of the Rolling Stones on the rickety record-player. Outside the window of the bedsit in Seaforth where the sweaty couple had lived when they were first married, the river Mersey frothed and spumed. The memory limped away to join others, equally significant, or insignificant, Emily wasn't sure.

She sighed hugely and the bed and the floor sighed with her. She pushed back the clothes with the stiff, mechanical movements of a zombie, put on the loose blouse, skirt, and old leather sandals she'd worn the day before, and plodded heavily out of the room, along the gallery of the hushful house that rarely woke — four of the bedrooms were largely unused and the clothes went damp on the beds.

Thorntons faced south-east and the sun shone through the low casement windows at the front, making dazzling crisscrossed patterns on the wooden floors, which were badly in need of a good polish, and a million particles of dust danced madly in the brilliant, slanting sunbeams. Imperceptibly Emily quickened her pace to pass through these spotlit patches, as if forced to walk on to a brilliantly lit stage when she preferred to stay in the wings. So encased was she in her own misery, she was unaware of anything in the house other than the space in which she walked and the dark and light areas she passed through, though she could smell the dust, as well as the dry rot, the woodworm, and possibly the death-watch beetle.

The tiled surfaces of the vast kitchen were silhouettes of untidiness, a New York skyline of boxes, tins, bottles and dishes, clean and dirty. This had once been Emily's queendom, a place where she had felt completely at home, and cleaning it had been a joy. She sighed again as she put the kettle on. It still felt warm, which meant Alex must have used it recently. Hopefully, she went into the big, square hall, which was dark and mottled with darker shadows from the trees outside, and knocked on the study door. No answer. She went inside. The curtains were drawn, the computer was on, the screen line after line of bright green print, and the couch where Alex had slept was crumpled. Emily picked up a tartan rug and folded it. She straightened the cushion on which his head had rested, holding it briefly against her face. It smelt of his black curly hair, his skin. She touched it with her tongue, as she had touched his skin all over, at another time, in another place. The cotton material felt dry and tasteless, as Alex might well do now, she wouldn't know. Apart from the crumpled couch, the room was otherwise spotless: books in stiff precision on the shelves, the papers on the desk neatly in piles. She imagined his long white hands putting the stapler back in its place between the bowl of paper-clips and the tub of variously coloured pens. There was a tier of three wire baskets holding files, the top one labelled HAUPTMANN-WAGEN in his square, bold script. It must be to do with the German contract he was so desperate to get.

The computer beeped and Emily jumped guiltily. The machine was linked somehow to the office in Skelmersdale. The green print melted into a single spot, which got tinier and tinier as it journeyed back into the screen, then exploded like a firework in a shimmer of multi-coloured stars. A chart appeared.

Emily shuddered. She couldn't get on with computers. She heard the kettle click and went to make the tea. On the wall directly in front of her, next to the phone, the diary-cum-calendar, showing a month at a time, was blank apart from a single entry in Emily's own shaky writing for Monday, 19 May.

'INTS.'

What the hell was 'INTS'?

She didn't even know what day it was. Yesterday, her mother had phoned. As she always called on Sundays, unless Emily had lost a day (it had happened before), today must be Monday. After further straining her sluggish brain, she eventually concluded that today was indeed the nineteenth.

Which meant that, later today, INTS would happen. INTS would come, or perhaps she was supposed to phone INTS, or INTS would phone her. It was her own fault, Alex would say. She was too bloody lazy to write whole words.

They would have had fun making sense of INTS once, she and Alex. Emily put her head on one side and a smile lurked around the pale, sad lips; International Nest of Traitorous Spies, Institute of Naughty Thwackers and Sadists.

Interviews.

Two candidates for the job as cleaner, at £3.50 per hour, Twelve till Four, Mondays, Wednesdays and Fridays, Fares/Petrol Paid, References Required, Responsible Persons Only Need Apply, Telephone Mrs E. Murphy, were due at ten and eleven o'clock respectively. Emily felt both daunted and excited. These days, cleaners were the only people over whom she had a scrap of influence, whose lives she could remotely affect, who took the faintest notice of her, who would listen. Consequently, to make her presence felt, she followed them around pointing out things that hadn't been done, becoming a more and more severe taskmaster, though she was always patient and polite. After all, she thought reasonably, if a job's worth doing, it's worth doing well.

'Not for three quid a bleedin' hour!' Mrs Betteridge had muttered angrily, when Emily had unfortunately shared the same reasonable thought with her three weeks ago. Other women had left, driven to distraction by Emily's constant interference, usually giving a week's notice and a lame excuse, but Mrs Betteridge had told her to screw the job up her fat arse and left on the spot.

9

'She hadn't cleaned the downstairs toilet properly,' a hurt Emily told Alex that night, when they ate their late-evening snack, the only meal they shared together. 'She said she was fed up scrubbing other people's shit.'

Alex laughed sarcastically. 'No one will do menial tasks any more. No wonder there's still so many people unemployed.'

'I thought if I offered another fifty pence an hour I might get a better class of person.' Emily was glad there was something to talk about. Thorntons, and its upkeep, was one of the few points of communication they shared nowadays.

'Don't go overboard, Em. It's fifty pence multiplied by twelve, another six whole quid, more than three hundred a year. Just think what people can do with three hundred quid, if they're careful. I thoroughly approve of the trickle-down effect, wealth from the rich trickling down to the poor, but we don't want to cause a flood.'

The 'Em' made her feel girlish, a bit giggly, the way she'd been when they first met at university. 'Yes, but don't forget how much we save on Eustace.' Eustace was their octogenarian part-time gardener.

'Eustace looks upon gardening as a hobby,' Alex said primly. 'People don't expect to get paid for their hobbies. Anyway, Eustace is past it. He's lucky to have a job of any sort at his age.'

There had been a time when Alexander Murphy, the well-known Marxist-Leninist, would have given a stranger his last penny. In his younger days, he had marched under banners too numerous to mention, all in support of left-wing causes. It was Alex who had organised the sit-in at university when students had protested against the rise in rents. An emotional man, he had almost cried when Mrs Thatcher was elected in 1979. Eighteen years later, in support of the forthcoming election, Thorntons had a 'Vote Conservative' poster in the living-room window, another sore point with Mrs Betteridge.

Alex's personality had changed some. It was a curious fact that the more money people had, the more tightly they held on to it. Instead of his last penny, Alex gave beggars stern lectures on the joys of work, which was available if they would only care to look. At least, he did until the incident with the beggar's dog. Since then, he had merely looked the other way.

And Emily, an empty pot when it came to politics, was easily influenced. Emily had followed her husband staunchly to the left, then loyally to the right. She loved him to distraction. She believed in him totally. Alex was much cleverer than she was, so his views, of necessity, must be correct, though occasionally, secretly, she felt just the teensiest, weensiest bit uneasy about his loudly expressed opinions on immigrants and the unemployed.

She supposed she should make herself respectable for the interviews with prospective cleaners, but couldn't be bothered to get changed or comb her hair. She slithered into the shadowy hall in her too-big sandals and looked at herself in the antique mirror. I look fine, she convinced herself, though all she could see was a fuzzy outline. 'Where's my big wholesome lass? Where's my ruddy-cheeked milkmaid?' her father used to cry when he came home. He'd been a big man himself, a barrow-boy in the East End of London, with a hearty laugh and a beguiling wink that could sell mountains of fruit and veg to captivated housewives. He was laughing when he died, literally, watching a repeat of *Steptoe and Son* on television. It was a heart-attack, 'But what a way to go, watching his favourite programme,' Emily's mum said tearfully. Emily was the youngest of the three Paynter girls, an afterthought, born ten years later than her sister Beryl. 'A bloody big afterthought,' Dad would laugh. Neither Beryl nor Katie had minded when Emily went to the best schools then to university. The money hadn't been there when they were young, they understood that. Emily was the only Paynter who didn't have a Cockney accent.

She turned away from the mirror, worried at what she might see if she stared too long.

The house ticked away its silence like a bomb waiting to explode. She should put on some records, or turn on the television. But she couldn't be bothered. A part of Emily had died after her children had left home and Alex had stopped loving her. She'd mislaid her plug. There was nothing left to connect her to life's electricity. There were mornings when she couldn't be bothered to get up.

Three weeks of dust and dirt had collected since Mrs Betteridge had walked out in a huff. Emily checked the telephone pad. There was Mrs Porter, due at ten, and Ms McNulty an hour later. She remembered the rather soft, childish voice emphasising the 'Ms', and hoped it didn't mean the woman was a feminist who would refuse to clean the lavatory. She must make clear everything that had to be done during the interview.

Emily heaped cornflakes into a bowl, sprinkled them with two tablespoons of sugar, and took the bowl into the living room, where she sat on the chintz-covered window seat to keep an eye out for Mrs Porter. It was the only thing she could be bothered to do, eat.

There were four marks on the window where Sellotape had secured the poster. Labour had been elected three weeks ago with a thumping majority. Emily was almost glad that Mrs Betteridge had left, because she couldn't have stood her look of triumph. There was even, incredibly, a Labour MP for their own, middle-class constituency. Alex had gone berserk and stumped off to bed in a sulk. *That* was when they'd last slept together, she remembered. He'd been asleep when she got in, and she'd been asleep when he got up.

Ten o'clock passed without a sign of Mrs Porter. Emily helped herself to more cornflakes. It was a bad sign, being late for her interview, an indication the woman couldn't be relied on. Mrs Porter proved her unreliability completely by not turning up at all. As the clocks, the house, and life itself, ticked towards eleven, Emily, stuffed to the gills with cornflakes, found herself praying that Ms McNulty would come. There's no way I can keep a big house like this clean all by myself, she thought piteously, though she had done once, and taken care of the needs of two teenaged children, as well as the welcome, urgent needs of a highly sexed husband.

Precisely on the dot of eleven, a rusty estate car turned full pelt into the drive, rattling over the gravel, spitting stones from the rear tyres. It screeched to a halt outside, and a small, slight woman leapt out and slammed the door as if she was in a tremendous hurry. She looked very young, with a great mass of white-blonde hair snatched casually on top of her head with a gold bulldog clip, and hanging around her pale, rather insipid face in soft wisps and ringlets. She wore jeans, a white sleeveless T-shirt with a low neck, and gold sandals. Emily frowned. It was only a cleaning job, but she might have dressed a bit more formally. Not exactly a business suit, but jeans and gold sandals!

She went into the hall and opened the door. 'Ms McNulty? I'm Emily Murphy. Do come in.' The words sounded strange. Her voice sounded strange. It was the first time for several weeks that she'd spoken face to face to another human being, apart from Alex, the girl behind the till at the supermarket, and her own reflection in the mirror. She twisted her expression into what she hoped was a welcoming and superior smile.

'Hi.' Ms McNulty shook hands politely, her small hand gripping Emily's with surprising strength. 'Call me Mae – spelt with an E.' Her voice was high and sweet and rather breathless, like a child's, and went oddly with the distinctive nasal Liverpool accent.

'How do you do, Mae?'

Emily didn't waste time with formalities because she'd forgotten what they were. She began to show Mae McNulty around the house. The woman wasn't obsequious, but she knew her place. She said little, merely nodding now and then with an understanding 'I see', as Emily pointed out what had to be done. Emily was conscious of the light, impatient steps following her heavy, stately ones, as she opened door after door. 'This is the morning room, the dining room, the living room, the snug.' Initially, it had been enjoyable touring antiques and second-hand shops in search of furniture suitable for a period property. Now, everything and everywhere had the look of being unused, unlived in, as indeed it was.

They went upstairs. Emily had forgotten to make the bed and put away the clothes she'd worn last week and the week before and the week before that. 'I've been rather busy this morning,' she said gruffly, sweeping up the disgustingly grubby garments and dumping them on the floor in a heap, 'to wash later', straightening the duvet, giving the pillow a shake, thankful that the bedding was darkly patterned and didn't show the dirt. As befitting someone who was a cleaner, Mae McNulty's clothing was pristine, her white cotton T-shirt straining delicately over well-formed breasts that made her look slightly top-heavy, like a character in a cartoon.

'I see.' Mae nodded.

'This is my son's room.' Emily opened the door of Gareth's bedroom. The first thing that met her eye was the collection of stones on the top shelf of the bookcase. She used to collect the children from primary school and they'd roam the beach and the sandhills of Formby, searching for stones. She remembered Gareth's excitement, the way his brown eyes, so like his father's, would light up when they found a particularly outstanding one – the blue one, for instance, which had little shreds of glass inside. Emily went over, picked up the stone and rubbed it against her skirt. She stared into it, as if it were a crystal ball and she could see herself skipping along the golden sands with Gareth and Mary on the day the stone was found. 'Gareth comes home most weekends,' she said. 'Mary, my daughter, sleeps next door.' Both these statements were lies. Emily had seen neither of her children since Christmas, and was too upset and ashamed to admit it.

Mae spoke at length for the first time. 'It's a lovely big room,' she said admiringly. 'Your son's very lucky. My lads have to share a room, and now our Craig's turned twenty, he complains about sleeping in a bunk bed.'

'Twenty!' Emily gasped. 'You don't look old enough to have a son of twenty – and I didn't think you were married.' She called herself 'Ms' and didn't wear a ring. Emily immediately regretted the remark. She always made a point of not getting on gossipy, familiar terms with her cleaners.

'I'm not married, not at the moment,' Mae McNulty said lightly. 'And I'm thirty-four.'

She'd had a baby at fourteen! Emily hadn't joined in the previous government's hysterical rant against single mothers, particularly those in their teens who apparently roamed the streets searching desperately for unsuitable fathers with the sole aim of getting a council house, but she wasn't sure if she wanted one cleaning her house. Still, Mrs Porter, who might well have been a model of propriety, hadn't turned up, and Mae McNulty had made no objection to scrubbing the Murphys' shit in either of the toilets.

They went down the rear stairs to the kitchen. 'The

washing-machine and dryer are in the utility room,'
Emily announced. 'I'd like the ironing done on Fridays.'
There was only the bedding and Alex's shirts; he insisted
on a clean one every day. A few years ago, he'd opted for
business gear: sharp suits, white shirts, a tie, instead of
the usual jeans and casual tops. But, he complained
bitterly, Emily seemed have lost the knack of ironing
collars and cuffs.

Mae nodded thoughtfully. 'I reckon I can fit that in,
though it's a big place to clean. Have you got an electric
polisher?'

'Yes. All the tools are in the utility room.'

'Would you like me to start straight away?'

Emily's miserable heart lifted in a rare moment of joy.
There was nothing she would have liked more, but it
wouldn't do to look too eager, let the woman know how
desperate she was. 'I've still got two more women to see,'
she said, trying to insert a hint of reproof into her dull
voice.

'Oh, well, never mind.' Mae hoisted her white plastic
bag on to her shoulder. 'You've got me number. Perhaps
you could let me know when you've made up your mind.
It's just that me Monday-Wednesday-and-Friday lady
died last week, and I need the bread quick, like.'

That put a different gloss on things. Emily could take up the welcome offer and it would look as if she were doing Mae McNulty a favour, though she hoped it wouldn't make her look weak at the same time. 'Well,' she said hesitantly, then shrugged, 'oh, I suppose that would be all right. But what about references?' she remembered.

'Me Tuesday-and-Thursday lady will vouch for me, and I'll give you the number of the daughter of me lady who died.' Mae wrote quickly and neatly on the pad beside the phone. 'Don't ring the second number just yet. Today's the funeral.' She looked sternly at Emily with her dusky blue eyes, skilfully and heavily lined with black kohl. 'Don't forget to ring those other women while you're at it, will you?'

'Which other women?'

'The ones coming about the job. I wouldn't like them wasting their time. Oh, and we haven't discussed petrol. It said on the postcard in the shop winder . . .'

'How far do you have to come? Actually, I haven't asked where you live.'

'Kirkby.'

Emily blanched. She'd never been to Kirkby, which consisted mainly of miles and miles of council houses, one of the largest estates in Europe. 'That's a long way.'

'It's not all that far on a good road. I love the countryside and don't mind the drive.'

They agreed on two pounds a day for petrol. 'You may as well get started,' Emily said pointedly. She could always change her mind if the references weren't good.

Mae put a red nail to her chin, chewed her bottom lip and looked thoughtful. 'What I'll do,' she said, after a while, 'is go round the floors today with a soft broom, then give everywhere a quick dust. Then I'll do the bathrooms and give this place a good going-over.' She waved her hand at the crowded surfaces, the grubby cooker, the fingermarks on the fridge. 'Wednesday, I'll polish the floors and vacuum the carpets.' She grinned encouragingly. 'I'll soon have everywhere looking spick and span.'

While Emily much appreciated Mae's obvious dedication to the task in hand, she felt a flutter of resentment at the idea of the itinerary being taken out of her hands. But Alex would probably claim Mae was merely showing initiative. 'I'll leave things to you,' she said stiffly. 'The utility room's through there. I think you'll find everything you need.'

'Ta.' Mae almost ran into the adjoining room. Emily hung around awkwardly until she emerged with a broom and several filthy dusters.

'Why don't you have a nice long soak in the bath?' Mae suggested. 'You look fair whacked. You said you'd been busy all morning.'

'I think I might.'

'Don't forget to ring those women first.'

Mae ran upstairs. Emily called the speaking clock and the weather and told both the cleaning job had been taken, just in case Mae could hear. She trudged up to the bathroom, her step perhaps a fraction lighter than when she'd come down that morning. It wasn't until the water was flowing into the old-fashioned bathtub that she thought it was an odd thing to suggest to someone that they have a bath. She removed her blouse, hesitated a moment, then sniffed it.

'Phew!' She made a face, remembering the girl from school who'd had BO and everyone had made the same sort of face behind her back. Had Mae noticed and dropped a not very subtle hint? Emily lowered herself into the water. Best not think about it.

The bath was long enough for her legs to float, and she lay listening to the broom banging against the skirtings on the landing and the gallery, and around the edges of the carpets in the bedrooms. Mae hummed loudly as she worked. Every now and then, a door would open and the sound would grow fainter, then louder when she reappeared. Emily found the sounds comforting. Any human sound was welcome in the normally deathlike house, which had once echoed to the shouts of the children playing, or fighting over the television, or Alex yelling for some grub or peace and quiet, or where the bloody hell was the *Radio Times*?

After a long soak, and with the water almost cold, Emily soaped herself all over. Her arms and legs were still good she noted, like tree-trunks but the skin glistened and they were the proper shape. It was her torso that had gone to pot. There was no waist left to speak of and her hips bulged with mounds of fat. Christ knows what her behind was like, she daren't look. The feeling of shapelessness turned to one of hopelessness as she clambered out of the bath and nudged the plug out with her big toe. Why was she bothering? Who would notice that she'd had a bath? Who would care?

She felt almost tempted to put her old clothes back on, but remembered the stinking blouse, thought of

Mae, wrapped a towel around her bulky body, and padded to the bedroom.

'You look much better.' Mae beamed, when Emily went into the kitchen, wet hair combed, feeling fresher. 'Less fraught. I've made us both a cup of coffee. You know, you should eat fruit for those spots.'

Mae was undoubtedly a good cleaner – the kitchen was already beginning to sparkle – but she suffered from a singular lack of tact. 'I eat plenty of fruit,' Emily lied huffily.

'Then it must be something in your blood. Have you tried garlic?'

Emily shook her head wearily as she sat down at the pine table, which could seat eighteen at a pinch.

'Do you take milk and sugar, Em?'

'Both,' Emily choked. 'One sugar.' *Em!* The nerve of the woman. She was wishing she'd interviewed the others when a mug of coffee was put in front of her and she remembered they didn't exist.

'You've got a lovely home, Em,' Mae said earnestly, sliding into a chair opposite. 'It's quite the nicest house I've ever seen. What does your husband do to afford a place like this?'

Emily's first instinct was to sack her new cleaner on

the spot for being a nosy bitch, but then she saw that her brown arms were covered with a faint gleam of perspiration and tendrils of fair hair clung damply to the back of her slender neck. Her cheeks were pink and there were beads of moisture, a dewy moustache, above her lips. Close up, she didn't look the least insipid, and all the dampness and the pinkness were a result of getting Emily's house clean while Emily had been lying in the bath. Mae McNulty had worked hard. She was worth humouring. Emily didn't even resent the fact that she was being paid by the Murphys to drink the Murphys' coffee, as she had done with her other cleaners. 'He's in computers,' she conceded graciously. 'He has his own company. It's expanding all the time.'

'Computers are all the rage, aren't they? Me kids keep nagging me for one. I told them they'll be lucky.' Mae smiled. 'Is he from Liverpool, your husband? You're obviously not.'

'I'm a Londoner, Lambeth. Alex was born in Northern Ireland, but his family came to Liverpool when he was five. We met in Manchester when we were at university.'

It was on the first day of the rent strike that she'd met Alex. There were dozens of students sitting on the floor in the corridor outside the Dean's office chanting, 'Low rents, no rent rises.' They were, in the main, law-abiding young people who had never done anything remotely rebellious before, and their voices throbbed with a mixture of fear and excitement. Then a tall, charismatic young man appeared at the end of the corridor. Someone said, 'Here's Alex Murphy,' and the heaving mass fell respectfully silent for the leader of the strike.

'Comrades, we need about a dozen hardy souls outside the main lecture hall,' the young man shouted. He had had the suggestion of an Irish accent in those days. 'There's a front-bench politician about to arrive, the bleeder's got a fucking title, and the pigs are on their way.' Alex Murphy's dark eyes burned two holes in his thin, intense face. His hair was black and thick and wild, like a bush in a storm, his forehead broad, his nose long and fine. Thin white hands folded and unfolded, nostrils pulsated, lean shoulders twitched. No part of him was still, as if not even the ferment he was brewing for the university authorities was sufficient to contain his abundant nervous energy – the protest was blamed on 'anarchists' on the six o'clock news.

'I'll come,' Emily said loudly. A voice in her head added, 'I'll come with you to the ends of the earth.' She rose from the crowd in her jeans and embroidered Indian top, her brown hair billowing down her back, her face glowing with bravery and purpose, like a mermaid emerging from a tempestuous sea, Alex said later. Their eyes met over the seething waves of their fellow students.

'Will you share my bed with me tonight, whoever you are?' Alex called.

'Indeed I will,' said Emily.

Everyone cheered and that was that. Alex was the only man she'd ever slept with. Emily sighed. That was that, and that was then, but now was now, and so very different.

Physically, Alex had hardly changed. He was merely older, his black hair tidier, and he had the suggestion of a beard, the intellectual version of designer stubble. He wore fashionable rimless glasses. But he was still recognisably the young man Emily had met in Manchester over a quarter of a century ago. She found him even more attractive now. She fantasised about them making love, as if he was as unattainable as Harrison Ford or Michael Douglas. That night, his lean fingers twitched restlessly when she told him about their new cleaner.

'She lives in Kirkby, in two council houses made into one. And you'll never believe this, Alex, but there's five generations live there. *Five!*' Emily repeated, still astounded. 'Her grandad, her father, Mae herself and her four children. And honestly, Alex, I nearly dropped dead when she told me, she's a grandmother herself! A grandmother, at thirty-four. Her teenage daughter has a baby girl. Of course, she's not married,' Emily finished primly.

'Who's not married, the mother or the daughter?' Alex was clearly intrigued, though usually showed little interest in all forms of human life inferior to himself.

'Neither are. Mae's divorced. Only one of her children is legitimate, I can't remember which. I found it all a bit confusing.'

'It all seems rather dodgy to me, Em. They sound a pathetic and inadequate lot. Did she have references?'

'I telephoned her Tuesday-and-Thursday lady earlier. She went into raptures. Mae is the best cleaner she's ever had.'

Alex looked dubious. 'She might be a con-woman. I should keep an eye on the silver.'

'We haven't got any silver.'

'On the valuables, then,' Alex said tetchily. He hated

being contradicted. 'I think I'll take my tea into the study.'

He disappeared. Emily knew she wouldn't see him again until she took him a drink at bedtime. 'I'll be up in a minute,' he'd murmer vaguely, though he hardly ever was, in which case it wouldn't be until late tomorrow night that they would see each other again. This was the couple who used to break down in tears when they had to part on Monday mornings when Alex returned to work. What had happened? Emily never knew quite who to blame: Mrs Thatcher, computers, Alex, or herself.

'Bloody hell,' Mae groaned, when she saw the tent set up on the lawn that stretched in front of her two houses. Or what purported to be a lawn. She'd been trying to grow one for years. Out of habit, she walked down the path of the house she'd first occupied before Dad and Grandad had moved in and the council had let them have the one next door. None of the kids crawling in and out of the tent seemed to be hers. 'Who gave you permission to put that up?' she demanded of one, a lad she didn't recognise.

'Your Dicky did,' the boy claimed.

'And where is he, our Dicky?' She couldn't abide the

name Dicky, but it had been hopeless from the start trying to make Richard stick in Liverpool.

The lad shouted back into the tent, 'Hey, Dicky, your mam wants you.'

'Is that Esmeralda?' a voice cackled, unnaturally deep for an eight-year-old.

Mae's lips twitched as her son, Dicky, emerged from the tent, doing his Charles Laughton as Quasimodo impression; shoulders hunched, arms swinging almost to the ground, one eye closed in his grotesquely squozen face. He loped down the path towards her. 'I've missed you, Esmeralda,' he lisped. Dicky knew this was a surefire way to make his mam laugh and forget about the tent.

'Oh, *you!*' Mae laughed and ruffled the silky blond hair as she went into the house. The front door was open and a dog lay in the hall, comfortably at home, although it didn't live there. 'Hi, Cecil.' She patted its head, which it acknowledged with a wag of its great hairy flag of a tail.

'I'm home,' Mae shouted, when she reached the lounge. Unknown to the council, the adjoining lounges had been made into one by the simple expedient of knocking between them a giant, arch-shaped hole, which had been neatly plastered and edged in red bricks. From various points within, her greeting was returned. Gradually, the McNultys converged on the room.

First Alice from one of the kitchens, a striking, milky-coffee-coloured girl, wearing flared yellow jeans and a rainbow-striped T-shirt, her black-brown hair a complicated structure of beaded strands and plaits. A red sequin nestled within the flare of her left nostril. She was carrying a half-peeled potato. An equally striking paler-skinned toddler, a girl, who had just learnt to walk, waddled close behind.

'Hi, Mum,' Alice sang. 'Our Craig phoned. He's working late. How'd it go today?'

'Okay, luv.'

'Nana!' The toddler held up her arms to Mae.

'Oh, listen to her! "Nana," she said. Who's a clever girl then?' Mae picked up her grandchild, Cloud, and gave her an affectionate shake, before falling gratefully into a striped armchair, Cloud still in her arms.

'You'd think she was a bleedin' parrot.' Jim McNulty stomped bad-temperedly into the room from the other kitchen. ' "Who's a clever girl then?" ' he repeated, in a high falsetto. 'Mind you, she's cleverer than our Eddie. Your dad didn't say a word till he was five.'

'Shurrup, Grandad,' Mae said mildly. 'You'll only upset him if he hears.' The pair had landed on her when the house they shared was demolished for a car park. Father and son had never got on, and Eddie McNulty, a widower of fifty-five, was particularly narked when his old dad pointed out his shameful shortcomings as a baby, which he knew was only done to rile him.

'I'll get on with the spuds.' Alice left, just as Eddie came downstairs.

'Didya get the job, luv?' he asked eagerly. Mae's father was a dapper man with dyed blond hair, exquisitely coiffured and heavily lacquered, and a pencil thin moustache. He wore a navy blue blazer and grey flannels. His shirt was pink, the collar turned rakishly up, giving Eddie a dashing, lounge-lizard air. Surprisingly, a lot of women were enamoured by his weak, handsome face, and he was quite justifiably regarded as a ladykiller.

'Yes, Dad. Four hours, three mornings a week, three pounds fifty an hour, and two pounds a day for me petrol.'

'Jaysus! How much is that?' Eddie's brain, well-practised in quick calculations in the betting shops of Liverpool, buzzed busily.

'Forty-two pounds without the petrol,' said a childish voice, and a smooth dark head appeared over the back of the settee in the other half of the room where the television was on. A girl of six regarded the company with cool, amber eyes.

'Shona, there you are, luv.' Mae blew a kiss at her youngest child. 'You're always so dead quiet.' The head disappeared and Mae said, 'You know, I'm not sure that kid's as backward as the teachers claim.'

'Your dad was the backwardest kid in the entire street, if not the whole of Dingle,' Jim sneered. 'Wore nappies till he was three.'

Eddie ignored him. 'Forty-two quid a week, eh! That'll do us proud, won't it, luv, along with the money from your other jobs?' His voice became a treacly wheedle. 'I don't suppose you could lend us a tenner for tonight, Mae? The cheque from the social didn't come through this morning. It's supposed to come Mondays,' he finished, slightly whinish.

'Scrounger!' his father hissed.

'You know the rule, Dad. No loans.' Mae shook her head. It wasn't a loan he was after, but a gift. She would never get the money back. She shifted slightly under the weight of her grandchild, who had fallen asleep. She felt tired herself, and had another job to go to in two hours' time, though she knew the tiredness would pass. 'No way, Dad,' she said flatly, when her father opened his mouth to protest. Eddie pouted and flounced up to the bedroom he shared with his da.

Now that everyone had gone, apart from Shona who didn't matter, the hot, bad-tempered expression in Jim McNulty's bright blue eyes faded, and he regarded Mae fondly. He loved her more than anyone in the world, and loathed the way his leechlike son ponced off her. He knew that there were a lot of people around who called her a slag because she'd had four kids by four different fathers. But in other ways, in the ways that mattered, Mae was the salt of the earth, the most decent person he'd ever known. 'What was it like, Mae, the new place?' he asked.

Mae's face lit up. 'Oh, Grandad, it's the most beautiful house imaginable! One of these old cottages, the sort you see in Hollywood films, with roses round the door, and black beams on the ceilings and loads of funny little rooms. You could hold a dance in the kitchen – you could even hold a dance on the table, it's so big. I was too busy to see much of the garden, but through the winder – latticed winders, Grandad, dead pretty — it looked lovely, natural, like, not neat rows of flowers like most gardens.'

'Don't work too hard, luv,' Jim said gruffly. She was too conscientious by a mile, he thought angrily, and he'd like to bet some of the snooty women she worked for took advantage of her sunny good nature and her willingness to put in more than a good day's work. She supported all the McNultys, looked after them, stood up for them, without a word of complaint, picking herself up and trudging serenely on, no matter what fate threw at her, including a violent husband and the early death of her mam — already abandoned by her shit of a dad when Mae was only a baby. It was Jim, a widower himself by then, who had raised her since she was eight, though she'd mainly raised herself on the streets. She was the fulcrum of their dull little lives and they ticked around her like fingers on a clock. The family would fall apart without Mae. Craig, the eldest, was working at the moment, but he was more often out of a job than in one.

Jim glanced around the space that had once been two rooms. There were separate carpets in each section, one mainly orange, the other several shades of purple. They clashed horribly. None of the various chairs and settees were related, and only one of the sideboard drawers had a handle. The gold-tone plastic shades on both lights were cheap and vulgar. He put a wrinkled hand over hers, noting how red and chapped the fingers were for such a young woman. 'I wish I could buy you a house like that.'

Mae's pretty face twisted into a smile that touched his heart. 'Don't waste your wishes on me, Grandad. I'm perfectly happy as I am, though I wouldn't turn down an extra fifty quid a week, and I've always fancied a nice garden. Anyroad, you know what they say, if wishes were horses . . .'

'. . . then beggars would ride,' he finished for her. He glanced around the room a second time. For all its shabby, disparate bits and pieces, it had a clannish warmth. And it had Mae. At that moment, there was nowhere else on earth he would sooner be.

'Having such a lovely house hasn't done the woman living there much good,' Mae said soberly. 'I've never seen anyone with such sad eyes, and she didn't half pong. I told her to have a bath.'

'You didn't, luv!' At times, she could be too bloody honest for her own good.

'Oh, I did it tactfully, she'd never have guessed why.'

'I'd better get on with the sausages. Alice is doing the spuds. We're having bangers and mash.' Jim disappeared into the other kitchen.

'I can't wait.' Mae sat, her tiredness ebbing, holding Cloud's warm body, listening to the meal being prepared and Dicky and his mates finishing off her attempts at a lawn. She was trying to work out what to do with the extra six quid she'd be getting from the new job. There was still the electricity to pay off after they'd got behind during the winter, and she dreaded to think what it would cost to get the car through its MOT. Shona needed a new coat for school in September, but that was months off, fortunately, and she'd see what could be got from the car-boot sale on Aintree racecourse, that's if she could wangle a few hours off from the supermarket where she worked Saturdays and Sundays. There were half a dozen other bills waiting to be paid.

Cecil came, laid his long nose on her knee and looked at her adoringly with his brown, luminous eyes. Mae patted his head. 'Good boy, nice boy.' He seemed to be there all the time. Someone said his previous owners had moved and left him behind. What else could she do but feed him?

Mae grimaced. Money, the root of all evil. Six pounds sounded a lot but was peanuts when you worked out what could be done with it. When her dad came down, all apologetic, and tried to borrow five quid instead of ten, his daughter told him politely to bugger off.

CHAPTER TWO

Emily Murphy woke, as she often had lately, with the sensation that noxious gases were swirling around her guts, reacting against each other to form even more poisonous fumes that curled their way in and out of her arteries and up and down her pipes and tubes, out of her pores, into her throat. She wanted to be sick, the way the woman in *The Witches of Eastwick* had been, vomiting toads and frogs.

'Perhaps I'm pregnant.'

If only.

In order to become pregnant, impregnation was a prerequisite. Unless she was an elephant with a seven-year incubation period, there was no chance of being pregnant.

She got up and drew back the curtains. For a moment,

she thought a celestial washing-machine had overflowed during the night, flooding the world with white foam. After several seconds of staring, transfixed, at this miracle of cleansing, she realised it was mist. Several feet of apparently solid mist was suspended over the garden. The taller trees and bushes thrust through the blanket of white, like decorations on a frothily iced Christmas cake. A pale creamy sun, which looked as if it had been doused in milk, was struggling to emerge through the skim of grey-white clouds.

It was a scene, almost unique, of spectacular, thrilling beauty, but it made Emily feel cold and very much alone, as if she was the only person left in this strange white world. Even the birds had been startled into silence. She couldn't hear a single solitary sound.

Then she remembered that Mae was coming today. She turned away from the window, the noxious gases abating slightly. Mae was bringing Vim, Windolene and other essential creams, fluids and powders, to bring every inch of Thorntons up to tip-top condition. Mrs Betteridge and her predecessors had made do with what was available, which wasn't much. Emily would give Mae the money for the goods at the end of the week. Alex said to make sure that she wasn't overcharged, that the prices were the same as those in the supermarket when Emily could be bothered to go and check. 'Ask for the bill,' he instructed.

Emily had a bath using patchouli oil from a dusty plastic bottle that had been a present from her sister, Beryl, several Christmases ago. She sprayed deodorant under her arms from a tin that had gone rusty with age. She put on an entire set of clean clothing, then removed the blouse and skirt, went downstairs, ironed them, and put them on again.

It was amazing how much better she felt. She brushed her hair and took some time plaiting it neatly, securing the ends with a stretchy circle of material that Mary had left on her dressing table.

She felt even better, though it made the years of wretchedness seem rather trite, the idea that things might have been improved with a good wash. She stared at her broad, pale face in Mary's mirror. It was still a pleasant face, but scarcely one you'd look at twice. She'd never been pretty, yet people used to tell her she was beautiful. It was a combination of rosy cheeks and a full red mouth, wide-apart hazel eyes and shining hair. It was shapely limbs and a large, shapely body. She'd looked fresh, healthy, bursting with life. She'd glowed. 'You look juicy,' Alex used to say, licking his lean lips. 'You look like overripe fruit. I could eat you all up.'

'So eat me,' Emily would reply. And he would try.

Wednesday was one of the days Eustace came to do the garden, though he was likely to turn up at any time during the week. She was relieved to hear the clip-clip of the shears when she went downstairs, which meant she wasn't alone. Eustace spurned all offers of anything electric, preferring to work with his hands. 'A Luddite,' Alex called him.

Eustace was a relic of an earlier age in other ways, an age when employees addressed their employers as 'sir' and 'ma'am', respectfully tugging their forelocks or tipping their caps, touchingly grateful to be paid wages. Eustace earned fifteen pounds a week, roughly fifty pence an hour. He had come with the house, one of the fixtures and fittings, like the battered dustbin that had been left behind or the rusty metal clothes posts.

Emily looked for him through the kitchen window, but there was no sign in the thinning mist. The shears had stopped. Sometimes she worried that Eustace might die on their property, and that she would find the old, unsightly body, which made her flesh crawl, with its grotesquely twisted hands and swollen feet, floating in the pond among the water lilies or spread over the strawberries. Even worse, in the little wooden shed, full of cobwebs, that smelt of piss. She'd even rehearsed dialling 999 for an ambulance and had worked out what to say if she was asked why she hadn't applied mouth-to-mouth. 'I don't know how, I'm afraid.' When she expressed her fears to Alex, he said casually, 'We'll dump the old git now, if you like. He passed his sell-by date years ago, anyway.'

Why had Alex become so hard, so ruthless? Emily's brain was as weary and lumpen as her body and didn't care for being taxed. But just thinking about Alex and the way things had gone brought on a terrible feeling of lethargy, and she sat staring at the table, her brain capable of merely a gloomy haze, until she heard Mae's car screech into the drive.

'Vim, Windolene, cream cleaner, toilet blue, air fresheners.' Mae thumped the articles on the table with a flourish. 'And here's the receipt. I wouldn't want you to think I was doing you, like.' She wore jeans and the same gold sandals and a bright blue T-shirt with matching eye-shadow. She must have had the window open in the car as her hair was an untidy bird's nest of wild yellow straw.

Emily flushed. You'd almost think she'd guessed that Alex had cast slurs on her integrity. 'I wouldn't dream of such a thing,' she said hastily.

She found things to do herself while Mae worked, somewhat unusually spurred on by the sounds of activity. She sorted through the bookcase, removing the books that Gareth and Mary would never want again – Mae might like them for her two younger children, presuming they could read. She got rid of the preserved flowers and grasses that had been dotted around the house for years. They crumbled to dusty fragments at her touch. When Mae had finished in the kitchen, Emily actually took the vases out to wash. She put the kettle on and went to the bottom of the stairs. Mae was on the landing with the polisher.

'Would you like a coffee, Mae?' Emily shouted.

'I'll be down in a minute,' Mae shouted back. She sounded puffed. Emily was tempted to tell her not to work too hard, but it was an easy temptation to resist.

When Mae came down, there were patches of perspiration under the arms of her T-shirt. She wiped her forehead with the back of her hand. 'It's hot up there. Airless.'

'Rest your legs for a while,' Emily said kindly.

'I'd sooner take me drink into the garden, take a look around. I'm dying to see it, proper, like.'

Outside the house, on the rough stone path that ran the whole width at the back, Mae grimaced. She hadn't realised that Emily had been looking forward to them having coffee together. Shit, the look on her face, a picture of bitter disappointment, when she'd picked up her mug and walked out. Mae felt humbled by the look of naked misery in the older woman's eyes. She felt in awe of it. It made her feel inadequate. She assumed there hadn't been a terrible tragedy. The woman's kids were alive and well and her husband was around. True, the kids had left home as kids do, as Mae's would one day – Alice was forever off to different parts of the country to protest against new roads that were being built, living up trees and down holes, sometimes taking Cloud with her, sometimes not – but it was something that happened to all mothers. It was if your kids didn't leave that there was something to worry about. Maybe her husband was having an affair, in which case the best thing to do was give him a good kick in the bollocks, or have a bit on the side yourself, not go into a decline. Every person Mae loved would have to be slaughtered in front of her very eyes before she would sink into a depression like Emily Murphy.

'Poor cow,' she whispered. 'Me, I'm not sensitive enough. I'm too thick-skinned.' She had little time for introspection.

She forgot about Emily as she contemplated the garden. Whispers of mist still remained, curling upwards, round and round, as if people were hiding in the bushes and behind the trees sending smoke signals to each other. Mae knew little about flowers, but she could recognise a few. She'd tried to plant them more than once in her own back garden, but they were usually trodden on long before they blossomed, either that or flattened with a football or a bike. If just one hardy shoot managed to flower, it would be picked, like a trophy, and she'd find it on the window-sill, solitary and pathetic, in a jam-jar. She'd given up, just as she might as well give up on the lawn at the front.

Oh, but she'd love a nice garden! And this one was perfect, more like several gardens joined together, all slightly different. The section she was facing comprised a lawn shaped like a broad figure eight, with a grey stone fountain more or less in the middle. But instead of water, ivy spurted upwards and downwards, circling the fountain like a skirt and spreading lacily on to the lawn. The dark, thick grass was scattered with clumps of buttercups and daisies, and surrounded by bushes and shrubs and sprawling plants that looked as if they'd been there for ever, and beyond them, a crumbling brick wall covered with lichen and white-tipped ivy. Mae crossed the grass and passed under a thick wire arch interwoven with trailing vines that smelt like wine. Everything was wet with dew left by the mist, and all around she could hear plopping sounds as droplets slid from leaf to glistening leaf.

'Oh!' She gasped in delight at the sight of several broken steps leading up to a rusty wrought-iron bench. It was like a grotto, covered with trees, the tops bent over and joined together to form another, much bigger, natural arch of slender boughs and leaves. She went up the steps and sat on the bench to sip her coffee and survey the winding moss-covered paths, which led to other mysterious sections of this wonderful, magical garden.

How could anyone be miserable in a place like this? The trees were enough to lift your spirits, no matter how low you'd fallen. Cherry trees and apple trees — she recognised them from the luscious pink and white blossom — oak trees and firs. She could see the tiny roof of a well — a real well! — and a pitted, decaying statue of a small girl draped in yellow lady's fingers. She could see purple anemones, creamy daffodils, the burgeoning buds of red and white roses, and all sorts of flowers she was too ignorant to know the names of. Through everything, she glimpsed a pond, blinking like a mirror in the sunshine.

Mae took a deep, invigorating breath. The air felt cool and slightly damp and was heavy with fragrance, a mixture of flowers and musk, smoke and cut grass. The bars of the bench felt cold through her jeans. 'I think I've died and gone to heaven,' she said aloud.

'Is that you, Mrs Murphy?' an old voice quavered, from behind the trees on the right of the grotto. Mae jumped, startled. She went down the steps and found a dilapidated wooden shed on the other side, curtains of cobwebs on its filthy windows. The oddest-looking man she'd ever seen was standing in the doorway, well over six feet tall and scarecrow thin. He wore a brown knitted sweater that was a tapestry of pulled threads and runs, and corduroy trousers stiff with baked earth and dirt. His swollen feet bulged through the frayed holes of his carpet slippers. He was a creature from a nursery rhyme or a fairy story, a product of the Brothers Grimm or Hans Andersen.

Mae smiled. 'It's not Mrs Murphy, but Mae McNulty, the new cleaner. You must be Eustace.' She held out her hand. 'How do you do?'

He shook her hand awkwardly, partly as if, like the woman he worked for, he was unused to human contact, and because his elongated fingers were twisted almost one hundred and eighty degrees with rheumatism. 'How do you do, miss?'

'Please don't call me miss, call me Mae.' She recognised the nose of a heavy drinker; burgundy-coloured and swollen, the enlarged pores running into each other resembling the surface of a miniature moon. His skin was an unhealthy yellow, lying floppily on the bones, as if he'd recently lost weight, and the deep, sharp crevices on his cheeks were ingrained with grime. There was grime in the lines that covered his neck, so that he looked as if he'd walked through the cobwebs in his den. He also looked very sick. The feature that proclaimed his strangeness more than any other was his eyes, one strikingly higher than the other, set in dark brown sockets. But they were gentle eyes, Mae noted, touched to the core by this dirty, shambling man whose twisted hands tended the beautiful garden.

'Mae.' He nodded, then repeated, 'Mae.'

She took one of his hands and stroked the curling fingers. 'Does it hurt much, luv?'

'Depends on the weather.' He looked bewildered by the attention he was getting. Emily must never talk to him.

'You keep the garden up a treat,' she said encouragingly. 'It's lovely.'

'I do me best,' he muttered.

'I'd better be getting back, else the boss'll accuse me of skiving.' She patted his bony shoulder. 'See you Friday, luv.'

Eustace rarely came on Fridays. It was the day he drew his pension and bought a lottery ticket from the post office, but his old heart shivered with an emotion not felt since his wife had died in childbirth nearly sixty years ago. Love! This Friday, Eustace decided he would come.

'She cleaned all the downstairs windows,' Emily boasted, as if Mae was her creation, built in the heavily haunted cellar out of bits of old vacuum cleaners, a clockwork

Mrs Mopp. 'If there's time on Friday, she's promised to do upstairs. Next week she'll clean outside if we provide her with a ladder.'

Alex shrugged. 'Well, if the flesh is willing, we'd be fools not to take advantage.' He was impressed with his strangely shining house, which smelt of lavender polish and pine disinfectant. This rare gem of a charwoman his wife had found did more work in one morning than their previous chars had done in three. It was satisfying to find the water in the lavatory a dreamy Pacific blue, and it stayed the same colour even after it was flushed. Scented air fresheners had been strategically placed for best effect, and the bath and toilet mats had been washed and restored to their original knobbly texture. Mae had diverted from the timetable to iron half a dozen shirts expertly.

'I was thinking,' Emily said earnestly, 'that I might up her wages to four pounds an hour, just in case she goes somewhere else for more money.'

'I shouldn't do that, Em,' Alex was alarmed. 'She might think she's indispensable.'

'She is.'

'But we don't want her to know that. She might get delusions of grandeur.'

'Oh, Alex! If there was a prize for exaggeration, you'd win. She's only a cleaner, not Mrs Thatcher or Tony Blair.'

Alex winced at the mention of Tony Blair. 'I should leave it, Em. Leave it for a few months, at least.' He picked up his tea. 'I think I'll take this into the study — oh, and it's Lady Thatcher, Em, not Mrs.'

Alex slid into the chair in front of the computer and clicked the mouse. A welcoming message flashed on the screen. 'Hi! Nice to see you. Step inside.' He got none of the satisfaction that he usually did from the cheerful, informal greeting he had written himself, which was written into all the machines manufactured by Murphy Computers. It was his intention to send a letter by email to his old friend from university, Heinrich Hauptmann in Frankfurt, but Alex paused before clicking the mouse again.

It wasn't the name of Tony Blair that had made Alex wince. He quite liked the guy. After all, he'd promised not to raise taxes, hadn't he?

No, it was Emily's casual mention of him winning a prize that had done it. Even now, thirty-seven years later, the memory of that terrible day could still make his stomach feel as if it were fighting a losing battle with a pair of pliers.

Alexander Murphy had never discussed the day with a soul. It was his dark secret. It wasn't anything depraved, criminal or corrupt. Indeed, some people, especially women, might think it rather sweet. Nor was it particularly a secret, the incident having been witnessed by the entire school, the parents of the fifth year, which included Alex's own (he had been eleven at the time), the teachers, and the wife of the local MP. He sometimes wondered if it was that fact, more than any other, that had made him turn, eventually, against the Labour Party.

Alex had passed the eleven-plus, naturally. He was the brightest pupil in the class. This was when the worst of his troubles had begun, because the secret had gone with him to grammar school, carried triumphantly by the other boys who'd passed with him, then told to the pupils who'd come from different schools. He was never allowed to forget it, not for a single day. The dreaded nickname had stayed with him until he was eighteen. With five A-grade A levels, the finest marks in the history of the school, merely a single mark dropped in Geography, Alex could have sailed into Oxford or Cambridge, despite his working-class background.

His father, an Irishman with a drink problem and a fine baritone voice, worked as a porter on the railways; his mother made industrial overalls on the treadle sewing-machine in the parlour, half a crown per garment, her fingers pierced to shreds from being caught under the needle when her eyes began to go. She was determined that her clever son would get on. She'd lived to see Alex get his degree and marry Emily, then died, presumably happy. As far as Alex knew, his father was still around. They hadn't seen each other in more than fifteen years.

Oxbridge was dismissed. Alex went to Manchester instead. No one else from school was going there. He could cast off his dark secret, say goodbye to the nickname, start afresh.

He was a vibrant, charismatic young man, Alexander Murphy, handsome, with a careless, untidy charm, all of which Alex was well aware. His head had already begun to swell when he was eleven, due to the enormous amount of intelligence stored within it, but the swelling had been temporarily constrained during his years at grammar school due to the off-putting, confidence-draining effect of his dark secret. At university his unhampered head swelled to monumental proportions.

It was only appropriate that Alex should win a first

class (Hons) degree and be top of his year. His subject was Mathematics.

It was also only appropriate that Alex should marry a girl willing to increase his ideas of his own importance, not deliberately but because she loved him so thoroughly. She adored him. Emily thought the sun shone out of his thin, hypersensitive bottom — Alex had a nervous stomach.

Mind you, he loved Emily every bit as much as she loved him. He was her god, she was his goddess, slightly lower down the scale of omnipotence. During the first years of their marriage, the time in Formby, he had been blissfully, ecstatically happy.

Then Melvyn Christopher had come to live next door. Melvyn had been to the same primary school as Alex. They had gone to grammar school together. 'Well, if it isn't old . . .' Melvyn's jaw had dropped in amazed delight. 'What are you doing with yourself nowadays?'

'I'm about to move house,' Alex said crisply, wondering why the hell he'd returned to Liverpool in the first place, and not moved down south or to the other side of the world where there was no chance of meeting up with his old enemies from school.

No way would he live next to Melvyn, park his car on

the joint driveway beside his old tormentor's, allow the Murphy children to play with the Christophers, watch Melvyn through the window of his kitchen, knowing that Melvyn was able to watch him through his.

He put the house on the market straight away, much to Emily's dismay. She liked it there; so did Gareth and Mary. But say, just imagine if the secret got out, if his children were told, or Emily. He could hear Emily's laugh: one of the things he loved so much about her was the delicious, throaty chuckle she'd inherited from her father, but he didn't care to hear it directed at himself. He enjoyed telling Melvyn that the Murphys were leaving 'this hovel' for Thorntons.

'How can you afford a place like that?' gasped Melvyn.

Alex shrugged. 'Easily.' In fact, he would be mortgaged to the hilt. If interest rates went up by half a point, the family would have to stop eating.

By then, Alex was already fascinated by computers. He had given up his job in the laboratory, where he was embroiled in fusty thermodynamics, to write programs for a small software company; dizzyingly complicated mathematical puzzles that only a genius like himself could solve. It is a fact that a tremendous amount of people think they're geniuses, usually men, and the games sold like hot cakes. Alex earned a royalty for each one sold. The Murphys' bank balance, so often in the red, travelled further and further into the black; three figures, four figures, five, and repaying the mortgage was a doddle. As his wealth grew, Alex's regard for those less fortunate than himself swiftly diminished in proportion. 'I've worked hard for my money,' he told himself and Emily, a statement that would have been met with contempt by the younger, nobler Alex. 'Why should I have to pay so much in tax so the work-shy can lie in bed all day and old-age pensioners take holidays in Spain?'

Also, Alex had discovered his forte. His brain, already scalpel sharp, was suddenly capable of thoughts and ideas way beyond the scope of ordinary mortals. *Anything* was possible with computers, undreamt-of concepts, almost supernatural.

Alex decided to go into business for himself. He borrowed again, hugely. Fortunately he had a sympathetic bank manager, Clive Fontaine, who could see into the future and understood the advantages computers could bring – he could sack most of his staff and employ part-timers to press the odd button, housewives mainly, who would need the money to support their redundant husbands. (Mrs Thatcher had already declared 'manufacturing' a dirty word; only the service industries mattered. Great Britain was about to become a giant theme park.) Years later, when the branch Alex dealt with was computerised, Clive Fontaine was the first to go.

Murphy Computers produced the Murphy-Gnome, smaller than the average computer, reliable, unflashy and competitively priced, a 'Best Buy', according to the magazines that judged these things and published tables. The Gnome had provided the Murphys with a hefty income over the years. Almost monthly, because the industry never ceased to advance, with the Internet, virtual reality, more and more powerful chips, a new Murphy-Gnome model came on to the market.

Somehow, somewhere, Emily had been left behind during Alex's plunge into this dazzling, exciting world. He thought about her occasionally. She seemed quiet. She looked different. She no longer appealed to him sexually. His secretary, a pale, sulky blonde whom he didn't like much but tolerated because she was efficient, turned out to be a tigress in bed. An occasional mauling from Gaynor offered the small relief that Alex needed nowadays. Most of his passion was directed towards computers. He empathised with their cool logic, admired their limitless powers — a computer costing less than a thousand pounds could send a manned spaceship to the moon. He adored them. They were his gods and goddesses rolled into one. He felt as attached to computers as an unborn baby is attached to its mother by the umbilical cord.

His wife, Emily — with only half a degree because she'd given up university during her second year to marry him and bear the children that Alex mostly forgot he had — came nowhere when compared to these marvels of technology that could work miracles. One of these days a computer would turn water into wine. Emily couldn't even iron a shirt.

Alex clicked the mouse and began to write the letter to his friend Heinrich's home address. As soon as it had been despatched, he would delete it from the files. Heinrich would do the same when he replied. Only the formal business correspondence that passed between Murphy Computers in Skelmersdale and Hauptmann-wagen's head office was stored and copied.

For Alex had another secret, shared only with his German friend. Unlike the first, this one was definitely corrupt and almost certainly criminal. In the not too distant future, Murphy Computers would become as famous as Microsoft and IBM, and Alex would become a multi-millionaire. Which, when you thought about it, was no more than he deserved.

'Hey, you.'

'Me?' Dicky McNulty pointed to his chest. What on earth did two such shifty-looking buggers want with him?

'Yes, you.' The shiftiest of the buggers nodded at the house Dicky had just left. 'Is that your house?'

Dicky nodded. 'Yip.' It wasn't his house, but in Dicky's experience, telling a lie was always (a) less likely to bring trouble on your head and (b) more interesting than telling the truth.

'Are you Rory Quinn's lad?'

'I am that,' Dicky lied again. Both of the men had beards, one as red as blazes, the other, the shiftiest, a brown one shaped like a trowel. Brownbeard's eyes were small and sharp, seeing everywhere. Redbeard's eyes were blue and round, and his skin was unnaturally pale. He had huge white teeth, almost too big for his mouth. The men were shabbily dressed — check shirts, tweed jackets, shapeless trousers – and had strong Irish accents. Dicky guessed straight away that they had something to do with the terrorist group it was rumoured Rory Quinn, his best mate's dad, was involved with. At this very moment, Mr Quinn was in bed, apparently sweating like a cob, his temperature still soaring, having caught a summer cold.

'What's your name?'

'Quentin,' Dicky said promptly.

'Quentin!' Redbeard laughed. 'That's a bloody stupid name to give a lad, particularly to go with Quinn.' He regarded Dicky with considerable sympathy. 'Do the other lads skit at you in school, Quentin Quinn?'

Dicky squared his shoulders and clenched his fists. 'They'd better not try.' He thought it unfortunate that a person for whom being anti-British was a way of life should have such a patriotically coloured face, so distinctly red, white and blue.

The other man dug his mate in the ribs. 'Shut the fuck up, Paddy.' He turned to Dicky. 'Would you ask your da to step outside, lad? Tell him someone wants to see him, urgently, like.'

'He can't see anyone. He's sick in bed.'

'Is he now?' The man made a fierce, angry face. 'Is his missus in, your ma, that is?'

'Yip. She's in the kitchen.' Mrs Quinn was also in the mother of all tempers. You'd think her husband had caught a cold deliberately, just to spite her. All Dicky had done was call for Quentin on his way to school and had been rudely told to sod off. Quentin had to stay in and amuse his da. She had to go to work, earning being more vital than learning. The Quinn girls, Moira and Norah, must have sensed what was on the cards and had made their escape early.

'Aw, fuck!' Brownbeard spat.

'Stop swearing in front of the lad, Mick,' the other man admonished. 'How old are you, Quentin?'

'Eight.' Dicky instantly regretted telling the truth, wishing he'd laid claim to fifteen, even older. He was tall for his age. 'Shit, I've heard swearing before,' he said dismissively. 'Loads of times. Loads and loads and loads of times. Every day, in fact. Every hour of every day—'

Brownbeard rudely interrupted Dicky's litany. 'We can't go in if Tilly's there, she'll kill us.'

'Can I take Mr – I mean, me da, a message, like?' Dicky offered generously. He was already late for school, but so what? It might be to do with planting a bomb, in which case he'd tell the bobbies.

The men looked at each other. 'What should we do, Mick?'

'I'm not sure, Paddy.'

The men transferred their gaze to Dicky. He tried to look loyal and committed to their cause, at the same time imagining himself in all the papers after he'd clatted on them.

'I suppose you could give your da a message,' Red-beard said thoughtfully. 'Just say Delilah, the three thirty at Haydock, is a dead cert.'

'Is that all?' Dicky was bitterly disappointed. On the other hand, it might be code.

'No, it's not all. Give him this package an' all. Carry it careful, like, and try not to let your ma see it. Stick it up your jumper before you go in. Say Sean Donovan will collect it when he's ready. Me and Paddy have to go back to London.'

For the first time, Dicky noticed Brownbeard was holding a Tesco's carrier bag. A bomb! This meant a reward, surely. He'd pretend to take it inside, then go straight with it to the bobbies. Both men helped Dicky stuff the package inside his sweatshirt.

'Just so's we know it's altogether safe and sound with Rory, make a sign out the bedroom winder once you've given it him.'

That might prove a problem. How was he supposed to burst into Mr Quinn's sickroom and make signs out of the window? Then his quick brain thought of a way. 'Okay,' he agreed.

'You're a fine lad,' Redbeard said approvingly. 'Your da's a lucky fella. Is Rory not a lucky fella, Mick?'

'For Chrissakes, Paddy, shurrup.' Mick nodded curtly at Dicky. 'Get a move on. We can't hang round all day.'

Fortunately, Tilly Quinn was hanging out washing at the bottom of the garden. Dicky slipped in at the back and made his way upstairs. He knocked on the bedroom door. It was a bonus to find Quentin reading the *Racing Times* to his ailing da. Both looked up in astonishment at Dicky's chirpy face when it appeared.

'What the bloody hell do you want?' the patient snarled, his face red and steaming.

'I've brought an important message from me grandad.' Dicky contrived to look hurt at this ill-natured greeting, and at the same time too nice to mind. 'He ses Delilah, the three thirty at Haydock, is a dead cert.'

'Oh! Ta, lad,' Mr Quinn said grudgingly. 'Tell your grandad it's much appreciated.'

Dicky went over to the window. The men were waiting on the pavement as expected. He made a thumbs-up sign. Redbeard waved his thanks and made a funny face. His mate slapped him hard on the back of the neck, and they crossed the road and got into a battered car. After several attempts to make it start, the car drove away. A few seconds later, another car backed out of the car park beside a parade of shops further along the road. Dicky could have sworn it followed the first.

'It's a great day outside,' he remarked cheerily when he turned round, feeling the need to offer some excuse for his overlong presence at the window. 'Pity you're missing it, Mr Quinn.'

Quentin came to the door and punched his mate playfully in the stomach. His fist came up against the package. 'What have you got there? Have you been on the rob?'

'Me?' Dicky's face was the picture of injured innocence.

'I'm fed up,' Quentin said seriously. 'Even school's better than being stuck in with me da.'

'I'm off.' The package felt as if it was about to drop out of Dicky's sweatshirt. If it really was a bomb, if it was already connected, it might explode.

Dicky opened the package in his bedroom. Plasticine!

He'd expected wires and clocks and timers, but there was only a big sweaty blob of Plasticine. It wouldn't have been so bad if there were different colours, but the whole bloody lot was a miserable blue!

'Shit!' Even so, it had come for nothing and was better than a pig's ear, but it was a waste of time taking a big blob of Plasticine to show the bobbies and expecting a reward. They'd call him a soft lad. He broke a bit off and moulded it into a spaceman, then broke off more to make a monster. Then he rolled both into a ball with his palms and slapped it on to the big piece. He put it back in the Tesco's bag, and shoved it under the bottom bunk where Craig slept, as far as it would go. Mam was tidy, but she was unlikely to go there.

He could hear his sister, Alice, pottering around downstairs, and Cloud, stupid name, whingeing about something or other. No one had heard him come in. It was boring here. Dicky supposed he might as well go to school, learn something.

CHAPTER THREE

'What do your kids do, Em?'

Emily and Mae were sitting at the kitchen table with their coffee. Unknown to Mae, Eustace was pining for her company outside.

'They both work in London. Gareth's a social worker in Tower Hamlets, and Mary works for a housing charity.' The children had stayed true to the ideals instilled in them by their father since they were little more than babies. Both worked for the common good, to make things better for those less fortunate than themselves. Money wasn't important. Emily supposed that, deep down at heart, Gareth and Mary still loved Alex, despite what he had become, but on the surface neither could appear to stand him. It was the reason they rarely came home. He'd betrayed everything he'd ever taught them, gone back on his word, forgotten his roots, or so they claimed on the rare occasions that Emily spoke to either of her children, which was usually on the phone. 'They live near each other,' she went on. 'They see my mother and my sisters regularly.' She sighed. 'We're a very close-knit family.' A close-knit family that she was excluded from, or that she'd excluded herself from. She wasn't sure.

'That's nice,' said Mae. She finished off her coffee. 'What would you like me to do now?'

Mae had been working almost three weeks for the Murphys, and Thorntons was in immaculate condition. It didn't take long, each Monday, Wednesday and Friday, for the lavatories to be scrubbed, a quick dust round, a rapid polish. The windows wouldn't need cleaning again for a while. Emily supposed Mae's hours could be cut, but remembered that she needed the bread. It might be a risky move. She might go elsewhere.

'You could take the curtains down and wash them,' she suggested. 'It will take weeks to do them all, but you could make a start today.'

'Right!' Mae jumped to her feet. 'I'll begin with upstairs. It's a nice windy day for drying, I'll put them on the line. It wouldn't do to put curtains in the dryer.'

She paused at the door. 'Oh, talking of kids, do you mind if I bring our Shona with me next week? It's half-term. She won't be any trouble, she's very quiet. Dicky's only eight, but he's got loads of friends and won't be stuck for somewhere to go. Our Alice would look after her, but she's stuck down a hole at Manchester airport, and me grandad's been left with Cloud.'

'I don't mind.' Emily always felt dizzy whenever Mae mentioned her complicated, tangled family.

To Emily's shocked surprise, Shona turned out to be yellow. Her father must have been Japanese, Chinese, something definitely yellow.

'She doesn't say much, do you, luv?' Mae patted her daughter's glossy black head and mouthed, 'She's a bit backward.'

Emily nodded dazedly. The child was undoubtedly pretty, but her strangely coloured eyes were blank, and Emily couldn't imagine getting used to her colour. 'My husband's in his study today,' she said. 'He has some important work that he'd prefer to do at home.'

'We won't disturb him, will we, Shona?'

'No, Mam.'

'You can come and help me take down the last of the curtains.'

'Yes, Mam.'

As Mae had predicted, Shona was no trouble. She was, in fact, quite a help, inserting the rings in the curtains that Mae had washed the previous week and had just finished pressing. There were more curtains waving on the line. Several years of heavy dirt had emerged in the washing-machine.

They stopped for coffee at one o'clock. 'Would you like a glass of milk, dear?' Emily asked Shona, wondering, being backward, if the child knew what milk was.

'Please.'

Shona drank her milk and disappeared. Mae assumed she'd gone into the garden, where Eustace was composing sonnets to his loved one, aching for her to come. Mae *would* come, eventually. Once she'd done her four hours, they would sit in the grotto and she'd ask about his hands, his poor feet, even though it meant she would be late leaving for home. She'd bought him two pair of socks, nice big ones that didn't pinch. Mae divided her time between the two lonely people who seemed to need her: coffee with Emily, a little chat with Eustace later. She felt sorry for them, and it seemed only right to make people happy if you could. Mind you, that's how she'd ended up with Shona, making a bloke happy she'd felt sorry for.

Shona was in the hall where the study door was open, Alex having gone to the lavatory to pee in the dreamy Pacific blue water.

A computer! She edged into the room, rested her arms on the back of the chair in front of the desk, and stared curiously at the screen. It was full of green writing. She leant over, pressed '1' and a line of print at the top of the screen jumped forward. Shona felt a surge of excitement. She wanted a computer more than anything in the world. She was about to press '2' then '3', when she heard the toilet flush in the hall. When Alex came into the room Shona was standing innocently just inside the door.

'Have you touched anything?' he demanded irritably. This must be the cleaner's kid, Emily had said she'd be coming today. He'd glimpsed Mae once when she was leaving. She looked a cheap tart and he wasn't surprised that she had a mixed race child.

Shona shook her head. 'No.'

'I'd like to get on now.' Alex returned to his chair. To

his further irritation, instead of the girl going away, she came and rested her elbows on the arm of the chair and stared with him at the screen.

'Have you got a fax modem?' she enquired conversationally.

'Of course,' Alex snapped.

'Are you going to fax the letter to Germany? Or will you send it email? Can I watch?'

'I shall send it by post.' He looked at her in astonishment. 'How do you know it's going to Germany?' How did she know about fax modems or email, come to that? She looked very young.

'It ses so. It ses Frankfurt, Germany.'

'You read very well.' Despite his impatience to get on, Alex was impressed. 'How old are you?'

'Six.'

He leant back in the chair. The small face close to his was a perfect oval, the hair a smooth black cap. And what peculiar eyes, tawny brown, almost orange! Unknown to Mae, Shona's father was Korean-American, a professor of biology at Boston University, Massachusetts, USA. She'd found him down a cul-de-sac close to Kirkby station, alerted by the groans. He had been lying in the gutter, having been robbed of everything he possessed, including his Gucci shoes. It was the last night of a cultural-exchange visit, and he was drunk out of his mind. She'd taken him home, feeling sorry for him, and provided him with a pair of Eddie's old shoes and other comforts.

'I expect you're top of the class for reading,' Alex said.

'Nah.' Shona wrinkled her button of a nose. 'It's so easy, I don't bother. I don't talk, even. The teachers tell me mam I'm daft.'

'Don't you care?' Alex was even more impressed. At school he'd thrived on flattery and approbation. What an arrogant little madam she must be!

'Nah.' She put her foot on the base of the chair and swung them both round. 'You're not daft, are you?'

'No,' Alex agreed. 'I'm not.'

'I don't mind talking to you.'

'Shona!' Mae appeared in the doorway. 'I thought you were outside. I'm sorry if she's been bothering you,' she said to Alex.

'That's all right,' Alex grunted. Surprisingly, he hadn't minded, feeling he'd met a rare personality similar to himself. 'Close the door, will you?'

Before the door shut, he glimpsed Shona's face

looking longingly back into the room, not at him but at the computer.

Alex had always found it hard to delegate, convinced that no one could do the job as well as he could himself. He checked everything, then double-checked it if it was particularly important. He was a lousy employer, trusting no one. At the factory he kept a close eye on his designers, checked regularly that the secretaries were hard at work, called in Despatch to ensure that orders were properly packed and sent out on time, prowled the workshop where the machines were assembled, mainly by women; from components imported from Taiwan, convinced his frequent visits kept his employees on their toes. He didn't realise that his sudden forays put everyone's nerves on edge. Where they'd had fingers, instead they had thumbs. If Alex had kept to his own office, Murphy Computers' output would have risen by ten per cent.

The covering letter to Hauptmannwagen, Alex predictably composed and wrote himself. The quotation had been typed and printed, and he'd read and reread all forty-one pages several times. It lay on his desk in a silver plastic folder, and was worth, he gulped when he thought about it, just over fifty million marks, roughly twenty million pounds in English money.

Once again he read the letter on the screen, which he'd been in the course of checking when he'd felt the need to go to the lavatory. It was short and to the point, just right. 'Quotation attached. Hope this meets with your requirements, blah, blah, blah', which was the stilted British way that apparently Heinrich's old man liked.

The old man was a stickler for formality. Tenders had been invited worldwide. On receipt, they would be placed securely in a safe until Thursday, 31 July. At 10.30 a.m. they would be removed in the presence of the eight directors of the company, one of whom was Heinrich Hauptmann, son and heir of the company's founder, and Alex's old friend, then taken to the boardroom where they would be opened. At least another week would pass while they were studied and compared, and the best quote chosen.

Alex had already deposited two million marks in Heinrich's private account in the Cayman Islands. The contract for installing the Peek-a-Boo watch system, as it was crudely called, in Hauptmannwagen's new car factories in Slovakia, Serbia and Latvia would come to Murphy Computers. Heinrich would see to that. It was a cinch.

Peek-a-Boo was a complex installation of tiny, hardly visible cameras fitted under the roofs of the workshops. They could pick up and pinpoint the most infinitesimal spot anywhere inside the building. On a monitor back in Frankfurt, an inspector could tell the time on a worker's watch. He could enlarge the watch until a single figure filled the screen. If that same worker happened to make an error or was slacking, he would be warned to watch his step by a tiny laser beam from the same camera that would jerk his attention without him realising. The workers would be unaware of the cameras and the laser beam, but would have the uneasy feeling that their every movement was under surveillance. It wasn't a case of big brother watching, but his smaller sibling with much sharper eyes. The system meant that Heinrich senior wouldn't have the expense of sending and maintaining more than a couple of German supervisors to keep the workers up to scratch. It could mainly be done from Frankfurt. It would deter theft, increase efficiency. If a worker sensed he could be seen pausing to blow his nose, he might think twice before blowing it. After all, jobs were hard to come by in those old eastern-bloc countries. They'd work their arses bare.

Alex put a Murphy Computers letterhead in the printer and ran off the letter. The envelope was too thick to print on, so he printed two labels, one for the front, one for the back, the computer automatically selecting the address on the letter. He put the letter inside the folder, put the folder in the self-sealing envelope, then sat and stared at the bulky package on his desk.

His entire future was contained within that innocent brown-paper parcel. Apart from the bribe to Heinrich, he'd spent five times that much installing a miniature version of Peek-a-Boo, though without the laser, free of charge, at Hawkins & Son, a small factory close to his own that manufactured washing-machines. The workers had been told it was to improve the central heating, otherwise there might have been a walk-out. It was imperative to make sure the system worked. It did. While the washing-machines were being assembled, the managing director watched his workers' every action on a monitor in his comfortable mansion overlooking Birkdale golf course. So far, three men had been sacked for thieving, the various expensive bits and pieces found in their possession as they were about to go home, much to their embarrassed and indignant surprise.

Alex rubbed his hands. In a minute he'd take the quotation into the main post office in Southport, hand it over personally to be sent by Parcel Force. It meant paying through the nose, but he would feel easier in his mind that it would get there safely.

The excitement – the risks he was taking – was playing havoc with his bladder. He felt the need to go to the lavatory again.

Alex was about to get into his car, a modest chocolate brown BMW with a cream leather interior, when he noticed Shona swinging from a rope on the giant oak tree in the front garden. He remembered stringing it over the strongest branch for Gareth and Mary when they had first moved in. The child's eyes were closed, she hadn't noticed him. She was in some blissful world of her own. Mary used to have the same expression. He'd asked her once, 'What do you think about when you're swinging?' She'd been older than Shona, about twelve.

'Nothing, Dad. I just enjoy the feeling. It makes me go all dizzy and dreamy.'

He wondered what it must be like to experience a

sensation that was purely physical, the brain uninvolved, the mind conscious only of motion. As a child, he'd never wanted a swing, or a bike to ride just for the pleasure, skates. Though he'd been good at team games, cricket, football, rugby. Not particularly strong, he was fiercely competitive, could run like the wind, and was an expert strategist. His temper could turn ugly if he was run out or roughly tackled. He liked to show off, be watched and admired. Swinging was an entirely aimless activity that he couldn't understand. Unproductive. No one would win or lose. No one would watch.

There was a slight, totally unexpected wrench when he recalled Mary involved in the same activity as the cleaner's kid. Gareth used to climb the rope and get lost among the branches. Dazed, Alex wondered if he was missing something. Had something rather valuable been lost along the years? He realised with a jolt that he had experienced a sensation that was purely physical when he'd made love to Emily; a sensation bloody well ecstatic, over the top, out of this world, fabulously magnificent, in fact. When Gaynor clawed him in her tigerish way, his brain never stopped working; in, out, I'm paying too much for those motherboards, must get a new supplier; in, out, contact Jock tomorrow about the design of speakers on the new multi-media; in, out, what's it all about?

What was it all about? Thoughts of his family melted from his mind like ice in a heatwave when Alex remembered the envelope in his hand. He looked at it, his stomach churning with excitement. It was about power and wealth and fame. It was about him, Alexander Murphy. No one else, nothing else, mattered.

He got in the car and drove away. Half-way to Southport, he remembered he hadn't told Emily where he was going. He'd forgotten to say goodbye.

Sean Donovan rang Rory Quinn a few weeks after Mick and Paddy had delivered the package. 'I'll be coming for the stuff tomorrer,' he grunted.

'What stuff?' Rory asked, bewildered.

'You know fucking well what I mean.'

'I fucking well don't.'

'You fucking well better had. Mick and Paddy brought it round not long ago.'

'I haven't seen Mick and Paddy in fucking months.'

'Are you playing fucking games with me, Rory?'

'I'm fucking well not. I haven't a fucking clue what you're on about.'

'You're treading on dangerous fucking ground, Rory.'

'Piss off, Sean.' With that, Rory Quinn slammed the receiver down angrily. But he felt frightened.

'A house not far from us got done over yesterday,' Mae told Emily. 'It was completely ransacked in broad daylight when everyone was out — cupboards emptied, drawers tipped out. They even went through the garden shed.'

'Oh dear! Was much taken?' Emily was terrified of burglars. Thorntons was so isolated. No one would hear if she screamed.

'That's the mysterious part,' said Mae. 'Nothing was taken at all.'

Tilly Quinn was glad not to have been relieved of the television, the video, not even her engagement ring, which had rolled under the bed still in its little blue box when the contents of the dressing-table drawers had been emptied on to the floor but, as she pointed out to Rory, it just showed what crap their possessions were, when burglars weren't interested in a single thing. She stared suspiciously at the ring. 'Are you sure this is a real diamond?'

'Didn't it cost twenty-five quid in Argos?'

'I think I might get it valued by a jeweller.' Tilly glared at her husband. 'Have you called the cops?'

Rory shuffled his feet uncomfortably. 'No, there's no point. Nothing's been taken. I don't want cops swarming all over the place, dusting for fingerprints and all that crap.'

Tilly was about to protest, when she remembered that the video had fallen off the back of a lorry. By reporting a non-burglary, they might end up in the dock themselves.

Mick and Paddy had been hastily summoned from their basement flat in Kilburn. They sat in their rusty car outside the Quinns' waiting for Quentin to leave for school. Two girls came out, Moira and Norah, tall and skinny but quite pretty in a dewy, Irish way.

'Cor! I wouldn't mind some o' that!' Redbeard snorted automatically.

Mick said nothing, but his little eyes watched the girls lewdly as they walked by. He tried to think of a way he could get at Rory through his daughters: take them hostage, try a bit of blackmail, threaten rape. A terrorist's job was rarely like that shown in the films. It was mainly dead dull, like now, waiting for that snotty-nosed kid of Rory's to appear.

Sean Donovan had phoned their London flat from Belfast the night before. 'Rory denies he ever got the package,' he said furiously. 'I've had his place turned over and it isn't there. Are you sure you give it the fella?' Sean sounded doubtful. Rory Quinn was only on the fringes of the organisation: he stored things, took messages and passed them on, but he'd always been trustworthy. He'd never let them down before.

'Sure I'm sure, Sean. I swear it on me ould ma's grave. We gave it his kid, Rory being sick in bed at the time. Perhaps he's sold it. Didn't he do time for bank-robbing some years back? Perhaps he's sold it to a mate. Perhaps he's got another job in mind for himself, so he's pretending he never got it.'

'Who, the kid?'

'No,' Mick said patiently. 'Rory, of course. Christ knows what two pounds of Semtex would go for on the open market.'

'In that case track down the kid. Find out if it definitely got to Rory. If he's two-timing us, then he's in deep fucking trouble.'

'Who, the kid?'

'No, you stupid arsehole, Rory.'

A lad appeared from round the back of the Quinns' house, but Mick and Paddy ignored him. He was at least six inches shorter than the boy they'd given the package to, and far rounder. He reached the end of the path, when a woman they recognised as Tilly Quinn came running after him. 'Quentin,' she screeched, 'you've forgotten your butties.'

Mick and Paddy looked at each other, jaws dropping, eyes popping. 'Quentin!' they said together.

Paddy edged the car forward so they were abreast of the boy. He rolled down the window. 'Are you Quentin Quinn?'

Quentin had already delved into his sarnies. 'Who wants to know?' he demanded, his mouth a chewy mass of bread and sardines.

'Who wants to know, Mick?' Paddy looked desperately at his partner.

Mick removed a five-pound note from a sticky plastic wallet. He handed it to Paddy, who handed it to Quentin. 'Does it matter?' Mick said.

'Does it matter?' echoed Paddy.

Quentin pocketed the note. 'I'm Quentin Quinn,' he acknowledged.

'Have you got a mate, taller than you, fair hair, freckles?' Paddy enquired nicely.

'Who wants to know?'

'Don't push your luck, kid,' Mick growled. 'Do you have a mate of that description or not?'

'I might have.'

'What's his name? Where does he live?'

'His name's Bart Simpson. He lives Scottie Road way. I don't know his address.' Quentin didn't like the look of the two geezers questioning him, but even if he had, there was no way he'd clat on a mate.

The men drove away and, seconds later, another car passed, also with two men inside. Quentin felt convinced it was after the other one.

Mae had gone home, having forgotten to take the shopping she had bought on her way there. She preferred not to leave it in the car: there was a piece of pork pie and a packet of streaky bacon that might go off in the sun. Emily peeped into the Sainsbury's plastic bag, which had been left on the draining-board. Along with the pie and the bacon, there were two tins of beans, apples, a thick-sliced loaf, sugar, and a bottle of orange squash. Feeling virtuous, Emily put the pie and the bacon in the fridge. It would keep till Mae came on Monday. She might even return for the groceries. Emily hoped so. In fact, she prayed so.

Oh, how she used to love Fridays at one time, the weekend stretching ahead, curling open like a beautiful flower. In the summer, they would go as a family to the beach, to the fairground in Southport, wander along Lord Street, have a meal. Winters, they'd visit the cinema, usually in Liverpool, tour the toy departments of the big shops: 'Can I have this for Christmas, Mum?' 'Oh, Dad, can I have that?' Alex would wink at Emily and say, 'We'll just have to see.'

On Sundays, when the children were older, Alex and Emily would stay in bed and Gareth and Mary would make a tray of tea, bringing it proudly and carefully into the room, four mugs, and all the Murphys would have the tea together on the bed. 'I really appreciate this.' Emily would smack her lips. The weak, insipid liquid always tasted like nectar.

Now Fridays were nothing, merely the start of another few days of emptiness and despair. Alex went into work on Saturdays, and more often than not on Sunday mornings, too, having a pub meal with a colleague before he came home, something he did almost every night. Yet Emily still had the gnawing feeling that Fridays should be special. When she was a child, she'd helped Dad on the stall. As a teenager, she'd shopped with her friends, or they'd lounged in each other's bedrooms, pretending to be bored with life but secretly happy. Later, there'd been parties and discos to look forward to. Later still, weekends with Alex, then weekends with Alex and the children.

The emptiness felt heavier after Mae had gone, the kitchen unnaturally tidy, scrubbed hygienically clean, like an operating theatre. Emily spread the things from Mae's bag along the worktops to make it appear lived in, used. She thought about making herself a chip butty, but it seemed too much trouble. She heaped a bowl with cornflakes and heaped the cornflakes with sugar. So much easier.

Perhaps she should start smoking. Or drinking. Perhaps she should ask the doctor for Prozac, or share her problems with a counsellor. Lots of people did nowadays, it was all the rage. But she'd feel ashamed to tell a counsellor that her husband no longer loved her. She might be advised to get her hair done, buy a sheer black nightie, arrange candlelit dinners. In other words, seduce him. Alex would think she'd gone mad.

Outside, birds sang, the trees rustled gently in the breeze. Far away, a dog barked urgently. Inside, everywhere was silent, except for the hum of the refrigerator, the creaks and groans of the house, the faint in and out of Emily's breath. How many people's lives were so utterly empty, so utterly devoid of sound that they could hear themselves breathe?

Emily was getting on her own nerves. She felt it imperative that she talk to someone, confirm she was alive. She'd call Gareth, not from the phone in the kitchen but in the living room where she could sit comfortably in an armchair and have a nice long chat.

She went into the hall, which was dark and murky and full of whispers, the early-evening sun now shining in at the back of the house. Shadows lay thickly, like strips of dense black velvet, which Emily felt convinced would slink along the floor, snakelike, curl around her body, around her neck, getting tighter and tighter until she choked to death. She hurried into the living room. More whispers, a faint, slight wind, a sigh, as if someone had just left the room as she'd gone in.

Shuddering, perhaps she was going mad, Emily's fingers trembled as she tapped out her son's number, but all she got was his answering-machine. She never knew what to say to answering-machines so, after listening eagerly to Gareth's voice, she put the receiver down. She'd call Mary. When she did, there was no reply.

'Mum. I'll ring Mum.' They normally only spoke on Sundays, but she'd think of an excuse for calling now. 'I'll ask for a recipe.' A recipe for what? As the number rang out, she tried to think of something it wouldn't seem foolish not to know how to cook after more than a quarter of a century as a housewife. Nothing had come to mind by the time several minutes had passed and she realised her mother wasn't in.

'Beryl!' Beryl was the sister she'd always felt closest to. By now, her fingers were frantic as they pressed Beryl's number. No answer.

'Where are they?' she murmured, fretfully and jealously. 'Why has everyone got somewhere to go except me?'

Her sister Katie had always seemed a somewhat distant figure, fifteen when Emily was born. Katie, with two daughters and three grandchildren, would soon be sixty. She must buy a present and a card. She'd ring Katie, say she was just calling for a chat. There had never been any need for excuses in the past, but the sisters had grown apart, at least Emily had. She'd got fed up with lying, saying stoutly, 'Oh, I'm fine,' when they asked how she was. Alex had always tended to look down on her family, with their rough Cockney accents and poor education, on the assumption that they were too dim to notice. But they had, and she didn't want them to know that she, too, had become an object of his contempt.

She was relieved when the receiver at the other end was picked up almost immediately. To her astonishment, it was Gareth who answered, her son. Emily gabbled something incomprehensible.

'Mum, is that you?' She could imagine him frowning at the phone. Her son, with his crisp dark curls, just like Alex, the same dark eyes, softer and kinder than his father's.

'Yes, love.' (*Oh, yes, love. It's your mother, and I miss you terribly.*)

'You sound different. Are you okay?'

'Oh, I'm fine, sweetheart. Absolutely fine. What are you doing at Katie's?'

'It's her birthday, she's sixty. We're going to the West End for dinner, eighteen of us. Bill's booked a room.' Bill was Katie's husband. Gareth's voice dropped a tone, became mildly disapproving. 'You forgot, Mum, didn't you? Katie noticed. She remarked that she hadn't heard from you.'

Waves of pain and remorse were washing over Emily.

She sat frozen to the chair. 'I'm sorry, sweetheart. Put Katie on and I'll wish her happy birthday.'

'Can't, Mum, sorry. I can see through the window and she's just getting into the car. We're already a bit late. Oh, look! Gran's dropped her stole.' Emily heard the faint beep of a horn. 'I'll have to run,' Gareth said quickly. 'They're waiting for me. The phone went just as I was going out the door. 'Bye, Mum. 'Bye.'

' 'Bye, son,' Emily whispered to the impersonal whining sound. She seized her plait and twisted it round and round until it hurt. Since when had her mother had a stole? Eighteen of them going out to dinner – and no one had thought to ask her! Would she have gone if they had, all the way to London? Of course not. It was all she could do to drive to the supermarket two miles away. There was a yellow Punto in the garage, two years old, with barely four figures on the clock. Emily had hypothermia, hypochondria, hypo-something. It was torture to leave the house. Yet she hated the house. She hated the whispers and the shadows, the feeling that old spirits lived there, phantom figures, grey, cobwebby ghosts that watched over her while she slept and floated mournfully in and out of the rooms.

The phone rang. Emily jumped fearfully, let go of the

plait and it fell back on her shoulder like a skein of old wool.

'Emily,' Alex said brusquely, his loud, sharp voice filling the room, 'I won't be home tonight. We're meeting up with some guys from the States who are staying in Manchester, useful contacts, that sort of thing.'

'Oh, no, Alex! Please come home.' She'd never pleaded with him before and wished she hadn't now. It was degrading, but the words had come out impetuously before she'd had time to think. Emily bent her head, waiting for the lash of his reply.

'For goodness' sake, Emily. I'm not often away, am I? Not like some husbands. It's only one night.'

'I'm frightened,' Emily whispered, grovelling.

Alex made a sound, like a little impatient sneeze, then made another. Emily wondered if they'd come from his nose or his mouth. She cowered over the phone. She'd done it now. He'd hate her. To her surprise, his voice when it came was relatively gentle. 'There's nothing to be frightened of, Em. Lock all the doors, bolt the windows, watch television, then go to bed. I'll be back in the morning.'

'The morning?'

'Well, it might be evening, I'm not sure. Night, Em. Sleep well.'

'Goodnight, Alex.' Yet again Emily spoke to a monotonous whine.

The silence before was nothing like the silence after she had returned the receiver to its cradle. The silence was so total, she felt as if she was buried in sand, or covered with snow, or nailed in a coffin six feet under the ground. Perhaps she'd lost her hearing.

She went over and switched on a lamp, and was relieved to hear it click. Her feet, in the large, shapeless sandals, were illuminated in the circle of yellow light. Were they her feet? Were these her hands? She held out her hands, large, capable hands. Who was she? A lost soul like the other invisible residents of Thorntons? A cobwebby wraith who floated from room to room? An unnecessary being, an irritant brushing against other people's lives, to be flicked away like cigarette ash or a piece of fluff?

She went over to the window. The dark green leaves on the big oak tree touched each other in the faint wind, spoke to each other. 'See that woman watching us? She's as mad as a hatter. Completely bonkers.'

The rope, the children's swing, rocked back and forth, the hemp worn now, hairy, like coconut matting. It looked like a noose, Emily thought. She briefly contemplated hanging herself. The thing was, she couldn't bear to miss Alex's reaction when he came home and found her heavy body swinging from the tree.

Then Emily did something peculiar. She laughed. It was a long time since she'd laughed, and it came out all rusty, like a key turning in an old lock, squeaky. But she could visualise Alex's face: the surprise, the shock, the horror. And the comments: 'His poor wife topped herself,' everyone would say. 'Mind you, she was a total nutter.' Once he'd got over it, he'd think she'd let him down. Alex had his pride, about ten times as much as other people. He couldn't stand anyone feeling sorry for him.

If she could laugh once, she could laugh again. So Emily did. And, as if the key was unlocking the door to a musty, unused room, allowing fresh air and sunlight to flood inside, Emily knew that if she didn't help herself, pretty soon she would indeed become a total nutter.

She walked round the house, locking doors and bolting windows, ignoring the ghosts that swept out of the rooms as she went in. But she didn't turn on the television. No way would she stay in this house on her own for another twenty-four hours. It was a question of survival.

No. She would get in the car and drive to Kirkby. Mae might need those groceries.

94

CHAPTER FOUR

The setting sun filtered through the hedges making a dazzling pattern of black lace on the yellow Punto as it sped along the narrow country lanes. For no reason Emily sounded the horn. She opened the window and sang. 'We shall overcome!'

By the time she reached the dual carriageway she felt quite insane, drunk with freedom and fresh air. She smiled a lot, not a normal smile because she'd forgotten how, more a fiendish grin, baring her teeth like the wolf contemplating Little Red Riding Hood. She waved through the open window at drivers coming from the opposite direction. The drivers took one look at her demented face and didn't wave back. Several children started to cry. Emily sang again: 'Get Me To The Church On Time', her father's favourite, and 'The Red Flag'.

' ". . . then raise the scarlet standard high, Within its shade we'll live or die . . ." ' she yelled defiantly, as she'd once done with Alex at student demonstrations. Now, though, with a Labour government in, it was no longer rebellious to sing 'The Red Flag', except if you were a member of the Labour Party, which had gone all respectable and middle-class under Tony Blair. ' "Tho' cowards flinch and traitors sneer, We'll keep the red flag flying here." '

Everywhere looked far more respectable and civilised than she'd expected when she reached Kirkby and its vast estate of houses. The sun was lower now, the air dusky. The blooms in the gardens of the rows and rows of neat dwellings glowed brilliantly, as if illuminated from behind.

The part of the estate where the McNultys lived was called 'The Flowers'. Emily found Daffodil Close quite easily. It was a cul-de-sac with about sixteen houses; Mae's two were numbers six and eight. The joint front garden was an expanse of lumpy soil, with only an occasional tuft of grass. Emily knocked on number six, slightly less manic than before, and smugly aware that she was doing a good turn and would be amply rewarded with Mae's warm, grateful smile, and hopefully the opportunity to meet the unconventional family she'd heard so much about.

The door was opened instantly by a small man with Mae's bright eyes and a face like an onion cut in half. He was old, going on for eighty. Tufts of grey hair sprouted from his large, pointy ears, making him look like a demonic pixie. His shirtsleeves were rolled up, revealing several faded tattoos. 'What?' he demanded rudely.

Emily was currently on too high a high to be disturbed by such a brusque greeting. 'Mae left her shopping at my house,' she said nicely. He'd change his tune once he knew why she'd come and turn all servile and appreciative. 'I thought she might need it over the weekend.' She handed him the bag. He opened it and glared at the contents.

'Where's the pie?'

'Oh, gosh!' She'd put the pie in the fridge and had forgotten to take it out again. 'I'm sorry, I put it—'

'And the effin' bacon?'

'I'm so sorry, I—'

'The bacon was for our tea.'

'I'm sorry.'

'We had to have tinned meat.' He transferred his glare from inside the bag to Emily. She found it so thoroughly intimidating that she apologised again, even more profusely, for something that wasn't her fault. It was Mae who'd forgotten the groceries, not her.

'I'm terribly, terribly sorry,' she stuttered.

'You must be the one she works for in Ince Blundell.'

'I'm Emily Murphy, yes.' The quickly acquired, unnatural high she'd been on rapidly sank to her usual natural low. Why did he need to spit out the question so nastily, as if he was asking if she was related to Saddam Hussein? A dog with a great orange plume of a tail strolled out of the house and began to sniff her shoe. She shuffled out of the way when it appeared about to pee against her leg.

The man smiled sarcastically. 'Clear your garage out okay, did she, our Mae?'

'Why, yes,' Emily gushed copiously, for some reason anxious to get into his good books. 'She did it wonderfully. She did a really good job.' The garage hadn't been cleaned for years. Alex would be pleased to find everything neatly put away, the rubbish in a row of plastic bags outside, the floor swept, the window cleaned. It had been his idea to suggest it on Thursday night when Emily said there wasn't much for Mae to do next day.

'Mae makes a good job of everything she does.' The

man's blue eyes seemed to bore right through her. 'What task will she be set on Monday?' he demanded angrily. 'Need the roof tiling, do you? Fancy a new chimney? Dampcourse want replacing? Any cows have to be milked? Paths laying? Want any walls knocked down or new ones putting up?'

It slowly dawned on Emily, listening to this tirade, that he disapproved of Mae clearing the garage, which did seem a bit of a cheek, but Mae hadn't objected. She never did, no matter what she was asked to do. 'Has Mae complained?' she asked, worried. She needed Mae, not just for her amazing cleaning powers but for the company.

'Mae never complains,' the man snarled. 'But I do. You see, I object to me granddaughter being exploited by people like you. Capitalist vermin! I suppose you're a believer in Victorian values, like Lady bleedin' Thatcher. Let's work the workers till they drop, till they sweat blood, but we're not paying 'em more than three pounds bleedin' fifty an hour, even less if we can get away with it.'

'Is Mae in?' Emily enquired tearfully. Perhaps she should have stayed at home with the ghosts.

'She's at work. You're not the only one she slaves her

guts out for.' He took a threatening step forward, and Emily feared she was about to be attacked.

'Thank you.' She backed down the path. Mae's grandfather began to follow, waving his fist, his half-onion face screwed in furious rage.

'Get her to change the engine in your car, why don't you? Maybe she could rewire your house, or cut down a few trees. She's handy with a chainsaw is our Mae.' When Emily crossed the road to the car, he was still shouting: 'Next time your husband has a shit, ask Mae to wipe his arse for him, the tight-fingered git.'

She was unlocking the car when she heard, 'Get her, Cecil. Go on, boy, get her!'

Fortunately, Cecil didn't seem inclined to give chase. Emily scrambled into the car and drove away, heart thudding.

She remembered now, far too late, that Mae worked behind the bar of an Irish club four nights a week, Wednesday to Saturday. A few minutes later, a shattered, shaking Emily stopped at a newsagent's and asked where the club was; no more than five minutes' drive away, she was told. She was in a much worse state than when she'd left Thorntons. At least the ghosts didn't shout insults, call her capitalist vermin. But she wasn't prepared to go home, back to them, and her over-whelming, all-consuming, suffocating, mind-bending solitariness. She wanted to say sorry to Mae about the garage. She'd tell her it was all Alex's idea, which was the truth.

It was half past eight by now, and the Irish club was crowded. At first, the man on the door wasn't prepared to let her in because she wasn't a member. 'I've come to see Mae,' Emily stammered desperately. 'Mae McNulty.' She hoped and prayed the man didn't know about the garage, or she'd be subjected to another tirade of abuse. He opened one half of the swing doors and screeched, 'Mae, luv. Someone wants to see you. What's your name, girl?' he asked.

'Emily Murphy.'

'It's an Emily Murphy,' the man yelled. Then, 'In you go, girl.'

Emily walked into a volcano of noise, an earth-shattering, ear-piercing din of music and singing, talking and shouting, glass banging and foot-stamping. It was like emerging from the safety and warmth of her mother's womb into a strange, bright world that she found frightening, yet she didn't want to go back to the comfortable place where she'd been all screwed up in a ball and felt more than a little bored. At the same time, she felt seriously conspicuous, a stranger, all alone, who must stand out like a sore thumb. She looked down at herself to see what she was wearing: an old, shapeless T-shirt the colour of mould, the dirndl skirt she'd made for herself just after Mary was born in the days when she was handy with a needle (and one or two other things). Those grotesque bloody sandals! Where the hell had she got them? They exposed all ten of her giant, plum-like toes — the nails badly needed cutting. Why hadn't she thought to change her clothes? What on earth would people think?

She glanced up, shame-faced, and felt even worse when she saw that not a single soul was looking in her direction.

I would have caused a stir — once. She sighed. And, once, Alex would have loved it here. But Alex would hate it now. 'The working classes at play', he'd sneer. She felt nostalgia for their student days, when they used to go to the same sort of club in Manchester, and Alex knew by heart the words of all the Irish songs. 'The Wild Rover', 'The Black Velvet Band', 'The Wild Colonial Boy'. They could make a pint of beer each last the whole night. With a Protestant mother and a Catholic father,

Alex was neither Republican nor Nationalist. The matter of Northern Ireland was one of the few things on which he had no firm opinion. Not even the brilliant, scintillating mind of Alex Murphy could come up with a solution.

Ah, recognition at last. Mae was waving to her from behind the bar where, with two other barmaids, she was trying to serve about twenty customers. She wore a black sequinned velvet top that revealed the tops of her creamy breasts, and long silver earrings. Her blonde hair was pinned untidily, but fashionably, on top of her head, with little ringlets dangling on her forehead and neck.

'What on earth are you doing here, Em?' she shouted, when Emily went over.

'You left your groceries behind and I thought you might need them. But I'm afraid I left your pie and the bacon in the fridge,' Emily shouted back.

'What? I didn't catch that, Em.'

'She's brought your groceries, but she's afraid the pie and the bacon were left in the fridge,' a man waiting beside Emily at the bar explained. He had an immense bass voice, full of resonance, easily heard above the din. 'Two pints of Guinness, Mae, luv, and a whiskey and ginger.' He turned to Emily. 'What are you having, Em?'

'Oh, gosh! I haven't brought a handbag. I've no money.'

'Make it two whiskey and gingers, Mae. One for Em here.'

'Actually, I never drink whiskey.'

'It'll do you good, Em,' the man said. 'Bring the roses back to your cheeks.'

On top of everything else she must look run-down. Oh, well, at least he hadn't ordered cod-liver oil.

'Find a seat somewhere, Em,' Mae said distractedly. 'I'll come and have a word when I'm less busy.'

'I met your grandad. I don't think he liked me much,' Emily said, the encounter still preying unpleasantly on her mind.

'Jim McNulty doesn't like anybody much,' the man beside her said, when Mae didn't hear.

'He set the dog on me.' Emily sniffed.

'Cecil!' The man laughed. 'It's not his dog, and Cecil's about a hundred years old and wouldn't hurt a fly.'

'Could you please tell Mae that I'm sorry about the garage?'

'Em's sorry about the garage, Mae,' the man boomed.

Mae looked startled. 'What? Didn't I do it right?'

'You did it perfectly. I'm just sorry I asked.'

'She's sorry she asked.'

'I haven't a clue what anyone's talking about,' Mae said.

'She hasn't a clue what we're talking about,' the man with the bass voice said to Emily.

'Oh, never mind.'

' "Oh, never mind," she said. Here's your drink, Em. Cheers!'

'Cheers.' At least the drink gave her an excuse to stay. Emily pushed her way through the crowds and saw an empty chair at an otherwise crowded table. 'Is this seat free?'

'No, it's fifty pence an hour to sit on,' a very elderly woman said.

Emily was about to move away, when the woman shouted, 'For Chrissakes, luv, I was only kidding. Sit yourself down. You're new here, aren't you?'

'Yes.' It was too wearing to have a conversation in such a racket. On the stage, a man in a canary yellow pullover with canary yellow hair was singing 'When Irish Eyes Are Smiling' in a high-pitched quivery voice that was rather appealing. He was very thin, and handsome in a dissipated, decadent way.

Oh, there was a karaoke machine. Alex would be

disgusted! Emily giggled, imagining telling him where she'd been. Just a few sips of the whiskey had gone straight to her head. It was all very pleasant and quite different from how she'd thought the day would end. The memory of Jim McNulty was beginning to fade. In fact, Cecil had seemed quite nice. Perhaps she should get a dog. And a cat.

Snippets of conversation wafted around her ears.

'And I said to him, I said to him, "All I want is two pounds of potatoes and a pound of soddin' carrots. I don't want to look at your dirty magazines."'

'That's a terrible way for a greengrocer to behave.'

To Emily's intense horror, the men on the next table were discussing Alex. Apparently they wanted to kill him in the most appalling way. Alex wasn't exactly the kindest of men, but was there any need to castrate him, or burn him alive? She turned to the men and said emotionally, 'Please don't talk about Alex like that.'

'What's it to you, girl?'

'He's my husband.'

Two of the men rose and stood over her threateningly. Emily cowered. 'You're Alex Ferguson's wife?'

'No, Alex Murphy's.'

'The woman's batty. Get her a drink someone.'

'Tony Blair's okay, but he's got no sex appeal. On the other hand, Gordon Brown could poke me for hours.' This came from the elderly woman who'd given Emily the seat.

'I always fancied Michael Heseltine meself,' said her companion, even older.

'I don't like blond men. They make me seasick.'

The man with the yellow pullover and matching hair was monopolising the karaoke machine, singing 'As Time Goes By', bent over the microphone as if he were making love to it. He wasn't exactly young, but Emily thought him very sexy.

Mae came over with a whiskey and ginger. She looked fresh and glamorous, her velvet skirt way above her knees. 'Enjoying yourself, Em?'

'Immensely. I think I'm drunk.' The club was dancing before her eyes, or the people were, or perhaps it was her brain. Everyone seemed to be talking very slowly in very deep voices, like a broken gramophone. 'People keep buying me whiskey.'

'Here's another on the house. Let yourself go, Em, it wouldn't be before time. I'd better be getting back. We're always dead busy on Fridays.'

'Slag!' the elderly woman spat, when Mae had gone.

'Who, me?' said Emily, startled.

'No, that Mae McNulty. Slag with knobs on.' She turned to her friend. 'Someone came looking for her at the community centre the other day, yeller feller with slitty eyes. Didn't know her surname, just Mae and a description. Knew straight away who he meant.'

'What did you tell him?'

'To sod off. No one like that round here, I said.'

People began to dance, properly dance, an Irish jig of some sorts. There was a fight in a corner, screams, a police siren, lots of policemen, ambulancemen with a stretcher, more dancing, more singing, more whiskey, more noise. Emily wondered why, in such a short space of time, the faces around her had become so hideously ugly: huge, bulging noses, swollen cheeks, big pop eyes, like hardboiled eggs without their shell. Even the man with the yellow pullover wasn't the least bit handsome close up – for some reason he was sitting beside her. His mouth was very thin and enormously wide, stretching from ear to ear. 'Are you a letter-box?' she asked.

She had no idea if he was or not. Suddenly, without warning, her head dropped forward on to the table with a thud and the glasses gave a little jump. She'd passed out.

The first things Emily noticed when she woke up next morning were:

(a) A yellow pullover on the bedroom floor.
(b) She had nothing on.
(c) There was someone in bed with her.

In regard to point (c) Who?

She could hear the person, behind her, breathing lightly, as opposed to Emily who was breathing heavily and wanted to scream.

Who was it?

Had she made love with this person?

Yes. Her thighs were sore and she could smell it.

Could it be Alex?

But if she and Alex had made love for the first time in, what was it, three years, four, surely she would have remembered?

Even more surely, if she'd made love to someone else, a complete stranger, she was even more likely to remember.

Unless it was Alex, all men's semen must smell the same. Or, to be grammatically correct, the semen of all men must smell the same.

She was scared to turn over and see who it was.

Say if it was a woman!

Last night she vaguely recalled an old woman professing an interest in Gordon Brown. It was an unfortunate fact, but as Emily had grown more bulky, she had become convinced she bore more than a passing resemblance to Gordon Brown.

Oh, gosh!

But women couldn't produce semen.

Phew!

How had she got home last night?

Had she come in her own car?

Who the hell was she in bed with? The more she stared at the yellow pullover, the more familiar it seemed. She'd seen it before.

There was a rustling sound and a click. Her unknown companion of the night had just lit a cigarette.

Emily took a deep breath and turned over. A thin man with a lovely tan, naked except for a smart moustache, was sitting up, leaning against the pillow, smoking.

'Morning, Em,' he said cheerfully.

'Morning,' Emily stammered. He knew who she was! Which didn't seem fair, as she didn't know him from Adam.

'Any chance of a cup of tea, luv? I feel as if I've just cleaned the bottom of a birdcage with me tongue.'

'In a minute.'

'Okay, Em.' He reached under the clothes and slapped her thigh in an intimate and companionable way. 'It's nice here, I like it.' He glanced around the room and nodded approvingly. 'Our Mae said it was nice.'

'Who?'

'Our Mae, me daughter who does for you. She said it was nice.'

She'd slept with her father's cleaner!

No.

Her cleaner's father. His name, if she recalled rightly, was Eddie.

Oh, Lord!

'I can't remember a thing about last night.' She gulped. Had she enjoyed it, for instance? Had he?

'That's not a very nice thing to say.' Eddie pouted, 'Doesn't do me ego much good, does it? Give of me best, and she can't remember a thing. Well, I'll remedy that in a minute. Wait till I've finished this ciggie.' He looked quite hurt. His eyes were paler than his daughter's, a light, milky blue. Like Mae, his features were small and neat, making him appear effeminate, especially with his bountiful blond hair all mussed — Mae had told her it was dyed. He looked like a nineteen-thirties matinée idol who wore silk pyjamas and smoked cigarettes in a holder. 'He's a bloody swine, me dad,' Mae, who rarely had a bad word for anyone, had commented more than once. 'Always got a string of women after him. I don't know what they see in him.'

Fortunately, since they were in bed together, Emily could. The idea of sleeping with a bloody swine quite turned her on, though she still couldn't get used to the fact that he was *there*! 'What do you mean, you'll remedy that in a minute?'

'I said, wait till I've finished this ciggie. Don't want to waste it, do I? Not with the price of fags nowadays.' There was silence. Emily watched in astonishment as the duvet began to rise, as if a small earthquake was taking place beneath. Then Eddie stubbed out his cigarette on the bedside cabinet, pounced on her, and provided rock-solid proof of what women saw in him.

Phew! Again.

'Won't forget that in a while, will you?' he crowed, after they had panted to an extraordinarily satisfactory climax.

Emily shook her head numbly. Never in a million years.

He sat up and lit another cigarette. 'I'm aching for that cuppa you promised.'

'In a minute.' She was still out of breath and riddled with pleasure. It had been great, not the same as with Alex but purely physical, enjoyable in a rudimentary, down-to-earth, entirely basic way, like someone scratching an unreachable part of your body when an itch was driving you insane. You didn't care who the someone was as long as they did it thoroughly. Eddie was undoubtedly thorough.

He pouted again. 'That's what you said before, in a minute.'

Apart from finding the pout quite adorable, Emily was otherwise unmoved. 'How did I get home last night?' she enquired.

'You passed out so I drove you back in your car. Nice little mover — the car, that is.'

She probed further. 'How did we get here? In bed, I mean.'

Eddie's face was a picture of virtuous innocence. 'Helped you upstairs, didn't I, else you'd have slept downstairs on the floor. Took your clothes off for you, seemed the proper thing to do, like.'

'Was I still passed out when we, when you . . . ?'

'Christ Almighty, girl, what d'you take me for? A bloody rapist?' He looked down at her indignantly, but she could tell it was faked. 'In fact, if you want the truth, it was more like you raped me. Put your arms around me neck, you did, and wouldn't let me go. I must say,' he remarked approvingly, 'you've got a strong pair of thighs on you. Felt like a fly, I did, trapped by a ten-ton spider.' He punched her playfully on the shoulder. 'It was great, I must say. Mind you, I'd had a bit too much to drink myself.'

Emily knew she should feel totally humiliated, but it was a measure of how low her *id* had sunk that instead she felt hugely flattered.

Then her cosy little love-nest suddenly fell out of the tree with a sickening thud. There were footsteps on the stairs, and Alex called, 'Emily! Em, are you there?'

In a trice, Eddie McNulty had rolled off the bed and under it, with the expertise of a man who'd done it many times before. Hands appeared from both sides, like an octopus on speed, and grabbed his clothes.

Emily reached the door and opened it just as Alex arrived. She didn't want him to come in and smell the sex, sense Eddie's presence. There wasn't time to put anything on.

'Alex.'

'Em.' He looked tired, agitated, as if he'd been up all night. His eyes narrowed slightly in surprise. 'Why, Em! I didn't realise you'd gone in for sleeping *in puris naturalibus.*' (He'd taken an A level in Latin.) 'You look different.'

He'd probably forgotten she had skin. 'It was hot last night,' she explained, flustered and embarrassed.

'Your hair's all mussed, your cheeks are pink. Oh, Em!' He put his wiry hands on her arms and began to push her back into the bedroom.

This was precisely what she had wanted for many years, what she had dreamt about, yearned for, alone in the bed, aching and pathetic in her need. Now Emily had no alternative but to do the unthinkable. She pushed him away. 'Sorry, Alex, but I'm dying to go to the loo.' There was no way she'd let him make love to her with Eddie under the bed. It would almost be like one of those sandwich things she'd read about, albeit with the extra filling of the mattress.

'So, it's not the proverbial headache this time,' Alex said spitefully.

'Only you could make such a snide remark, Alex,' Emily said, in her coldest voice. She wanted to hit him. He'd ignored her all this time, then expected her to fall into his arms the minute the whim took him, which she would have done willingly if it hadn't been for Eddie. Now, she was almost glad that Eddie was there and she'd had to reject Alex — let him realise that she wasn't just there for the asking. What's more, she really *did* have a headache, a thumping, clanging headache, which was probably a hangover from last night.

Alex looked sulky. 'You'd better put some clothes on. I'd forgotten, there's people downstairs and they'd like breakfast.'

'There's no food!'

'You don't appear to be of much use anywhere in the house, Emily,' Alex said, with a nasty smile. 'You're no good in the kitchen, or the bedroom.'

There were a few old eggs in the fridge, but she had forgotten about Mae's bacon and the pork pie. Emily cut the pie into slices and fried them with the bacon. The visitors, an American couple in their fifties, might think it a peculiar local dish, like Yorkshire pudding or Cornish pasties. Alex was still showing them round the garden and she hadn't met them yet. She watched through the window as she prepared the food. The man was small and tubby, with bright, button eyes and a loud check suit. The woman had dramatic toffee-coloured hair, cascades of it rippling down her back, and a beaked nose like a hungry bird of prey. Enviably lean, she wore white jeans and a red silk shirt. It was another glorious morning, everywhere drenched in sunshine.

Emily tapped on the window when the meal was ready, and forced her face into a smile. Her adventures of the night before, finding Eddie in her bed this morning, the narrow escape when Alex had come home, his unexpected advance, and making breakfast for two Americans which, due to her thumping hangover, made her want to be sick, were beginning to take their toll. Her head felt as if it was crammed with old newspapers. Yesterday there had been nothing of any description to occupy her mind, and today there was too much. Was Eddie still under the bed? Would Alex decide to go upstairs and change? Would Eddie tell Mae that he'd slept with her employer? Would Eddie want to do it again?

Oh, yes, *please!*

Alex came into the kitchen with the visitors. To Emily's astonishment, before they could be introduced, the woman swooped down on her, arms open wide, like an eagle who had spotted a particularly desirable lamb. 'This is an unhappy house,' she intoned loudly, in a deep, funereal voice, hugging Emily so hard she almost choked. 'I sensed it the minute I came in. In years gone by, people have suffered here and died.'

'Of course they have, honey,' her husband said amiably. 'It's an old place. People are bound to have suffered here and died.'

'True,' Alex concurred, annoyed.

The woman released Emily with a dramatic flourish, and regarded the men with, there was no use denying it, totally mad, black, glistening eyes. 'Men have no awareness of the spiritual. You sense it, don't you, Emily, babe? You sense those sad souls wandering around your house, in and out of the rooms, up and down the stairs, seeking something, who knows what? Salvation, escape, the companionship of other listless spirits like themselves.'

'Sometimes,' Emily said awkwardly. Could she bring herself to stay alone in the bloody house again?

'What rubbish, Em,' Alex snapped.

'Honey, sit down and eat your breakfast,' the man pleaded. He winked at Emily a touch desperately. 'She's driven all our friends back home into moving house. Naturally, they don't tell us their new address. Back home, we're friendless.'

'That's understandable,' sneered Alex, who'd clearly had enough of the American visitors.

'Something can be done about it.' The woman pierced her egg with a fork, and Emily's stomach heaved as a piece of Mae's pie was dipped into the yolk. Yellow-streaked, it was waved in the air, and the woman fixed her great, mad eyes on Emily. 'This house must be purged, the spirits banished, washed away.'

'What with?'

'With a sponge and water, babe. Wash every inch of every wall, every ceiling, every floor, and don't forget the doors and windows.'

'I see,' Emily said faintly.

'Honey, please!' the man wailed. 'Look, don't take any notice of her, she's talking garbage.'

Alex snorted agreement.

When breakfast was over, to Emily's horror Alex took the American into his study, and she was left with the wife.

'Another thing, babe,' the woman said earnestly, leaning across the table and clasping Emily's sturdy hand in her clawlike one, 'your toilet lid and seat were up.'

'I'm so sorry, it's Alex, he always forgets to put them down.'

'That toilet in the hall is in the worst possible place, directly opposite your front door. Your good luck comes flowing in, then disappears right down the toilet.' She squeezed Emily's hand till it hurt. 'This isn't just an unhappy house, babe, but an unlucky one as well.'

'Oh, Lord.' Emily groaned despairingly. Would nothing ever go right?

'Wash your walls, keep the toilet lid down, then everything will be all right.'

'Will it?'

'I promise, babe.'

An hour later, the visitors left with Alex, who was taking them to Skelmersdale to look around the factory. A drained, exhausted Emily immediately went upstairs in search of Eddie. There was no sign of him in the bedroom – perhaps he'd sensibly gone to hide in another. She was about to search elsewhere, but jumped when the wardrobe door creaked, then swung open, and Eddie stepped out wearing one of Alex's suits, the pale blue linen one with twenty per cent silk content.

'Hiya, Em. I peeped through a crack in the door to make sure it was you.' He began to preen himself in front of the mirror, adjusting the lapels of the jacket, smoothing the sides of the pants. 'What d'you think?'

'It looks nice,' said Emily.

'Blue suits me, goes with me eyes, like. I'll keep it, if you don't mind. Bit of a reward, sort of thing, for bringing you home and that business in bed. Your husband won't miss it, will he? Must have about twenty suits in there.'

'I think he might – miss it, that is.'

'Tell him it got lost at the cleaners'.'

'Alex is not the sort of person to accept an explanation like that.' Alex would sue the cleaners all the way to the House of Lords if he thought they'd lost his suit.

'You'll think of something, Em.' In the mirror his eyes met hers, challenging her to challenge him. He was telling her he valued himself very highly. Eddie McNulty wasn't prepared to tour Liverpool servicing lonely, frustrated housewives for free. He wasn't a very nice man, but Emily needed him. Any remnant of any pride she might have had left vanished in a puff of smoke. She decided that a row with Alex in the distant future over a missing suit was well worth what had happened last night – and what she hoped would happen again.

'Does Mae know you brought me home?' she asked.

'She might do, luv, I dunno. Why?'

'Won't she be wondering where you are?'

Eddie shook his head. 'She works all day Sat'days and Sundays in the supermarket, doesn't she? She won't know I'm not at home.'

'I'd sooner Mae didn't hear about last night.'

'So would I,' Eddie said fervently, rolling his eyes. 'Else she'll pin me ear back for the rest of me life. Come on, girl. I still haven't had that tea, and I wouldn't mind a bite to eat, either.' He smiled a charming smile. 'And don't bother with a pudding, Em. I'll have you for afters.'

And Emily – once, oh, a long, long time ago, it felt

like a thousand years, a fierce and vocal feminist – let the side down completely and nodded eagerly. She couldn't wait.

Alex called to say he wouldn't be home till eight that night, so Eddie stayed till seven. Emily took him to Kirkby in the car, dropping him off some distance away from Daffodil Close so they wouldn't be seen. He wore the blue linen suit, with his own clothes in a plastic bag. He would tell Mae he'd got it in a car-boot sale. She'd never guess it originally cost five hundred quid.

Emily picked him up in the same place next morning after he'd been to Mass. When he left that afternoon, he rooted through the wardrobe and helped himself to one of Alex's shirts to go with the suit. Emily watched from the bed, where she lay sated, drugged with sex, tired but happy, feeling at least faintly desirable for a change. If you looked at it one way, men paid for sex all the time so it seemed the ultimate in feminism for women to do the same, though perhaps it was a touch unusual to pay with your husband's clothes.

CHAPTER FIVE

'Excuse me, missus, but would you know a lad lives round here name of Bart Simpson?'

The woman looked up from the doorstep she was scrubbing. 'Sorry, luv. Never heard of him. Ask at the pub.'

'We already have.'

Mick and Paddy returned to the car, parked in an old, narrow street off Scotland Road, not far from the centre of Liverpool. 'I'm fed up asking people, Mick,' Paddy complained. 'Either they've never heard of him or they look at us as if we were eejits and laugh themselves sick.'

'Is he a little chap with bright yeller hair?' one young lad of about ten had asked only yesterday. 'Talks American, like.'

'No, he's quite tall for his age, and his hair's not

125

exactly yeller, more a creamy colour,' Paddy had replied. 'Speaks with a Liverpool accent.'

'In that case, I don't know him.' The lad grinned, made a face and tapped his head, as if he was addressing lunatics. 'Someone's having you both on.'

'What did that young feller mean yesterday, d'you think, Mick, that someone was having us on?'

'I dunno, Paddy.' Mick tapped his teeth thoughtfully. 'But I think it's time we went back to Kirkby.'

Detective Sergeant Watson and his partner, Detective Constable Jones, were sitting in their unobtrusive grey Sierra at the far end of the street. They were hard men with steely eyes and bullet heads, their faces set like concrete in expressions of permanent suspicion. Their hair was short, sternly trimmed and the colour of mud. They considered themselves as unobtrusive as the car, in their plain, dark clothes, yet every single thing about them down to their size twelve shoes, screamed *COPS!*

'What in fuck's sake are they up to?' Watson mused.

'Christ knows, Sarge.'

'I mean, what the hell was this Bart Simpson kid doing in Kirkby when he lives round here?'

'Haven't a clue. I asked a couple of the chaps back at

the nick, and they reckoned we were on a wild-goose chase.' They'd also looked rather amused, Watson couldn't think why.

'What's it short for, Bart?'

Jones thought hard. 'Bartholomew, I reckon.'

'Ha-ha-ha.' Watson squeezed every ounce of sarcasm he could muster into the laugh. 'As if anyone round Scotland Road would call their kid Bartholomew. They must be stupid if that's what they think.'

'Well, Sarge, they're Irish, aren't they?'

Watson nodded understandingly. 'Yes, mate, there's that.'

They watched in silence for a while as the suspects returned to their car, where they appeared to be having an animated conversation.

Jones said, 'I wonder where the stuff is?'

'Christ knows. I reckon that's what all this is about. They've lost it. They gave it to the wrong kid, this Bart Simpson, when it should have gone to Rory Quinn's lad. Now they're trying to find him to get it back.'

'We should have waited that day, the day we saw them hand the package over. We should have waited and made sure it stayed inside the Quinns' house.' Jones spoke with a faintly accusing air. He was only the junior partner, though ten years Watson's senior, having been unfairly passed over for promotion numerous times. It wasn't him who decided procedure. It wasn't him who'd decided to follow the two Irishmen and leave the stuff behind.

'For fuck's sake,' Sarge exploded, and his rage was awesome to behold. 'I didn't expect two pounds of Semtex to go in the Quinns and come shooting out again like a fucking yo-yo, did I? I thought it would be there until Sean Donovan came to collect it. Then we could have caught him red-handed. He's the one we're after, he's the fucking terrorist, not those two stupid wankers down the street.'

'Donovan arranged to have the Quinns done over, we know that much.'

'I know we know that much. We also know it wasn't found there.'

'I've thought of something,' Jones's concrete expression cracked briefly as he frowned. 'It mightn't be a bad idea to go over the place ourselves. Prove, once and for all, that the stuff's not there. Then we can concentrate on finding this Bart Simpson.'

'Not ourselves, not us. The Super would blow his top

if he found out. It would be more than our jobs are worth.'

'Of course not us.' The promotion process was grossly unfair, Jones thought bitterly. How in hell had Watson been made sergeant when he appeared to have shit for brains? Perhaps he should join the Freemasons – his wife was always nagging him to. 'We'll get our snitch to do it.' He was convinced he could hear Watson's shitty brain grinding slowly and rustily as he thought the matter over.

'You might be on to something there,' he said eventually. 'Let's get back to Kirkby, and concentrate on Rory and Sean. We'll forget about Mick and Paddy for now.' As Jones started up the car, Watson said irritably, 'Their names get on me fucking nerves. Why can't they have good solid English names like we do?'

Michael Jones glanced incredulously at his partner. 'I haven't a clue, Patrick.'

They backed round the corner and headed towards Kirkby, at the same time as a battered car drove out the other end of the street and headed in the same direction.

The snitch was bloody fed up. It was awkward sometimes, being a double agent. It meant that for the second time in as many weeks he'd been asked to turn the same house over. He supposed he'd better appear willing, make a good job of it for the sake of appearances. He emptied drawers, flung the contents of cupboards and wardrobes on the floor, scattered cushions, dragged the bedclothes off, upturned the mattress, looked in the fridge, ate half a scone. Half-way through, the doorbell rang several times, but he ignored it and went out into the shed where he emptied several tins of paint, which he hadn't thought to do the first time. He turned over some freshly turned earth in case the package had been buried, revealing nothing but rows of half-grown spuds.

'It's not there,' he reported back to Detective Sergeant Patrick Watson, just as, unknown to them, he'd reported back to Sean Donovan ten days before. 'Not a sausage.'

'What the hell are burglars coming to?' Tilly Quinn screeched at her husband that night after they had assessed, yet again, that nothing was missing. 'Is this some new sort of fashion, or have burglars become particularly fussy these days? Is someone trying to wear us down? Psychological warfare, I think it's called. Or is it a novel form of consumer research? In a roundabout and very hurtful way, someone's trying to tell us that everything we own is worthless, and the whole house needs kitting out with entirely new stuff. Next time, perhaps they'll leave a questionnaire.' She paused for breath. 'The bugger didn't even finish me scone, and it was made with butter too. And why pour paint on the floor? Why not steal it? It was good paint that, Solo, only requires a single coat. I got it with me Sainsbury's Reward vouchers because someone sitting no more than six feet away promised to paint the lounge. I'd sooner it'd been taken, I really would, let someone else have the benefit, rather than see it wasted.' She paused for more breath. 'And that stupid bitch next door, she saw him! Saw him digging up the spuds. Thought we'd taken on a gardener. A gardener, if you please. Who does she think we are, Lord and Lady Muck? She said he was a titchy feller about sixty. Kitty Branagh saw him going down the path and said he was a big chap in his twenties. Next door said he was white, Kitty claimed he was a China-man. Someone's powers of observation are pretty crap, I must say, and I don't know if it's next door's or Kitty Branagh's. And you, Rory, don't just sit there like a bloody pill garlic, *do* something.'

'What?' Rory asked helplessly.

'I dunno, do I?' Tilly shrieked. 'Men have got

bigger brains than women, or so you're always telling me. I tell you this much, Rory Quinn, if we get done over one more time, I'm going back to me mam's and taking the kids with me. So, put *that* in your pipe and smoke it.'

Much as Rory loved his wife and children, he could think of nothing he could do.

'You look well, Em,' Mae said, when she arrived at noon on Monday. 'Far more alive than usual.' She plunged on, even more tactlessly. 'Your spots look better too, not quite so angry.'

Emily hadn't touched a cornflake all weekend; she'd had far more important things to do. She thought Mae looked tired. More than tired, completely washed out, with hunched shoulders and heavy eyes. Instead of jeans and T-shirt, today she wore a thin cotton frock, which gave her the air of a teenaged waif. Emily felt a motherly concern. 'I didn't know you worked in a supermarket at weekends,' she said. It meant the woman had scarcely stopped working since she'd tidied the Murphys' garage last Friday.

'Who told you?'

'Oh, er, someone mentioned it on Friday night.'

Mae laughed. 'Friday night! You enjoyed yourself, I must say. Did me dad get you home all right?'

'Yes, thank you. He was very kind.'

'I hope he behaved himself.'

'He behaved like a perfect gentleman, Mae.'

'That's not like him. He can be a bloody swine, me dad. Went to a car-boot sale yesterday and came back with a lovely suit for only a few quid. I said to him, "I bet you didn't think to keep a lookout for a coat for our Shona, did you?" It wouldn't have crossed his mind. All he thinks about is himself.' She went over to the utility room. 'I'll give the place a quick dust over, then do the carpets. I haven't cleaned the carpets in more than a week.'

Emily opened her mouth, wanting to say, 'Why not give it a miss today? Sit down, Mae, and we'll have a coffee and a natter.' But the words wouldn't come. It went against everything that she'd come to believe in over the last few years. Employers employed employees to work. Employers weren't supposed to feel sorry for their workers and tell them not to bother. She let Mae go ahead. Her footsteps weren't so lively as usual, and even the vacuum cleaner sounded half-hearted, as if infected by the weariness of its user. Emily wondered if it was the Murphys' fault Mae felt so tired. Perhaps there hadn't been time to recover from tidying the garage before she'd had to go to the club; dragging all those sacks of rubbish outside, putting away the heavy tools that Alex never used, moving ladders and leftover bags of sand and cement, sweeping the cobwebs off the ceilings and the walls, picking up all the loose screws and nails off the floor and putting them in a box because she couldn't bear to throw them away. 'They might come in useful one day. Me grandad's always on the lookout for the odd screw,' she said innocently, oblivious to the *double entendre*. No wonder Grandad had been so angry.

I should never have asked. It's all Alex's fault.

Uneasy and full of guilt, at one o'clock she called Mae down for coffee. 'It's a bit early, isn't it, Em?'

'I'm longing for one myself, that's why. Would you like a chocolate biscuit?' She'd actually been to the supermarket that morning in the car and bought a trolleyload of groceries.

'Oh, it's nice to get the weight off me feet, Em,' Mae said thankfully, when she sat down. It turned out she was worn out because she'd been up all night with Cloud, who was cutting more teeth. 'Our Alice took herself off to Colchester to demonstrate against animal exports, and she didn't come back last night.' On Friday, Craig had arrived home with the news that he'd got the sack. 'That's the fifth time he's been made redundant, and he's only twenty. He's a bright lad, our Craig, got five GCSEs, but they've never got him anywhere.' This morning, Shona had refused to go to school, which wasn't a bit like her. 'So I couldn't get on with me washing. I had to physically drag her to the gates and make sure she went in. She's as thick as two short planks, that girl. She needs her schooling more than most.'

'Never mind, Mae,' Emily said soothingly. 'You can have a rest when you go home. You don't have to work in the club till Wednesday, do you?'

'No, but Monday and Tuesday evenings I do a bit of office cleaning, six till eight. Brings in a bit extra, like. Oh, well,' she jumped to her feet, 'I'll finish off downstairs, then give the bathroom and the lavatories a wipe round.'

'Don't kill yourself, Mae.'

'That's what you pay me to do, isn't it?' Mae replied, with a sunny, utterly guileless smile.

Guilt returned in waves so high that Emily felt as if she were drowning. 'Have another cup of coffee, please.

You worked so hard on Friday, why not take it easy for a change?'

'You're ever so different today, Em. Almost human.'

Emily *felt* almost human. She brought over the coffee pot. 'By the way, someone mentioned on Friday night that there'd been a man in Kirkby looking for you.'

'Did the someone say what he looked like?'

'If they did, I can't remember.'

Mae looked unperturbed. 'Oh, well, he'll find me if he wants to. Let's hope I don't owe him money, that's all.'

Emily told Mae about last Saturday's visitors. 'The woman, I never discovered their names, said this is an unhappy house, that it's haunted. She sensed lost souls everywhere.' She'd often wanted to talk to someone about the ghosts, someone apart from Alex, that is, who always pooh-poohed the notion in a very offensive way, accusing her of being neurotic and unbalanced. It would be a relief to hear from someone who was sensible and impartial that the ghosts didn't exist.

'What nonsense!' Mae said predictably. 'This is a lovely house, and it's got a lovely atmosphere. I hope you're not thinking of washing down the walls or nothing. It'd take for ever. As to tightening the screws on the lav, a man could have a nasty accident if it fell down in the middle of a wee. That poor woman only said it was an unhappy house because she's an unhappy person.'

'That's what I thought.'

'Okay, so it's haunted,' Mae shrugged, 'but in the nicest possible way, as if they want to know you, be mates, like.'

Emily's scalp prickled. 'They?'

'The ghosts.' Mae gave a little shiver, more of delight than fear. 'Little warm draughts and tinkly laughs when you go in and out the rooms, whispery hellos and goodbyes, sort of thing. Haven't you felt them, Em?'

'I was aware of something,' Emily conceded faintly.

Mae looked concerned. 'You're not scared, are you?'

'Occasionally.' From now on, she'd be terrified out of her wits. Twice in the last few days she'd had confirmation of what she'd always suspected. Thorntons was haunted.

'Don't be scared, Em. They don't like it if you're scared. It offends them, because they don't want to hurt you. They just want to be friends.'

'I'll try to remember that in future,' Emily said,

wondering if she should buy a tent and camp in the garden.

Eustace had always been a simple man with simple needs who thought simple thoughts. His mind resembled a telephone directory or a train timetable, where the facts were laid down in plain, printed English, and there wasn't a single question or exclamation mark. Eustace knew his place, which was right down at the bottom of life's shit-heap. He did as he was told, and took what he was paid, even though it was peanuts, and it never crossed his simple mind to question anything that had happened throughout his plain and simple life.

When he'd been sold with the house after more than a quarter of a century of loyal service, left behind by the previous owner, a shady individual heavily involved in a protection racket who'd felt obliged to quit the country hastily and seek sanctuary in the Algarve, Eustace considered himself an old family retainer being passed on from one great dynasty to another.

He lived in an isolated two-roomed cottage about a mile away from Thorntons; one bedroom, one living room, with a lean-to primitive kitchen perched precariously on the back. There was a lavatory at the bottom of the untidy, overgrown garden (like builders with run-down houses, and hairdressers with lousy hair, Eustace, the gardener, only used his talents in his place of work). He mostly rode to the Murphys' on an old sit-up-and-beg bike that had belonged to his mother, and which he kept in as-new condition. On the days when his legs had difficulty turning the pedals, unknown to the Murphys Eustace slept on sacks in the garden shed with a bottle of whisky as company and to keep him warm.

It had dawned on Eustace a few years ago that one day he would die, and it seemed only natural to make out a will leaving everything he possessed to his employers. The Murphys had been very kind to take him on at all, and there was no one else to whom he could bequeath his great wealth. His wants had always been few, simple, and lately food of any sort had made him feel sick, so he existed on mugs of tea and whisky. His only other expense was the lottery ticket he bought once a week. There was a substantial sum of money in his Post Office account. He also possessed a rare collection of stamps that he had put together as a boy, and a leather case of precious coins, all of which would go to the Murphys.

Of late, Eustace's thoughts had started to veer wildly off their usual narrow, simple path, and he felt muddled.

It was all Mae's fault. He adored her. He was besotted. Within his ancient, tall, bent, stiff, twisted, disgustingly smelly body beat the heart of the lithe handsome young man he'd once been. Why leave his wealth to the Murphys, he thought, who'd never so much as brought him a cup of tea in all the years he'd worked for them, asked how he felt, bidden him good morning or good-bye?

But Mae had. For the first time in his life, Eustace felt bitter. As soon as he was up to it, he'd ride his bike to Formby, see his solicitor, change his will, and leave all his worldly possessions to his beloved.

'How've you been over the weekend, luv?' Mae enquired, when she finished work and came to see him. For more than an hour, Eustace had been quite literally panting as he waited. He couldn't remember the weekend; the forty-eight hours had been spent in a drunken haze.

'Not so bad, Mae,' he quavered. Such trite words. If only he could bring himself to say how he really felt, quote the poetry he'd written, tell her that her beauty was glorious to behold, that he would lay down his life for her, that she made him want to dance and sing. But he hadn't the nerve.

'D'you feel all right?' she asked solicitously. 'You're out of breath, you're panting.' She stroked a withered hand and he began to pant even louder. A part of his body that had lain dormant for many years sprang into action. Eustace almost choked. Mae slapped his back. 'Shall I fetch you a glass of water?'

'No, ta,' he gasped. 'How was your own weekend?'

'Busy.' Mae sighed. 'Dead busy.'

'What you need is a rich husband.' He might have proposed himself, had the age gap not been so great.

'A husband's the last thing I want,' Mae said, with feeling. 'I've had one already, haven't I? I swore I'd never have another. They're more trouble than they're worth.' She sighed again, a sigh of contentment, because it was so lovely sitting on the iron bench, Eustace's bony body pressed against her, the sun beaming down on them, breathing in the sweet scents of the garden, which were strong enough to muffle the smell of the old man. Delicate tendrils of feathery leaves fell from the branches plaited thickly through the arch, dangling in front of their eyes, trailing around them protectively, like a cloak. She actually felt less tired than when she'd come, because for some reason Emily, usually such a hard taskmaster, had insisted she take it easy.

'It's funny,' Mae said, 'but the only man who ever treated me bad was the one I married.' She spoke so softly that Eustace couldn't properly hear the words she said, but was content to listen to the soft, breathless voice. As she continued and he caught the occasional phrase, he realised that, in a way, she was talking to herself, hypnotised by the sun and the magical, fairy-tale garden that he nurtured with his crippled hands, lazy for once with nothing to do but tell herself her own life story, a story she might have forgotten as she went from job to job. It was as if she was reminding herself of how she'd come to the point where she was now. 'Craig's father, he was a lovely little feller, Kevin, his name was. Only thirteen when we did it, fourteen when our Craig was born. I had to leave school, so I never saw him again for years. By that time, I'd had Alice. Her dad was eighteen, and I was a year younger. I was working as a waitress in this Indian restaurant that his family owned. I called him by his surname, Ali, because his first name was a bit of a mouthful. We fell in love, and were going to get married, but when his dad found out all hell broke loose because a marriage had already been arranged for him back in India, or something. Ali was packed off to Delhi like a shot, in buckets of tears, poor lad, and I got the boot as soon as Ali's dad found out I was expecting. I called her Alice, the nearest name to Ali I could think of. Did I say the restaurant was vegetarian? So, you see, it's not surprising our Alice turned out the way she did.'

She paused and Eustace nodded sleepily. He had only the barest idea what she'd just said, but murmured, 'Yes, luv,' to encourage her to keep talking.

'Anyroad, not long after that I met Kevin again. He'd just joined the Army, there being no work about that he could find. Now, you'll think this is really weird, but Kevin was Irish, the seventh son of a seventh son. He'd been born with second sight and swore he'd never reach twenty-one. If it weren't for that we would have got married, because he really took to Craig, and Craig, why, he adored his dad for the short time he knew him. I didn't love Kevin, but as I said before, he was a lovely feller, and not so little by then. True as I'm sitting here, he got killed in Northern Ireland the week before his twenty-first.' Mae gently flicked away an ant that was crawling up her leg, 'I went to his funeral. It was dead sad.'

'Dead sad,' echoed Eustace.

'By then, I was on the pill, and had got a council house in Kirkby. Me grandad said I was amoral, whatever that means.' She cocked her head sideways and said thoughtfully, 'I think it's something to do with liking sex too much. I could never see the harm in doing it with a feller who felt the same way.' She laughed drily, and Eustace did the same. 'Funnily enough, I didn't sleep with me husband before we got married, which is the biggest mistake I ever made. If I had my way, I'd make it the law that everyone should sleep together before the wedding, make sure they're compatible, if that's the word. Me husband was worse than an animal, hit me when I wasn't prepared to do the disgusting things he wanted. After three months I told him to sod off. It was a good thing I hadn't given up me council house. He was a copper and he'd moved in with us while we waited for a police house to come empty. Fortunately one hadn't by the time I chucked him out. I've no idea if he knows that Dicky was born six months later, seeing as how I never asked for maintenance. I'd sooner work myself to a standstill than touch a penny of the bugger's money.'

She shook her head furiously, and Eustace noticed the way the little curls danced on her slender neck.

'After that, I decided not to have any more kids, but I was coming home from work one night and I found Shona's dad lying on the path by Kirkby station. He was a person of Oriental disposition, dead gorgeous in an Oriental way, though he came from somewhere in America, Boston I think it was. I took him home, he was in a terrible state, drunk as blazes, and robbed of everything; watch, camera, money, even the shoes he stood up in. He was crying, I was patting him, like, trying to make him better, one thing led to another, the way it does if you're not careful, and I ended up with our Shona. I never even knew his name, but he left his hankie behind with his initials embroidered on the corner, T.A. I kept the hankie to show Shona in case she ever asks about her dad. Me dad and grandad hadn't long come to live with us, and not long afterwards, the council let us have the house next door.' Mae smiled brilliantly. 'So, all things considered, everything's turned out almost perfect.'

'Are you still here, Mae?' Emily appeared. She'd been waiting for Mae to shout that she was leaving, which she usually did after speaking to the Murphys' repulsive gardener. 'I was worried you might have fallen asleep somewhere.'

Mae jumped to her feet. 'Strewth! I'd forgotten the time. I've just been telling Eustace here the story of me life.'

Emily's lips tightened jealously. She was the one who paid the wages. If anyone was entitled to hear the story of Mae's life, surely it should be her.

For the past few weeks, Alex Murphy had been able to think of nothing but the Peek-a-Boo quotation, which by now would be lying snugly in Hauptmannwagen's safe in Frankfurt. He couldn't wait for the safe to be unlocked, the quotations removed, and the decision process to begin, at which point in his chain of thought, Alex would descend into panic. The waiting was killing him.

His friend, Heinrich, had confirmed that four of the seven directors had been sewn up, pledged to go for the Murphy bid. 'It's a cinch, stop worrying,' he had said, the last time Alex called. 'They'd probably go for the Murphy system, anyway. I've seen the plans, haven't I, though I know I shouldn't, and it's *glazend*, a brilliant scheme, exactly what the old man's after.'

If they didn't – go for it, that is – he'd be in a terrible hole. Alex's entire design team and his top technicians had spent months on the project, neglecting the firm's basic bread-and-butter work. All that money gone in wages, then there was the backhander for Heinrich, not to mention the experimental system installed for free in Hawkins & Son. But there wasn't a penny profit to show in return, not yet. An updated version of the Murphy-Gnome was late going into production, and wouldn't be on the market for several weeks. Any minute now that fact would be picked up by the people who noticed these things and commented on them in the trade press. Murphy Computers would be accused of a lack of enterprise in allowing the firm to be left behind, a fatal thing to do in the world of computers, where machines had already been superseded by the time their purchasers got them home and plugged them in. This wouldn't matter if, no, *when* he got the Hauptmannwagen contract, and the firm would go into a higher league altogether, though they might continue producing computers for anoraked nerds as a sideline.

In the meantime, Alex was up to his eyes in debt (unknown to Emily, he'd remortgaged Thorntons). Borrowing had never bothered him in the past; in a way, owing money was a challenge he enjoyed, the responsibility resting solely on his shoulders. All he had to do was work harder, employ more people, produce more machines. But now that responsibility had been taken away. What if Heinrich fell under a bus before the end of July? The uncertainty, the idea of his entire future being in someone else's rather untrust-worthy hands — after all, the chap had taken a back-hander — was driving Alex berserk.

With all this on his mind, he thought it impossible for his feverish brain to become involved with other worries.

But it had.

He came home on Monday night, slightly earlier than usual, faintly surprised to find that there was actually food in the house, proper food, the sort you cook.

'Well, you're never usually here to eat it, are you?' Emily said, when he remarked on the fact. 'It's no use buying groceries when they'll only go to waste.' She'd bought the food for Eddie, who ate like a horse, and whom she was expecting the following day.

For once, the illogicality of Emily's reply (why was the fridge crammed with food if he wouldn't eat it?) went over Alex's head. Earlier that day he'd taken Gaynor, his secretary-cum-mistress, to lunch. Over coffee, she had dropped a bombshell, and suggested it was time he got a divorce so they could marry. Hauptmannwagen and the Peek-a-Boo system had been pushed to second place in his thoughts.

Alex had never considered himself a conventional person, not in a world where unconventionality went hand in hand with greatness, but at the same time he had never envisaged himself becoming known as a 'divorced man', having a 'second wife', or 'starting a new family'. His marriage was undoubtedly stale, but Emily was held to him by memories that even this new, cold-blooded, cold-hearted Alex couldn't deny. Emily was part of him, attached to him almost physically, as wholly and as importantly as, say, his right arm, or possibly the slightly less useful left. He couldn't discard her.

He ate the snack in silence, Emily toying with a ham roll. He assumed she was sulking, upset by the way he'd spoken to her on Saturday morning. Thinking about it, it had been an impulsive, unfair thing to say. When had Emily ever rejected him by pleading a headache? When had Emily rejected him full stop? Never, Alex acknowledged. She'd wanted to go to the loo, a perfectly reasonable excuse. If those crazy Yanks hadn't been there, they would have made love later. Common sense told him that Emily would always be there for him. Always.

'I'm sorry, darling,' he said.

'What for?' The times that Alex had apologised for

anything could have been counted on the fingers of one hand and Emily looked suitably impressed.

'For Saturday morning. I was horrid, wasn't I?'

'Saturday morning? Gosh, don't worry, Alex. I'd forgotten all about it.'

She'd forgotten all about it! Two bombshells in one day. He stared at his wife, stunned. She was bloody miles away, chin resting in her hands, eyes cast down demurely. For a moment, Alex saw the apple-cheeked maiden he'd married, his big, gorgeous girl, his magnificent Emily. A day plucked itself out of all the days they'd spent together, the day they were returning from that terrible farmhouse holiday in Somerset, where they'd not been given nearly enough to eat. Gareth was four, Mary two. The traffic was horrendous, holdups everywhere, the rain torrential, the sky black and sinister, with thunder in the distance. They'd had a Marina in those days, a clanking old bucket, full of rust and falling to pieces. Emily was in the back with the children, who were hungry and fretful. Alex felt fretful himself as they crawled and splashed through the bouncing rain, the windows full of steam, the wipers working only fitfully. He could scarcely see the car in front due to the downpour. He was worried that the worn tyres might skid on the wet surface. They passed an accident on the other side of the road, a bad one: blue lights flickering all over the place, ambulances, stretchers, the police hunched in their oilskins, directing the diverted traffic. Through the mirror, Alex saw Emily calmly shield the children's eyes. Head bent, brown hair shimmering in the half-light, she was singing: 'There were ten in the bed and the little one said, "Roll over." They all rolled over and one fell out. There were . . .' She paused. 'NINE,' Gareth shouted. By the time they'd finished the song, Alex had joined in. She sang more, told stories, played games, and Alex felt that he and his children were quite safe with Emily, his wife, their mother, their all-powerful guardian angel, as they drove through the storm. The Marina became a rusty haven on wheels. They were one unit, one soul shared among four. Humbly, privately, he submitted himself wholly to Emily during the journey home, knowing that he would have gone to pieces without her. She kept him sane. She kept him within himself.

Then, slowly, the mists of time faded and he saw the Emily of now. In the near future, when he was invited to number ten Downing Street with other industrialists of repute — Richard Branson came to mind because they were two of a kind (Alex had already decided he'd tell Tony Blair bluntly to his face he hadn't voted for him, but was slowly coming round to thinking the guy might be okay) – did he really want to introduce this big, slab-faced woman with ratty hair as his wife?

Well, no, not really. But he didn't want to introduce Gaynor, either. She had lousy taste in clothes, he couldn't stand those anchor-patterned blouses she went in for. He didn't like her all that much, and she wasn't exactly great in bed.

Oh dear, he was all confused.

So, did he need Emily any more? Okay, she was part of him, but so was his appendix, which was superfluous and could be removed, leaving him still whole with only a scar. Without Emily, without his appendix, Alex could manage very well on his own, thanks all the same.

At least, he thought he could. He stared at his wife, lost in her daydream, and felt angry. How dare she ignore him? He'd give anything to know what she was thinking about.

His bladder was giving him hell. He went to the lavatory and left the wooden seat up so that, as usual, all the Murphys' good luck went straight down the toilet during the night.

CHAPTER SIX

Mae had decided to air the rugs and give them a good beating, something Emily had never done, even in the days when she'd been a perfect housewife.

'Dirt becomes embedded, even if they're vacuumed regularly,' Mae said knowledgeably. She kept calling Emily outside to watch the dust exploding off the rugs and mingling with the brilliant sunshine as they were thoroughly roughed up with the cane carpet-beater she'd found in the garage. 'I give each rug me ex-husband's face, so I quite enjoy it.'

Mae had brought Cloud with her, and hoped Emily wouldn't mind. Alice still hadn't returned from her Sunday stint demonstrating against animal exports. 'Me grandad usually looks after her, but he's got a hospital appointment.'

With the memory of her encounter with Jim McNulty still fresh in her mind, Emily managed to ask charitably, and she hoped, sincerely, 'Is it something serious?'

'No, just an ingrowing toenail that gives him gyp.'

Cloud was an adorable child, a year old, with pale, dusky skin, and the most extraordinary blue eyes. According to Mae, who was surprisingly frank about things, her father was a young Serbo-Croat refugee from Bosnia whom Alice had met up a tree during violent protests against the Newbury bypass. 'Me grandad said the United Nations should have our Cloud as a mascot.'

'They couldn't have a prettier one.' Emily kept going out to play with the little girl, who was sitting happily on a shady patch of grass, playing with an assortment of odds and ends: an empty washing-up liquid container, a plastic ball, Mae's car keys. She was attached to a tree by her reins and a length of rope. 'Because,' said Mae, 'she's just started walking and might make it as far as the lily-pond if she's left to her own devices.'

Emily busied herself in the kitchen between her visits to Cloud. She was making a cake for Eddie when he came the next day, humming to herself. In the garden, Mae beat the rugs and sang. Cloud cooed on the lawn. Somewhere deep within the trees and hedges, Eustace pruned and clipped things. Thorntons had an air of occupancy about it for a change, a feeling of busyness.

It's all rather nice, Emily thought. Like having a little family around, not including Eustace, of course. Then the day was made almost perfect when she heard the front door open and a voice called, 'It's only me, Mum.'

'Gareth!'

'I was worried about you, Mum,' Gareth said, after she'd hugged and kissed him and patted him to make sure he was real. 'You sounded very peculiar when you rang on Friday night.'

'I'm fine, love,' she assured him. She hadn't felt fine on Friday night, but things had changed since then. 'What on earth are you doing in Liverpool?'

He'd had to come to Manchester for a case conference that involved social workers from two different boroughs, he explained. 'It was over at eleven o'clock, so instead of going back I decided to come and see my mum.'

'It's lovely to have you,' Emily breathed. 'Come and meet Mae. And Cloud.'

After Mae had been introduced to Gareth, she watched Emily as she picked up Cloud and perched her expertly on her broad hip. 'Isn't she gorgeous?' Mae heard her say. Why, Em looks quite lovely, she marvelled. Her eyes smarted with unexpected tears. Poor cow, she's so proud of her lad. Her face is shining, radiant, I think you'd call it, as if her batteries were run down and they've been recharged. She misses being a mother, that's all that's wrong with her. She misses having someone to love and love her back, make her feel special, like. That husband of hers is a rum sort of geezer altogether. Very odd. Most peculiar, if you ask me.

Emily thought Gareth was much too thin. He'd always managed to tear at her heart, far more than Mary, who wasn't nearly so vulnerable. Gareth was oversensitive, easily hurt, impractical, clumsy with his hands. She noticed how badly his shirt had been ironed, and gave a little, inward sob, imagining her impractical, clumsy son struggling to look after himself.

If only he lived nearer, I could do his washing and ironing, she thought wistfully. She watched through the window as he played on the grass with Cloud. He was so like Alex, almost a mirror image of his father at the same age, yet his personality was entirely different. He was Dr Jekyll to Alex's Mr Hyde. He was Alex without the furnace burning inside, Alex without the manic eyes and bulging brain. She recalled how gutted he'd been when his father had changed sides, become one of the hated capitalists he'd taught his children to loathe. And how scathing Alex had been when his son had decided to become a social worker, 'And waste his life on society's drop-outs and inadequates,' he sneered.

'Damn you, Alex,' Emily swore, years and years too late.

She made sandwiches and took them outside. 'Let's picnic on the grass,' she suggested. 'The way we used to when we first came here.' It seemed only natural that Mae should join them, and they sat in the shade encircling Cloud.

Gareth was relieved that the visit home, made purely from a sense of duty, had turned out to be an unexpected treat. He'd anticipated finding his mother, whom he loved dearly, missed badly, and worried over constantly, looking sullen, feeling neglected, and nothing like the mum he used to know. She was so much under the influence of his father that she'd actually come to think like him. It was a pleasant surprise to find her looking so much brighter, and on such friendly terms with the cracking new cleaner; in the past they'd always been at daggers drawn. He was thinking idly that he must ring his sister when he got back to London, tell her, when a girl came wandering into the garden. Her almost black hair was plaited in dreadlocks and threaded with beads, and her skin was the colour of cinnamon. She wore a skimpy scarlet T-shirt that left her gleaming midriff bare, and a brightly patterned wrap-round skirt. As she approached, Gareth saw that her huge, limpid eyes were chocolate brown. This wasn't a girl but a goddess, a beautiful, enchanting, utterly desirable goddess.

He tried to stand, but his legs wouldn't obey. He struggled manfully to regain control of his body, to stop his head from thumping so powerfully, prevent his heart from beating so dangerously loud and fast, to douse the fires that were crackling furiously in his stomach. And make his legs work.

'Well, if it isn't our Alice,' Mae cried. 'Hallo, luv.'

'I've been knocking on the front door for ages,' Alice said, 'but there was no answer.' Her wonderful eyes locked, like two magnets, on Gareth's. She didn't even glance at her mother.

Oh, God, thought Gareth, her voice droppeth like the gentle rain from heaven upon the place beneath. It is twice blessed . . .

'I thought I'd come and collect Cloud, case she was in your way, like,' Alice muttered, without removing her luminous gaze from Gareth. She was floating towards him in slow motion. Any minute now, any second, they would meet, touch, and be lost for ever.

'We've loved having her,' said Emily.

'Where've you been, luv?' asked Mae.

Alice appeared to be only half aware of the question. She blinked before answering, then resumed eye-contact with Gareth. 'In the police station, in a cell. I was bound over for causing an affray.'

She was everything he'd ever wanted in a woman. Gareth's bones moaned with longing.

'You haven't met Em, have you, luv? Em, this is our Alice.'

'Nice to meet you, Em,' Alice more or less said.

'And this is Em's lad, Gareth.'

And Gareth, his body his own again, got to his feet and held out his hands to his destiny. 'Hi, Alice.'

'Hi, Gareth.'

'Let me get this straight,' Alex enunciated carefully, to make sure he'd got it right. 'What you're saying is that my son has fallen crazily in love with a girl called Alice. Alice is seventeen, and has spent the last few days behind bars for assaulting a policeman. Alice has an illegitimate

Serbo-Croat-Indian-Irish daughter called Cloud. Alice also happens to be the illegitimate mixed race child of our cleaner. Is that it?'

'Apart from the fact that Gareth is *our* son, not just yours, Alex, I'm pretty sure you're right. That's it. Oh, and Alice is just as smitten. She fell in love with him. It was terribly romantic. Mae and I cried a bit when we watched them together.' Emily sighed dreamily.

'I don't like the idea of you fraternising with the cleaner. I reckon it's about time Mae was given her cards,' Alex said brutally. 'The Murphys and the McNultys are becoming too involved.'

More involved than you'll ever know, thought Mae, glancing at the cake she'd made for Eddie. She said blithely, 'Don't be ridiculous, Alex. You couldn't meet a nicer girl than Alice. Gareth's coming to Liverpool again this weekend. He was even talking about getting a job here.'

'But, Em, it means we could have black grandchildren!' gasped a scandalised Alex.

It was Emily's turn to be brutal. 'Who bloody cares? I certainly don't. And a few years ago you wouldn't have cared either. In fact, you'd have been thrilled to bits, proud. Alice does the same sort of things you used to do yourself. And me. Honestly, Alex, I don't know what's come over you lately, I truly don't. You've become a dreadful hypocrite not to mention a racist.'

Another bombshell! Alex already felt as if every one of his nerves was being expertly twanged by a heavy-metal guitarist playing 'Let's Fuck The Wealthy, Don't Let Them Screw The Poor', a song he'd composed at university and, these days, carried an unwelcome and sinister message. He wished, desperately wished, he could sink into blessed unconsciousness with instructions not to be revived until the beginning of August. What with Hauptmannwagen, Gaynor nagging him several times a day to get a divorce, his son infatuated with a young unmarried mother whose imperfections Alex felt too tired to list again, and now Emily speaking to him in such an unaccustomed and insensitive manner, he was convinced he had already gone beyond the end of his tether, that he was suspended, not in Limbo like normal people but in some sort of vile, choking Purgatory where he was slowly suffocating to death. Yet he was usually such a calm person, usually so self-controlled.

'That's him!' said Paddy, his tombstone-like teeth gleaming in triumph. 'That's him there!'

'Yes, that's the bugger we gave the package to.' Mick started up the car and moved it nearer to the school entrance. It was going-home time, half past three.

'Shall I give the little feller a bit of a duffin' up, like, in the back of the car? I won't hurt him much.'

'No, you eejit, we want to know where he lives, don't we? We'll follow him, that's all.'

Two cars followed Dicky McNulty home to Daffodil Close; one limping noisily, all indications of who had made it and what model it was having dropped off or been stolen or rusted away. The other vehicle was grey and unobtrusive.

The occupants of both cars watched eagerly, noting the name of the road and the number of the house the boy entered. The first car drove away. Paddy and Mick would ring Sean Donovan who'd arrange for the place to be done over, and if the package was there, it would be found.

In the other vehicle, DC Jones said to DS Watson, 'What do we do now, Sarge?'

Watson looked strangely grey and subdued, like the car. 'I'm not sure. I'll have to think about it.'

'What's there to think about? Let's have the place done over.'

'I'll think about it,' Watson said again.

'Look, the little arsehole's come out again.' Having deposited his school-bag, Dicky had emerged, and was sauntering cockily down the path, picking his nose, eating an apple, and whistling a tune. 'You can bet your life he never gave that package to Rory Quinn. Kids round here, they're nothing but thieving scumbags. I bet he stole it.'

'Don't jump to conclusions quite so hastily, Michael.'

'*What?*' Jones wondered if he was hearing things. Until today, until that very minute, Sergeant Patrick Watson had never jumped to a conclusion that wasn't instant, never mind hasty. He led his life according to his own personal creed, upon which every single judgement was made: (a) every man, coppers excepted, was a criminal; (b) every child was a criminal-in-waiting; and (c) every woman, coppers included, was a whore. 'Are you all right, mate?' Jones enquired solicitously.

'I'm not sure.'

Before Jones could delve into whatever psychological undertones or overtones might lie behind that remark, their junior prey had crossed the road and was about to walk past the Sierra. He leapt out and grabbed the kid by the ear. 'What the fuck have you been up to?' he asked, in his most threatening voice, carefully cultivated to send shivers down the spines of the most violent and danger-ous crooks. And motorists.

'Sod off!' Dicky squealed, otherwise appearing en-tirely unthreatened. 'Let go of me ear. It hurts.'

'It's meant to hurt, you thieving little arsehole. Is your name Bart Simpson?'

'Are you soft or something? Course it's not.'

Jones's fingers tightened on the lad's ear. 'What is it, then?'

Dicky squealed again. 'Mind your own bleedin' business. I've done nothing wrong.'

'Oh, yes, you have, scumbag. Where's the package you robbed off Rory Quinn?'

'I don't know what you're talking about. Let go of me ear, or I'll tell me mam.'

'Oh dearie me,' Jones quipped wittily. 'I'm terrified, I really am.'

'Eh! Eh, you!' An elderly woman carrying a shopping-bag came storming up. She was at least five feet tall, and her old face was twisted in a scowl of fearful rage. 'Leave the lad alone, you pervert.'

'Mind your own business, missus,' Jones snarled, hanging on to Dicky's ear. He waved his free arm contemptuously at the woman, as if he was swatting away a troublesome fly.

'I'll do no such thing.' The old woman went into action. She reached in her bag for the first thing that came to hand, a packet of something frozen in a plastic bag, and with a gesture almost Olympian in its grandeur, she swung it three times around her head, before thwacking it against the side of Jones's skull. He screamed in pain and released Dicky, who retreated to his front garden to finish his apple and watch. The policeman responded immediately to the blow, and those that followed, with the automatic instincts of a trained rat. In one smooth, seamless movement, he assumed the attack position, and raised his right hand (no longer the hand of an ordinary forty-five-year-old copper but a lethal weapon), ready to strike the ould biddy's raddled neck, kill her, take the bitch out, when he became aware that Watson was tapping on the windscreen of the car. He paused and glanced at his superior, who was shaking his head and mouthing, 'No, no, no.'

Jones's hand went limp and resumed its everyday function. He cowered against the car as blows continued to rain down on him, and he thought how undignified the whole thing was.

'If you don't scarper sharpish, I'll call the cops,' the woman said menacingly.

'Madam, we *are* the cops.'

'Then I'll call different cops. Go on, away with you. Away.' She flicked her hands at him disdainfully. 'Away.'

'Why didn't you give us a hand?' Jones panted resentfully as he started up the car, blood trickling down his neck. 'We should have run that ould bitch in.'

Watson laughed his famous sarcastic laugh. 'For protecting an eight-year-old kid? She'd get a medal, and our names would be mud all over Merseyside.'

'How do you know the thieving little wanker's eight?'

'He looks about eight, I suppose. And don't jump to such hasty conclusions, Michael, I told you before. He seemed quite a decent lad to me, quite a bright little feller, as a matter of fact. And we don't know for sure that he's stolen anything.'

Jones narrowly missed crashing the car. What in fuck's sake was wrong with Watson? Had he had a Damascene conversion, or something? Any minute now he'd announce he was off to Rome to kiss the Pope.

My son, Patrick Watson was thinking, his entire being soggy with emotion, and heady with the powerful scent of late-blossoming love. My son, my son.

He'd known all about Dicky, naturally. He was a copper, he knew everything, but this was the first time he'd seen him, having kept well out of the way to avoid being caught for maintenance. Anyroad, he'd never been interested in kids, even if they were his own. Yet as soon as he'd seen Dicky enter the house in Daffodil Close where Patrick had spent the three months of his marriage to Mae McNulty, he'd realised who he was. His son, dammit. At the sight of Dicky's chirpy, handsome face, he felt overwhelmed with an unexpected thrust of longing to be a dad, a real flesh-and-blood dad. He'd like to read to the little lad in bed, *Winnie the Pooh*, *Brer Rabbit*, *Toad in the Hole*. He'd like to take him to football matches, where they'd eat crisps and meat pies, and share a few beers when the lad got older. He'd like to help him with his homework, as long as it wasn't hard and didn't involve figures.

His son!

And Mae's son.

Mae!

His feelings for Mae had always been somewhat ambiguous. He was never sure whether he wanted to kill her, or put her on a pedestal and worship at her feet.

He loved her, he hated her. He never wanted to see her again, but yearned for her to take him back.

Perhaps he hadn't behaved too well when they were married, but what else were women for except to shag until you dropped? You shagged them whenever you felt like it, and in any position, posture, place, situation you felt like shagging at that particular time. Least, so he'd been brought up to believe by his dad. But perhaps his dad hadn't been the world's best teacher.

Mae had turned out to be an awkward bitch. 'You don't own me,' she claimed.

He thought he did.

'You only married me. You didn't buy me.'

He thought he had. Who'd paid for the marriage licence?

The night she'd thrown him out he'd cried himself to sleep in his old bedroom at home, where pictures of naked women in lewd poses adorned the walls.

Next morning, his dad said to him gruffly, 'You should have slapped her round a bit, son.'

'But I did, Dad, I did.'

'You should have taught her what's what.'

'I did that too, Dad, honest.'

'Made her see who's boss.'

'Oh, for Chrissakes, Dad, I did all those things, least I tried, but she didn't want to know. That's why she chucked me out.'

Dad shook his head, utterly bewildered. His own wife, Patrick's mother, who was long dead, had allowed herself to be knocked stupid throughout their dismal married life, and had never complained once. (She would have got a thick ear if she had.) 'I don't know what the world's coming to, I really don't. Women don't know their place any more. I'm glad I'm old and haven't got long to go, 'cos the future terrifies me.'

So what was Patrick Watson to do now? Now he'd seen his kid and badly wanted to get to know the little feller. Could he start courting Mae again, send her flowers, like, buy her chocolates, that sort of crap? He wondered if there were night-school classes where he could be untaught all the things his dad had taught him about how to treat women. Could he learn to be a gentleman? Could you be a copper and a gentleman both at the same time? He wasn't sure.

Questions, questions. Patrick Watson was unused to asking questions of himself, and his head hurt.

'What are you thinking about, Sarge?' Jones enquired.

Patrick had forgotten Jones was there, though someone must have been driving the Sierra. 'Just shit, mate. Just some shit.'

Jones sneered inwardly. What else would a person who had shit for brains be thinking? 'That house in Daffodil Close, shall I ask our snitch to do it over?'

'I'm not sure, Michael. I'm not sure.'

In that case, Jones decided he would take the matter in hand himself.

There was something highly provocative and possibly unhealthily sexy about watching your lover remove your husband's underpants before getting into bed with you.

But it had to stop. Alex was beginning to notice. The other day he'd gone haywire when he couldn't find the pale grey tie with the crossed cricket bats or tennis racquets or billiard cues or some other sporting emblem embroidered on the front.

'Do you have to do that?'

'Do what?' It was twenty exhilarating minutes later. Eddie was back in the white silk underpants, rooting through Alex's drawers, seeking his reward, having carried out his duties to Emily's entire satisfaction.

Emily was sitting up in bed admiring his lean, tanned body. Having nothing to do all day except bet on horses and make love to women, he spent his spare time sunbathing in the garden, while his daughter worked herself to the bone to provide food for the table. He was a complete rotter, an utter creep, totally worthless, utterly despicable. Emily knew all this but, for the moment at least, she couldn't live without him. He made her feel whole and feminine. She would also have liked to feel desired, but wasn't wholly confident whether Eddie came to get his hands on her or the contents of Alex's wardrobe.

'Do you have to take something of my husband's every time you come?'

'What harm does it do?' His rather womanish mouth pouted in a discontented *moue*. 'He's got so much stuff, he'll never notice.'

'Actually, he has. If he finds anything else has gone missing, he might start to suspect Mae.'

'Oh, well, we can't be having that, can we?' With a flamboyantly petulant gesture, Eddie slammed the drawer shut. He came and sat on the bed. 'What are we going to do about it, then?'

'I don't understand.'

'You don't expect me to come here for nothing, do you?'

After giving this serious thought for a while, Emily said eventually, 'I can't see why not. It doesn't put you out in any way. I pick you up, take you home, feed you. Is it such an effort to make love to me that you have to be tipped, as it were, with items of my husband's clothing? It's almost like employing a gigolo.'

She was annoyed when Eddie glanced at himself conceitedly in the wardrobe mirror, lightly running his fingers through his dyed blond hair, as if he rather fancied the idea. 'Mind you,' Emily went on slyly, 'I doubt if many gigolos are great-grandfathers. They're usually vigorous young men.' He hated being reminded that he had grandchildren – at first he'd tried to convince her he was only forty-four – and never mentioned Cloud, his great-granddaughter.

'I'm vigorous,' he said stoutly. He glanced in the mirror again, flexing his rather puny muscles, then turned back to Emily, his weak, handsome face screwed up earnestly. 'Would you mind if I was frank, Em?'

'I wouldn't mind if you were Frank or Eddie.'

He had no sense of humour and didn't see the joke. 'Frankly, luv, you don't turn me on. It's a bit of an effort, like. I've got to wind meself up, sort of thing. Pretend I'm with someone else, as it were.'

'Who?'

He wrinkled his nose and shrugged. 'That woman in *The X Files*, f'rinstance, I'm not sure if she's Mulder or Scully. Or the newsreader with the melon-shaped face.'

'Peter Sissons?'

'Come off it, Em. She's not a young woman. 'Bout my age.'

'Anna Ford?'

'That's who I mean, yes.' He smacked his lips. 'Anna Ford.'

Emily sighed. Crouched, toad-like, deep in the pit of self-loathing, she fully appreciated his dilemma. Were she a man, she wouldn't fancy herself, either. 'So, where do we go from here?' she asked humbly. Did she hate herself enough, was she desperate enough, to offer money? Was Eddie contemptible enough to take it?

She was taken aback when he said, 'You could do something with yourself.'

'Such as?'

He regarded her thoughtfully for a long while, got up, walked around the room, looked at her from several different angles, came back, seized her chin, rotated her face, moved it up and down and sideways. Emily wanted to giggle, because he was taking it all so seriously. She also wanted to cry, because it was obvious she presented an almost insurmountable challenge.

Eventually Eddie spoke in hard, crisp tones. 'Get rid of them spots, they look awful. Your skin needs rejuvenating, it's too grey, get some nourishing cream. Go on a diet, lose weight, do exercises, wear makeup, get some decent clothes — your underwear's a real turn-off. Get your hair cut, have it tinted. Use scent, it's sexy. Have you never heard of jewellery? Or nail polish? Or high heels? Or sheer tights? Stockings and suspenders would be even better.' He paused and nodded. 'I think that should do it.'

'I see,' said Emily. 'And what do I do when the transformation is complete? Send you a letter and a photograph?'

'Course not, luv.' He patted her arm affectionately, and gave an encouraging grin. 'I'll give you a hand, see you through, as it were. Women have always been a sort of hobby of mine. I like to see them looking nice. Fact, if things had turned out different, if life hadn't been so cruel and unfair, I'd have started a beauty parlour of me own.'

It was Eddie who was cruel, Emily knew that much, walking out on his wife when she was still pregnant with

Mae, not even returning when his wife died, so that his father, Jim, had been left to raise Mae. He thought the world owed him a living, and whined when the debt wasn't paid. He put nothing into anything, and expected something back.

Still, he was all Emily had, and he seemed willing to invest in her, put whatever talents he possessed into doing her up, as if she were an old, neglected house, or a run-down car.

'When shall we start?' she asked.

'What about now?' He jumped off the bed and rubbed his hands together excitedly. 'We'll go to the supermarket and you can get the face cream and the makeup and one or two other things at the same time. They might have a video of exercises you can do.'

In the supermarket, Emily didn't complain when he put a bottle of expensive aftershave in the trolley. As soon as she was beautiful again, Eddie could get stuffed.

It was one thing being a snitch, but another thing altogether being 'persuaded', to put it mildly, to turn over houses virtually every other week for only a few quid at a time. He couldn't even pinch anything,

'Otherwise they might call the cops,' said the cops. Even if he found the Semtex the fuzz were after, he'd been told to leave it where it was and report back.

The snitch had been watching number six Daffodil Close all morning from his car and was bored out of his wits. Two children had come out, obviously on their way to school. Then a young woman emerged (great body, daft hair), with a baby in a pushchair, shortly followed by a chap of about twenty, which meant, according to the cops, that only the woman of the house was left. Lazy bitch, thought the snitch. Why didn't she take herself off to work?

He was jolted out of his reverie by a tapping on the window of the passenger door, and his first thought was that his long wait had been spotted by some nosy ould woman with nothing better to do, suspicious of what he was up to. Instead, it was a sharply dressed yellow geezer, smiling at him, all friendly, like.

'I wonder if you can help me, sir,' the geezer enquired, when the snitch rolled down the window.

'Tell me what you want, and we'll see,' growled the snitch, feeling considerably chuffed at being called 'sir' by this Oriental Adonis, a Yank from his accent, tall, broad-shouldered, perfect features for a wog. The aroma of expensive aftershave drifted into the car and the snitch sniffed appreciatively.

'I'm looking for a woman, probably in her early thirties. Lots of blonde hair, about five feet four or five, pretty – exceptionally pretty. Her name is Mae. I'm afraid I don't know her surname.' The geezer regarded him anxiously with his strange, amber-coloured eyes.

The snitch would have liked to help, he really would. The description fitted exactly the woman whose house he was watching. But if he revealed that Mae McNulty lived right across the road, then there would be a reunion or a confrontation or whatever, and Christ knows what time she'd leave for work. The snitch badly wanted to get home in time to see *Neighbours*.

'Sorry, mate,' he said apologetically, though he felt a bit rotten. 'I've lived around here all me life,' (a lie), 'and I've never known a blonde woman called Mae.'

The amber eyes looked forlorn. 'Thank you, sir, for your time,' the chap said politely.

He hadn't been gone more than ten minutes when Mae McNulty emerged, got into an ancient Cortina estate, and drove away, by which time the snitch was worried that the girl with the baby might only have gone to the shops and would return at any minute.

As soon as Mae disappeared, he got out of the car and walked purposefully past number six. It looked empty, no sign of life. The television was on in the house next door – a good thing, because it would deaden any noise he might make while ransacking its neighbour, searching for the sodding Semtex.

The snitch turned on his heel, walked casually back to number six and down the path at the side to the rear door. If there was only a lock involved he could deal with it in a jiffy, but inside bolts meant he'd have to break a window – risky in a built-up area in broad daylight. To his surprise, the door opened at the turn of the knob. Some people! They deserved to be done over. Fancy leaving a door unlocked in this day and age, what with so many suspicious characters hanging around. It was unbelievable, it really was.

He paused nervously when he entered the kitchen and a dog strolled towards him. 'Nice doggy,' he whispered. The dog wagged its tail. 'Friendly doggy.' The snitch liked dogs. He opened the fridge and gave the dog a string of sausages, which was sitting on a plate.

Next door's television was on much too loud. If *he* lived here, he'd complain, the snitch thought indignantly. And if they refused to turn it down, well, he'd take the matter up with the council. There was a lack of community spirit around nowadays, people had no idea how to behave towards each other. No one *cared* any more.

There was nothing in the kitchen cupboards that resembled two pounds of Semtex. The snitch stepped over the dog, who was making hard work of the sausages, and went into the lounge, where he found a great, yawning hole in the wall, and two men sitting on a settee in the other half of the room, which he assumed must be number eight, watching television.

'Holy Mary, Mother of God!' he gasped.

If only he'd kept his big mouth shut he wouldn't have been noticed, but at the sound of his voice both men turned. The snitch assessed them quickly. One was old but tough, a chap to be reckoned with; the other, a poncy individual still in his pyjamas, was considerably younger, but a blatantly useless git.

'Jaysus, Mary and Joseph!' the older man screeched, and promptly fell over the settee in an effort to grab the intruder. His companion turned pale and knelt on the floor, where he began to cross himself repeatedly.

'Forgive me, Father, for I have sinned,' he intoned, in a squeaky, desperate voice.

But before Eddie could confess a single sin, the snitch had escaped through the front door and got clear away.

CHAPTER SEVEN

'There's been some dead peculiar things happening to us lately, Em,' Mae said conversationally, when she and Emily sat down in the kitchen to have their coffee. It was mid-afternoon and the sun had just begun to creep through the latticed window, dancing on the freshly polished, stainless-steel sink, so brightly that it hurt the eyes to look. Everywhere gleamed. Emily had made scones, and the smell of baking mingled with lemon disinfectant and the scent of the roses in a glass vase on the window-sill. The house was peaceful, still, the spirits at rest. The day felt good. For Mae, life was a constant struggle to survive, to keep her head above water, which she somehow always managed to do. It gave her the sense of being lucky, on the winning side. Mae was happy, as she usually was. Until recently, Emily could see little point in wanting to survive, but now things were different, changing, there was hope. Emily wasn't yet happy, but she hoped she would be soon.

'What sort of peculiar things?' She never ceased to be avidly interested in her cleaner's affairs.

'We had a burglar, in broad daylight, too! Me dad and grandad chased him away, so all he took was a pound of sausages. Poor feller, he mustn't half have been hungry,' she said tenderly. 'I hope he had somewhere to cook 'em – they'd taste awful raw.' Mae was probably the only person in the world who'd make excuses for a burglar. 'Then, when I went to collect me child benefit from the post office yesterday, the woman said some chap had been in looking for me. She recognised the description he gave, and the fact he knew me name was Mae. The thing is, Em, she said he looked Hawaian.'

'Hawaian!'

'Hawaian. Or he might have been from Tahiti, she couldn't be sure. Course, she didn't tell him she knew who I was. He might have been from the Social Security, or something. They can be dead underhand, that lot. The weirdest thing of all,' Mae continued, 'was this morning our Dicky got a letter. Someone had only sent him a twenty-pound note. There was a message, "Buy yourself something nice," was all it said. Nothing to say who it was from.'

'I bet Dicky was thrilled.'

'He wasn't thrilled for long. I took it off him. I said he could have a quid, and the rest'll go on a coat for our Shona.'

'Didn't he mind?' enquired Emily, genuinely interested.

'Of course he minded, but he's a good lad, our Dicky, and he soon saw sense when I explained me financial position, which is dire. The dog was sick, poor thing kept vomiting, same day we had the burglar, as it happens, and I couldn't afford to take him to the vet.'

'Isn't Dicky's father the one you married? Maybe it was him who sent the money,' Emily suggested helpfully.

Mae's laugh tinkled around the sunlit room. 'You must be joking, Em. Patrick Watson is king of the louses. I wouldn't even let Dicky have his name. Did I ever tell you the things he did to me?'

'No,' Emily was all ears.

'Oh, my God! No wonder you threw him out,' she gasped, quite a long time afterwards, when Mae had finished describing her ex-husband's disgusting behaviour. They then discussed Gareth and Alice, whose relationship had blossomed quickly to the point that they had decided to throw current convention to the wind and get married. The date had been set — Saturday, the thirtieth of August.

'You don't mind if the reception's held here, do you, Mae? The house is so much bigger, and if it's a nice day, we can all go in the garden.'

'Good Lord, Em, no. I don't mind a bit. I can't think of a nicer place to hold a wedding reception. Think of the lovely photos we can take. It means we'll be related in a way.' She looked at Emily warily, remembering the stiff, formal, withdrawn woman she'd first encountered. 'Will you mind?'

'Of course not,' Emily said warmly. 'In fact, I can hardly wait.'

Eustace could be seen, hovering outside the kitchen door. It was time for Mae to go home, upstairs still unvacuumed and the bathroom and toilets still uncleaned. But Emily didn't give a damn.

'Didn't Mae come today?' Alex demanded irascibly that night.

'Of course she did,' replied Emily, equally irascible. 'Mae has never let me down.' She had made up her mind to increase Mae's wages by a pound an hour, but wouldn't tell him yet, if she told him at all. It was worth it, if only for the company. Listening to Mae was better than a talking book. 'Why do you ask?'

'She usually dusts my study on Wednesdays, but it hasn't been touched.'

'She was probably too busy,' Emily snapped.

'Huh!' was all Alex could think of to say. He couldn't come to grips with this new, aggressive Emily, who didn't hang on his every word and agree with everything he said. She looked different, too, since she'd started wearing makeup, a fraction better than before. Even so, he tried to think of something to take her down a peg or two. 'Why have you started wearing all that muck on your face?' he asked primly. 'It doesn't suit you.'

'Why, thank you, Alex. You say the nicest things.'

She was quite unperturbed, so Alex pressed further. 'In fact, it makes you look like a man. You look like Gordon Brown in drag.'

'Even nicer. You look . . .' She stared at him, trying to think of something more insulting to call him, and was suddenly aware that he looked terrible. His face was drawn and lined, thinner; in fact, his whole body was thinner. Was he eating properly? She had never seen

Alex's eyes appear so dull before, so heavy and listless, yet with a touch of something — could it be panic? Since when had his shoulders begun to stoop like those of a very old man? She felt both frightened and concerned. 'Alex, darling, you look dreadful. Are you ill? I think you should go and see the doctor.'

For the briefest of moments their eyes met, and during that brief moment, Alex felt the strongest urge to throw himself in her arms, sob his heart out, tell her everything; about Hauptmannwagen, remortgaging the house, how bloody worried he was. Even about Gaynor, because Emily, his Emily, would understand, forgive him, help him, take half the load. He could face the coming weeks with Emily at his side, supporting him.

And Emily shared the moment with him. There was the faintest flicker of what they'd had before he'd fallen under the spell of Money, become besotted with the power of Money, the feel of Money in his wallet. Its smell. Money had come between them, causing far more havoc than another woman. Money had torn their marriage apart. She wanted to remind him of the things they'd once planned to do together when the children had left home: drive around the States, for instance, or work in an orphanage in India for a few weeks every year. But now Money held Alex in such a sweet, seductive embrace that he couldn't bring himself to leave Murphy Computers for more than a few days. They hadn't had a holiday in years, yet they'd always managed to get away when things were tight, before Money appeared on the scene, and even if some of the holidays had been dire, they'd had a laugh, they'd enjoyed themselves if only because of the camaraderie that existed between them, the wholesale passion, the knowledge that they meant everything to each other.

Emily lifted her hand, wanting to touch him, wanting to suggest they went on holiday because he looked ill, he needed a break, she was worried about him, and couldn't they at least try to start again?

But she had left it too late, because Alex said hoarsely, 'Jesus, Emily, you've changed. You certainly know how to get under a chap's skin. For a minute there, I thought you meant it.'

'But I did . . .' Emily watched, horrified, as Alex slammed out of the room, slammed into his study and slammed the study door. When she went to listen, he was typing away furiously on the computer. She put her hand on the knob to go in, still wanting to sort things out, but the sheer unreasonableness of the way he'd just behaved, the silly petulance, reminded her of other times, the bad ones, the years when she'd got fatter and fatter and more and more unhappy, and Alex hadn't noticed, or hadn't cared. If there was something seriously wrong, he'd be off to the doctors like a shot – he'd always been a bit of a hypochondriac. She decided not to worry. He'd probably overstretched himself at work, which had never particularly bothered him in the past. If she tried to make peace, she'd only end up having her head bitten off, and tomorrow Eddie was taking her to get her hair done.

Eddie had pooh-poohed the idea of using an upmarket hairdresser in Liverpool or Southport, and instead was taking her to a salon in Bootle.

'But will they be any good?' Emily cried anxiously, as she drove them there. She'd never been to Bootle and didn't trust it. And she hadn't had her hair done since her wedding day, and looked upon it as worse than visiting the dentist.

'It's Bootle, not Bosnia.' Eddie was sarcastic. 'They're quite civilised there, women have their hair done every day, and mostly they look much better than you, Em.'

'I've never had a perm in my life.'

'There's a first time for everything. It's a shaggy perm.'

'It sounds a bit indecent.' Emily wriggled nervously. 'I might look awful.'

'You look awful now, but you won't when Daphne's finished with you.'

'Who's Daphne?'

'The hairdresser, of course. She's a friend of mine with her own salon, gives me a trim once a month.'

In return for what? wondered Emily.

She was quite taken with Bootle when they reached it, a small town on the Mersey and a rather startling mix of the very old and the very new: a big modern shopping centre, throbbing with people, and lots of narrow streets of Victorian terraced houses, the bricks dark brown with soot and age. The slate roofs dazzled in the inevitable sunshine of what was turning out to be a perfect summer. Since Labour had been elected, there'd been scarcely any rain.

Her anxiety returned when Eddie directed her into one of the narrow streets and she saw Daphne's. The name was painted in gold on a black background on what was merely an end house that had been converted into a shop by enlarging the front window. The pink and mauve striped curtains were decidedly grubby, and the window needed a good clean. Eddie got out of the car, and she contemplated driving away and leaving him stranded. Perhaps Eddie guessed her thoughts, because he came round and opened the door. He looked very smart today, dressed from top to toe in his immoral earnings.

'Stop worrying, Em. Daphne's a top-notch hairdresser and a great beautician. She could have worked at an exclusive Mayfair salon if she'd wanted. You'll be transformed.'

Transformed into what? 'Why didn't she?'

'She preferred Bootle. I know the shop looks run-down, but Daphne's let things slide a bit lately. She's retiring in a week's time to the Isle of Man. Come on, luv,' he urged impatiently. 'We're a bit late. Oh, and by the way, as well as being great at her job, Daphne's also a total nutcase, so don't take any notice of what she says.'

A bell clanged lustily when Eddie pushed open the door. Two rooms had been made into one, and they entered a long pink and mauve grotto, as vividly and as starkly lit as a theatre stage with several fluorescent tubes, despite the brilliant sunshine outside. The striped wallpaper matched the curtains, the tatty, threadbare towels were pink, the tiled floor mauve. Two women in pink plastic gowns, pink nets tied round their pink rollers, were already seated beneath dryers that were spotted with rust but basically mauve. One woman smiled at Eddie, the other winked.

'How are you doing, girls?' Eddie said smarmily.

'Ah, you've come.' A small woman in a pink nylon overall piped with mauve appeared from a room at the back. She had silver hair cut in a thick fringe on her forehead, curling inwards just below her ears. As she came towards them, it was like watching a new coin spinning on its side in the sun, so bright was she and so swiftly did she walk. She kissed Eddie briefly on the cheek.

'That's a nice suit, Edward.' The woman fingered Alex's pale blue linen jacket. 'Is there silk in that?'

'Yes, there is, Daph. And I tell you this much, I didn't get it in Burton's.' Eddie laughed uproariously at his own joke, the only ones he understood.

Emily decided that, today at least, she hated Eddie McNulty. She found herself being pushed forward to be introduced to Daphne, whom she might possibly hate, too, but decided quickly that she wouldn't because she looked so nice. Daphne's age was indeterminable. She looked about fifty, but might have been younger, might have been older. Whatever her age, she had bone structure most women would kill for, the sort that stayed for life: a small straight nose and high, moulded cheekbones. Her eyes were large, an unusual dark green flecked with gold, and they glowed with an inner tranquillity that Emily envied. Her makeup was tasteful and discreet. Now that they were close, Emily thought she detected wrinkles in the pale, translucent skin, a whole network of them, but then Daphne turned her head and the wrinkles disappeared, or perhaps they hadn't been there at all.

'So, this is Emily,' she said warmly, in a soft, sing-song voice, taking Emily's hands.

'I told you she was a challenge.' Eddie spoke as if he'd brought something to be mended, something so far past its prime, so long out-of-date that the parts were no longer available and it couldn't possibly be repaired.

'Of course she's not a challenge. What a thing to say. She's beautiful. Come and sit in front of the mirror, Emily, and let's see what we can do to make you even better. Pass us a gown, Eddie, luv.'

A pink plastic gown was draped over a bemused Emily, who hadn't been called beautiful for so long that she didn't believe it for a minute. Daphne bent and whispered in her ear, 'Take no notice of the cheeky bugger. Beauty's in the eye of the beholder, and Edward's mainly attracted by powder and paint. But he's useful to have around in an emergency, like an old raincoat you keep in the car in case it rains, if you know what I mean.' She gave Emily's shoulder a significant squeeze, and it did Emily a power of good to hear her lover (their lover?) being compared to an old raincoat.

Daphne ran her hands up and down Emily's neck, which was very relaxing. 'You've got a lovely neck, sturdy but shapely.'

Emily stared at herself in the gold-tinted mirror, and her reflection stared back through a gold-tinted haze. Actually, she didn't look too bad. Then she noticed that Daphne, standing behind her, had shed at least several decades and looked no more than twenty-one. She caught the older woman's eyes and Daphne winked. 'Does wonders for a girl, this mirror. Always have a last look in it before I go out.'

'But it tells a lie,' Emily spluttered.

'Not if you believe it,' Daphne said enigmatically. 'You are what you believe you are. If you think of yourself as beautiful, not just with your mind but with your heart and your soul, with every single part of you, then so will the world. They'll see it in your eyes, hear it in your voice. They can tell by the way you walk. It's all a matter of faith, and confidence.'

'Ha, ha,' Eddie sneered.

Daphne turned on him. 'You can just take yourself to the pub, Edward McNulty,' she said firmly. 'Don't think you're going to sit there making snide remarks the whole time Emily's here.'

'I'm skint, Daph,' Eddie sighed.

'Are you ever anything else? Take five quid out of the till, and if I find you've taken ten then you're in trouble.'

'But look at me,' Emily wailed, after Eddie had gone. 'Look at my hair, look at my skin, my figure. Look at my clothes. How can I ever convince myself I'm beautiful?'

'You won't until you've made the effort,' Daphne murmured, in her lovely sing-song voice. She was still stroking Emily's neck, massaging it gently. Their eyes met again in the mirror, and Emily felt as if she was being hypnotised, that she would emerge a few hours later looking just the same but feeling like Julia Roberts, and Eddie would sneer, 'Ha, ha,' and the whole thing would have been a waste of time, because the feeling would never last. Within an hour, she'd be back in

Emily Murphy's body and with Emily Murphy's face.

'It's about time we started.' Daphne undid Emily's plait and seized a pair of scissors. The transformation had begun.

Over the next few hours, Emily's hair was cut, washed, put into rollers, dabbed with nauseous-smelling liquids, washed again, dried. She was moved from mirror to sink, from sink to mirror, then back again. Then a revolting rubber bathing hat full of holes was forced on to her head, and Daphne's assistant, a young girl called Tina, began to poke in the holes with an evil-looking instrument to pull through Emily's grey strands, which were then daubed with a foaming blue liquid that smelt even more nauseous than the ones before. While the blue liquid 'took', she had a mud pack, and Tina rubbed cream into her hands, and did her nails, painting them a frosty pink.

Never, thought Emily, exhausted, as she sat in front of the supposedly flattering gold mirror, had she seen a sight so utterly hideous, so grotesquely obscene, as the one that met her eyes now. She looked like a sadly beached whale, covered in mud, with a head like a giant, foaming, balding, blue tassel.

'Bloody hell,' she groaned.

'You're coming on nicely, Emily,' Daphne sang. 'Won't be long now.'

Nevertheless, she enjoyed herself. She felt very much at home in the vividly lit, strangely smelling pink and mauve grotto that hardly seemed part of the real world outside, more like a spaceship hovering on the brink of the furthest universe; the women, with their roller-covered, pink-netted heads, dressed in identical pink plastic uniforms, sitting under mauve metal helmets, resembled a crew of aliens. And Daphne, with her bright silver hair, neither young nor old, moving quickly yet calmly to and fro like a moth on Prozac, the ship's captain.

There were customers in and out throughout the day who asked where Emily lived, and if she worked, did she have any children, what did her husband do? She had several cups of tea, but virtuously refused biscuits – she'd already lost four pounds. She listened to several life stories, including Daphne's. She had been born in the house next door but one and 'took over the rent book' from her mother. 'I started the salon just after I got married in nineteen fifty-nine. When Joe died I moved into the flat upstairs.'

'Eddie said you're retiring.'

'That's right, luv.' Daphne's green eyes sparkled. 'I'm off to the Isle of Man next week, Douglas. I've loads of friends there.'

'We'll miss you, Daph,' an elderly customer said, with genuine regret. 'You've been doing me hair for nearly forty years.'

'Has the business been sold?' Emily enquired.

'There's not much to sell, luv. The place is only rented, and the equipment's not worth much – it's so old. I don't know what's going to happen to it. How does that face pack feel?'

'Hard,' said Emily. 'Like concrete.'

'It's time it came off. Tina, see to Emily, there's a luv. Clean her face and shampoo the tint off. I'll blow it dry, but we won't let her see herself in the mirror till after she's had her facial.'

Half an hour later, a perspiring Emily sat on a reclining chair, with Daphne on a stool beside her, and a sweet-smelling cleansing cream was gently smoothed on to her face, followed by apple-scented toner, then moisturiser. 'I won't bother with a base, Emily,' Daphne murmured. 'You've got strong skin, you don't need it. I don't believe in plastering stuff on. I'll just use a breath of powder. Close your eyes, while I do the eyeliner. I'll not use much mascara, you've got nice long lashes. Did you know that? As for the shadow, I'm using mink on the lids, rose beige on the outer eye. I'm telling you this so's you know what to buy, like. Everything's Max Factor.'

'Thanks, Daph,' Emily murmured. She felt pleasantly languid.

'Don't mention it, luv. Now, remember what I said before, won't you? It's all in the mind. You are what you tell yourself you are. You're better than Edward McNulty any day, so don't let him piss you around. Any minute now it'll be time to leave the bugger behind. The storm will be over, and you won't need that old raincoat any more.'

'For goodness sake, Daphne. You should have been a philosopher.' Emily opened her eyes and stared into the face only inches from her own. Lord, it was *massively* wrinkled, a whole cobweb of wrinkles, etched deeply into the skin, particularly around the fine mouth, under the eyes, across the forehead. Daphne was incredibly old. Then Daphne's lovely green eyes glowed with amusement. She shook her shining hair, moved back a little, and it was like watching a magician, because Daphne suddenly became incredibly young. 'That's what my husband used to say. Come on, luv, take a look at yourself in the mirror. We won't use the magic one, just an ordinary silver one that never tells a lie.'

So Emily sat before the ordinary silver mirror, in which she saw an older version of the girl who'd married Alex: a captivating, if slightly overweight creature, with bouncing, silver-streaked, shoulder-length hair, and large, mysterious eyes, so skilfully made-up that the fine kohl liner and subtle shadow were scarcely noticeable. The blusher made her face appear thinner, her skin was no longer grey. And there was a bow in her pink-painted lips that she'd never known she had. She was beautiful. She tossed her head, and the soft waves and curls fell gently back against her face, making her feel feminine and wholly desirable.

A feeling of elation swept over this refurbished and much improved Emily, a sense of power that no amount of Money could bring. From this moment on, things would change. She intended to do something with her life, she wasn't yet sure what, but something.

'What do you think?' asked Daphne, her hands on Emily's shoulders, smiling.

'It's a miracle, thank you.'

'Don't thank me, luv. It's you that worked the miracle. You turned the water into wine, not me.'

'How much do I owe you?'

'Nothing, luv. It's on the house.'

'Oh, but I must . . .' Emily began, but Daphne put a small finger on Emily's newly discovered lips, and said, 'This is me last week and I'm not charging anyone. It's been a pleasure, Emily.'

'Well, thank you.' She hadn't just improved outside but inside, too, because Emily stood up and warmly embraced the woman. Such spontaneous, affectionate gestures, extended either way, had been long missing from her life. 'Thank you, Daph,' she said again.

As Emily drove out of the street, she glanced back at the hairdresser's to check it was there, to ensure it hadn't been merely an illusion and that she'd dreamt the last few hours, or that Daphne's actually was a spaceship, which would vanish like the Tardis in *Dr Who*.

'That was all very strange,' she said to Eddie. 'I feel as if I've had a brain transplant.'

'Told you Daphne was a nutcase, didn't I? It comes from being in a convent all that time.'

'She was a nun?'

'Only until she was about thirty. Not bad, is she, for a woman of seventy-five?'

'Not bad at all,' Emily said faintly. *She'd been sharing him with a very old old-age pensioner!*

'Anyroad, Em, you look great, a real stunner.'

He squeezed her knee, and Emily was surprised that she resented the rather familiar gesture. Who did he think he was? She didn't want to appear ungrateful, but she'd sooner not sleep with Eddie McNulty again. 'I think I'll send her some flowers.' Tomorrow, first thing, she'd order a great bunch.

'Who, Daph? She'd appreciate that. It's a pity she's closing down,' he said, with a sigh. 'That place is a little gold mine. If I had the dosh, I'd take it over meself, put a sauna, a few bikes and rowing machines in the upstairs, and turn it into a beauty and fitness centre. Cleopatra's, I'd call it, the face that sank a thousand ships.'

'It was Helen of Troy, actually, and she launched the ships, not sank them.'

He sighed again. 'It's always been a dream of mine to run a beauty parlour sort of thing.'

'So you've said before.'

'I'd be good at it.'

Emily glanced at the weak, bland, handsome face, so

completely devoid of anything resembling character yet able to charm an awful lot of birds off an awful lot of trees, and said, 'You certainly would.'

'In no time at all I'd have a whole chain. Hey, Em, you should have turned left for Ince Blundell.'

'I'm not going home. I'm going into Liverpool to buy clothes.' He was irritating her, but she remembered that he was ultimately responsible for the woman she was now. After she'd acquired a new wardrobe she'd treat him to dinner.

Alex had never left her short of money. For years now, a large sum had been transferred into Emily's personal account every month, and only used when she made her pathetic forays to the supermarket to buy pathetic amounts of food, so the bulk of the money was still intact. What need had Emily Murphy for the things that other women found so vital to their everyday existence, clothes, jewellery, cosmetics to name but a few? Other items, which would have made life fuller, videos, books, records, for instance, it had never crossed her mind to buy, because she couldn't visualise anything improving her sluggish, half-dead half-life. As to household items, new curtains, pretty dishes, designer bedding, the occasional ornament, why, Emily had not bought so much as a magnet for the fridge since her children had left home. She'd never even thought to bring flowers into the house from the wonderful garden until Mae had done it for her.

Under the circumstances, Alex would surely have approved if he could have seen Emily go crazy with her credit card for the first time in her life, go completely demented. The madness glinted in her eyes, as if she were drunk, though she was completely sober. She felt as if she had just been released from a long period of solitary confinement and had joined the world again. She would have gone even madder, had Eddie not lent a restraining hand from time to time. 'Hang on, Em. Two outfits is enough for now. Don't forget, you need to lose a couple more stone and then they'll be too big. Same goes for underwear. You don't want to waste money.'

'Oh, yes. Oh, no.' She made do with a cornflower blue linen suit with a straight skirt and fitted jacket, and a flowing, chiffony dress, splashed like an artist's palette with numerous shades of pink. She kept the dress on, bought a pair of silver sandals to go with it, and two other pairs of shoes. With a cry of exultation, she chucked her old clothes in a bin, and charged into

Marks & Spencer for underwear. She bought tights. She bought nightdresses. Then bought the makeup that Daphne had recommended in George Henry Lees, where she sprayed herself with several expensive perfumes, bought two large bottles, then galloped over to the jewellery counter.

'Hang on a minute, Em,' Eddie said again, breathless beside her. 'They're clip-on earrings, and your ears are pierced.'

'Are they?' She'd forgotten. 'Are you sure?'

'I can see the holes, luv. They're nearly closed up, but not quite.'

'I remember now. Mary and I had them done together just before she went to university.'

'Those pink ones go the gear with your new frock, Em. I'll help you put them in.'

'And a necklace, I must have a necklace,' Emily cried greedily. 'And another necklace and earrings to go with the blue suit.'

'Gold would look better, more tasteful. A nice fine chain and some little studs.'

'Gold, then, real gold,' Emily panted. 'I don't want plated. And I don't want little studs, either. I want big ones, huge.'

'She's just won the lottery,' Eddie explained, to the alarmed assistant. 'Calm down, Em,' he whispered. 'You're making a show of yourself. Daphne said people will think you're beautiful because of how you walk. They'll take you for a bloody carthorse from the way you're charging around.'

'Oh!' Emily subsided with a hiss. 'Oh, Eddie. I feel a bit sick.'

'I'm not surprised, luv,' Eddie said kindly. 'You woke up as Boris Karloff and ended the day like Cher. Come on, let's have something to drink. Anyroad, the shops'll be closing soon. You can come shopping another time when you feel a bit calmer, when you've got used to yourself, as it were.'

'Am I really beautiful, Eddie?' she enquired plaintively.

'All women are beautiful, but as Daphne said, only if they think they are, only if they believe it.'

'I think I believe it.'

'Well, in that case, as from today you are.'

Alex emerged from his study when he heard the key in the front door, ready to tear a strip off his wife. He had found he didn't like being in Thorntons by himself, especially after it had gone dark. He felt lonely, he needed company, even if it was only Emily, and even if she was usually in another room. At least he knew someone was there. As the hour got later, he also began to worry. It was years since Emily had been known to go out in the evenings, and she had never stayed out late.

'It's past eleven o'clock, Emily. Where on earth have you been till . . .' His angry voice trailed away when he saw the gorgeous, flushed, splendiferously pink woman with tumbling silver-streaked hair in his hallway. 'I'm afraid you seem to have come to the wrong house,' he mumbled reverently. By Christ, she was a cracker. Big, but a cracker all the same. By some strange coincidence her key must fit the Murphys' front door.

'For goodness sake, Alex,' the cracker laughed, a lovely throaty laugh he remembered well, but hadn't heard in a long time, 'it's me, Emily. I would have phoned to tell you I'd be late, but I seem to have forgotten our number.'

'Emily! Where have you been? What have you done to yourself? You look different.'

'I've been to see Daphne, the hairdressing ex-nun,' she gurgled, possibly drunkenly. 'Then I went to dinner with a friend.'

'But you haven't got a friend.'

'Well, I definitely didn't have dinner with myself, which means I must have.' She laughed again. 'I feel a little bit tiddly. Well, quite a lot, actually. I had to leave the car in town and get a taxi home. It's all the champagne we had to celebrate.'

'Celebrate what?' Alex demanded jealously. He felt wholly disorientated and, for the first time ever, as if he was no longer in charge of his life when he'd always been so much in control, so organised. Things rarely happened unless he decreed they should. Emily wouldn't normally visit a hairdresser without discussing it with him first, not to ask his permission, of course not, he wasn't that sort of man, but merely to seek his approval, which was a different thing altogether. He was cross with himself, because the situation was so trivial, so utterly insignificant, when compared to the other things on his mind, Hauptmannwagen, mainly, which was really something to worry about. He also felt unreasonably cross with Emily for looking so phenomenally gorgeous when he'd got used to her being plain. Why hadn't she done it before – before he'd got involved with Gaynor, for instance? Never, not in a million years, would he have taken up with that paltry little blonde if he'd had this beautiful creature to take to bed.

'Oh, we were celebrating all sorts of things,' Emily said vaguely. 'Nothing that would interest you.' She and Eddie had drunk a toast to Daphne, to wish her well in her retirement on the Isle of Man, they'd drunk to the weather, then to the government, to each other, to Emily's dress and Emily's hair. On the way to find a taxi, they had passed Emily's bank. She'd used her credit card to acquire a mini-statement and discovered she had more than seven thousand pounds in her account.

It was then, feeling a recklessness and audacity that she didn't know she had, that she made up her mind to start her own business. She'd vowed to do something with her life, so why not do it now? Why wait and cast around for other things? She'd had no training, no experience of any type of work, other than as a house-wife and a mother – valueless and disparaged occupa-tions in the sour, post-Thatcherite nineties. In a way, it was an easy decision to make, because there was a business, waiting on a plate as it were, ready for her to start.

'How much rent does Daphne pay?' she asked Eddie. 'I'm not sure, forty or fifty quid a week.'

'Could you find out? Ask if there's a lease available. A lease gives more security than rent.' She had no idea how she knew such a thing – she must have read it somewhere.

'Of course, luv,' Eddie said, his vacuous face puzzled. 'But why?'

'I think your dreams are about to come true, Eddie. It depends on costs. The price of hairdryers, for instance, the decoration, the sauna you suggested, the rowing-machines, how many staff we'll need . . . but if everything's affordable, if everything works out the way I hope, then I'm offering you a job as manager of Cleopatra's Health and Beauty Salon.'

'What's in the bags?' Alex asked. He'd only just noticed she was laden with carrier-bags, at least a dozen.

'Just stuff.'

'What sort of stuff?' Was his voice getting older as he spoke, becoming quavery, querulous, fainter? Was his body letting him down, as well as the whole world?

'Clothes and stuff. Are you all right, Alex? You sound a bit odd. I hope you're not coming down with a cold or something.'

'Oh, I'm fine,' he said bitterly. 'Would you care if I wasn't?'

'More than you ever cared about me. I haven't been fine at all, not for years and years, not until now.'

'Em!' He wanted to apologise, he wanted to faint, he wanted to die, he wanted a huge hole to open up so he could throw himself in and weep and wail that life was shit, that he'd made a terrible mess of everything.

Emily crossed the hall and went upstairs. She walked lightly, gracefully, not in the usual plodding, heavy way that had so much got on his nerves. Half-way up, she turned. 'I forgot to say I'm going to London for the weekend to see Mum and the children. Do you have a message for Mary?'

'Mary who?'

'Mary Murphy, she's your daughter.'

Alex's brain began to melt and trickle down his throat. Before it could melt altogether and he had no senses left, he said, 'Give her my good wishes.'

'I think I'll remember that. "Mary, your father sends his good wishes." Thank you, Alex. I'll leave late tomorrow afternoon, after Mae's gone. Alice is taking Cloud to stay with Gareth, so I'll ring first thing in the morning and see if she would like a lift. I must remember to get the child's car seat down from the loft. Oh, by the way, did I tell you Gareth and Alice are getting married in August? On the thirtieth. It's a Saturday, so you might be able to spare a few hours off work. Otherwise you can just send your good wishes.'

'But, Emily,' Alex said feebly, 'I was going away for the weekend myself, to Frankfurt to see Heinrich.' He needed to be in the vicinity of his quotation, to be near Heinrich, listen to his assurances that everything was going to be all right.

Emily raised her combed and subtly drawn eyebrows. 'So what?'

'The house, we can't leave it unoccupied. Someone might break in.'

'In that case I'll ask Mae if she'd like to stay, though we'll have to make up the wages she gets from her other jobs. It will give her a break. She'll have to bring Shona, but she's no trouble. Well, goodnight, Alex. Or perhaps I should say goodbye, as I probably won't see you again before I go. I hope you have a nice time in Frankfurt.'

CHAPTER EIGHT

Dicky McNulty had guessed by now that there was something peculiar, not quite right, about the blue Plasticine. Hadn't Quentin Quinn's house been done over twice? His own house would have got the same if there hadn't been someone in. And that snotty policeman who'd nearly torn his ear off had demanded to know where 'the package' was. They must have seen those two geezers hand it to him outside the Quinns' house that day then take it inside — he remembered the grey car that had followed when the Irishmen drove away — and assumed he hadn't given it to Mr Quinn, which Dicky found highly offensive, even though it was true. Did he look like a thief?

He had pulled the Plasticine into little pieces, expecting to find something hidden inside: jewels, maybe, or drugs. If it was jewels, he'd keep them till the fuss died down then take them to a fence to sell. Dicky had no idea where fences lived, if they had shops or offices, if they advertised themselves in the *Liverpool Echo*, but someone in his class at school might know. He'd buy himself a Sega games system, a whole pile of games, and something for his mam: a ladder, she was always on about wanting a ladder. If he found drugs, Dicky wasn't quite sure what he'd do. Drugs were dangerous, he knew that much. People killed for drugs. Either that, or drugs killed them. And if his mam found him with drugs, she'd never forgive him. He decided that if it turned out to be drugs, he'd put them back in the Plasticine and squeeze the whole lot through the Quinns' letter-box one night when it was dark and no one was looking.

However, when he looked, the Plasticine was empty. Dicky rolled the shreds into little balls, threw them at the wall, collected them and patted them back into a shapeless wad. He stared at it, frowning deeply. Perhaps it wasn't Plasticine at all, but something different, something valuable and highly sought after, like, like . . . Dicky put his imaginative brain to work . . . like the liver of a prehistoric animal, for instance, that collectors all over the world were anxious to have. Or a precious substance that jewellery was made from. He made himself a ring, but it looked dead horrible. He preferred the idea of the liver. Anyroad, whatever it was, the Quinns' house had been torn apart twice by men looking for the stuff, and since so many people, including the cops, were after it, Dicky felt he'd like to keep it for himself. He'd never owned anything worth much before, and rather liked the sensation. It made him feel a bit special, rather important, a sort of juvenile Mr Big.

On the other hand, it was a bit risky storing the parcel under the bottom bunk where Craig slept. It was one of the first places a burglar would look, should a burglar get this far, and although Dicky had surveyed the house quite thoroughly, he couldn't find anywhere more secure.

'Did they go through your airing cupboard?' he asked casually of Quentin Quinn.

'Yes, they threw everything out, and me mam had just done the ironing. She had a fit.'

'What about the bathroom, behind the board on the bath, like?'

'They kicked it in,' Quentin said gloomily. 'Me da still hasn't fixed it. It's dead draughty in there when we have a bath.'

'The fridge?' Which was a stupid question, Dicky

realised straight away, as Mam would be bound to notice it. His great-grandad, being shortsighted, might even fry it for their tea one night.

'Yes. They searched everywhere, Dicky. They emptied the paint out the shed, me mam's never stopped moaning about it, and even dug up the garden.'

'Right,' said Dicky.

It would appear there was no hiding-place for his piece of precious, mysterious Plasticine, until one Friday night his mam came home and said she was spending the weekend at this house where she worked in Ince Blundell. Looking after the place, sort of thing.

'You'll be all right, won't you, luv? You'll have your mates to play with,' Mae said anxiously. She was looking forward to the peace and quiet of the next few days with only Shona for company, but especially as a rest from her various jobs. Emily, who since last Wednesday appeared to have risen again like Jesus Christ and emerged a totally different person, had offered to cover the wages she would have earned, with an extra twenty quid on top. 'Jim and Eddie will both be here, as well as our Craig. Cloud won't be in your way. Em's taken her and our Alice with her to London.'

Dicky thought immediately of where he could hide

the package, in a house that was miles from nowhere, according to his mother, where the coppers would never dream of looking. 'Can I come with you, Mam?' he asked, in a weak treble.

'But you'll be bored out of your skull, Dicky, without your friends.'

'Not if I'm with you, Mam.' He put his hand in hers and regarded her beseechingly with his large blue eyes, which were suddenly moist. Blinking furiously, he managed to raise a tear, which ran heart-wrenchingly down one rosy cheek.

'Jaysus, luv,' Mae gasped, alarmed. 'You're not being bullied at school, are you?'

Just as if anyone would dare bully Dicky McNulty, he thought indignantly. 'No, Mam. But I don't feel all that well. I'd sooner be with you and our Shona.'

'Well, in that case, luv, of course you can come.'

When Eddie heard about Mae's weekend plans, he announced himself unwilling to be left with his dad for two entire days without her there to protect him. Eddie felt hurt. Emily hadn't mentioned anything about going to London on Thursday. She must have decided after the taxi had dropped him off. He felt very possessive about Emily, his new business partner, and the woman he had moulded with his own hands, as it were, like Rex Harrison had done with Audrey Hepburn in *My Fair Lady*. He'd been looking forward to spending Saturday at Thorntons and would have expected Emily to be looking forward to it even more. Mind you, now they were to be business partners, it mightn't be a bad idea to cut out the sex. Poor Em, it would break her heart, but she'd get over it.

Jim McNulty also found the notion of a weekend break irresistible. 'It'll be like staying in a five-star hotel, if what you say about the house is true.'

Then Craig emerged from the bedroom where he'd been lying on his bunk, completely broke and jobless, and said he wasn't prepared to stay in this house all by himself. He was a prepossessing lad, Craig, with brown curly hair and an open, guileless face, so like his Irish dad, sadly killed in Northern Ireland.

Mae saw mountains of bedding to be washed before they left on Sunday evening when Emily was expected home, meals for six instead of little snacks for her and Shona. There goes my peace and quiet, she thought. But, taking all things into consideration, she far preferred her family around. Look what peace and quiet had done to Emily Murphy!

'We'd better take some food, otherwise we'll eat the Murphys out of house and home,' she said cheerfully. 'If you'll quickly get your things together, then we'll be off.'

Jim McNulty sat in the front of the estate car beside his granddaughter, Eddie got in the back with Craig, who had Shona on his knee, with Dicky squeezed between them.

'What have you got there, luv?' Mae nodded at the plastic carrier-bag on Dicky's lap.

'Just some books to read,' Dicky said virtuously. 'School books.'

'Good lad,' Mae said approvingly.

Cecil, the dog, sat on the step and, for the second time in his long life, watched sadly as a car containing everyone he loved drove away, probably, if previous experience was anything to go by, never to be seen again. Then the car stopped, a door opened, and a voice shouted, 'C'mon, Cecil boy, else you'll be left behind.' Cecil gave a little joyful yelp, and leapt inside, where he licked every face within reach with the deepest and most heartfelt gratitude. If only he could tell these people how much he adored them.

As Mae McNulty and her family left for Ince Blundell, in a car parked some distance away from Daffodil

Close two men were jumping about agitatedly, in so far as it was possible to jump about while sitting down.

'Did you see that, Mick?' Paddy shouted. 'Did you see what the lad was carrying? A Tesco carrier-bag!'

'I suppose there's a lot of them about,' Mick grunted. If the truth be known, he was fed up to the teeth with the whole fucking business. It was weeks since they'd brought the damn stuff to Kirkby, though it might have been months, and it felt like years. All they'd done since was search for a lad called Bart Simpson who turned out not to exist, arrange for houses to be done over, and sit in their fucking cars getting bored fucking rigid watching out for who knows fucking what. Why didn't Sean Donovan just get another two pounds of Semtex, for fuck's sake? Was it difficult to get hold of? How much did it cost? If it was cheap, if he knew where it could be got, then Mick would willingly have bought the bloody stuff himself, pretend he'd found it hidden in a rosebush in the Quinns' garden, thus bringing the whole boring business to a fucking end. Trouble was, he thought huffily, he wasn't privy to such sensitive information as the source of explosives or their cost. Oh, no, he wasn't to be trusted with the really important stuff. Not for him the excitement and the thrill of being a genuine terrorist. He was right at the very bottom of the organisation's shit-heap: a foot-slogger, a delivery-boy; he didn't have a single stripe. Why, he wasn't even provided with a decent car.

The problem was that Sean Donovan had mounted his very high horse, and announced it was a matter of principle, a question of honour, that the stuff be recovered from wherever it happened to be. Even if more could be got for twopence a pound, Sean wanted the original consignment found, the one Mick and Paddy had been despatched with to give to Rory Quinn. 'Otherwise,' Sean said, in his deep, gravelly, sinister, threatening voice, 'I'll never be able to trust any one of yis again, will I?'

'No, Sean,' Mick had agreed.

Paddy nudged him with his elbow, nearly breaking a rib. 'Well, come on, Mick, get a move on.'

'Get a move on where?'

'After that car, eejit. The one with the lad in with the Tesco carrier-bag.'

Neither noticed (one of the reasons they didn't have a stripe) the anonymous grey Sierra that followed them off the estate as they pursued Mae McNulty and her son with the Tesco carrier-bag to Ince Blundell.

'Who d'you think lives there, then, Mick?' Paddy asked when the car in front turned off the pretty country lane.

Mick edged slowly forward until they could see a large tiled cottage through the trees and bushes that screened it from the road. 'How the hell should I know?' he snarled. 'I haven't got an electoral roll tattooed on me arm.'

'Let's find a shop somewhere and ask. And don't get shirty with me, Mick. There's no need for it.'

'Thorntons,' Michael Jones murmured. 'Bet that cost a bob or two.' The car in front had driven off, and they'd stopped outside the house and were watching the occupants of the car in front of the car in front unpack the contents of the boot and go inside. Jones was especially interested in the lad with the plastic bag. 'That's where that blonde-haired bint works.'

'Who?' enquired his sergeant, Patrick Watson.

'The mother of that ratbag kid. I thought someone should find out about the family,' he added pointedly. Watson appeared to have lost interest in the case. 'Mae

McNulty, her name is, and a real slag, by all accounts. Pile o' kids, all by different fathers. It would seem some blokes aren't all that particular where they dip their wick.'

'She looks quite an attractive woman to me,' Watson said, in the ridiculous namby-pamby voice he'd recently started to use. 'Who lives there?'

'I didn't think to ask. It didn't seem important.'

'If the little lad has brought the Semtex with him, it's important now. Ring the nick and they'll look it up on the computer.'

Am I supposed to do everything meself? Jones thought bitterly, as he reached for the mobile. He probably doesn't know how to work the bloody thing.

Patrick Watson was watching Mae, Mae and his son, together, thinking of how things might have been if only he'd acted differently, or if Mae had been a bit more accommodating. After all, he hadn't hit her all *that* hard. Lately, he'd been trying valiantly to reform himself by thinking only of pleasant, gentle things, like green fields full of daisies, with woolly lambs gambolling on the fragrant grass, of trees bulging with blossom (he preferred pink), monks chanting psalms, starry skies, babies crying, though that didn't work, and he'd nearly murdered one.

He had forced himself to be nice to people, to be understanding, patient, think positively, not to jump to conclusions, to take each day as it came, not bear grudges. He'd been watching Tony Blair on telly and practising a similar smile. He spoke evenly, softly, politely, never raised his voice. He said 'please' and 'thank you', had stopped swearing and begun to take pains with his grammar. He opened doors for people. He was, all in all, a much nicer guy, and the thing was, he rather liked himself, which he never had before, not that he'd given it much thought, not that he'd cared.

Surprisingly, very quickly, he'd noticed that other people had started to like him, too. Not Jones, his partner, who for some reason was always in a terrible temper, but the women coppers at the station, for instance, whom he used to regard as a shower of dykes, had suddenly become all friendly, asking his advice on questions of procedure or cases they were working on, which was only right and proper, him being their superior. But he'd frightened them off before, and they'd avoided him like the plague.

Lately, the world seemed to have got brighter, lit by a luminous golden light. People looked happier, kinder, they smiled a lot. There were more flowers about, the air smelt balmy and was sweet to breathe. He began to notice butterflies and listen to the pretty song of the birds.

Patrick Watson was preparing himself for the day he introduced himself to his son, to Dicky. He thought about Dicky a lot, usually with a lump in his throat, the same lump he used to have when he had been thrashed nightly by his own dad, usually for the most insignificant reason, or for no reason at all. His mam would be sobbing quietly downstairs, and in the next bedroom, Monica, his sister, would be wondering if she'd be next. Genuinely, with all his heart and soul, he wanted to be a good father to Dicky, a proper dad, which was one of the reasons he'd sent the lad twenty quid, though he was still too nervous to reveal who it was from. There would be plenty of time to introduce himself. He swore to himself that never, never would he lay a finger on *his* boy, never speak to him unkindly, never make him feel small, never . . .

'The name's Murphy, Alexander Murphy,' Jones said abruptly, switching the mobile off. 'Lives there with an Emily Murphy, presumably his wife.'

'What?'

Shit, thought Jones, astounded, are those tears in

Sarge's eyes? He looked away, embarrassed. 'I said, the name's Murphy, Alexand—'

'All right, Michael. I heard you the first time. I was miles away, sorry, mate.' Watson put his hand on Jones's arm in a gesture of apology, and Jones shied away as if he'd had an electric shock. They weren't footballers, and he didn't like being touched by another man except in a fight. Then he had the most appalling thought, really shocking. Had Watson decided he was gay? He noticed that the man hadn't had his hair cut in ages. It was quite long, curling around his rather nicely shaped ears in quite an attractive way. Oh, Jesus! He felt himself grow hot.

'Is something wrong, Michael?' Watson asked gently.

'No, Sarge.' Jones rolled down the window for a whopping great spit to hide his confusion. 'It's just you couldn't get a more Irish name than Murphy. I wonder where he comes from? Perhaps this is where the Semtex was meant for all along. We've been concentrating on Rory Quinn when we should have set our sights on Alexander Murphy.'

Within ten minutes of the McNultys arriving at Thorntons:

Shona had invaded Alex's study, switched on the computer, and was trying to find the Internet.

Dicky had hidden the carrier-bag in the lily-pond beneath a heap of stones.

Cecil was trying to catch a goldfish with his paw in the same pond.

Eddie was in the bedroom trying on Alex's clothes.

Jim had found a snug little room with a television and a cupboard containing several bottles of fine brandy, as well as a box of expensive cigars that the master of the house kept for visitors. He helped himself to everything, put his feet on an embroidered stool and watched *Star Trek* on BBC2. He was, at that moment, a sublimely contented man.

Craig was on the phone to his best mate, Peter, who had emigrated to Australia the year before. His mam wouldn't let him use the phone at home. 'Hi, Pete. Guess who this is? It's Craig. Yes, Craig McNulty. How's things going, mate?'

Of the McNultys, only Mae was above reproach, as she tried to catch up on the work she should have done during the week but had neglected because all she and Emily had done was gossip. She mopped the kitchen floor, polished the worktops, then started to prepare the tea.

Poor Eustace, whisky-sodden, muddled and not at all well, was cowering in the shed, where he had been just about to settle down on a pile of filthy, evil-smelling sacks with half a bottle of Haig. He could hear voices, music, a dog. Had Thorntons been invaded? Would he be put up against a wall and shot? He was getting quite frantic when Mae found him, explained that the invaders were merely her family, and invited him inside for a cup of tea and something to eat.

'No, ta, Mae.' It wasn't his place to go inside, he'd feel uncomfortable. 'Anyroad, I'm not hungry.'

'But what are you doing here, luv? I thought you'd be well home by now.' Her pretty face was furrowed with anxiety on his behalf.

'I was going in a minute,' he lied. 'Didn't feel up to the bike ride, not just yet.'

'In that case, sit in the arch, and I'll fetch you a cuppa. Once I've got the meal on the go, I'll take you home in the car and tuck you up in bed. You'll probably feel better after a good night's sleep. I'll try and pop in and see you in the morning.'

So Eustace sat in the arch, trembling like a young man

on his first date as he waited for Mae to take him home and tuck him in. He tried to remember when he'd last changed the bedding, and thought it was probably around nineteen ninety-three. One of these days he really must get to Formby to change his will in favour of the woman he loved so dearly. But lately he had had trouble merely walking on his long, stringy, painful legs, let alone riding a bike. The furthest he could stagger was to the small sub-post office to collect his pension, and buy his weekly lottery ticket. (Eustace was unaware that he was supposed to check the numbers, and assumed that the government would write and tell him if he'd won.) Fortunately, the post office had an off-licence, and the pension was quickly exchanged for a week's supply of booze.

After tea, when Eustace had been taken home and tucked under his grey, rotting blankets, the McNultys deserted their various activities inside the house and roamed the beautiful, wild garden, separately and to-gether. Night was beginning to fall, the sky was dusky, the new moon a faint blur, and the air thickly scented with the heady fragrance of herbs and a thousand flowers.

Dicky was swinging dreamily from the rope on the

oak tree at the front, listening to the gentle creaking of the branch above, and the soothing swish of the rope. If it hadn't been for the mysterious Plasticine, he wouldn't be here, but he was glad he'd come. This place really was the gear, dead cool, excellent. He hoped his mam would soon be able to come again.

Sharing a rare and unaccustomed spirit of friendliness, Jim and Eddie, father and son, walked together through the garden.

'Isn't it still?' Jim murmured, moved by the utter quietness and the tranquillity of their dark, leafy surroundings. Used as he was to the sound of never-ending traffic, the hoot and wail of the various emergency services, of children playing in the street outside, of frequent fights, of the jingle of ice-cream vans, of the television, which seemed to be on all the time, now his ears felt almost numb, strangely empty, when all he could hear was a faint rustle as birds settled down for the night, and a slight shuffling of little creatures in the undergrowth, creatures, Jim realised with a pang, about which he was totally ignorant. He was nearly eighty, yet he knew so little. There was so much to learn, yet you were allowed such a short span on this mortal plane, and he'd never had the opportunity to study. He thought of all the books he'd wanted to read, the music he'd wanted to listen to, the things he'd wanted to do. Paint, for instance. He'd always wanted to paint. He felt sad, thinking of the opportunities that had been denied him. Ah, but now he was doing an Eddie, blaming the world when it was himself who was to blame. What was there to stop him from painting now, even if he used kids' paint, not the proper, expensive sort? It was never too late to learn.

'Isn't it still what, Dad?'

'Nothing, son.'

Eddie's thoughts were miles away from Ince Blundell. He'd never liked Thorntons, which he considered a dump, and gardens were nothing but a pain. What were trees but lumps of disease-ridden wood with slimy leaves that dropped in the autumn, littering the streets and staining his shoes, particularly if they were suede. In Eddie's mind, it was 2002, and Naomi Campbell had graciously agreed to open the newest branch of the Cleopatra's chain of health and beauty salons in the West End of London. Quite a crowd was there, including Fergie. He looked across the dazzling white, black and chrome room for his business partner, Emily, and there she was, looking radiant and almost as slim as

Naomi. It was Eddie, though, who was the cynosure of all eyes, the man responsible for this glitteringly successful company that had recently been floated on the Stock Exchange; *Mister* Eddie, as he was known, who seemed to have grown younger in the intervening years, and acquired a more noble profile. His hair, more luxuriant than now, was combed in the cutely bouffant style that had become his trademark.

Meanwhile, Craig McNulty was on his knees in the failing light, inspecting the flowers, astounded that such delicate stems could support such heavy blossoms, bewildered by the startling beauty of every single thing; the petals, for instance, so perfect, so impossibly perfect, each one exactly matching the other, and arranged around the thing in the middle, whatever it was called, as if they'd been drawn with a compass and protractor. And so many colours, too, rainbow upon rainbow of colours and hues and tints and shades. And the leaves: he'd always thought of leaves as exactly the same shape, leaf-shaped, but there were round leaves, fan-shaped leaves, pear-shaped leaves, oval ones, fat ones, long, thin ones, little thin ones, and some big enough to eat your dinner off, all threaded with a skeleton of intricately patterned veins, and all in entirely different shades of green, ranging from an almost white green to a green that was nearly black. Craig was a nice lad, but the least sensitive of Mae's children. His thoughts rarely strayed beyond Liverpool Football Club's performance in the league (lousy at the moment), a beer with his mates (difficult when you had no money), women (impossible for the same reason), and the need either to find a job or to keep the one he had (Craig wasn't a sponger, and tried very hard to do both). But now he found himself wondering about the flowers. He was mystified by how such absolute perfection could emanate from a single tiny seed. He'd like to find out, he wanted to know. It was called botany, he remembered that much because they used to do it at school and it had seemed dead boring. He'd like to go on a course, learn about botany, become a gardener. He stood up and planted his feet in the rich, soft soil, watered only that afternoon by Eustace, who could have taught Craig a thing or two about gardening. Craig's boots sank into the earth, and he experienced a strange, most unusual sensation that made him feel almost lightheaded, as if he'd actually grown there, like the flowers.

Even Shona, who had recently been in communication with the White House on the Internet, was enchanted as she pushed her way through the leathery leaves of the miniature forest.

'I wish we could live here for always, Mam,' she said to Mae, who was sitting in the arch, sipping the sherry she had bought on her way back from taking Eustace home. Cecil slept, snoring gently, his nose resting contentedly on her feet.

'So do I, luv,' Mae said softly. 'Oh, so do I.'

'Well, blow me,' gasped Patrick Watson, using the phrase in its innocent, unworldly sense.

'Fucking hell,' Jones roared coarsely, pointing to the screen of the computer. 'Will you read that!'

The youthful Alexander Murphy would have been proud to know that he was on police records. Indeed, he would have been desperately hurt if for one moment he'd thought the strikes he had organised at university, the demonstrations he had led, the marches he had headed, the dodgy, highly suspect organisations he had joined in order to overthrow the establishment he loathed had gone unnoticed by the powers-that-be.

This, however, was not the information that so shocked the two policemen. 'Typical student activist,' was all the newer, kinder Sergeant Watson felt bound (almost) to sneer when he read it. Like most activists, Murphy seemed to have calmed down when he left university for the real world where, no doubt, he'd got a job and found himself paying taxes like everybody else, and complained bitterly about the irresponsible way students behaved nowadays. There were no more entries after 1971, when he'd left with a degree; a jolly good one, Jones recognised, with a certain amount of envy.

Both men were aware that the entry might not refer to the Alexander Murphy now living in Ince Blundell. The record showed he had been born in Belfast in 1950 to Eileen Murphy (née McClusky), and Liam Murphy (OR/CI). The family had moved to Liverpool when their son was five.

'What does OR/CI mean?' Patrick asked.

'"On Record, Classified Information",' said Jones. 'I'll look him up. This might be interesting,' which was when they found the information that would have caused the present Alexander Murphy's nervous stomach to have a nervous breakdown. Poor Alex, he had never suspected that his inoffensive da with the fine baritone voice had once been one of the most notorious terrorists in the whole of Northern Ireland.

Jones pressed the mouse and the words rolled up the screen. The men read, fascinated. In those days, in the forties, Liam O'Connell, a Catholic, had been top of the Royal Ulster Constabulary's 'Most Wanted' list. But in 1950 he had redeemed himself, at least in the eyes of the RUC. For Liam had fallen in love with Eileen McClusky, a Protestant woman, and double-crossed his own organisation by revealing a plot to murder her brother, which meant he was wanted by his own side, desperate for revenge. After years spent living in hiding, the couple, now with a son, Alexander, had made their way to Liverpool, where they changed their name to Murphy. According to the occasional checks made since, Liam Murphy had led an uneventful, law-abiding life working as a porter on the railways. There'd been no entries for over fifteen years, and no way of knowing if Liam O'Connell/Murphy was still alive.

'It all sounds very romantic and idealistic,' Patrick said dreamily. 'Risking your life, like, for the love of a good woman.'

Jones ignored him. He was feverishly tapping keys. It should be easy to establish if the Murphy who'd gone to Manchester university was the same Murphy now living in Ince Blundell; credit-card records, hire-purchase records, bank records. Within minutes he had found what he was looking for.

'It's the same person,' he said triumphantly. 'Alexander Murphy, who took delivery of two pounds of Semtex earlier today, is the same Alexander Murphy who was such a pain in the arse at university, and the one who has an Irish terrorist for a dad. I think we might be on to something, Sarge.'

'And what exactly would that be, Michael?'

'A conspiracy, a giant conspiracy. I'd like to bet this Alexander Murphy chap is what's called a sleeper. He's been lying low for all these years, but all the while he's been secretly in contact with the organisation. There could well be a bomb factory in that house.' Jones rubbed his hands together, scarcely able to contain his excitement. If he was right, promotion loomed pleasurably ahead. 'I think we should raid it.'

Watson shook his head. 'Not yet. I'll arrange for twenty-four-hour surveillance, but don't forget, Michael, the original plan was to get our hands on Sean Donovan. If there's a bomb factory in Thorntons, then one of these fine days Donovan's bound to turn up and *then* we'll nab him. As for that kid, Dicky McNulty, he's just an innocent dupe. Donovan and Murphy are merely using him as a go-between, his mam being the cleaner, like. It wasn't Rory Quinn those two prats were after, but Dicky all the time.'

'He's taken his time delivering the stuff,' Jones sneered. 'It's been weeks since he got it.'

'That's probably all part of the plan,' Patrick Watson said sagely.

It was early when the McNultys settled down peacefully for the night in Thorntons, where the subdued ghosts were wondering what had hit them.

Down in London, Emily Murphy was wide awake and enjoying the high life.

The housing charity that her daughter, Mary, worked for was holding an auction in a Mayfair hotel of items donated by celebrities to be followed by a party. Mary invited her freshly furbished mum to come with her (she might not have invited the old one). The auction went well, thousands of pounds were raised, and Emily bought a long cream silk scarf for fifty pounds; it had belonged to Joanna Lumley. She draped it around her neck. It went perfectly with her new blue linen suit.

'Are you enjoying yourself, Mum?' Mary asked later,

at the party. She was a slightly smaller, considerably thinner version of her mother.

'Oh, yes, sweetheart.' Emily was drunk again, but only slightly, on wine. It helped her cope with the unaccustomed attention she was getting. People kept asking Mary who she was, wanting to be introduced.

Mary linked her arm. 'You look gorgeous, Mum, really striking.'

Then, just as the party was about to finish and nearly everyone had gone, the Chancellor of the Exchequer, Gordon Brown, who'd been at another function in the same hotel, came in. He had the sweetest smile, thought Emily, as they shook hands. She was relieved that Alex wasn't there, as he would only have made a sour political comment. She wasn't even the tiniest bit hurt when the Chancellor enquired, 'Have we met before, Mrs Murphy? There's something very familiar about your face.'

At the exact moment that his wife was shaking hands with one of Britain's top politicians, Alex Murphy had just begun to sample the low-life in another country, as his friend Heinrich Hauptmann took him on a tour of Frankfurt's red-light district.

Had Heinrich always been such a repellent, odious

creature, Alex wondered, so utterly repulsive, so comprehensively obnoxious? Had he always been so coarse? Had they really been such good friends back in Manchester? Okay, so Heinrich had been an ugly bugger even then but, accompanied by a youthful, courteous charm, it hadn't seemed to matter. But now the youth had gone and the charm was non-existent, along with any suggestion of good manners, including the ability to say 'please' or 'thank you'. They had corresponded regularly, but hadn't met since their student days. The older Heinrich had a face that put Alex in mind of a large, pink, shiny blister, and was so sadly lacking eye-sockets that his mean, angry little eyes protruded in a way that was quite revolting. His once lean body was covered with a thick layer of tough, hard, unhealthy fat, and he thrust himself about clumsily, with a certain amount of effort. It was too late now, but if Heinrich had been bent on a life of total debauchery, which, if tonight was anything to go by, would appear to be the case, then his best plan would have been to do a Dorian Gray, i.e. have his portrait painted, make a pact with the devil, and let the portrait take the strain.

Yet this was the man to whom Alex had entrusted his entire future. He had come to Frankfurt to talk business, seek comfort, receive assurance that Heinrich had everything sorted, that their plan couldn't possibly fail, but Heinrich thought he was there for a weekend fling, to get away from Emily, have a wild old time. Alex was having a lousy time, but couldn't back out or show his reluctance. It was imperative that Heinrich think well of him until Murphy Computers had the Peek-a-Boo contract, which apparently meant behaving like a drunken, lascivious slob.

For one thing, he didn't like being led. In every situation, Alex automatically assumed the frontal position. He expected people to look to him for direction, for inspiration, for the next move. Instead, he found himself being dragged from one seedy club to the next, even seedier, with Abba hysterically belting out from every loudspeaker, and Heinrich drinking more and more, mixing his drinks with a total lack of caution so that his face turned puce and he got louder and ruder, openly fondling the hard-eyed, hard-faced girls who surrounded them everywhere they went. In one club, a small dingy room painted wholly black, he disappeared for a while, returning with his stubby nose tipped with white powder. In another, he ordered champagne, which was warm when it came and tasted sour. He seemed to expect Alex to pay for everything; the champagne cost the equivalent of fifty pounds. The inevitable girls came and sat with them. Alex had a smattering of German, and knew enough to understand when they tried to persuade him to buy more. He refused. The girls went away. Heinrich frowned.

Only a light drinker, two pints of beer was Alex's limit, which he'd managed to stick to so far, despite Heinrich's taunts that he was an *altfrau*, an old woman, that he was ruining the legendary drinking reputation of the Brits. Now, though, the champagne had gone to his head, and was eating away like acid at his stomach. He felt queasy. The weekend was turning out to be a nightmare.

'Come, Alex,' Heinrich bellowed, 'let's have something to eat.'

Alex sipped red wine in the restaurant, a dangerous thing to do, but he didn't want his friend (*friend?*) thinking him a complete cissy. He watched, smiling (well, trying to), while Heinrich shovelled down a curry and drank copious amounts of red wine, then lit a very expensive cigar.

'Now,' Heinrich slammed his glass on the table, burped loudly and exhaled a virulent cloud of curried breath, 'now I need a woman. Let's find a whorehouse.'

'Well, actually, Heinrich,' Alex said, with a sinking heart, 'I'd prefer to go to bed.'

'You can go to bed with a woman,' Heinrich shouted. Everyone in the restaurant turned to look.

'I'd prefer to go to bed alone in my hotel, if you don't mind. I'm rather tired, Heinrich.' Alex waved a hand limply. 'The journey, you know.'

'For Chrissakes, Alex, how far did you come? From Australia? The North Pole? It's only a piddling little five-minute flight from Manchester. What are you, Alex, a man or *ein Maus*?'

A mouse, a mouse, tonight I'm definitely a mouse, Alex screamed silently. He paid the bill and got wearily and somewhat shakily to his feet, feeling the wine, the beer and the champagne swilling ominously around his guts, a deadly cocktail. Oh, hell, the things you did for money, so degrading. But it was too late now. As soon as he'd got his all-important contract, he'd never again have anything to do with Heinrich Hauptmann. He did his best to grin suggestively. 'Okay, then, so it's a woman.'

Alex didn't want a woman, he wasn't up to it: his sex drive had shrivelled to nothing with worry. Even if it had been throbbing manfully and the mixture over-rich, he wouldn't have wanted a prostitute. Furthermore, he'd got the impression from somewhere that a suspiciously large number of prostitutes in these parts were actually men, transvestites, and the more feminine they seemed the bigger the chance that they were not. He thought longingly of Emily, who had gone to London to stay with her mother, which this time yesterday had seemed the dullest thing in the world but now seemed the most welcoming. He needed Emily at the moment, the way he needed her in the car that time on their way back from Somerset in the storm. He needed the protection of her large, capable arms. He heard her voice, firm and full of courage, singing to their children, 'There were ten in the bed and the little one said, "Roll over . . ."' It sounded a million times better than Abba.

He followed reluctantly as Heinrich barged his ungainly way to an even more squalid club, which Alex assumed must be a brothel. (His only knowledge of brothels came from the paintings of Toulouse-Lautrec.) They were immediately joined by the inevitable girls. Heinrich, the bastard, ordered a magnum of *Champagner*.

Alex decided quickly that the only way to avoid letting Heinrich think he was an undersexed wimp was to choose a woman, go with her to her room, tell her he was impotent, or that he'd lost his penis in the war (the

Falklands would do, blame the Argies), pay the fee, hopefully a reduced one, and escape back to his hotel.

Any woman would do. How did you go about these things? What were you supposed to say? He turned to the heavily made-up woman in the chair next to him and twitched his lips nervously.

'Okay, darling,' she said, in a husky, thickly accented voice, 'I'm Helga. And who are you?'

'Maurice. Maurice Smith.'

Helga was possibly the ugliest of the lot, but what did it matter? She had pockmarked skin, a quite impressively huge nose, and a mountain of blue-black curly hair. To Alex's surprise, her eyes were quite nice: warm, friendly. They regarded him kindly, slightly amused.

She was taking him to her flat around the corner. On the way, he remembered he hadn't paid for the bloody *Champagner*, and was glad. Which was the last thought Alex had before he slithered to the ground, out cold, right in front of a shop that sold computers, his head coming to rest only inches away from the Murphy-Gnome.

The McNultys woke to another glorious morning. Jim got up first and went down to make tea. He brought a cup to Mae; the other buggers could get their own.

'Ta, Grandad.' Mae sat up in bed and beamed at him. 'It's like being on holiday, isn't it? I can't believe we're only a few miles from Kirkby. It's as if we're on the other side of the world.' She glanced through the window. 'I can't wait to see the garden. I bet it feels different so early in the morning, fresher, full of dew. Oh, Grandad! It would be like Paradise, living here.'

Jim regarded his granddaughter tenderly. She looked very much the lady of leisure in the Murphys' big bed, her face flushed with well-being, with no job to go to and nothing in particular to get up for except a walk around the garden. For today, at least, no lousy employer would piss her around. Jim would willingly have given everything he owned, including his life, for what it was worth, if only his dear Mae could always look as radiant as she did now.

Emily lay in her old bed in her old room in the house where she'd been born, drowsy with contentment, feeling the early morning sun caress her face like a gentle lover. Dishes rattled downstairs. Mum was up. The years fell away. She was a child again, a teenager. She had woken in this same spot, with the same sun warming her face, on the day she left for university where she was to meet her husband and where the course of her life would change.

The day stretched ahead invitingly. She was going to Camden Market to shop with her sisters — it was lovely seeing them again — then they were going back to Beryl's for lunch. Tonight Mum was looking after Cloud, and she was taking Gareth and Alice to dinner. Emily thought briefly about Alex, and how dreadful he'd looked lately. But no doubt he was having a whale of a time in Frankfurt and hadn't given her a single thought.

In Frankfurt it was raining heavily. Alex Murphy opened one bleary eye, then another, and found himself in the arms of Steve, an ex-miner from Bolsover.

CHAPTER NINE

Alex was too shocked to faint or have hysterics. At first, he merely stared at the heavily made-up face so close to his own, slowly taking it in, recognising the pockmarked skin, the big nose, the same eyes, which were open and watching him with the same amused expression. Yet there was something different, something odd, something missing. It was then that the shock hit him, and the waves steamrollered over his body, squeezing out every drop of breath. Where was the curly black hair? *Helga was almost completely bald.*

'How do you feel?' Helga asked, in a fairly deep baritone.

Alex had no breath left to answer. He lay there as still and as lifeless as a tree that had been buried under tons of earth for so many billions of years that it had turned to coal, a rather appropriate metaphor considering the former occupation of his companion, of which he had yet to learn.

'Cat got your tongue?' Helga quipped, in a strong North Country accent.

Alex found a voice, not his, but it would do. 'Are you a man?'

'Yes.'

'Last night, did we do anything?' *(Please God, dear God, I'll do anything, anything in the world if you make him say no.)*

'No.'

(Thank you, God. Thank you very much. Even so . . .) 'Why is your arm around my waist?'

'It's only a little bed, mate. I'm holding you on, otherwise you'd drop off.'

'That's kind of you, thank you. But would you mind removing it, the arm?'

'If that's what you want.'

The arm was removed. Alex dropped off the bed. He sat up and leant against a chest of drawers, saw that he was fully dressed and that everything appeared to be intact. None of him had been interfered with. He had a hangover, only mild. His shock abated, he began to feel better, even intrigued by the situation he found himself in.

'Are you all right?' 'Helga' enquired, leaning over the bed. He was wearing a modest pair of striped winceyette pyjamas, which contrasted quaintly with his over-made-up face, which already looked grotesque on someone so convincingly bald.

'Fine, thanks.' Alex scrambled to his feet and found a chair. 'Are you English?' he asked, impressed by the calm way he was handling things. A lesser man might have turned to violence, even murder.

'Yes. That's why nothing happened last night. Wouldn't want to fool a fellow Brit.' (Alex thanked God for nationalism.) 'Steve's the name, Steve Weatherspoon, from Derbyshire. Bolsover, to be precise. And you're Maurice, if I remember right.'

'Am I? Oh, yes, Maurice Jones.'

Steve grinned engagingly. 'Last night it was Smith.'

'Was it?'

'It's all right, mate, you don't have to tell me your real name,' Steve said equably. 'Most blokes don't. Would you like a cup of coffee, Maurice? Or would you prefer to get the hell out of here PDQ? I'll understand if you do.'

After the traumas of the previous night, Alex felt quite safe. There was something essentially trustworthy about Steve. He seemed entirely harmless, even if his occupation was a trifle bizarre. The room they were in — obviously an attic with its steep, sloping ceiling and protruding dormer window — which he would have expected to be sordid, was relatively pleasant, uncluttered. The only things that jarred were a dressing-table full of cosmetics, and several gaudy frocks hanging outside the wardrobe door. The window overlooked a park and he could see the topmost branches of tall trees swaying lazily, and hear rain falling on the roof and muted traffic outside. If there were other residents in the building, they were keeping very quiet.

'I'd like a coffee, thanks,' he said.

'Then I'll put the kettle on.' Steve sprang out of bed and went into what appeared to be a tiny kitchen.

'Would you mind very much doing me a favour?' Alex shouted.

'Anything, mate, as long as it's legal.'

'Either wash your face or put your wig back on. I find the way you look now a touch distracting. I'm not quite sure who or what I'm talking to. Are those eyelashes false?'

'Could they be anything else, Maurice? They're an inch long, and a bugger to put on.' He emerged five minutes later, his face scrubbed clean, wearing jeans and a white T-shirt, bearing two cups of coffee. He was very sunburnt, and appeared to be a perfectly normal bald young man with a large nose, probably in his early thirties. 'Better?' He grinned.

'Much. You don't wear . . . well, those things you had on last night all the time, then?'

Steve shuddered delicately. 'Christ, mate, no. They're just for the job.'

Alex had always been a wholly self-centred person, even when he was young and relatively noble, a Marxist-Leninist, when he had ranted against inequality and marched in support of the masses more unfortunate than himself. But it was concepts that Alex believed in, principles, ideas. He didn't give a toss for people individually. He never thought about their lives, how they lived them, how they managed. Nevertheless, he found himself curious about Steve, a transvestite pros-titute based in Frankfurt. It seemed a rather unusual career move for an evidently heterosexual young man from Bolsover.

It turned out that Steve had been a miner like his dad and his grandad before him, like his uncles and his older brothers. 'Then bloody Thatcher reared her head out of the slime,' he said bitterly. 'Couldn't wait until every single pit were closed, couldn't wait to get her own back on Arthur, could she?'

'Arthur?'

'Arthur Scargill. Don't tell me you've never heard of King Arthur?'

'Of course. In fact, I met him once, many years ago. We were at the same demonstration. I can't remember what it was about.'

Which meant that Steve immediately took Alex for a fellow traveller on the path of socialism, a path that was getting narrower and narrower all the time. Alex didn't disabuse him of the idea. Neither did he argue. Nor did he feel it wise to point out that the woman Steve so reviled, who Alex so admired, had been ennobled for services to her country and was now 'Lady'. In so far as Alex was capable of liking another human being, he quite liked Steve, who had rescued him from Heinrich Hauptmann and hadn't taken advantage of his drunken state. There had been no need to bring him back to his flat. He could have left him where he was, out cold in a shop doorway. *And* helped himself to Alex's wallet and credit cards. Alex didn't bother to check if his valuables had been touched, because he just knew, somehow, that they hadn't.

Anyway, how could you argue with the fact that more than a hundred thousand men had had their jobs brutally removed then been left to rot when the pits shut down and nothing had been put in their place? Okay, so the economics were sound but even Alex, when faced with one of the victims of the pit massacre, the human proof, a young man bursting with integrity, could see it wasn't exactly fair, possibly a bit of an insensitive thing for a government to do.

'Of course, I did all the courses, plastering, bricklaying, electrical,' Steve continued bitterly. 'I even got me HGV licence, but I couldn't get a job, least nothing decent. I was proud of being a miner. I wouldn't have been proud of being pissed around in a factory for three pounds an hour. Apart from which, how was I supposed to support me wife and kids on that *and* pay me mortgage?'

'I don't know,' Alex said truthfully. He was married! He had children! 'But are you proud of what you do now?'

'No, course not, but I earn good money, and I'd do anything for me family. All the same, I miss them a lot. They think I'm a builder — you know that programme, *Auf Wiedersehen, Pet?* — but there's not so much of that about since the Berlin Wall came down. Two years ago I was about to go back home with me tail between me legs, another failure, when I saw a documentary on telly so I turned to this.' He gestured towards the dresses. 'It was hard at first, but I soon got used to it. Would you like to see a picture of me wife and kids?'

There wasn't a soul in Murphy Computers who would have dared suggest Alex look at a picture of their family, knowing he would have contemptuously waved it away. But, for the moment, Alex had forgotten all about computers, about the Peek-a-Boo system, quotations, and the reason he'd come to Frankfurt in the first place. He willingly took the photograph of Steve's attractive wife and their two attractive children. 'Very nice,' he said sincerely, handing the photo back. 'Very nice indeed.'

'Are you married, Maurice?'

'Yes, I think I might have a photo with me.' It had nestled in his wallet, untouched, for many years, the photograph he had taken of Emily in the garden holding Mary in her arms with Gareth clinging to her leg. 'Mind you, that was taken quite a while ago. The children have grown up since then. Gareth's getting married shortly,' he remembered.

'She's a stunner, Maurice, your wife, and your kids look great. What do they do now?'

'Mary works for a charity, Gareth's a . . .' Alex paused, staring at the photograph so hard that the figures seemed to come alive. Had Emily just moved? Had her smile just broadened? He used to have a larger version of the same photo on his desk at work, so that he could glance at it several times a day and count his blessings. He vividly remembered the day it was taken. Afterwards, Emily had passed Mary to him, then taken a photo of Alex and the children sitting on the grass. Gareth had rested his chin on his dad's head and linked his chubby arms around his neck, while Alex's own arms were around his baby daughter. Gosh, times were good then, he thought, or perhaps he said it out loud. So much love, so much laughter. Looking back, he was dazzled by the memory of what life had been like in the very ordinary semi-detached house in Formby. They'd been so poor; no, not poor, but it had been a struggle to make ends meet. He could see nothing wrong with striving to make things better; after all, too much contentment and the world would stagnate and rot. But somewhere along the way, Alex realised, he'd lost touch with everything that really mattered, and the awareness was alarming. Could he put things right, or was it too late?

'Are you okay, Maurice?' The kindness in the voice of the young man who'd been reduced to such indignity to support his family was too much. Alex did something that would have shaken Emily rigid. He burst into tears.

He told Steve everything: about the contract that had taken a small fortune to prepare; about Heinrich and the dreadful time he'd had last night touring the red-light district — 'I hope you don't mind my saying that, after all, it's your place of work' — about Emily, the butterfly who'd turned into a caterpillar, then become a butterfly again. But now he couldn't catch her, not that he'd given it much of a try. 'She's been very withdrawn lately.'

'Well, perhaps she found *you* withdrawn during the time you were making all that money.'

'Perhaps.' Alex sighed tearfully.

'I can't understand people who want more and more money,' Steve said, a touch severely. 'If I could just earn two hundred and fifty quid a week back home, I'd be a happy man. Three hundred, and I'd be on top of the world. I just don't get what drives people like you. Why do you want more than your share?'

'I have no idea,' Alex confessed. (He would tomorrow.) He even told Steve about his dark secret, the day that had haunted him since he was eleven.

Steve didn't laugh. 'I guess it must have been embarrassing, Maurice.'

'It was the worst day of my life, worse even than yesterday, and my name isn't Maurice Smith or Maurice Jones. It's Alex Murphy.'

At midday, the rain stopped, the sky brightened, the sun came out. Alex thought he had better make his departure. For the first time he felt slightly awkward when he shook hands with Steve and flesh touched flesh, despite them having spent the night together in a very small bed. 'Thanks for everything. You've been . . . well, you've been a mate.' It wasn't his sort of language, yet it seemed right for the moment. He wondered if he should offer compensation for a lost night's income, but Steve might be offended. (Alex was definitely not himself today.)

'It's been nice meeting you, Maur— Alex.' Steve smiled, but Alex thought he looked lonely, desolate, at being left. Perhaps he should stay.

'What will you be doing with yourself this afternoon?'

'Duty calls. It's Saturday afternoon, so I'll be work-ing.' He made a face, but still managed to grin. 'Got bills to pay, you know. Anyroad, I hope you have a safe journey back.'

'I hope you have a safe life. What you're doing is very dangerous.'

'So was working down the pit. Cheers, Alex.'

'Goodbye, Steve.'

There was a newsagent's on the ground floor of Steve's apartment block. Alex bought a street map of Frank-furt. He had expected to spend the weekend with Heinrich and wasn't due to return home until next morning. If he changed it, went back today, Mae was looking after Thorntons and would leave as soon as he appeared, which meant he would be there alone until Emily came home tomorrow. If he had to spend the night by himself, he'd sooner spend it in Frankfurt. Heinrich had probably rung his hotel by now and would be wondering where he was. It would be diplomatic to give him a ring, say he was still with Helga, an excuse of which Heinrich would thoroughly approve. Alex prayed he wouldn't suggest a repeat of last night's performance.

There was a row of phone booths outside the newsagent's, and it turned out that Alex had had no need to worry.

Heinrich answered the phone in a voice that was nothing like his usual guttural foghorn. No number, just a wretched, whispered, 'Hallo.'

'It's Alex. You sound rough. What's wrong?'

'I feel *krank*, Alex. Very *krank*. I have the *Kopfschmerzen*. I badly want to *erbrechen*.' He was very sick. He had a headache. He wanted to vomit. 'I enjoyed myself too much last night.'

'I'm so sorry you feel bad, Heinrich,' Alex lied. 'I hope you feel better soon.'

'You must come to Frankfurt again. Last night was *wunderbar*, despite today. Did we have a good time, or didn't we? I hope you gave that woman a good poke.' He managed a weak, coarse laugh.

'What do you think?'

Alex replaced the receiver. The booth was plastered with calling cards, all highly suggestive, printed in English and German. 'Luscious Asian beauty offers intimate massage.' 'Ex-headmistress chastises naughty little boys.' One caught his eye: 'Helga, English model, has a surprise in store for you.' For some reason, Alex felt sad. He took down the card and put it in his pocket. He wasn't sure why.

He went back to his hotel and changed his crumpled business suit for jeans and a casual shirt, then spent a restful and relaxing afternoon in Frankfurt. He visited the museum of arts and crafts, admired the sculptures in the Liebighaus, and the paintings in the Stadel. His hangover having completely gone and his stomach feeling unusually composed, he ate a fiery goulash in a restaurant called the Scarlet Pimpernel, and followed it with ice cold vodka. He shopped, bought himself two shirts, and finished off the day listening to New Orleans jazz in the Jazzkeller. That night, he had the best sleep he'd had in years and woke up thoroughly refreshed.

It was a bright, totally rejuvenated Alex who caught a taxi to the airport. He felt extraordinarily laid back about everything. Heinrich, quotations, Peek-a-Boo, none of it seemed important when compared to the trauma of other people's lives. If it all went wrong, well, he could always start again. He boarded the plane, feeling almost giddy as the stress that had been weighing him down for weeks lifted. He vowed never to let himself get into such a state again.

The vow lasted approximately ten minutes. On the flight back to England, Alex's worries returned, crawling on to his knee, tweaking his nose, twisting his ear, worming their way into his brain. In a fortnight he would know his fate. Could he stay sane that long? And who said it wasn't important? Okay, so he'd said it himself. But it was more than important: it was a matter of life and death. No, more important even than that. If he didn't get that contract, everything he'd worked for would be lost, and why the hell should he have to start again at his age?

'Well, your weekend didn't do you much good, Alex. You look worse than when you went away.'

'If I want your opinion, I'll ask for it,' Alex snarled. *She* looked fine. *She*'d had a marvellous time. Oh, it was all right for women, wasn't it? Not a care in the world. All they had to do was sit back and let their husbands selflessly work their guts out on their behalf. Look at poor Steve!

She'd brought him a present back from London, a tie to replace the one that had gone missing, which meant he'd had to hide the shirts he'd bought for himself as it hadn't crossed his mind to buy a present for *her*. But then, *he*'d been on an important business trip, while all she'd done was enjoy herself in London, waving one of Gordon Brown's scarves in front of his eyes and having shaken hands with Joanna Lumley, or some such nonsense.

It didn't help when he went into his study and found reams of guff had arrived by e-mail from the office of President Bill Clinton.

'Emily,' he screamed, 'that kid of Mae's has been at my computer.'

'Don't be silly, Alex. Shona's not exactly top of the class at school. The girl wouldn't know one end of a computer from the other.'

Takahashi Ariake, known as 'Taki' to his numerous friends, drove through the flat Cambridgeshire countryside with the top of the MG sports car down. He made a handsome, romantic figure, with his golden skin and tawny eyes, the wind casually ruffling his thick glossy black hair. Many an admiring eye was cast in his direction.

Taki was in fact a Romantic in the literary meaning of the word, an avid reader of the poems of Wordsworth, Byron and Coleridge, and the novels of Sir

Walter Scott. Among his various interests, he was a sometime poet himself, writing wildly idealistic, starry-eyed verses of deeply purple prose. This was how Taki saw the world, as a romantic place full of happy endings.

He was also one of those rare individuals who had been blessed with the sweetest of natures from the day he was born, and nothing had happened during his thirty-two years on earth to change it. Those years had been fortunate for him. He was the only child of moderately wealthy parents, who owned a chain of small supermarkets in the Chinatown district of New York. A brilliant brain, and no financial problems to worry about, meant that Taki had sailed through Harvard, emerging with the highest honours and scores of job offers. After working in industry for a while, he had eagerly accepted a lectureship in the biology department of Boston University. He loved university life. He was sublimely unaware of the backbiting, the jealousies between colleagues, the intrigue and scheming that went on at most universities across the globe. No one schemed or plotted against Taki. Fifteen months ago, he had been appointed a professor, the first Korean-American to reach such an eminent position, making him one of the youngest professors in the entire establishment. Since then, his adoring students addressed him affectionately as Prof.

With an apartment in an old brownstone in the downtown area of Boston overlooking the Granary Burying Ground, where Paul Revere and Benjamin Franklin's folks were buried, Taki felt very much a part of the country in which he had been born, though he was only a first-generation American. He was a committed fan of the Boston Red Sox and had a season ticket to the Lyric Opera. At the moment he had three mistresses, all beautiful women, and all aware of the others' existence. None seemed to mind. So far he had never married, but assumed he would, one day, when his life would continue to be as perfect as it already was.

There was only one thing that bothered Taki, not deeply, not often, but it niggled at him from time to time. He was not so detached from real life that he didn't realise there were some pretty nasty people in the world: Saddam Hussein, Hitler, Pol Pot were some of the worst examples. But at the opposite end of the scale there were people who were so supremely nice that they soared above the average human being, though they rarely achieved the fame of their diametric opposites. Taki had once met one of these people. Her name was

Mae, and she lived in a place called Kirkby on the outskirts of Liverpool, England.

And that was all Taki knew about her.

It had been seven years ago, and he had been in the UK to address a conference on genetics at the University of Liverpool. Afterwards he had gone for a drink with a group of men he scarcely knew. They had ended up on what the Brits called a 'pub crawl'. By closing time, when he was liquored up to his brain, he had gone to the gents', and come out into the saloon, instead of the parlour, where he had met a crowd of chaps who at the time seemed inordinately friendly. They had slapped his back, admired his watch, were impressed with his camera, commented on his shoes, and warned him not to carry so much cash around in his wallet when he paid for a final round of drinks. He remembered nothing more until he opened his eyes and found Mae bending over him. She was on her way home from work and had been alerted by his groans. At first he thought he'd died and gone to heaven and that this sweet-faced person with a halo of golden hair was a welcoming angel. Then he became aware that he was lying on a hard, dark pavement, pressed against a wire fence, and the sweet-faced person said, 'It's a good job I stopped the car by the station to post a letter, else I'd never have heard you. Where do you live, luv, and I'll take you home?'

'Boston, Massachusetts,' Taki whimpered.

She giggled, and he could still hear the sound to this day, that little tinkling giggle. 'Well, you'd better come back with me, then, and I'll sort you out.'

He had sprawled on the back seat of the car, tried to assess his injuries and was relieved to find he didn't have any. His unconsciousness had been due solely to drunkenness. He was, however, without his watch, his camera, his wallet containing all his money and his credit cards, his Gucci shoes and Armani tie, the latter a present from a girlfriend. Fortunately, the thieves hadn't noticed the matching socks.

In the house where she took him, of which he had only the vaguest memory, Mae helped him to a couch, then knelt beside him and washed his face, all the while making soothing, cooing, clucking sounds, which Taki found surprisingly erotic. To his horror, he felt quite turned on. He was far less disturbed than most people would have been by the fact that he had been robbed. The watch and camera could easily be replaced. He had had about fifty pounds left in his wallet, only seventy or eighty bucks, and there were travellers' cheques in the safe at the hotel, along with his passport. The credit cards were insured and could be cancelled with a phone call. The tie he didn't care for, and he could always buy another pair of shoes. He was more upset with himself for getting so comprehensively drunk.

'I'm sorry,' he kept saying. 'So very, very sorry.'

'As if you could help being robbed, you poor thing,' Mae said tenderly, gently stroking his brow. Taki could scarcely contain himself.

He stared into her lovely blue eyes, moist with concern, and noticed that she was so affected by his plight that her soft lips were trembling. Her abundant blonde hair tumbled around her face and lightly brushed against his own, and the featherlight touch made him giddy with desire. But Taki was a gentleman. Under no circumstances would he consider taking advantage of any woman, let alone this Good Samaritan, this angel of the night, this genuinely Romantic heroine who might have graced the pages of Sir Walter Scott, and who had rescued him, if not from great peril, then from a rather awkward predicament. He was determined to contain himself, but the effort was so great it burst from his mouth in an agonised, racking sob.

'Oh dear,' cried Mae. She bent her head and kissed him.

Next morning, when it was barely light, she drove him to the station. 'I'd take you to town, but I work from six till eight, and perhaps it would be wiser if you left before the kids come down. Also, me dad and grandad have just moved in, and it wouldn't do for them to find you here.'

She gave him a pair of her father's shoes. 'He hardly ever wears them because everybody laughs.' She also gave him his train fare.

'I'll return the money, and the shoes, Mae,' he promised. Taki always kept his promises, as a true Romantic should. But the next night, after he had cashed the travellers' cheques and had a new wallet in his pocket stuffed with notes, he realised he didn't know her address and would never remember where she lived, having gone to and from the house in darkness. He hadn't even asked her surname. It had been a strange, unexpected night, full of the best and worst of things: getting drunk, getting mugged, making love with Mae, which had been such a joyful and rapturous experience. He would never forget it.

He took a taxi to Kirkby, but the houses all looked

the same. Even if he passed Mae's, he would never recognise it, he realised sadly. After a short while, he asked the driver to return to town. The day after, he went back to Boston.

And that was how the matter had remained for seven years, until June, when Taki had arrived in Cambridge, England, to spend a three-month vacation with his friend Bert Pullman. During the seven years he had thought of Mae occasionally. He felt guilty. What would she think of him? As a fly-by-night cad who had taken advantage of her body, her money and her father's shoes. He was not a vain man, but he minded being badly thought of by someone he respected so highly, admired so much. So, while in England, he resolved to seek Mae out, repay the debt. Not the few cents she'd loaned him, of course not, but a gift, something valuable, so that in the future she would remember him with warmth in her heart. She had given herself to him, yet he'd left her with nothing to remember him by.

So far he'd been to Kirkby half a dozen times — Bert had let him borrow the MG. He had walked the streets, describing Mae to strangers, to the folk in shops, the post office, the library, some sort of community centre, bars. All professed total ignorance of Mae's existence. Yet Taki felt sure that some were lying, either out of perversity or the need to protect her from possible ill tidings or unwelcome demands. On one occasion, he'd thought he'd cracked it. 'Ask Tilly Quinn. She knows everyone round here, the nosy bitch,' he'd been advised, somewhat sourly. He'd gone round to the address he'd been given, had rung the bell several times, but there'd been no answer, despite there being a hell of a noise going on inside, as if the place was being torn apart.

He considered putting up posters, 'DO YOU KNOW THIS WOMAN?' followed by a description, but after due consideration decided he wouldn't relish the same sort of posters pinned around Boston describing *him*.

So, what was he to do? He was getting desperate. In another month or so, on the first of September, he would return to Boston in readiness for the new students due in the fall.

Perhaps the shoes were the key. He'd kept them. They were in a leather satchel on the passenger seat, along with a few toiletries and a change of clothes. They were nasty things: lightweight black and white plastic brogues with an extravagant amount of punched holes, the sort gangsters wore in films. He always brought them, in case Mae had forgotten him and he could remind her by producing her father's shoes.

Without realising it, he'd become so used to the journey that he'd driven through several counties and was now on the M6, driving north, to Liverpool.

Taki smiled cheerfully. He wasn't sure exactly how, but he'd try to think of a way to find Mae through the shoes.

CHAPTER TEN

Eustace was greatly disturbed by the recent appearance of a helicopter that flew over the house several times a day. 'It's spying on us,' he said fearfully to Mae. 'I can see them watching through binoculars.'

'Don't be silly, luv,' Mae said kindly. 'You're getting paranoid. Why would anyone want to spy on Thorntons?'

'I don't know.' Eustace shivered.

'It's probably just the Army doing exercises or something.'

'It's a police helicopter, Mae.'

'Well, they're probably up to the same thing.' Mae was a tiny bit disturbed herself about things inside. It was as if the entire house had been tipped up and put back again, making everything move slightly, so that whenever she looked in a cupboard or drawer, nothing was quite where she expected it to be, but to one side or further back or behind something else. The same went for the utility room and the garage. It was almost as if the house had been done over, yet nothing appeared to be missing. Or perhaps it was the ghosts, she thought, when she found the vacuum-cleaner on the left of the electric polisher – it should have been the other way round.

'I hope you're not playing games with me,' she said severely when she went upstairs. 'We've been friends up until now.' She decided not to say anything to Emily, in case, like Eustace, she was being paranoid. Which reminded her: she still hadn't told Emily about the men who had come to fix the phone, when Mae had been unaware that anything was wrong.

Anyroad, Emily hadn't been there all week to tell. Rather surprisingly, she had had things to do, and had already left by the time Mae arrived and, oh, it was lovely to have the house all to herself. She cleaned and polished ruthlessly, and played a blissful game of make-believe that all of it was hers, that she lived within its gleaming atmospheric splendour with the ghosts and her large, extended family.

On Friday, Emily arrived home just as Mae was about to leave. She had black paint on her lovely new hair and on her cheek, which was a really funny coincidence because Eddie had come home with black paint on his hands only the day before and refused to say where he'd been. She said as much to Emily.

'Isn't life strange?' Emily commented sweetly, though she didn't explain what she'd been up to.

In fact, Daphne had left Bootle for the Isle of Man ten days before, Emily had taken a five-year lease on the salon, one year payable in advance, which had made an immediate, huge hole in her bank balance and caused the landlord to jump for joy because he had never thought he'd get rid of the damn place. It only confirmed his long-held belief that there was a fool born every minute. Now, she and Eddie were busy renovating the salon from top to bottom. Tina, Daphne's young assistant, had almost finished her apprenticeship and had agreed to stay on and look after the hairdressing side of things with an assistant even younger than herself.

Eddie had decided that everywhere had to be black, white and silver, and Emily bowed to his apparent instinct in such matters. Cleopatra's walls were already black, and tomorrow they would paint the old floor tiles silver. Two black and silver dryers were on order, as well as a massage table, which would go in its own cubicle behind silver polyester curtains, Eddie explained, rubbing his hands together gleefully. A plumber was coming next week to replace the existing pink basins with virginal white, and the fluorescent lights had already gone. Half a dozen spotlights now graced the newly pristine white ceiling. Shortly, the upstairs bathroom would be converted into a sauna just big enough to hold one fat woman or two thin, by which time there might be enough left to buy a few items of exercise equipment. The first supply of hair products and cosmetics would be provided free on condition that an agreement was signed to use the same supplier from there on. If she ran out of money, Emily would just have to draw out of the Murphys' joint account, which she had only used in the past to settle large household bills. She wouldn't mention anything to Alex, because if he heard about Cleopatra's he'd only sneer.

It was all very exciting, very satisfying. Emily could almost appreciate Alex's preoccupation with the business he had started himself, which had become so hugely successful. Perhaps she should have taken more of an interest from the beginning, though she vaguely remembered that she had and that he had shrugged her away with a curt 'You wouldn't understand, Em. It's way above your head, I'm afraid.' Having your own business wasn't just to do with making money, more a feeling of being involved in something tremendously important. Emily felt useful again.

Mae left, but not before asking if it was all right to bring Shona next week. 'School broke up today, and I don't like leaving her. Poor kid, she doesn't seem to have any friends. Her school report was abysmal. I should really have a word with the teachers about her and our Dicky, but with me working most nights I can never get to the parents' evening. I missed it as usual last night. They'll think no one's interested in the McNulty kids at school.'

Unknown to Mae, at least one of her children had been represented at school the night before. The Parent Teacher Association had provided the refreshments. It was to be hoped that the headmaster never discovered that one parent and one teacher had associated in a way not provided for in the written constitution.

Detective Sergeant Patrick Watson had always found it difficult to visualise his hard-eyed, hard-nosed partner, Jones, a man with such a dour opinion of the world, doing normal uncopperly things, like, well, wearing pyjamas, for instance, owning a house, growing flowers, having a wife, playing with his kids, putting up wallpaper, that sort of crap.

Yet Michael Jones did indeed own a house, where the walls were nicely wallpapered and the garden was full of pretty flowers. He also had an amazingly pleasant wife, and two perfectly respectable teenage children who were doing well at school.

When Jones claimed he had to be home early for a parents' evening, Patrick, only recently a proud parent, asked what a parents' evening was.

That night, showered and wearing his best suit, a refreshing example of a model, caring father, he made his way to Dicky's school in the hope that it wasn't too late to attend on his son's behalf. He knew Mae wouldn't be there because she worked in the Irish club on Thursdays. He found a crowded car park and the road outside was lined with more cars. He was in luck. After some subtle questioning (after all, he was a policeman experienced in such matters), he established which class Dicky was in and the fact that he went under the name of McNulty, not Watson. This hurt at first. In fact, he felt extremely cross and his immediate reaction was to seek Mae out and wallop her, but reason prevailed. He remembered that he had recently acquired a conscience and the knack of looking at things in more ways than one. Why should Mae let Dicky use the name of the man who had never even acknowledged the lad's existence?

He had to wait in the classroom in a very long queue for a very long time to speak to Dicky's class teacher, and managed to keep his patience by thinking of little woolly lambs and starry skies, and the teacher, who was only young and extremely desirable with a great pair of tits.

'Ah, yes, Dicky McNulty,' she said, when eventually it was Patrick's turn and he took the chair on the other side of her desk. A cardboard sign showed her name to be Ms Kirsty Turner. She was even nicer close up, with hazel eyes and nut-brown hair and a cute little turned-up nose. 'He's an extremely bright boy, top of the class in most things.'

'Takes after his dad,' Patrick said modestly.

'I can see that,' Ms Turner smiled. 'Have you read his report?'

'I'm afraid not. My wife and I are divorced.'

'I see.' Ms Turner smiled again, but this time the tip of her pink tongue emerged and rolled provocatively over her pink lips. Her eyes narrowed in an erotic and suggestive manner. 'I'm in the throes of divorce proceedings myself.'

Patrick's heart beat a modicum faster. The atmosphere in the classroom, lined with the innocent drawings of young children and pictures of baby animals, had begun to pound with an almost tropical sultry heat mixed with a liberal dose of carnality. Was that steam rising from the gaps in the floorboards, so sadly left to rot and crumble by the previous government? 'Are you really?'

Ms Turner fluttered her long nut-brown lashes. 'Have you remarried?'

'No. I'm a copper. I never seem to have had the time to start a new relationship.'

'I love policemen,' Ms Turner breathed huskily.

'I wouldn't say I was averse to schoolteachers.' Patrick gulped mightily as he felt the toe of her shoe rub against his ankle. Christ, think of all the nooky he might have had if only he'd been nicer sooner.

'What are we going to do about it, then?' Ms Turner looked at him challengingly.

'Well, Kirsty, how about a drink when this is over?'

'I'll be about another half an hour.'

'In that case, I'll wait in me car outside.' Patrick shook hands, as he had seen the other parents do, and felt Ms Turner's finger tickle his palm.

'As I said before, there's no need to worry about Dicky,' Ms Turner said loudly. 'He's doing fine.'

He'd forgotten all about Dicky, Patrick realised as he returned to his car, trembling with lustful anticipation. Still, his intentions had been honourable, the thought had been there.

July the thirty-first. In Frankfurt, the quotations would be removed from the safe and opened. Alex couldn't bring himself to leave the house and go to work. Even he was able to assess how useless he'd been recently, that some of his staff suspected he'd completely lost his marbles. He kept asking the same questions twice, forgetting people's names, wandering in and out of offices, not sure which was his. Gaynor kept out of his way, too scared to speak. He felt as if his nerves were exposed, hanging from his body in fringes, like little pink worms. He hurt if he was touched. He couldn't sit down. Yesterday, when one of his designers had put a hand on his shoulder, Alex had yelped and nearly hit the roof.

So, he remained at Thorntons. At long last, after so many years, Emily was the only person he wanted near him on this fateful day and during the week ahead, when his entire future was on the line, in the hands of the repugnant Heinrich Hauptmann.

Where was she? Alex emerged from his study, where he had slept on the settee, expecting to find Emily in the kitchen where she belonged. He was beginning to resent that she hadn't invited him into her bed since she had gone through her astonishing metamorphosis. He was too nervous to approach her himself.

Alexander Murphy, too nervous!

Yes, it was true. On top of everything else, Alex had been feeling very vulnerable lately, scared of being rejected. His *id* had shrunk to the size of a peanut. He imagined making love to Emily in the hopeless way he had imagined the same thing with Doris Day when he was ten, as if Emily, like Doris, was way out of his reach. When he came home in the evenings, he would find quite a tasty little snack waiting, but his wife preoccupied with things other than himself, often writing in an efficient-looking notebook. If he hadn't known better, he would have said she was doing accounts.

'What's that?' he asked resentfully one night.

'Just stuff. Just some stuff. I'll do it in the den.' With that she got up and left.

Last night she looked at him over a different notebook to say, 'I'm making a list of the guests for Alice and Gareth's wedding. Mum's hired a coach, there's almost fifty people coming from London. Mae's asking about twenty. I was wondering, Alex, if we could try to find your father.'

'How?' Alex asked simply. He'd been surprised fifteen years ago when his father had announced he'd been offered a job in Mexico. It seemed an unusual place to have need of a redundant railway porter with a drink problem who was getting on in years. Surprise was followed quickly by relief. By then Liam Murphy had become something of a pest, unable to cope on his own since Alex's mother had passed away, frequently dropping in on the family of his only child, unannounced, unwashed and, inevitably, the worse for drink. Emily, though, felt a sense of responsibility: she had fed him, done his washing, bought him clothes, and seemed to think Alex should show some sense of filial duty.

'Your parents supported you until you were twenty-one. You wouldn't be where you are today if it wasn't for them.'

'What nonsense,' Alex protested at the time, convinced he'd done everything on his own.

Emily said now, 'It would be lovely if we could find Liam in time for Gareth's wedding. He adored the children. I can't understand why he's never written, never even sent a card.'

'Probably too drunk to remember. I think you'd be pursuing a lost cause, Em, trying to find him. He might have left Mexico years ago. He could be anywhere in the world.' He could even be dead, Alex thought, and tried to get his head round the fact that he might possibly be an orphan, but it was already overflowing with so many other pressing concerns that there wasn't room for a single one more.

When Alex emerged from his lair on 31 July, Emily was nowhere to be seen; neither was her car. Last night she hadn't mentioned she was going out. Perhaps she'd gone shopping. Alex sulked around the house, the feeling of being neglected adding to his list of woes, until Mae arrived with Shona.

'I'm afraid my wife is out. I suspect she's only gone to the supermarket. She'll be back soon,' he said, in the surly, haughty voice he reserved for cleaners and their ilk.

'I doubt it,' Mae said cheerfully. 'She's been out all day every day for weeks.'

'Has she? Where?' demanded a startled Alex.

'I don't know, luv.'

Mae immediately went upstairs. Shona, frustrated at being denied the use of the computer by the presence of the master of the house, sat at the kitchen table and began to kick her heels against the chair. She looked like a doll in her tiny T-shirt and pale blue jeans.

'Do you have to do that?' Alex said irritably.

'No.' She stopped and regarded him gravely with her big, tawny eyes. 'You don't half look in a state. Your karma is all wrong.'

He remembered that this was the child with the remarkable intelligence, possibly equal to his own. 'My what?'

'Your karma. You should become a Buddhist. I'm going to be a Buddhist when I grow up.'

'You don't say,' Alex sneered.

'I shall pass along the Noble Eightfold Path until I reach Nirvana. Do you want to know what the eight things are?'

'No, I bloody don't.'

'I might go to Tibet,' Shona said thoughtfully.

Alex threw himself into a chair. 'Why don't you go

now? You're getting on my nerves,' he barked, quite forgetting he was addressing a six-year-old.

Shona rolled her eyes impatiently. 'People overreact to the burdens of existence. Nothing's ever as bad as it seems.'

'Yes, it is.'

'Everything turns out all right in the end.'

'No, it doesn't,' Alex said pettishly. 'It didn't turn out all right for the people who were killed in Bosnia.'

'No, but they will have been . . .' She paused, searching for the word. The smug little bitch wasn't quite so brainy as she thought. '. . . reincarnated by now into a better life.'

'What if they were reincarnated in Rwanda?'

'You're just being silly, Mr Murphy. It's too complicated for you to understand.'

'I reckon so,' Alex sighed, defeated.

The telephone rang. 'Shall I get it?' Shona asked.

He nodded gloomily. 'If it's my office, say I'm not here.'

Shona trotted to the phone. She had to climb on a chair to reach the receiver. 'It's a man with a foreign accent,' she said eventually. 'He sounds very bad-tempered. His karma is even worse than yours.'

Heinrich! Why was he in a bad temper? Something must have happened. *Oh, God, please, God, make everything be all right.*

'Hallo there, Hein—' he began jovially.

'Where is the *Kostenvoranschlag*, Alex, you fucking swine?' Heinrich spoke as if he had razor blades in his throat.

'The *what*?'

'The quotation, you ape, you mental throwback. They opened the safe this morning *and yours isn't there!*'

'But I sent it. It must be there. How can it possibly not be there?' Alex's exposed nerves began to do handstands all over his hypersensitive body.

'How can it possibly be there when it's *not* there?' Heinrich snarled.

'It *must* be there. I paid an extra fee for proof of delivery, which came a few days after it was sent.'

'Whatever, Alex, your quotation wasn't in the safe.'

'That can't be true.'

'It *is* true. Am I lying? Do you think I *wanted* it not to be there? You've let me down, Alex. I had five directors lined up, all ready to support you. I promised them girls, I promised them . . . well, all sorts of things. You've made a fool of me. This is the end of our business relationship, Alex. Do you hear? This is the *ende*.'

Alex winced visibly as the receiver in Frankfurt was slammed down so hard that it hurt his hypersensitive ear. Which was just about the last thing he felt before his body went entirely numb. He managed to shuffle into his office like a very old man holding on to the wall, followed by a curious Shona.

Who could he blame?

Parcel Force! It must be. They'd delivered it to the wrong place, got the wrong signature. He'd sue them till the teeth rattled in their thick, stupid heads. The proof of delivery was in a filing basket on his desk. He picked it up with numb fingers, read it with numb eyes. Hauptmann-wagen, Blumenstrasse 115, Frankfurt. Delivery of the package had been accepted and duly signed for.

Wait a minute! He'd written enough letters to Hauptmannwagen over the last year to know the address off by heart. It was Blumenstrasse 15, not 115.

How fortunate it was that Alex felt numb, otherwise who knows what he might have done in revenge for the delivery of his precious package to the wrong address? Set fire to Thorntons, for example, or murdered the small child watching him so sweetly wide-eyed from the door, followed by the mother who was singing tunefully upstairs. 'Who's sorry now?' Mae warbled.

Instead, Alex merely picked up the phone with the intention of tearing Parcel Force off a strip a mile wide, then giving them the name of his lawyer. But no, not yet. He switched on the computer, inserted the appropriate disk. He'd have the proof in front of his eyes. He would read the address to them. He distinctly remembered running off the labels from the covering letter. He pressed the file reference. The letter appeared on the screen. Alex's blood turned to ice. His heart leapt to his throat.

Hauptmannwagen, Blumenstrasse 115, Frankfurt, Germany.

So, who could he blame now?

He could track down the fucking wanker who'd signed for the package and had not bothered to redirect it when he found it wasn't for him. And stab him between the eyes.

He could do the same thing to the Parcel Force guy in Germany, for a reason that would come to him eventually.

But ultimately, when all was said and done, when everything had been taken into account, the only person genuinely to blame was Alex himself.

Alex sank his tired head on to the keyboard. Letters, numbers appeared, scattering wildly over the screen.

It was as if he was writing himself a jumbled letter with his forehead, Shona thought, creeping closer. 'What's the matter?' she whispered.

'I've blown it,' Alex croaked. 'I sent the letter to the wrong address. I've lost the contract. It's all my own fault. I'm ruined.'

It wasn't his fault, it was hers. Shona distinctly remembered pressing 'i' when the same letter was on the screen several weeks ago, and the line had jumped forward. She wasn't a dishonest child but, all things considered, it seemed wiser not to say anything. Mam would only lose her job, a far greater tragedy than Mr Murphy losing his contract. Mam needed the money more than he did. Anyroad, in the infinite scheme of things, everything happened for a purpose. At some time in the future, this crazy, distraught person (whom she quite liked) would discover it had all been for the best and would thank Shona if he knew what she'd done.

'Oh, God!' Alex muttered, his head still buried in the keyboard. 'A thunderstorm! How appropriate just now. A bad one, too. I've never known such a deafening racket.'

Shona glanced through the window at the clear blue sky, the sparkling golden sunshine. The only sounds to be heard were the chirruping of birds and her mam singing upstairs.

Perhaps it wouldn't be a bad idea to leave Mr Murphy alone.

Apart from one or two odds and ends Cleopatra's was ready to go. Leaving Eddie alone to drool over the diminutive patch of the United Kingdom over which he would shortly rule, Emily drove into Liverpool to place an advertisement in the *Liverpool Echo*.

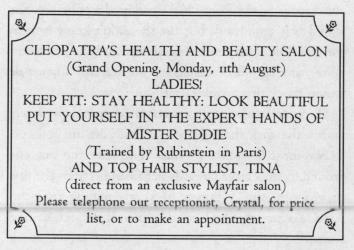

CLEOPATRA'S HEALTH AND BEAUTY SALON
(Grand Opening, Monday, 11th August)
LADIES!
KEEP FIT: STAY HEALTHY: LOOK BEAUTIFUL
PUT YOURSELF IN THE EXPERT HANDS OF
MISTER EDDIE
(Trained by Rubinstein in Paris)
AND TOP HAIR STYLIST, TINA
(direct from an exclusive Mayfair salon)
Please telephone our receptionist, Crystal, for price list, or to make an appointment.

Eddie would have liked his photograph included, but it was sure to be seen by someone he knew, or the buggers from the Social and he'd lose his benefit. He wasn't prepared to out himself until the business was a success, and he optimistically expected to be off the Social by Christmas.

As for Emily, she had realised a childhood dream. Crystal was a name she had hankered after since she was four.

Having placed the advert, and an announcement of Gareth and Alice's forthcoming wedding, Emily returned to the multi-storey car park where, to her dismay, she discovered the Punto had developed a puncture. She stared at it aghast, not because she didn't know how to mend it (Alex was above such things, and she had learnt a long time ago) but because she was wearing a new pale lemon frock that would get filthy.

'Trouble?' a pleasant voice enquired, from somewhere within the dark shadows of the dimly lit car park.

She turned, slightly nervous. There was no one else around. A man came towards her from between the cars parked opposite, a bunch of keys dangling from his hand. To her relief he looked eminently respectable and reassuringly safe, in a lightweight tweed jacket, check shirt and khaki trousers. His whole appearance was as pleasant as his voice. A fiftyish man with crisp black curly hair, a rugged face, the skin like bronze, well-cared-for leather, piercing dark blue eyes. She was surprised to note how sexy his mouth was, particularly when he smiled and his narrow lips turned up a fraction on one side (the left). Emily had never been the sort to notice such things, not even before she met Alex, and certainly never since. She'd only become aware of Eddie's various attractions as a drowning woman would notice a log floating by to grab in desperation.

'I seem to have a puncture,' she said pertly, though she hadn't intended to sound pert.

'Well, we'll soon take care of that. Is your spare tyre okay?' He had an Irish accent, the deeply lyrical, musical sort, perfect for reading Brendan Behan and J. M. Synge aloud, or singing haunting folk songs.

'It's never been used.' Emily unlocked the boot. 'Are you sure about this? I could always call a garage.'

'I'm sure absolutely. It will only take a wee minute.'

'The tyre was all right when I left.'

'Oh, well, it's the way of these things,' he said, smiling his disturbingly crooked smile. 'Tyres, like people and life itself, can be desperately unpredictable.' He removed his jacket, then rolled up the sleeves of his shirt, revealing broad shoulders and strong, muscular, bronzed arms. Emily opened the boot, and he seized the jack with a pair of large, capable hands, the sight of which caused her to give a delicious little shiver. 'Have we met before somewhere?' he asked.

'If we have, I don't recall it.'

'You look familiar, but from a long, long while back. Is your name Emma? I'm afraid the surname escapes me, that's if I knew it.' He was working swiftly, jacking up the wheel, undoing the nuts and bolts, lifting it away.

'It's Emily.' Surely she would have remembered meeting a man like him.

'Em! They called you Em. I must have thought it was short for Emma.'

This was truly remarkable. 'Who did?'

He stopped working, rested on his haunches and regarded her thoughtfully, a touch of a grin on his leathery face. 'People. You were always with a crowd.' He clicked his fingers triumphantly. 'Manchester University.'

'Gosh, that was years ago, more than a quarter of a century,' Emily remarked, impressed. 'What subject did you take?'

'I didn't. I worked there, laboratory technician on paper, general dogsbody in fact. I wasn't there long.

Went to Australia shortly afterwards. Swimming-pools.'
He grinned.

'But you remember me! That's amazing.' Emily was
monumentally flattered.

He lifted the spare tyre as if it weighed no more than
a feather, and regarded her almost shyly. 'You're at
liberty to laugh, but I had a bit of a crush on you.'

'I wouldn't dream of laughing. I feel quite touched.'
For some reason she also felt rather tearful, and at the
same time elated. There was something romantic and
unreal about this meeting. She felt as if the finger of a
smiling fate was pointing directly at her for a change.

'I suppose that's why I remember you so clearly, my
first love.' The spare tyre was on. He had nearly finished,
was tightening the last few bolts. 'I hope you don't mind
me saying that you've scarcely changed.'

Emily blushed and supposed she couldn't have changed much or he'd never have recognised her.

'Don't forget to get that tyre repaired. You don't
want to be without a spare.'

'I won't. Thank you very much for everything.'

He smiled and her knees turned to jelly. 'It was a
pleasure – Em.'

She couldn't just let him walk out of her life, not a

drop-down-dead gorgeous man like this who had once had a crush on her. Emily swallowed, took a deep breath, and said in a rush, 'Look, could I buy you a thank-you drink? You've been so very helpful.'

'I wouldn't say no. It wasn't exactly hard work, but it's given me a thirst. A pint of bitter would go down a treat.'

'There's a pub just round the corner. What's your name, by the way?'

'Martin McCutcheon,' said Sean Donovan, who was anything but safe, and definitely not pleasant, having killed seven men with his bare hands during his violent life, and was all set on killing another if he could discover from Emily where the traitor was.

If she hadn't suggested a drink, he would have done it himself. Sean Donovan was aware of the effect he had on women. She'd been a pushover from the start. He'd been following her for days, waiting for the right moment. It was a simple matter to let the air down from a tyre, then wait for her to return. He *had* seen her before, but not in Manchester, and was glad she was a looker — it would have hurt his pride to suck up to someone with a face like the back of a bus.

Sean had never given a toss about the Semtex, not once he had realised he hadn't been betrayed, that the mix-up was due solely to desperate incompetence on the part of his ragged army. (There were only twelve soldiers in it, including himself, and the other eleven would be gobsmacked if they could have seen him now, with his smiling Irish eyes, his quirky smile, and heard him string together three whole words without a single blasphemy.) But Sean had kept up the pressure, scared the wankers shitless, insisted they find the stuff. What else was there for them to do with peace breaking out all over the place on the island of Ireland?

Anyroad, there was another, altogether more pressing thing on his mind. He had only been four when his father and his father's friend had been betrayed by the traitor Liam O'Connell. Both men had been shot, his father fatally. Throughout his entire childhood and into his youth, Sean's mother had shown him O'Connell's photograph every single day, waving it in front of his eyes, her face quite mad with hate and the desire for revenge. 'Get him for me, Sean. Get him.'

To Sean's everlasting regret, he had never been able to find the man responsible for his father's death before his mother herself had died. Fifteen years ago he thought he had. A friend had recognised O'Connell in a Liverpool pub. He had changed his name to Murphy. Sean was on his way to take the bastard out in person when, for the second time in his life, O'Connell/Murphy had disappeared off the face of the earth. Perhaps some sixth sense had told him he'd been spotted.

There was a streak of common sense, or possibly an innate decency, buried deep within the man who was Sean Donovan. He had never believed that sons were responsible for the sins of their fathers. He had been shown the house where the son of O'Connell/Murphy lived, witnessed the man with his wife and two children, so it had been true when he said he had seen Emily before. He had left them to get on with their lives. He had no quarrel with Alexander Murphy.

But now, by strange coincidence, Murphy had come back into his life.

Sean knew how police minds worked. He knew what was going on. He had eyes, he had ears. Ever since the cleaner's kid, interfering little sod, had moved the Semtex to the Murphys', the house had been watched, the phone had been tapped. The cops, thick as pigshit, automatically suspected anyone with a name like Murphy to be a terrorist. Under normal circumstances,

Murphy would be behind bars by now while the law tried to build a case against him, except the law was waiting for him, Sean Donovan, to turn up so they could catch him and Murphy together. Red-handed.

Under the same normal circumstances, Sean would have just sat back and laughed. Let the cops spend their scarce resources on trying to trap an innocent man, but he urgently needed to get inside Thorntons. It was an isolated house down an isolated lane, so what was there to stop Liam O'Connell/Murphy having lived there for years without anyone apart from his family having known?

Which was why he wanted to talk to Emily.

CHAPTER ELEVEN

Heinrich Hauptmann's *ende* had not proved completely final. Alex had managed to persuade him to come to Thorntons for the weekend in the hope of salvaging something from the wreckage of his thwarted ambitions.

'I'll need a girl,' Heinrich warned.

Where did you get a girl? Alex had no knowledge of such things. He'd never needed anyone to get him a girl, he thought, with a sense of smug and superior satisfaction. He'd always got his own, as had Heinrich in the days when he had been merely a conventionally unlovely person. Would it be tactless to ask Gaynor, his secretary, if she would be willing to partner Heinrich at dinner? What happened afterwards would be up to them. Gaynor had needed little persuading to become Alex's mistress. If she turned down Heinrich's advances, he'd just have to be taken to a club of sorts in town, and a girl found for him there.

'It's Heinrich Hauptmann,' he told his secretary. 'We've written to him often enough. His father owns one of the biggest car manufacturers in Germany.'

Gaynor's little round grey eyes looked at him blandly. Their relationship had fizzled out of late, Alex not being in the mood for distractions. 'Will your wife be there?' she asked, in her colourless voice.

'Of course. The dinner is at my home. It's purely business. I merely thought it would make for a pleasanter atmosphere if we were four, two men and two women. Heinrich won't feel a gooseberry, as the saying goes.'

'Okay, I'll come.'

Gaynor watched him leave the office, her face expressionless. Until recently, she had thought herself in love with Alexander Murphy, which was the reason why she'd needed little persuading when he'd first asked her out. She considered him the most interesting man she had ever met: handsome in an intellectual way, with his thin, arrogant face and never-still eyes, excitable and impatient, stimulating to be with. Gaynor had been thrilled when they had started an affair. She was thirty-five, her parents were dead, her two brothers had married and moved away from Liverpool. Alex was only the second man she had slept with, the first being the fiancé many years ago who had dumped her the day before the wedding. Gaynor was lonely, so lonely that she cried herself to sleep several times a week. She wanted a husband and longed for children, but somehow she seemed to have been overlooked. Gaynor was forced to concede that, although she did her best with herself, she was a quite unremarkable person, neither fat nor thin, tall nor short, pretty nor plain. Her brothers used to say she looked like a cat with her small round face and small round eyes, and that she had about as much personality. Perhaps it had been wrong, premature, to badger Alex about a divorce, but Gaynor was desperate. He was the only man to show interest in years, but when he began to make excuses, stopped asking her out, she realised she meant nothing to him. He had no intention of getting divorced. He had been using her as he would probably have used any woman who happened to be his secretary.

Anyway, she wasn't interested any more. Alex had changed: he was no longer the man she had thought she was in love with. The excitability had become hysteria, the impatience had turned to rage. And he wasn't handsome, either. In fact, he looked awful, grey and pinched, as if he was terribly ill, or something was weighing heavily on his mind. Gaynor was convinced he was on his way to a massive nervous breakdown. It might be because the business wasn't doing too well. She had heard the furious arguments with the bank manager on the phone, knew there had been articles in the computer press that the firm was lagging behind. What had happened to the German contract that was so important? Perhaps that was the reason Heinrich Hauptmann was coming to dinner. In the meantime, the staff seemed to have little to do, and were vainly waiting for Alex to give them some direction.

This Heinrich Hauptmann sounded interesting, a bachelor in his forties. She didn't care if he was rich or poor as long as he was nice, but, Gaynor thought bitterly, if things went the way they usually did, he probably wouldn't take a blind bit of notice of her.

'Saturday, Alex? But I shall be busy. Why didn't you ask first before inviting Heinrich for the weekend – and your secretary to dinner?'

'Busy doing what?' Alex demanded angrily of his

wife. She looked lovely in a floaty white skirt and red
silk T-shirt, her bountiful brown hair framing her rosy
face, as it had once done on the Rubenesque Emily of
old.

She shrugged. 'Things, stuff.'

'I have rarely asked you to entertain my friends
before, Emily,' he said stiffly.

'Only because you didn't want them to meet me. You
were ashamed.'

'That's not true,' Alex protested, though it was.

'Has something gone wrong with the Hauptmann
contract? Is that why Heinrich's coming?' Emily didn't
know much about it, but it was around now that Alex
had expected a decision as to whether the quotation had
been accepted. She had no idea how much depended on
it, that the house had been remortgaged, the company
was in trouble, that they were living on an overdraft that
the bank expected to be repaid soon.

'Well, yes.' Alex sighed. 'Things got mislaid, though
none of it was my fault, naturally.'

'Naturally,' Emily said, though she didn't believe him.
If it had been someone else's fault she would never have
heard the end of it – he'd have been in a furious rage for
the rest of his life. Instead, he was unusually subdued,

even a touch pathetic. Emily couldn't help but feel alarmed. She still loved him, and decided to do her level best to make the weekend a success. Cleopatra's would just have to do without her for a couple of days, though Eddie would be cross with them opening the following Monday. 'What time is Heinrich coming?'

'I'm meeting him at Manchester airport about mid-day. I'll take him for a drink on the way back. We'll probably be home about four or five o'clock.'

'Shall I have dinner ready for, say, half seven?'

'If you wouldn't mind, Em. Make it something substantial, Heinrich eats like a horse. I doubt if he'd want salad. Oh, and get plenty of wine.'

'All right, Alex,' Emily said comfortably. 'Don't worry. Everything will turn out all right in the end.'

He smiled wanly for the first time ever. 'I hope so, Em. I really do.'

Even when the children lived at home, the dining room at Thorntons had been used only rarely, reserved for Christmas and when family came to stay. Next day, Wednesday, Mae gave the large square room an extra clean, making sure there wasn't even a suggestion of a cobweb in the black beams that lined the walls and crisscrossed the low ceiling. She polished the heavy oak table and the eight matching chairs, two of them carvers, dusted the bulbs in the red-shaded wall lights, gave the tapestry cushions on the window-seat a good shake.

She returned to the kitchen where Emily was frantically turning the pages of a cookery book. 'The room looks nice. All you need now is some nice food to eat in there.'

'What shall I do, Mae? I've forgotten how to cook.' The dinner was important. She didn't want to let Alex down, even if the times he'd let her down were too numerous to mention.

'Here, let's have a gazzer. I can help you get stuff ready on Friday. I'll give your good crockery a rinse, an' all. It's probably got dusty in that cupboard.'

'Oh, Mae, what would I do without you? I'm a bag of nerves. What if I burn it, or if it's underdone? What if I drop things?'

'Stop worrying. What about soup for the first course? Or smoked salmon? Isn't that what they have in posh hotels?'

They decided on kidney soup for the first course, with smoked salmon as an alternative, pork and apple casserole, followed by sherry trifle with lashings of cream, because, as Mae said, 'You can't go wrong with trifle, and if this chap's a gannet, then he can help himself to more. Though you'll have to cut the kidneys up yourself, Em. The way our Alice goes on about eating animals, I can't bring meself to touch offal in the raw no more. Even mince can turn me stomach.'

When Emily went to the supermarket, the bill came to nearly a hundred and fifty pounds, what with half a dozen bottles of decent wine, the button mushrooms, the asparagus, the pork, and all the other bits and pieces, which seemed an awful lot to pay for a dinner for just four people. Not only that, she'd asked Mae if she wouldn't mind taking a night off from the club again to wait on them.

'It's not that I want it to look as if we have a maid, I'd just feel happier with you here. I'll compensate you for your wages and pay extra on top. Please, Mae, you'd be doing me an enormous favour.'

'Well, if you put it like that, Em, of course I'll come. I'll wear black so's I look like a professional, eh!'

Emily paid for the food using the card from the joint account. All the hoarded housekeeping money had gone on Cleopatra's. In fact, she was slightly overdrawn, but

the monthly standing order was due to be paid in shortly
and the overdraft would be cleared.

Would there have been never-ending rain, thunder and
lightning if the Conservatives had been re-elected? Was
Blessed Tony Blair a sun-god, a bringer of perfect
weather upon the country who had recently (and
wisely?) chosen him and his bright-eyed, bushy-tailed
New Labour MPs to govern it?

Who knows? But if this glorious dry spell continued,
there would soon be no water left for the charismatic
new leader to walk on.

It was another hazy, golden, sun-drenched afternoon
when Alex returned to Thorntons bringing with him his
old friend from university, Heinrich Hauptmann. Emily
had never met Heinrich. He had left Manchester as she
arrived. She didn't much like what she saw. He reminded
her of the piece of pork she had bought the other day,
pink, damp and fleshy, but she greeted him charmingly,
kissed his cheek, poured him a drink, asked if he would
like to rest after the journey. Alex was unnaturally full of
bonhomie, almost grovelling, which Emily found most
distressing. It was like watching a lion in a circus, the
king of the jungle reduced to silly, degrading tricks.

Heinrich opted for a stroll around the garden, which was at its brilliant best that day, a mass of roses, marguerites, pansies, almost every flower you could think of that bloomed in August. Their scent was magical. Even Heinrich, who didn't give the impression of being sensitive to nature, remarked on it.

Emily returned to the kitchen. Mae was coming at six, Gaynor, whom she had also never met, an hour later. She poured a glass of wine to sip as she stirred the soup, though it didn't need stirring, checked that the trifle had set properly, and that the casserole in the oven hadn't burned.

Promptly at six, Mae arrived in the brief black skirt and low-cut sequinned top that she had worn in the Irish club. She produced a frilly white apron from her bag. 'I forgot I had this. It's from when I used to be a waitress.' She looked like a maid in a pornographic movie when she tied it around her neat waist.

Outside, in the sweet-smelling garden, Heinrich said to Alex, 'The old man's not too impressed with the various schemes that arrived, particularly not when I told him about yours.'

'If you could possibly persuade him, Heinrich . . . ' Alex was desperate. The bank manager had phoned yesterday. He knew all about Peek-a-Boo. Alex had convinced him months ago that the whole thing was a cinch. He wanted to know if a decision had been made in Frankfurt. Alex said he was still waiting to hear, but he couldn't stall much longer. If things couldn't be turned round, he'd lose the business or the house, possibly both.

'Trouble is, Alex, old chap, the old man's such a stickler for formality. Your quotation wasn't there by the proper date. It's a sign you could be unreliable in other ways.'

'I told you, it wasn't my fault,' Alex whined. He couldn't abide people who whined. He'd actually sacked a man in Despatch once because his whining, complaining voice had got on his nerves.

'It's never done for the man at the top to blame others, Alex,' Heinrich said reprovingly. 'The ultimate responsibility rests with yourself.'

Alex swallowed bile. How dare the fucking wanker lecture him? What did he know about responsibility? The man was a walking insult to men all over the world; a disgustingly corrupt scab on the face of society, who'd been born rich and had never done a decent day's work in his life. He loathed the bastard with all his heart. 'You're right, Heinrich,' he said, through teeth that felt as if they had been cemented together. 'Nevertheless, I'll give you a copy of Peek-a-Boo to show your father. If you could convince him he's cutting off his nose to spite his face by sticking to his precious formalities, I would appreciate it very much.'

'How much?' Heinrich asked slyly.

All Alex could see was red. It was as if the entire world was suddenly drenched in blood. He took several deep breaths before replying, by which time things had returned to normal, though there was still a red tinge in the air. 'I'm rather cleaned out at the moment,' he choked, 'but if you manage to talk your father round, let's say the same as before.'

'Done.' Heinrich smacked his fat lips with satisfaction. 'By the way, I drove past Blumenstrasse 115 the other day, the address your quotation was wrongly sent to. It's a little shoe repairer's. Very dusty, very dark, very closed, otherwise I might have stopped and asked why they didn't redirect their wrongly addressed mail. Such an irresponsible thing to do, or should I say, not to do.' He chuckled.

And Alex saw red again.

The meal had been cooked to perfection. Emily was justly proud on her own and Mae's behalf. However, perfect food does not automatically a good dinner party maketh. A lively atmosphere is essential, sparkling conversation, convivial company.

At Thorntons that night the atmosphere was deadly dull, the conversation virtually nil, and the company didn't want to know each other.

Emily tried, she really tried, but all Heinrich wanted to do was eat. When he wasn't eating, he was drinking. Whenever she spoke to him, he either didn't answer, or answered with his mouth full, and the sight of the mashed-up food on the green-tinted tongue made her feel slightly sick. Alex was very red and very quiet. He held his knife and fork tightly, the knuckles showing white on his thin hands. He was mad about something, almost bursting with scarcely suppressed rage. As for Gaynor, Emily had spoken to her on the phone in the past, so knew she wasn't a deaf mute, but so far tonight she hadn't spoken. It didn't seem possible to describe someone as being the colour of water, but somehow it fitted Gaynor perfectly.

The only lively moments occurred when Mae came in to collect the dishes or bring the next course. Unaware that this was a dinner party for the dead, she would ask brightly, 'Did you enjoy that? Shall I pour you some more wine?' Alex ignored her, Heinrich held out his glass, and Gaynor gave a little squeak, which might have been yes or no.

Only Emily would reply. 'It was lovely, Mae. And yes, I'd love more wine.'

As all things come to an end, good or bad, so did dinner. A glowering Alex produced cigars, and Gaynor spoke at last. She asked for the bathroom.

Emily escaped to the kitchen to tell Mae all about it. 'It was *awful*. Terrible. I'll never hold a dinner party again.'

'It sounds quite funny to me, Em. The sort of thing you tell your grandchildren. Anyroad, the dishwasher's stacked so I'll be off. I promised to lend a hand at the club if they're busy.'

In the dining room, Heinrich was saying bluntly, 'If you asked that anaemic little blonde for me, I don't fancy her.'

'We'll go into town, find a club,' Alex said tiredly. He'd had enough of Heinrich Hauptmann to last a lifetime.

Heinrich winked. 'What about the *Kellnerin*? She'd do very nicely.'

'I'm sorry, what?'

'The servant, the waitress. Would she,' he winked again, 'you know?'

'Mae? Christ almighty, Heinrich, she's our cleaner.'

'Who cares? She has a great body. I could fuck her for hours.'

'Do you really have to be so *disgusting?*'

Oh, Jesus! Alex groaned inwardly, now he'd blown it, but the remark had come out quite spontaneously. He was casting round desperately for a way of turning it into a joke, but to his horror, Heinrich flushed and looked as if he might cry. He got up and left the room without a word, leaving Alex with no idea what to think, thinking about nothing, thinking about everything. The dinner party had been a disaster, though he had to concede that Emily had done her best.

Heinrich made for the garden, he needed to be alone. The kitchen was empty, the dishwasher chugged away, the maid had gone. She wouldn't have fancied him, no woman would touch him unless they were paid. And Alex hated him, everyone hated him. As a human being, he was a total failure. Heinrich stuffed his hands into his pockets and stamped through the darkening grass, his body and brain torpid with misery. It was strange, but in a perverse way, he gloried in his failure, as if the only way to cope was to make himself more and more objectionable, give people a real reason for their obvious disgust.

Age had treated Heinrich Hauptmann cruelly. As a young man, his ugliness hadn't seemed to matter. He had managed to overcome it with a cheerful, upbeat attitude to life. But this was difficult to hold on to as he became older and his skin grew rougher, his neck thicker, and his eyes protruded more. When he looked in the mirror, his reflection stared back at him obscenely, as ugly as the proverbial sin. He became aware that he made people feel uncomfortable, he could see it in their eyes, just as he had seen it in Emily's eyes throughout dinner, and he had responded by gorging like a pig. Yet inside he was the same man he had always been, generous and kind, a man who liked to have friends. But human beings seemed incapable of seeing beyond the flesh that formed so heavily and disagreeably on his face. They took him for a monster, so Heinrich behaved like one, becoming more and more debauched as time went on, almost revelling in the odious persona he presented to the world.

'Do you really have to be so *disgusting?*' Alex, his friend, had just asked.

Heinrich sighed miserably. Every now and then he was brought to his senses by a remark like that. Usually, for a while afterwards, awash with shame, sunk deeply in despair, he would quite seriously consider becoming a hermit or a monk. He began to think about it now, but became aware that there was someone in the garden with him. He could hear breathing and a soft, snuffling sound, as if the person was crying.

'Who's that?' he called.

'It's Gaynor,' a woman's voice replied softly, a touch sadly.

'Gaynor?'

'The woman who sat opposite you during dinner.'

The anaemic blonde. He managed to locate her in the flower-scented darkness. She was sitting on a bench within an arch of curving trees. 'Are you all right, Gaynor?'

'I'm fine, thank you.'

If there really was a God, and if he was as good as people were led to believe by experts in religion and all things holy, then by rights Gaynor and Heinrich should have come together that night. They were both nice people. They were alone together in a lush and highly romantic setting. She hadn't disliked him. Had Heinrich bothered to look deep into Gaynor's round grey eyes, he would have witnessed sympathy and understanding. As one who also read people's eyes and saw only disinterest and boredom, Gaynor had recognised the pain in his. She was sensitive to the misfits of this world. She knew exactly what Heinrich was up to. While she shrank further into her shell as if to prove she was a nobody, he exposed himself to show that, yes, he was every bit as repulsive as people thought. Throughout her life, Gaynor had always been convinced that there was a great big party going on just round the corner, somewhere out of sight, to which everyone had been invited except her. But Heinrich, another outsider, gatecrashed the party, an uninvited, unwanted guest.

Gaynor would have been a perfect match for Heinrich, and he for her. They could have had a wild old party on their own.

But maybe the atmosphere wasn't quite right. The little creatures that inhabited the garden found their innocent slumber interrupted by bad dreams that August night. They wondered if there was about to be a storm, and their restless twitching created a sense of unease, so that dusk fell more heavily than usual over this normally peaceful place.

It made Gaynor shudder. 'I think I'll go inside,' she said.

'Hmm,' Heinrich murmured idly, having already forgotten her name again.

There wasn't to be a storm. Something far worse was afoot at Thorntons. Murder! And the perpetrator and the victim were already there, just waiting for the act to be carried out.

Emily found Alex alone in the dining room. He was smoking a cigar, something he did rarely. 'Where are Heinrich and Gaynor?' she asked in surprise.

'Dunno,' he grunted.

'Shouldn't you be looking after them? Heinrich at least. I'll find Gaynor in a minute.'

'I suppose.' He spoke listlessly. He was wearing a dark grey suit and a white shirt, a combination that Emily had always thought made him appear particularly attractive, but now the whiteness of the shirt merely emphasised the pallor of his haggard face, while grey echoed the shadows beneath his dark, lacklustre eyes.

'Alex,' she said kindly, 'there's something wrong, I know it. Why won't you tell me what's going on?'

Alex wasn't sure what he wanted right then, but it

wasn't kindness. There was probably nothing on earth other than a quick and instant death that would have lessened his sense of frustration with the fact that he was no longer in charge of his own destiny, and that it would be days, if not weeks, before he would know for sure whether he had lost everything or had been saved. He turned on Emily, filled with resentment that she had a life when, just lately, he seemed to have none, that she looked so happy when he was sunk in the furthest depths of despair. 'I could ask the same question,' he snapped. '*You* tell *me* what's going on. Why are you never here, for instance? You scarcely listen when I speak to you. You disappear into the den as soon as I get home.'

'I only asked because you seem worried about something, Alex. I thought you had a problem. There's no need to turn on me.' He was his own worst enemy, Emily thought impatiently, accusing her of exactly the same things he'd been doing to her for years. It was hard to feel sympathy for someone so completely unaware of their own failings. 'I'll look for Gaynor,' she said. 'I'm not being a very good hostess, leaving the poor woman to her own devices. I wonder if she's still in the bathroom.'

The subtly shifting shadows on the stairs and the

gallery, the muffled rustlings and whispers, no longer bothered her. She'd got used to them, the sounds were friendly, as Mae had assured her.

Emily knocked on the bathroom door. There was no answer, and when she looked inside the room was empty, though she heard the faintest suggestion of a far-off sigh. Gaynor was obviously elsewhere. Emily paused on the landing to watch a half-moon drift through a bank of fluffy, silver-lined clouds. One of these days she'd have to tell Alex what was going on, about Cleopatra's. She could almost hear his disdainful laugh. He might even laugh if he found out about Eddie — 'How pathetic, Emily, sleeping with our cleaner's father. Have you no pride?' It was difficult, though, to imagine his reaction if he knew about the afternoon she had spent in the Adelphi with her gorgeous Irishman, Martin McCutcheon. Oh, God! A frisson of almost unbearable delight swept through her at the memory of their lovemaking; so impossibly romantic, so highly emotional, yet almost violent in its intensity. It was like a film, a genuine brief encounter, begun in a car park instead of a station. She wouldn't be seeing him again. They were merely 'ships that had passed in the night', as Martin had said, stroking her breasts. Which was how Emily wanted it. She hadn't the strength of character for a proper affair. (Eddie McNulty, who considered himself a stud of the first order, would have been outraged were he privy to her thoughts.) She wasn't up to keeping secrets and telling lies: it wasn't in her nature. Over dinner, Martin had told her he had come to Liverpool to see an old friend, and was returning to Australia in two days' time. 'And I have to be in London tomorrow, have a word with the big cheese before I go.'

'I'll never forget this afternoon.' Emily sighed blissfully.

Sean Donovan, for whom such afternoons were ten a penny, sighed with her. 'Nor will I, my dearest Emily. But you have a husband, a family. They must come first.' He was only being kind in letting her think that he had been bowled over. He quite liked her. The last two hours had been exceptionally pleasant. Alexander Murphy was a lucky feller. He reached for one of her broad, sturdy hands, and gently kissed the knuckles one by one. 'Tell me about your family.'

Emily felt the blood flow more sweetly through her recently ravished body at this supremely romantic gesture. 'There's not much to tell.'

Sean listened attentively as she told him about Murphy being in computers, her kids living in London. 'So, there's just you and your husband left at home?'

'That's right, yes.'

No mention of her father-in-law, the traitorous Liam O'Connell/Murphy. Was it possible she knew something of his background? Was his presence, or at least his whereabouts, deliberately kept concealed? It was difficult to ask a direct question without raising suspicion, and the man responsible for the death of his father would escape into the unknown yet again.

There was only one thing for it. He'd have to take a look around this house of theirs, Thorntons, for himself.

Emily's reverie on the landing was broken by the sound of Heinrich's raised voice downstairs. 'But I insist, Alex,' he was saying, 'I positively insist.'

'All right, if that's what you want. Heinrich would like to go home,' Alex said, when Emily appeared. He looked even more shattered than when she'd left him only a few minutes before.

'But will there be a flight at this time of night?' Emily wondered aloud.

'Possibly not. I don't really care. If necessary, I'll catch the train to London, and go to Heathrow.' Heinrich knew he was only living up to his reputation by appearing extremely boorish, but he had an overwhelming desire to be alone. He didn't want to wake up and have to face Alex in the morning, spend the day with him. 'Do you really have to be so *disgusting*?' Alex had said.

'I'll give you a lift to the station,' Alex said dully. Heinrich had taken umbrage. It really was the *ende*.

Not quite.

'I'd prefer it if you called a taxi, thanks all the same. Oh, and don't forget to give me that copy you promised, Alex. I'll take it with me, see what I can do.'

'I'll be going too.' Perhaps Gaynor had been there all the time. If so, no one had noticed. 'Thank you for the lovely dinner.'

The two policemen were scarcely visible in their car parked just inside the entrance to a field almost within sight of the Murphy's house. 'That's the last of the visitors gone,' one remarked, when a taxi drove away with a single passenger in the back. 'Still no sign of Donovan, though.'

'And there won't be. From what I hear, Donovan's all

about. He'll know the place is being watched. He'd have
to be mad to show his face around here.'

At that very moment Sean Donovan's face was peering
through the kitchen window of Thorntons watching
Emily tidy up. He was dressed from head to toe in black.
Emily would have been shocked had she been able to see
the brutal expression in the eyes she had thought so
beguiling, and the cruel twist in the lips that had kissed
her so lavishly only a few days before. Sean had been
hiding in the greenery for hours, ever since the sun had
dipped behind the crumbling wall at the rear of the
property. The cops were fools if they thought he would
approach the place from the front. He recognised Mae
from the description Mick had given him. It was her lad
who'd taken the Semtex, which was hidden somewhere
round here. Sean didn't care about the Semtex. After
nearly half a century of festering hate, his only interest
was in finding Liam O'Connell/Murphy to kill, if not
tonight then as soon as he could get his hands around
the neck of the traitorous bastard.

During dinner, Sean had crept furtively round to the
front of the house to check if lights were on in other
rooms where his prey might be, but only the hall was lit.

He crept back to the rear, watched Mae stack the dishwasher, talk to Emily, then leave in a car with an old, tired engine. The woman guest came into the garden, and shortly afterwards the man. They spoke briefly, then returned inside, the woman first. Not long afterwards, two more cars left. Emily and Murphy were alone. If this was the place where Liam O'Connell had hidden himself, now was the time for him to make an appearance.

What would he look like now that he was seventy, Sean wondered. The photograph his mother had given him was in the wallet in his jacket pocket, next to his heart. He was a tall man, his mam had said. The son, Alexander, looked nothing like him, dark when his dad had been fair.

Emily put the kettle on. She made a cup of coffee, and sat at the table, drinking it alone.

Once again, Sean crept round to the front. There was a light on in a downstairs room. He approached eagerly, heart thumping, but it was only Murphy in what appeared to be a study. He was staring vacantly into the screen of a computer, which hadn't been switched on, his chin resting in his hands.

It would seem that Sean was wasting his time. He

relaxed his taut body and returned to the back, where Emily was still drinking coffee. There didn't seem to be much communication between the Murphys. The moon had slipped behind a cloud, and he could barely see the various paths that led to the wall he had climbed over to get in. The car he had hired was parked two miles away with several others in an ordinary suburban road. He paused by some sort of arch, unsure which way to go, just as Eustace emerged from his shed, having awoken from a drunken slumber and anxious for a piss.

The tall lanky figure with matted grey hair loomed before the Irishman who had murder in mind on this enchanting night. So, *this* was where the bastard had been hiding. With a muted, almost inhuman roar, he leapt at Eustace, who tottered forward several startled steps before tripping and falling face down into the lily-pond with only the gentlest of plopping sounds.

As he lay there, Eustace was scarcely aware of the hand pressing lightly between his shoulder blades preventing him from coming up for air. The water tasted of mildew and old earth, and was soothing to his aching joints. He made no attempt to struggle as he lived his life again during his last moments on this earth. He was a little boy again, with brothers and sisters he'd almost forgotten he had; he was courting Julia, he watched Julia die, and briefly kissed the tiny nameless dead baby girl who had killed her, he came to Thorntons, where the neglected garden was wildly overgrown and full of weeds. Eustace had brought it to perfection entirely on his own. He saw himself planting the larch and the willow, the magnolia and the cherry trees, firming the soil with his large, capable hands. He persuaded roses to climb the walls, trailed clematis around the windows and the doors, coaxed ivy up and down trellises and in and out of arches and around trees. And the flowers, thousands of flowers, millions, they bloomed and wilted before his closed, fading eyes. The flashbacks turned hazy, just as Eustace had when he became ill, and his hands twisted, his feet hurt, his head ached, and he had to drag himself around his beloved garden. Then Mae came and, oh, he still hadn't made out a will in his dear Mae's favour.

Oh, Mae! was Eustace's last simple thought before he died, painlessly, but so easy to kill, no trouble to anyone right up to the end.

CHAPTER TWELVE

Dicky McNulty quite missed the blue Plasticine. There didn't seem much point in having it when it was so far away. He'd been wont to get it out to play with if he was bored. When he went to Ince Blundell for their Alice's wedding, he'd fetch it back. There'd been no sign of Mick and Paddy or the cops for weeks, so hopefully the heat had died down. He supposed none of them had had anything to do with the gerbil that had come last week, complete with its own cage and a supply of toys and food. All he'd done was put a gerbil at the top of the list when Ms Turner had asked the class to write an essay, 'The Things I Want Most in the World', only because he thought it looked good. A few days later, like a miracle, there was a gerbil on the back doorstep when he came home from school, much to his mam's annoyance.

He was already quite fond of the little animal, which he had christened Bambi, but to his dying day, Dicky would regret not putting a trip to Disneyland first in the list, or tickets for the World Cup in France next year. Quentin Quinn was eagerly awaiting the arrival of a Harley Davidson, but had so far been unlucky.

Jim McNulty had bought a set of children's paints and a drawing pad and spent a lot of time painting pictures of the garden, though the parched, patchy lawn, with an occasional clump of defiant dandelions, surrounded by a broken-down fence, didn't offer much inspiration. He thought longingly of the garden at Thorntons.

Craig McNulty had caused a frisson of excitement in the local Job Centre, and a sense of usefulness within the staff, when he asked to go on a course. Most of their clients produced devilishly clever reasons for refusing any sort of training, and to have a client request one was a unique and thrilling experience. Craig had already started work as a trainee gardener in Calderstones Park, with one day a week at college studying botany.

Alice McNulty wanted her wedding to be a statement of her love for animals and her support for all things natural and green. Having searched the charity shops of

Liverpool for a wedding dress, she had come across a coarse hopsack garment the colour of oatmeal with a wartime utility label in the back, which would be perfect, and a pair of canvas boots with rubber soles that were only a size too big. On the day, she would make a daisy chain for her hair. She was disappointed when Mam flatly refused to hire a bunny rabbit outfit for Shona, who was to be bridesmaid, and had instead purchased a plum-coloured silk dress through a neighbour's catalogue. Had the silkworms suffered, Alice wished angrily to know. Gareth would be wearing a pure cotton denim outfit made in the United Kingdom, where the workers were only moderately exploited.

Shona McNulty was fed up with being clever, and sometimes wished she were thick. She was probably the only person in Liverpool, if not the world, who would have liked to know Alex Murphy better, because she could talk to him as an equal.

As for Eddie McNulty, he was rarely seen these days in Daffodil Close. 'It must be a woman,' Mae said knowingly to Emily. 'There's nothing else that would make him get up at six o'clock in the morning and come back at midnight. Whoever she is, she's wearing him out. He looks fair whacked when he gets home.'

Mae was happy enough to bust. Craig had a job he loved, even if he was only paid a pittance, which meant she had to help out with his bus fares and make him a packed lunch each day, and Alice was marrying a sweet boy and they clearly adored each other. And what a bonus that the mothers-in-law should already be the greatest friends. She'd always wanted the very best for her children, what mother doesn't? and now it would seem that Craig and Alice had found the best there was. Mind you, she was running up a terrible debt with the wedding, even though the young couple didn't want a conventional affair with cars and formal clothes and all those other things that cost the earth, and it was fortunate that the reception was being held at Thorntons. Shona's dress had cost thirty-five pounds, and a pair of decent grey trousers for Dicky was fifteen, and she still had to get him a new white shirt and shoes. Craig was giving his sister away and would need something respectable. Perhaps Dad would lend him something for the day. And there was no way she'd buy herself an outfit for her daughter's wedding in a car-boot sale, which meant she'd owe her next-door neighbour's catalogue company well over a hundred and fifty quid by the time she chose something. Fortunately, Emily was well aware of how Mae was placed and had offered to pay for the food, which had to be vegetarian. Naturally, Mae would help prepare it. Still, she'd cope, somehow or other, just like she always managed to cope. It might be possible to squeeze in another little job to clear the debt.

While in such a happy frame of mind, Mae wondered why she should wake up on Sunday morning with such a bitter taste in her mouth. It stayed with her throughout Mass, even after she had taken the Host, and on the way home from church she had a feeling of foreboding. Something bad was about to happen. Or perhaps it already had.

Emily Murphy felt as if she had caught up with herself. After all those years of doubting her own existence, mixed with a sense of aching nostalgia, she had at last come to terms with the fact that she was a forty-five-year-old woman with a life of her own and two grown-up children who had left home. Gareth had got a job with Sefton Council and was coming back to live in Liverpool in a few months' time. He and Alice would stay at Thorntons until they found a place of their own. Emily was pleased, of course, but not quiveringly, pathetically pleased, as she would once have been.

On the Sunday morning after the dreadful dinner party, she rose early with the intention of going to Bootle to carry out any last-minute touches that might be required at Cleopatra's, which was opening next day, picking up Eddie at an agreed location on the way. She slipped into a royal blue satin kimono, tying the belt tightly around her ever-decreasing waist, and strode confidently through the shafts of bright sunlight that lay sharply across the polished gallery floor.

Normally, Alex would have gone by now, despite it being Sunday, but he seemed to have been staying off work a lot recently, and the trouble was, she didn't like leaving him in the house all day alone. It seemed unfair that what should have been an exciting time was spoiled by a constant, niggling concern that he was in some sort of trouble that he refused to reveal. She would never cease to want the old Alex back, the one she had married, but in the meantime, the until recently detached, confident, bright-eyed Alex, who breezed through life and scarcely noticed she was there, would do in preference to the physical and emotional wreck he seemed to have become.

Damn! Emily chewed her lip worriedly as she made herself a cup of tea and carried it into the dew-drenched garden. Her feet were bare and the grass felt cool and refreshing. Steam rose from the wooden roof of the garden shed as the sun gradually crept across. Flowers, dazzlingly wet, were slowly unfolding for the day. It all looked impressively beautiful, yet there was an odd feeling about, a strange unpleasant tingling in the air. Emily felt the hairs prickle on her neck, as she realised that not a single bird was singing on that lovely morning.

She had no idea what made her go straight to the lily-pond, as if the garden itself was leading her to the place where the genius who had created it had met his end.

'Eustace!' she screamed when she saw the thin body lying face down, half in, half out, of the murky water. Without hesitation, she plunged into the pool which was only a few feet deep, and lifted and dragged the body on to the grass. She was about to apply mouth-to-mouth resuscitation, but realised it was too late. Eustace was unquestionably dead, with the suggestion of a smile on his creased face. There scarcely seemed to be anything of him now that the saturated clothes clung so closely to his fragile body with its sharply protruding bones. Emily shed tears for the old man who had tended her garden with such care and devotion for so many years. She knew it was hypocritical: her concern was far too late.

Then she went indoors and raised Alex to tell him the news.

'Oh, God!' Alex looked shocked, which was just as well, as Emily might well have left him on the spot had he made an offensive comment.

He called the police. Two uniformed officers arrived quickly in a car with the blue light flashing, causing some consternation to the occupants of the unmarked police car parked within sight of the house, who had unwittingly allowed a murder to be committed only a few metres from them. They hurriedly contacted the local nick to find out what had happened.

One of the uniformed men called an ambulance. It was undoubtedly an accident, the medics said knowledgeably, as they hoisted the body on to the stretcher. The pathologist would determine the cause of death.

The ambulance doors slammed and, as if this was the signal they had been waiting for, just as an orchestra waits for the lifting of the conductor's baton, the birds throughout the garden threw back their heads, opened their beaks and began a slightly late, full-throated dawn chorus, so that Eustace was driven away to the sound of an affectionate musical farewell from his feathered friends.

Both Emily and Alex had to confess they had no idea why Eustace should have been there during the weekend. 'He works for us, sorry, worked, for just a few days a week, any time between Monday and Friday,' Emily tearfully told the officer, who seemed to be in charge. 'He usually went home about four o'clock.'

'He's been sleeping in here.' The other policeman emerged from Eustace's shed. 'There's what looks like a bed made out of sacks, as well as a half-drunk bottle of whisky, also a load of empties.'

'Gosh, I didn't know. His bicycle must be around somewhere.' It was shameful to admit, but she knew nothing whatsoever about Eustace, and neither did Alex, only where he'd lived. No, they didn't know if he had any relatives, any friends, how old he was, if he frequented a particular pub, which doctor he was registered with. Emily had to rack her brains to remember his surname. 'Ramsbotham, Eustace Ramsbotham,' she gasped, relieved. How awful if she'd had to say she had no idea.

The sit-up-and-beg bike was found tucked behind the

garage, where it must have been put so that no one would know its owner was still there.

'We'll take a look around his place.' The policemen made to leave. 'We'll be back in touch soon.'

'Why do they need to be back in touch?' Alex asked petulantly when the men had gone. 'What's it got to do with us?'

'Oh, shut up, Alex. You make me sick,' Emily said tersely. 'I'm going to telephone Mae. She was very fond of Eustace. I know she'll be upset.'

Alex retired to his study, hurt, and with no intention of adding a dead gardener to his already long list of worries. He was sorry about Eustace, naturally, but just wished the chap had had the good sense to die on his own property.

Sean Donovan's hand had left no mark on Eustace's frail, blotched body. His liver had almost rotted away, his stomach contained no food, he had drunk almost half a bottle of whisky in the hours before his death, which was officially pronounced 'Accidental'. The body would be released shortly for burial.

'Will we be allowed to go to the funeral?' asked Mae, still distraught several days later.

'I don't see why not, though I've no idea who's organising it,' Emily replied.

'Then I'll make up a wreath with flowers, *his* flowers from the garden, if that's all right with you, Em.' The poor, sad old man, she should have looked after him better, thought Mae. Done his washing perhaps, made him the odd meal. 'I feel terribly guilty,' she sobbed.

'Try not to upset yourself, dear,' Emily said gently. 'After all, he was eighty-five. He had a good innings, as my mother always says. And he was working right up until the end. Not many people manage to do that.' (Working for fifty pence an hour, a hard voice reminded her. Mae wasn't the only person to feel guilty, and she had far less reason, if any at all.) 'We've got the wedding to think of. It's just over two weeks off, and I've got other things to do.' On Monday, Cleopatra's had got off to a flying start, and Mister Eddie was delighted. 'I'm afraid I'm going to have to leave you on your own again today. I'm already terribly late. Will you be all right?'

'Yes.' Mae sniffed.

'Talking of the wedding, we'll need someone to keep the garden tidy in the meantime, cut the grass and clear the weeds.'

'Shall I ask me grandad?' Jim had loved the garden that weekend they'd stayed.

'It would be marvellous, Mae. You always seem to be coming to my rescue. I honestly don't know what I'd do without you.'

When Alex returned home early from work the telephone was ringing. He was already in a foul mood, but then he always was these days. An apparently empty house only added to his bad temper. He picked up the receiver in the kitchen and snapped the number.

'Is that Alexander Murphy?' a cultured male voice enquired.

'Yes,' growled Alex, ready to bite the chap's head off if he was toting double glazing, new kitchens, outside cladding for the walls, or insurance. (Alex was already insured for every eventuality, apart from sending critically important mail to the wrong address.)

'This is George Dobbs, of Dobbs and Curtis, solicitors, Formby. I would very much like to arrange a meeting in my office between our two selves and Mrs Emily Murphy. Could you suggest a time that would be convenient to us all?'

'What's it about?' Alex asked guardedly. What else

had gone wrong? Was he being sued? He no longer had faith in anything. It could only be bad news.

'It's regarding the will of my late client, Eustace Arthur Ramsbotham. Yourself and Mrs Emily Murphy are the sole designated beneficiaries.'

'You don't say!' Alex felt a small bubble of hope rise up within his jaded body. 'How about tomorrow morning, nine o'clock?'

'Ten would be more convenient,' George Dobbs said smoothly.

'Then ten it is.'

Why else would Eustace make a will, Alex thought excitedly, unless he had something to leave? And what else had Eustace got to leave apart from his house? The house was little bigger than a rabbit hutch and falling apart, but the plot it stood on was substantial, big enough to take two large detached properties, or a couple of pairs of semis. The land was worth forty, fifty thou, possibly more. And if he could raise the cash to have the building work done himself, then he'd make a bundle, between a quarter and half a mill. Alex rubbed his hands. Even with the first option, there'd be enough to get him out of his current hole, placate the bank manager for quite a while.

Emily took some persuading to keep the appointment with Dobbs. 'I've got things to do,' she wailed. 'Couldn't we go late one afternoon? It can't be all that important. If Eustace had been worth anything, he would have bought himself a decent pair of shoes.'

'I know it's highly inconvenient, Em, but we owe it to Eustace,' Alex said, stiffly virtuous, having kept his hopes of a windfall to himself. 'Just imagine the poor soul, cycling all the way to Formby to make out a will in our favour.'

'If you put it that way.'

George Dobbs was a small, plump individual with smooth baby cheeks and lots of important silver hair. He beamed at them benevolently through his half-moon spectacles, the look of a man about to impart good news, Alex thought hopefully.

He spent ages reading through the first part of the will, full of legal jargon that even Alex couldn't understand. A few minutes later, from what Alex *could* understand, he and Emily had been bequeathed everything that had belonged to the late Eustace Arthur Ramsbotham, in particular, (a) a stamp album, (b) a case of coins, and (c) the contents of his Post Office Savings Book.

'There is, let me see, a balance of two hundred and seventy three pounds and eightpence,' Dobbs said, leafing through the little blue plastic book. 'I got this from Mr Ramsbotham's house yesterday. I should point out that the furniture is only fit for burning. In fact, the place needs fumigating.'

'The album, the coins, are they worth anything?' Alex asked plaintively, his dreams shattered for the second time within the space of a few weeks.

'Alex!' Emily nudged him sharply.

'I have them here.' The solicitor picked up a plastic bag from behind his desk. 'They're rather dusty, I'm afraid, and also quite worthless. The album's full of those cheap, fake stamps all boys collect. I used to have one myself, though of course you can have it valued to make sure. The coins were given away free during the Festival of Britain in nineteen fifty, with packets of tea, I do believe. They're some sort of base metal. They probably made money on the case, which cost a pound. It's only cardboard made to look like leather.'

'We'll treasure them always,' Emily murmured.

'Mr Ramsbotham thought they were worth a fortune,' George Dobbs said, smiling fondly.

Alex breathed on his nails, polished them on his sleeve, tried to look casual, and said, 'I thought he owned his own house.'

'No, no. The house was rented, though no rent had been paid in years. The owner knew no one else would want to live there, and the longer Mr Ramsbotham stayed, the more the land would be worth. By the way, the owner is willing to clear the place, so that expense won't fall on your good selves.'

'Great!' By now all Alex wanted to do was leave, the coins and stamps could be dumped in the nearest garbage bin for all he cared.

'There is one more thing,' the solicitor said, with an unreal cough and an air of false geniality that Alex found suspicious. 'I hope you don't think this too personal a suggestion, but my client has left no provision for the costs of his burial. If your own circumstances are such that the money in the Post Office account could be diverted towards the funeral, the gesture would be highly appreciated. Otherwise, I'm afraid Mr Ramsbotham will be buried in a pauper's grave.'

'We can't possibly have that!' Emily cried promptly and generously. 'Can we, Alex?' She turned to Dobbs. 'Please spend anything you need and let us have the bill.

Eustace was such a wonderful worker, it's the least we can do.'

They drove back to Thorntons in silence. How could being left money cost money? Alex wondered, dazed. Had someone put a curse on him? Had Lady Luck deserted him for ever?

When they arrived home, Emily immediately climbed into the Punto.

'Where are you going?' Alex demanded.

'I have to see someone.'

'What about?'

'Oh, you know, stuff.' She started up the engine and drove away. 'I've no idea what time I'll be back,' she shouted through the open window.

Alex, feeling neglected and very alone, opened the stout oak door (he must remind Emily that the hinge needed oiling), stepped into the hall, and – this seemed to be happening a lot lately – was conscious of a faint agonised moan, a hushed whisper, a slight cold breeze that ruffled his hair, yet there wasn't a breath of wind outside.

'Who's there?' he asked shakily, and was rewarded with another desperate moan. Jesus! Why had he never believed Emily all the times she had claimed the house was haunted? He hurried into the kitchen and made himself coffee. By rights, he should go straight to work where Gaynor would make coffee for him, but he seemed to have lost all interest in computers. The very sight of them turned his stomach.

He sat down at the table. Shit, it was quiet in here, with just the groans of the shifting house to be heard, and the song of the birds outside. Yet it used to be so different, with a rosy, smiling Emily bustling around, the children running in and out with their friends. The place had seemed full of life. Alex frowned, remembering. Thinking about it, he'd quite like to have those carefree days back.

By God, he'd made a mess of things. At the moment, he was actually strapped for ready cash. He daren't draw more out of the bank, and the amount he owed on his credit card was soaring all the time. Even the two hundred and odd quid from Eustace would have come in useful, but Emily had given it away and offered more, which was understandable as she had no idea how tight things were cash-wise. He wondered idly if the bank had honoured the monthly standing order transferring funds into her personal account, not that she'd notice if they hadn't. Until recently, Emily had spent scarcely anything on herself, or the house. It was only over the last few weeks she'd bought clothes and food had started to appear.

His hands tightened on the coffee cup. *Which meant she must have literally thousands saved.* Help, it seemed, was at hand. Alex slammed the cup on the table, hurried into the study, and took the folder containing the family's bank details from the desk drawer. Emily's statements weren't among them. Knowing her, she probably just chucked them away. But the account number was. He rang the bank, gave the number, and asked for the current balance.

'Hold on a minute, sir,' a young woman said courteously. She came back quickly. 'That account is in the name of Mrs Emily Murphy. I'm afraid I can only give that information to the account-holder in person.'

'But she's my wife, for Chrissakes,' Alex thundered.

'I'm sorry, sir, but that is the rule.'

A few minutes later, Alex rang the bank again with the same request, this time assuming a shrill falsetto. Fortunately, a different woman answered. 'Your account is one hundred and thirty-two pounds overdrawn, Mrs Murphy.'

'It can't possibly be!'

'I'm afraid it is.'

'But where have I spent all this money?' Alex whispered.

'I don't have cheque details to hand, but within the last four weeks, drawings on this account total more than seven thousand pounds.'

'*Seven thousand pounds!*'

'Seven thousand pounds.'

'Thank you.'

'No problem, Mrs Murphy. Thank you for calling.'

Seven thousand fucking pounds! Within the last four weeks Emily had spent seven thousand sodding, fucking pounds!

What on?

He couldn't ask without disclosing that he'd been spying on her account. What the hell was she up to? This wasn't a bit like Emily.

His heart was thumping. Alex was very worried about his heart. Another day like today, and it would give up on him altogether. He threw off his jacket, undid his tie and went into the garden, urgently in need of some fresh air.

Eustace's bike was propped innocently against the

wall outside. Alex bared his teeth and kicked it. It fell to the ground with a crash. He kicked it again. He felt better. He grinned, leapt on the spokes of the back wheel and danced on them for several minutes until every one was bent. This was good. He was enjoying himself. He danced on the front wheel, turned the seat round so that it pointed backwards, then, with almost superhuman strength, managed to twist the handlebars upwards until something snapped and they fell back limply. Alex picked up the wrecked bicycle and flung it against the wall. It looked like something that might have come from Damien Hirst's tortured brain, and Alex almost felt himself again.

The phone rang, and he answered it quite chirpily. It was George Dobbs, solicitor.

'Further to our recent conversation, Mr Murphy, I've just thought of something.'

'And what might that be, pray?' Did Eustace's extra long body require an extra long coffin, which could only be acquired at great expense, or had he been a member of an obscure religion that required a minister to be flown in from somewhere like Haiti to officiate at the funeral? If so, Dobbs could go screw himself.

'It's Mr Ramsbotham's bicycle. I understand it once

belonged to his mother, so it must be very old, and was always kept in beautiful condition. I know very little about such things, but I reckon that bike must be worth quite a bit. I thought I should let you know before it was dispensed with.'

CHAPTER THIRTEEN

The police surveillance carried out so far on Thorntons and its residents hadn't produced anything even faintly suspicious. The phone calls in and out were mainly to do with a wedding at the end of August, now just seven days away. The Murphys had few visitors, and the police were convinced that Sean Donovan, who was rumoured to be in Liverpool, had never been near Ince Blundell. The snitch had done the house over when everyone was out without finding the Semtex. 'Mind you, I'd need a week to go over a big place like that properly,' he said. 'I didn't have time to touch the loft or the garden.'

The gardener had recently popped his clogs by falling into the lily-pond, but he was an old feller, pickled to the gills, it was all quite above board. He had left all his worldly goods to the Murphys, but from subsequent recorded phone conversations, this seemed to have turned out to be a loss rather than a profit.

Sergeant Patrick Watson had conferred with his superiors, and it had been decided to continue surveillance until the day of the wedding. Once it was over, and if nothing had happened, the police operation would be wound down. The helicopter had already been called off after the crew complained bitterly that they were fed up spying on bloody flowers. But a wedding provided the perfect opportunity for an assignation between Murphy and Donovan, what with a large number of guests, many of them strangers to each other. From what he'd overheard, Patrick knew there were fifty people coming by coach from London. He needed to keep his eye on that wedding, and he knew exactly how he would do it.

'How?' his partner, Michael Jones, asked scathingly. He was fed up to the teeth, if the truth be known. Watching Murphy had been *his* idea, yet Watson seemed to be getting all the credit. Frankly, he'd be pleased if the whole operation was deemed a waste of time, effort and expense, and Watson fell flat on his bovine face.

'I'm going as a guest, old chap,' Patrick said, which floored Michael Jones completely. And 'old chap'!

Lately, the turd had started to talk as if he'd gone to Eton.

It was all Ms Kirsty Turner's idea. Patrick was by now wholly in love with Kirsty and she with him. It was Kirsty who had told him that Dicky, his son, longed for a gerbil, and Patrick had supplied one forthwith. (Dicky would have been horrified had he known that the father he had never met pored over his essays and admired his neat sums.)

'From how you describe Mae, she wouldn't dream of turning you away if you arrived at the reception with a wedding present,' Kirsty, who had been told every detail of Patrick's work and knew all about the Murphys, said reasonably. 'You said there was no animosity when you broke up, that you were merely incompatible. As you were Alice's stepfather for a short while, and you saw the notice in the *Echo*, you came to wish her and her husband good luck.'

'I suppose I could.' Patrick was truly ashamed of his past, and had made light of the break-up of his marriage. He prayed Kirsty would never discover that the incompatibility he spoke of arose from the fact Mae had professed an unwillingness to being beaten stupid or made violent love to at the drop of a hat.

'Next time we go to town,' Kirsty said, 'we'll buy a present, nothing too ostentatious, just a nice set of coffee mugs or some pretty towels. And don't forget, darling, it would make an ideal opportunity to introduce yourself to Dicky. I still can't understand why you haven't already.'

It was raining steadily in Frankfurt when the small, bent figure of Otto Vogler let himself into the dusty darkness of Blumenstrasse 115. Overhead, black clouds plodded heavily across a watery grey sky. (Which was no more than Germany could expect, for this was not a country that had recently plumped for a teenaged government, led by a slightly balding Christ-like figure with a face like Peter Pan's and an ability to control the weather.)

Today would be the last time Otto would visit the shoe-repair shop where he had worked for just over half a century of his long life. He was giving up. He had just come out of hospital, having had a lung removed, he was nearly blind, and what had once been a satisfying and fulfilling occupation had been hijacked by glitzy places where you sat shoeless on a stool for ten minutes while your footwear was badly repaired for twice as much as he charged.

For years Otto had found himself with little to do. He still came to the shop because it gave him a sense of purpose, and was a change from his featureless apartment, though he barely made enough to pay the rent. His time was mainly spent listening to the wireless. He even closed for lunch, as if it mattered any more.

He switched on the light, which seemed dimmer than he remembered – it was six or seven weeks since he had been in – but didn't conceal the state of the shop. Dust, dirt, everywhere, and the smell was foul, as if a small animal had died and was rotting away beneath the ancient floorboards. He was too tired to clean it. Each day he woke up more weary, slightly sicker, more despondent than the day before. He could see no point in going on. He had no family; he had never married. The thing that bore down on him most heavily was the sense of disillusionment with what the world had become. Otto had spent the Second World War in Yugoslavia fighting against his own countrymen, and had thought the successful battle against Fascism would lead to something breathtakingly great, a new order, a fresh way of running things; equality, liberty, fraternity, as the French might say. But it had all stayed the same, with capitalism as king, and socialism a lost cause.

With an effort, he stooped to pick up the post that had arrived while he had been away. Nothing but circulars and bills. He put them beside the till to take with him when he left. Every last bill would be paid, even if he had to use his pension to finish them off. He was a man of honour. No one would ever say that Otto Vogler had left unsettled debts.

He ran his fingers over the till, which was as old as the shop itself and possibly a museum piece by now, like himself, he thought, with a rare glimmer of amusement. An assistant, usually a woman, used to operate it, write receipts, take the money in the old days when he was busily repairing shoes in the small room at the back.

'You old fool, stop being so maudlin,' he told himself sternly. He had come to collect whatever personal items he wished to keep before leaving the shop for ever. There were a few books, a scarf, an umbrella, several cheap pens, writing paper. He put them together on the counter, and wondered if the old wireless was worth taking.

It was then he noticed the letter; rather more than a letter, more a package, very bulky, in a large brown envelope with a British stamp. He recalled signing for it on the morning he was taken sick, which meant he had

had to leave early for the first time in his life and hadn't been back since. In the meantime, the letter, the package, had slipped his mind. He opened it curiously, hoping it might be from some of his old comrades in London, still fighting a losing battle against the inevitable: the mixed economies, the social democracies, the 'Third Ways' that the politicians dreamed up. He could read, if not speak, English well. He had taught himself as a young man, anxious to enjoy the works of Shakespeare and Dickens in the original.

This seemed too grand, though, to come from one of those societies run by old men with no funds to speak of, Otto thought, as he pulled out an expensive silver folder. He reached in his pocket for his reading glasses, with their thick, heavy lenses, perched them on his nose and went into the workshop, where he sat at his bench and switched on the bright, overhead lamp he used to work by.

After a few minutes, he threw down the file with a humph of disgust. He had more or less got the gist of the contents. What had this got to do with him? What did he, a man who had worked all his life with his hands, with lasts and leather, a hammer and tacks, know about computers? He turned to the front page. By now he wasn't surprised to find the covering letter wasn't for him, though it was his address, but for Hauptmannwagen along the road, one of the multinationals he loathed, forever spreading their greedy tentacles further and further around the earth.

And what sort of person was this, this – Otto peered closely at the name at the bottom of the letter – Alexander Murphy, who had invented the evil, heinous system to spy on his fellow men, as if they were rats in a laboratory, so that their every move was watched, noted, judged? People like Murphy would sell their souls for money, he thought, with the utmost contempt.

He picked up the file again, and this time read it through from beginning to end, taxing his fading eyesight to the furthest limit. When he finished, he put it on the bench with a heavy heart and heavy eyes. So, this was what the brave workers in the old eastern bloc were to be subjected to. Instead of the iron hand of Communism, a rather more intangible evil would control their bodies, their minds, their souls. Even in Great Britain, the cradle of democracy, a country loud in its advocacy of civil rights for others less fortunate, the system had already been tried out, successfully it would seem, and without the workers' knowledge. Hauptmannwagen were invited to inspect a similar installation at Hawkins & Son, in a place called Skelmersdale, should they so wish.

What should he do now? An honest man would pass on this – this quotation, to its proper destination with apologies for the delay, but an honourable man would see that his duty lay elsewhere.

And Otto Vogler had always been an honourable man.

What, an astonished Eddie McNulty wondered, were his old black and white shoes doing in the middle of the window of a video rental shop in Kirkby town centre? (The sweet and tobacconist had turned down the twenty-five quid a week Taki Ariake had offered to display the shoes, on the grounds that people would laugh. The owner of the video shop liked making people laugh, and anyway thought the whole thing a touch surreal and terribly romantic, though this Mae must be a hefty piece if she took size ten.)

There was a note under the plastic stand on which the shoes stood.

ANYONE WITH KNOWLEDGE OF A WOMAN CALLED MAE, AND/OR THE PERSON WHO OWNED THESE

SHOES IN 1990/91, PLEASE CONTACT TAKI ARIAKE ON
THE FOLLOWING NUMBER. A REWARD IS OFFERED.

Under different circumstances, Eddie would have been on the phone like a shot after the reward. The shoes were his. And they weren't old, either, he'd only worn them half a dozen times. He was as passionate about clothes as any woman, and always remembered where and when he had bought things and how much they had cost, or took a guess at how much they had cost some other woman's husband if they had been in return for services rendered. He had bought that particular pair of shoes the day the Gulf War started, to go with his pinstriped suit, and they had mysteriously disappeared about three months later. Mae had sworn she knew nothing about it, but from the note it would appear she had.

The different circumstances were thus: Eddie McNulty was now Mister Eddie, who managed and was a partner at Cleopatra's, which was doing great business and looked certain to be a success. As soon as Emily had made enough to cover her investment, they intended to open another branch in Liverpool, Seaforth or Waterloo. Mister Eddie wasn't the sort of person who rang up and claimed rewards — it was like finding someone's cat. And he didn't like the shoes any more, either. They looked cheap.

Nevertheless, the situation was intriguing. He'd like to know how this geezer, Taki Ariake (peculiar name), had come by them, and what exactly his daughter had to do with it. He'd give him a ring from the salon tomorrow, and tell him to stuff his reward. Mister Eddie was only calling out of the goodness of his heart.

The young receptionist at Hawkins & Son had been chosen for her flashy good looks, which gelled perfectly with the flashy reception area, with its thick, pearl grey carpet and stainless steel and leather furnishings. No regard had been paid to the tact and good humour required in a post at the very vanguard of an aggressive, upwardly thrusting company.

'Good morning, Hawkins & Son. How can I help you?' the receptionist enquired falsely, when the phone rang on Tuesday morning at five past nine. Privately, she thought, 'Fucking hell, it's only five past nine. Some people must think I live here.'

'*Guten Morgen*. May I please speak with the chop suey,' a halting, guttural voice enquired courteously.

The receptionist wouldn't have recognised courtesy had it picked her up and thrown her to the ground. 'The what?' she demanded rudely.

'Your chop suey. I would like to speak to him if it is not inconvenient.'

'I don't understand what you're on about. Would you mind speaking more clearly?'

At that moment, Hawkins's son chose to put in an appearance. He was a loutish person, almost thirty, of limited intelligence and no visible appeal to man or woman. Nevertheless, the receptionist covered the receiver with her hand and flashed him a hypocritical smile. 'I've got this stupid foreign creep on the phone who wants to speak to our chop suey.'

The caller had begun to spell his request, his voice by now desperate with the effort of trying to make himself understood, and she wrote the letters down, her fingers edgy with impatience. 'Shop steward! Well, why didn't you say so in the first place?' She covered the receiver again and spoke to Hawkins's son. 'Have we got a shop steward?'

'Of sorts.' The man grinned mockingly. The unions had been emasculated under Thatcher. Nowadays, they were about as much use as a mouse in a circus.

'In that case, can this creep speak to him?'

'It's her, actually. Bessie Riddick. She works in Packing. Put him through, it won't hurt. Give Bessie a thrill. She's so fucking old and hideous, I bet she hasn't had a thrill in years.'

This decision, taken so lightly and so contemptuously, would shortly bring Hawkins & Son to its knees and cost the firm several million pounds in lost production.

The message was on the answering-machine when Taki returned from a day spent punting on the Cam with a delightful young lady companion. There had already been several calls laying claim to the shoes and asking for the reward. A few simple questions had revealed the callers to be bogus. This caller, though, didn't want anything for his trouble. He merely left his number, and pooh-poohed any suggestion of a reward. Taki rang the Liverpool number, feeling more hopeful this time.

'Cleopatra's Health and Beauty Salon,' a woman's firm, pleasant voice answered.

'Can I speak to Mr Edward McNulty?'

'Hold on a moment, he's in the middle of a massage.'

The voice rose a fraction. 'Mister Eddie, there's a call for you.'

From two hundred miles or so away, Taki heard a light masculine voice say, 'Don't move, luv. I'll be back in just a minute to do your thighs. Hello, Mister Eddie speaking.'

'This is Taki Ariake. I've just received your message about the shoes.'

'Oh, yes, the shoes. They're mine, least they were when I last saw them. I'd very much like to know how you came by them, mate.'

'I believe it was your daughter who gave them to me, my own shoes having unfortunately been stolen.'

'Our Mae? The little bitch. She swore she hadn't a clue where they'd gone. I'll give her a piece of me mind when I get home.'

Then Taki knew with utter certainty that his quest had been successful. He'd found his Good Samaritan. 'But it was a gesture of pure kindness on Mae's part, Mr McNulty,' he protested fervently. Mae hadn't exactly saved his life, but she had rescued him from a certain amount of embarrassment. If the police had found him lying in that alley, drunk out of his mind, it wouldn't have enhanced his reputation had the news got back to Boston.

Mister Eddie said, a touch proudly, 'That sounds just like our Mae.'

'I would very much like to thank her personally, if that is possible. I had meant to return the shoes, and the money she loaned me, but I'm afraid I lost her address.'

'You can keep the shoes, mate, and as I said before, I don't want any reward.' Mister Eddie reeled off an address. 'Try and come early morning or late evening. If Mae's not there, someone'll tell you where she is.'

'Who was that?' Emily enquired, when Eddie replaced the receiver in the salon.

'Just some bloke, sounded like a Yank to me,' Eddie replied nonchalantly. He had already forgotten about the incident by the time he returned to the cubicle and began pounding and squeezing the thighs of a plump, wholesome housewife of about twenty-five. Christ, this was a job in a million. He wasn't quite sure what he'd done to deserve it but it would appear that every dream he'd ever had had come true.

The phone rang again and Emily answered, 'Cleopatra's Health and Beauty Salon.' It was a woman wishing to make an appointment for a facial on Saturday afternoon. 'I'm terribly sorry, but Mister Eddie is completely booked up that day,' she said. They had decided to lie, rather than say Eddie wouldn't be available on Saturday. It looked bad, when the place had only been open two weeks. But Saturday was the wedding, which he didn't want to miss. Emily wouldn't be there on Friday either, as she had the food to prepare.

Emily uttered a sigh of contentment. Cleopatra's was buzzing. Upstairs, the various items of exercise equipment were creaking and groaning with use. There was someone in the sauna. Tina was just finishing off a perm, and a customer in a silver gown was waiting for a blow-dry. In the cubicle at the far end of the room, Eddie was giving Mrs Lord a full body massage. She sometimes worried what Eddie got up to behind the silver polyester curtains, but whatever it was, the customers seemed to like it, and kept coming back for more.

It had been Emily's idea to paint the little backyard white, buy a plastic tree and some cheap garden furniture, so customers could wait outside if the weather was nice, or cool off with a cold drink after a session of vigorous exercise. Which reminded her: she must buy some more Coke and lemonade for the fridge.

The small expense involved had turned out to be more than worth it. Several women were in the yard right now, she could hear them chatting away happily. As far as she was aware, they hadn't known each other when they came in. But Cleopatra's was becoming almost like a club, a place where working-class women came to meet their friends, get to know others, to be pampered, relax, exercise, be made beautiful, or to submit their bodies to manipulation by Eddie's expert hands, or their faces to his equally expert knowledge on how they should be made up. Charges were reasonable, much less than half the cost of similar establishments, where the surroundings might well be more plush and the equipment more expensive, but the atmosphere could not possibly be more friendly.

Of course, Mister Eddie was the star attraction. He seemed to have a natural affinity with women, just as Van Gogh had had an affinity with paint, and Yehudi Menuhin with the violin. He gave each individual woman his total attention, as if how they looked, or how they felt, was of genuine concern. And it *was!* Nothing was faked.

Emily picked up the phone and dialled Thorntons. 'I just rang to see if you were all right,' she said, when Mae answered. Eustace had been buried on Friday afternoon, and Mae had cried bitterly throughout the service.

To Emily's relief, she sounded her old cheerful self. 'I'm fine. I'm sorry I made such a show of meself in church, but I'm over it now. I'm just glad I was privileged to know him, that's all. He was such a nice old man.'

'We have the wedding to look forward to on Saturday,' Emily reminded her.

'I know, Em. Me grandad's cut the grass and done a bit of weeding. He's just about to tidy up the shed, get rid of those old sacks, like.' Mae's voice lowered to a whisper. 'Your husband's home again, shut in his study. I don't know whether to offer him a cup of coffee or not. I bet he's had nothing to eat all day. Should I take him something?'

Emily pulled a face. 'If you wouldn't mind, Mae. A coffee, and perhaps a bite to eat – a sandwich.'

She rang off. Oh, *Alex!* What on earth was she to do with him?

Alex was in his study playing Hearts on the computer, a game he had once been able to do in less than a minute, but now couldn't manage in ten. He had lost the knack, which wasn't surprising as his brain seemed to have acquired the consistency of cotton wool. He saw everything through a blur of white, frothy clouds. His thought processes were equally unclear. For Alex was unable to adjust to the fact that he had made a mistake, that his imminent downfall was due entirely to his own incompetence in sending the most important letter of his life to the wrong address. He badly needed another person to blame. Things wouldn't seem quite so tragic if they were someone else's fault. But now he no longer trusted himself to make a decision; which was why he was neglecting Murphy Computers, leaving the firm to run itself.

Emily had left early that morning, done up to the nines in white and pink. Had she spent that entire seven thousand quid on clothes? Where was she going? When he had asked one day last week, she merely answered vaguely, 'Oh, just some place.'

What sort of reply was that? What did it tell him? Of course she was going to a place. Even if it was only the end of the road, it was a place. He wasn't prepared to demean himself by probing, demanding to know exactly where the bloody place was. He concluded that she had found herself a job, a lowly position of some sort because she wasn't trained for anything else, and was too embarrassed to tell him. What did Emily know of the world of work, of responsibility, when she had been a housewife all her life?

Alex whistled 'Colonel Bogey', and watched himself twiddle his thumbs. His nails needed cutting. He looked for scissors on his desk, but gave up when they weren't in their usual place. So what if his nails grew long? They might come in useful one day.

The desk was in a state. (Mae wasn't allowed to touch it.) The study stank, mainly because he scarcely left it. What was a man who owned (for the moment) a house with five bedrooms doing sleeping in his study night after night? After a long, hard think, Alex concluded it was a relic of those far-off days when he was too busy working to sleep for more than a few hours.

In the kitchen, Mae was humming as she worked: dishes clinked, which reminded him that he was famished, but there was no one around to feed him any more. Outside, the oak tree groaned as Shona played on the swing. Every now and then he heard Jim McNulty's gruff voice as he came in to speak to his granddaughter. The sounds of life in his own house, in which he played no part, made him feel extraordinarily alone, as if he were one of the damned ghosts that haunted the place. Did Mae know he was there? Did anyone? Suddenly Alex felt desperate for company. Anyone would do.

The phone rang, and he stared at it vacantly. It might be Murphy Computers with a problem. He hoped not as he wouldn't be able to solve it, which was probably why the firm hadn't bothered him in ages. On the other hand, it might be Heinrich to say he had managed to talk his father round. Before he could answer, the receiver in the kitchen was picked up and he heard Mae give the number. It would appear that the call wasn't for him but, shit, it would at least have offered the opportunity to *talk* to someone, use the voice that God had given him. He tried to think of a reason to go into the kitchen that wouldn't make him appear as anxious to speak to the cleaner, her grandfather or her half-caste kid as he actually was. He practised one or two.

'Is that kettle on for coffee?' But the kettle mightn't be on.

'Was that phone call for me?' Of course it bloody wasn't.

'Do you know where the aspirins are, Mae?' Good, very good, Alex. He'd go for that.

He was about to get up, when there was a knock on

the door. Thank Christ, oh, thank the Lord. 'Come in,' he shouted.

A nervous-looking Mae appeared, bearing a mug of coffee and a sandwich on a tray. 'I thought you might be feeling peckish, like, so I've brought you a bite to eat.'

'Why, thank you, Mae. That's very welcome. By the way, do you know where the aspirins are? I have a touch of a headache.' Cunning, Alex, extremely cunning. If she says, 'They're in the kitchen', then follow, taking the tray with you, and say you'll have the coffee and sandwich out there, a natural, friendly thing to do.

'They're in the medicine cabinet in the kitchen, Mr Murphy. Shall I fetch them for you?'

'Actually, it's getting a bit stuffy in here. Will I be in your way if I have this in the kitchen?'

Mae gave an all-embracing smile that Alex found quite warming. 'Of course not, luv. You look a bit pale and wan. I'm not surprised to hear you've got a headache. In fact, you look quite run-down. What you need is a good strong tonic.'

'I've been working very hard lately,' Alex said pathetically. He hadn't done a stroke in weeks.

'Well, it's about time you stopped and had a rest,'

Mae chided, which bucked Alex up no end. At least *someone* cared, had his interests at heart.

Mae fussed around, refusing to let him take the aspirins until he had eaten something, otherwise it might upset his stomach. 'Em said it's rather sensitive.' She refilled his cup, fetched him cake, carefully doled out three tablets, reminding him of his mother who had done the same thing when he was a child and had been studying too hard and really did have a headache. In his present fragile state, the memory almost brought tears to his eyes.

He stayed while Mae cleaned the fridge, and they talked about the wedding. She was amazingly easy to talk to. It was, after all, his only son who was getting married, and he found himself getting quite caught up in the arrangements. He had had no idea the food was to be vegetarian because Emily hadn't bothered to tell him, or that Alice was getting married in what was virtually a sack, or that Gareth was wearing denim. He thought it all rather amusing and, well, admirable in its way.

'She wanted our Shona dressed as a rabbit,' Mae said, 'but I put me foot down to that,' and Alex burst out laughing for the first time in weeks.

Mae decided that Mr Murphy wasn't at all like the

ogre she'd imagined him to be. He had a lovely laugh. Why, the years had just fallen away and he looked young and quite attractive, not the least bit stern.

'You should laugh more often,' she said. 'It does you good, better than a tonic.'

It was talking to her that had done it, Alex realised. He felt almost human again. She was kneeling in front of the fridge, bending to wipe the bottom shelves, so that her jeans were taut on her hips and thighs. Jaysus, she had a great figure: slim, but shapely. He'd never noticed before. When she straightened up, she tossed back her great mass of untidy blonde curls with an entirely feminine gesture that made him catch his breath. No wonder Heinrich had preferred her to Gaynor.

Alex watched slyly, fascinated, as she began to put the food back with quick, efficient movements. What lovely arms, he thought, as she reached for a jar of pickles: brown and slightly freckled. And she had a genuinely swan-like neck. And magnificent breasts, which bounced teasingly each time she twisted and turned between the worktop and the fridge. And a very kissable mouth. He was trying to imagine what she would look like naked, when Mae caught his eye and gave him a brilliant smile.

'What will you not be wearing for the wedding?' he

asked. Thank God she wasn't a mind-reader or she would never have smiled at him like that.

She giggled. 'I'm not Lady Godiva, am I? You mean what will I *be* wearing. A blue suit. I bought it from a catalogue.'

'To go with your eyes.' Alex had already noted that they were a deep forget-me-not blue.

'That's right. Em's got this lovely lilac frock, so we won't clash. That reminds me, Mr Murphy, Em said you might need a suit cleaning for Saturday. I'll get it done if you like, seeing as you're so busy.'

'Why, thank you, Mae,' Alex said gratefully. What on earth would this family do without her? 'I'll look one out later.'

The garden shed was beginning to lose its smell of sickness and stale whisky now that Jim McNulty had chucked away the sacks that poor dead Eustace had slept on, along with dozens of empty bottles. Also waiting for the binmen were several ancient, rusted garden implements that were of no use to anyone.

Now Jim was clearing the shelves of all sorts of muck: bottles without labels containing murky-looking liquids, cardboard packets so old that whatever might be in them had faded long ago with time, tins of rock-hard paint and varnish. Once he'd done and the floor was swept, there might be an hour to spare before Mae finished work, which meant he would have time to start a painting. He had already made up his mind to paint the well, Impressionist-style, Monet – or was it Manet? Whoever it was that painted lily-ponds and gardens. It was the only reason he'd agreed to do a bit of gardening for the Murphys, so that he could paint. Mind you, the missus hadn't turned out to be so bad, and Mae was quite fond of her. He'd seen little of Mr Murphy, so couldn't judge, but their lad Gareth was a credit to his mam and dad.

Jim sang to himself, a rare occurrence for he was basically a tetchy person, but he found his spirits uplifted by the feel of the warm sun on his back through the newly cleaned window, as well as the wonderful garden. He was convinced he could quite happily stay there for ever. An old man's thoughts, he told himself, but didn't care.

'"Yours till the stars lose their glory,"' he warbled happily. It had been his favourite song during the war, particularly when sung by Vera Lynn. What a fine-looking woman she was. Still going strong, still able to sing like an angel.

'What's this?' He took down a tin of what looked like mud-coloured emulsion, if the colour around the rim was anything to go by, and found it had no lid. The inside was stuffed with pieces of paper.

Lottery tickets!

Jim McNulty regarded the tin with disgust. He thoroughly disapproved of the lottery, that monument to greed. It was nothing more than a scam, merely another shabby, underhand method dreamed up by two-faced, conniving politicians to transfer even more wealth from the poor to the rich. Jim felt angry whenever he thought about it. Ordinary working-class people, without two ha'pennys to scratch their arses with, went without necessities to buy tickets in the hope of realising their dreams when the odds against winning were millions to one. He'd recently read that there was a greater chance of dropping dead before the draw was made than coming up with the right numbers.

Christ! It was like an oven in here. The temperature had soared to an uncomfortable level. Would the time ever come when he would stop getting so het up whenever he thought about the injustices in this world, the massive con-trick being perpetrated by the high and mighty upon the poor and weak? He ran his finger around his soaking collar, and was conscious of his heart pounding unevenly in his chest. He felt dizzy. Not a stroke! Please, God, not a stroke. He was bound to die in the relatively near future, but he had a dread of being incapacitated, of being unable to move or speak, of being a burden to his darling Mae, who would insist on looking after him.

He managed to stagger outside, where he sank on to the grass in the shade, still clutching the tin, and took several deep, rasping breaths. To his relief, he quickly felt better. Perhaps it was the air in that damned shed.

CHAPTER FOURTEEN

On Wednesday when she came to Thorntons Mae was alone. 'Me grandad's taken our Dicky and Shona to Southport for the day. The holiday's almost over, and the poor little things haven't been anywhere special.'

Over the last two days, Alex had managed to avoid thinking about the nightmarish path his life had recently taken by concentrating on nothing but Mae. His feelings were rather awkwardly mixed. She had been the subject of a turbulent wet dream, the first he had had since he was twenty. At the same time, he wanted to bury his head in her neat but ample bosom and be mothered, and wasn't sure which service he needed most. Neither seemed on the cards: he didn't want to risk losing the best cleaner in the world by making his dual needs public and Mae taking umbrage. He decided to claim another headache. In his current delicate state, sympathy was enough.

He had been watching for her through the study window. When he saw the car drive in, he went out to the garden, then assumed surprise when he came into the kitchen and found her there, adorable in jeans and a yellow T-shirt. 'I didn't hear you come,' he said jovially.

To his dismay, after informing him of the reason why she was by herself, Mae seemed unwilling to meet his eyes and was in no mood to talk. Before Alex had time to tell her about his mythical headache, she mumbled, 'I promised Em I'd do the bedrooms today. Her mam's sleeping over on Saturday night, so I'm putting on fresh bedding.' She departed, laden with a broom, dusters and a tin of polish.

For more than an hour, an agitated Alex stayed in the kitchen listening to the thumps and bumps coming from upstairs, until he really did have a headache, yet it didn't seem as if a shred of sympathy was about to come his way. At half past one he made coffee, an act that would have shaken Emily rigid had she known, and called Mae down.

'You shouldn't have bothered, Mr Murphy,' she said, when she came in, all flushed and dishevelled, and looking a mite uncomfortable, Alex thought. Little diamonds of perspiration sparkled on her brow.

'Please call me Alex.'

'I was going to make a drink meself in a minute.' She stared into the cup, still unwilling to meet his eyes. 'Actually, Mr Murphy, Alex,' she said, without looking up, 'this is dead embarrassing, but I found something in the pocket of your suit, the one I took for cleaning – it'll be ready tonight, by the way. I wasn't sure what to do with it. I nearly threw it away, but thought to meself, You never know, one day he might be looking for it. I didn't want the cleaners to find it, 'cos they know your address, like. I wondered if I should just put it back after the suit had been cleaned, but was worried Em might see it.'

'What is this mysterious "it", Mae?' Alex asked curiously. He hadn't the faintest notion what she was talking about. Since when had he carried anything embarrassing in his suit pocket?

'It's this.' Mae produced a card from her white plastic handbag and laid it in front of him on the table.

'HELGA, ENGLISH MODEL, HAS A SURPRISE IN STORE FOR YOU' followed by a German telephone number.

'Oh, that!' Alex managed a strained laugh. 'It means nothing, Mae, I assure you.'

Mae shook her head, almost irritably. 'It's none of me business, Mr Murphy. You don't have to explain yourself to me. I just wish I could have thought of a way of giving it back without you knowing.'

'I wouldn't want you to think I frequented prostitutes,' Alex said stiffly.

'As I said, it's none of me business.' She looked at him squarely for the first time, and he was conscious of concern in her blue eyes. 'But if you did, it would be a terrible shame. I hope you don't mind me saying this, but it's obvious you and Em are going through a bad patch, and she loves you ever so much.'

'Really!'

'There's no need to be sarcastic, Mr Murphy. She really does.'

'Then where is she when I need her?' Alex demanded pitifully. 'I'm in the most terrible jam, Mae.'

'Does Em know?'

Alex shifted uncomfortably. 'I haven't told her yet.'

'Then perhaps you should,' Mae said sternly. She leapt to her feet. 'Well, I'd better be getting on with the bedrooms.' She paused at the door. 'Do you mind if I ask you something?'

'Depends what it is.'

'What was the surprise that Helga had in store?'

Alex grinned. 'She was a man. Oh, and thank you, Mae, for keeping this to yourself.' Any other cleaner would have given the card to Emily, in the hope of watching the subsequent drama unfold.

Later, after Mae had gone, he wandered into the garden. Eustace had certainly done a great job out here. He'd never really noticed before, there'd never been the time. Mind you, it was a bit late to notice now, when he was about to lose it. He sniffed the highly scented air. His mind felt unusually lucid for a change, his body less tense, his limbs looser. He tried to think lucidly about nothing in particular, but it didn't work. It was no good smothering reality beneath a ridiculous teenage urge to make love to the cleaner. Reality returned. There was still no word from Heinrich, and that morning he'd had an extremely terse letter from the bank manager wanting to know when 'borrowings' would be repaid. At that moment, in the sun-filled garden, surrounded by cascades of colourful, gloriously pungent blooms, and birds twittering away in the trees, Alex didn't feel as if it was the end of the world. If he lost his company and his house, there'd still be enough left to buy a smaller house, start again with a smaller company — perhaps some of his staff, the few he regarded as friends, would agree to come with him.

But even as he thought this Alex knew the feeling wouldn't last. He remembered thinking in more or less the same way on the plane back from Frankfurt, and it had lasted roughly ten minutes. Any minute now he would start bubbling over with *Angst* at his complete lack of business acumen in borrowing so much for what he thought was a certainty, when common sense should have told him that there were no certainties in this world. He had been too greedy, too headily over-ambitious. Until very recently he had already had a highly successful, still expanding company. Had he left Murphy Computers to proceed normally, in another ten years it might have reached the position he hoped to be in when he acquired the Peek-a-Boo contract. He could still have become a multi-millionaire, more slowly but without the hassle.

He strolled up and down the leafy paths and thought soberly about Emily. It was time he told her that they were about to lose the house. It was unfair to keep it to himself because he was ashamed to admit his failure. He decided to tell her after the wedding.

Alex had reached the pond where Eustace had taken his last, choked breath. The lilies stared up at him vacuously, their petals waxen, reminding him of the old man's dead, white face. He shuddered and returned to the house.

Mae had left a plate of sandwiches in the fridge. He took them out, poured a glass of milk and sat at the vast table. By Christ, it was quiet in here. Apart from the buzzing of the fridge, the silence was total.

Or was it? Could those little desperate gasping sounds upstairs be the plumbing? Why was there a suggestion of a breeze inside when outside everything was completely still?

Alex shuddered again. It would seem as if every inch of this damned property was haunted. He'd be glad to get away. How on earth had Emily stood it all those years?

Perhaps she hadn't. He recalled the long hours he had worked, the little time they had spent together, how much Emily had changed from the happy, bouncing woman he used to know. Over the last few weeks he had needed Emily badly, yet he hadn't been there for her for years.

He would turn over a new leaf, Alex vowed. From

now on, he would be there for Emily whenever she needed him. But as the hours passed, and the late August sky turned misty purple, and the birds in the garden settled down for the night so that everything was silent, except the ghosts, still Emily didn't return, and Alex began to wonder if she would ever need him again.

With a sigh, Rajendra Ali placed a candle in a brass holder in front of the shrine, already dressed with vine leaves, sweets and exotic fruit. From the first candle he lit another, then a third. The marble statue of Vishnu shimmered palely in the flickering orange flames. It should be the mother who lit the first candle of the day in preparation for family prayers, but Rajendra's mother had died when he was twenty, and Vandana, his wife of sixteen years, had never borne a child, to Rajendra's unending shame.

What had he done in a previous life, he wondered, to bring such misery upon the present one? He must have committed a great, horrendous crime, or an act of the most grotesque cruelty.

He knelt in front of the shrine to Vishnu, the creator, and prayed that he would create a child for him. For what use was a man who was unable to plant his seed in a woman to bring another life on to this wondrous earth? It would be bearable, just, if the fault were Vandana's, but unbearable knowing it was his. His own father, Mahesh, had sired only one child, Rajendra himself, though confessed he had wanted more, whereas Vandana came from a large, extended family. She had four brothers and three sisters, all married, all with children, as well as scores of cousins, nieces and nephews scattered all over the globe. Here in Birmingham, two of her brothers lived less than a mile away, both younger than Rajendra yet already with six children between them. Whenever they met, he was aware of the pity, or it might have been contempt, in their eyes for the man who was less than a man.

His father came into the darkened room, where the heavy brocade curtains were tightly drawn, bearing sweets from their factory for the shrine. He knelt beside his son, not speaking. Rajendra wondered if he was praying for the same thing, in Mahesh's case, a grandson, though in this country, where women were emancipated, a girl child might well be in a position to keep her elderly relatives in their old age.

Vandana, for instance, was pursuing a career in the law. Rajendra had been fourteen, Vandana twelve, when he first saw her and had been told she was for him: a tiny child, thin as a bird, great dark mischievous eyes above her veil. They had been married six years later. When Rajendra was twenty-one they came to England, he for the second time. As time went by, and there were no children to bear his name, the day came when Vandana shrugged her shoulders and announced that she was going to university. 'I might as well do something with my life.'

She was totally westernised, nothing like the smiling little girl he had first met. Rajendra would have liked to have shared with her the tragedy of his loss, their loss, but Vandana apparently didn't care if she became a mother or not. In a way, her indifference was a blessing, for it meant she never thought to allot blame.

Rajendra rose to his feet, leaving his father silent before the shrine to Vishnu, and went into the kitchen where he made a cup of sweet tea. It was early, not yet eight o'clock, and brilliant sunshine flooded the room. Vandana, whose indifference included all things Hindu, no longer prayed, and had already left for the solicitor's office where she worked.

Just one child would do, Rajendra thought, a son, a daughter, I wouldn't care. He sat at the table, his bent shoulders aching with misery.

'Is it really such a burden?' a quiet voice murmured, and Mahesh Ali came into the kitchen to join his son. Both men were immaculately dressed in white shirts and dark business suits.

Rajendra hadn't realised he'd spoken aloud. 'I have no burdens, Father. It is the lack that I find so intolerable.'

'There are other things in this world to delight a man. Business in our factory improves week by week, month by month. I thought I was rich when I owned a single restaurant, but now you and I are rich beyond our wildest dreams. Money can make up for many things, my son.'

'Money has bought me much, Father, this beautiful house, for instance, the best clothes, a good car, but it will never buy the thing I want more than any other. A child. A father works for his family and his family's future. I work for no one but myself. Vandana is quite independent.' Rajendra's hands tightened on the cup until his knuckles whitened. His eyes burned with an unhappiness that tore at his father's soul. 'Sometimes, I can see no point in going on. I would give up all I possess in return for that one single thing. Lately, I think about nothing else night and day. It occupies my dreams.'

Mahesh Ali went over to the window and thought-fully regarded the neat flower-beds, the crisply green lawn. What would happen if he told his son the truth? It was something he had contemplated frequently for more than a decade, but always rejected because of the disruption it might cause: the arguments, possibly a broken marriage, even divorce — anathema to a Hindu. But his fervently Hindu son might well consider divorce if he learned that it was not him who was unable to have children but Vandana. Would his longing for an heir override his faith? And for how much longer could Mahesh continue to allow his faith to override the love he had for his only son?

He turned and looked into Rajendra's tormented face. 'You already have a child, my son,' he said softly. 'You have a daughter. Her name is Alice. Do you remember the first time we came to this country? You were only eighteen. We had a restaurant in Liver-pool, and there was a girl working there called Mae . . .'

It was Friday, the day before the wedding. Mary and Gareth had arrived home together late the previous night. Mae came early, bringing with her Alice, Cloud, Shona, and her grandfather. Jim would mow the lawn and trim the dead heads off the flowers, so the garden would look its best for the guests to stroll or eat in.

Emily had started baking soon after sunrise. Too rushed to put on makeup, her skin was clear, her cheeks pink, her eyes shining with health and confidence.

'You've been busy, Em,' Mae said, when she came into the kitchen and saw the surfaces covered with trays of vol-au-vents and tartlets with a variety of vegetable and cheese fillings, all waiting to cool before being stored in the fridge till tomorrow. 'Shall I start putting some of these away?'

'If you wouldn't mind, Mae. I suppose I could have been making all this and freezing it for weeks. I didn't think of it until this morning.'

'I'll make some flaky pasty for turnovers in a minute. I'm a whiz at flaky pastry.'

'You're a whiz at most things, Mae.' Emily stopped working for a minute and regarded her cleaner fondly. 'You know, none of this would be happening if you hadn't come to work here. Gareth and Alice would never have met.' Nor would she have met Eddie, who had changed her, and her life, out of all proportion for the better.

Emily didn't know, of course, but there were other,

darker, things that wouldn't have happened if Mae hadn't come to Thorntons. There would be no Semtex hidden in the lily-pond, for instance. The police wouldn't be watching the house or listening to their calls. A man with vengeance in his heart would not have crept through the garden one night, and Eustace would still have been alive. Alex's quotation would have gone straight to Hauptmannwagen in Frankfurt and been accepted by now, and he would be on his way to monumental riches, more arrogant, more supercilious and even more unbearable than before.

Worse was to happen, but that wasn't until tomorrow. Today was today, and totally perfect. The weather was ideal, but would the time ever come when it wasn't? The earth was gradually turning below the brilliant sun so that it was already embracing the garden with its warmth. The sky was cloudless, a pale, powder blue.

Gareth and Alice were sitting in the arch framed by lacy, trailing leaves, hands clasped tightly, quietly contemplating the start of their life together. The sensation of happiness that they shared at that particular moment was so great, so intoxicating, that both held their breath, not daring to speak in case they broke it.

Cloud trotted after Jim McNulty as he cut the dead

flowers off their stems. 'Careful, luv,' he said, as the baby reached for a rose, 'you'll prick your little fingers.' He regarded her with love. He was a lucky man, for Cloud was his great-great-granddaughter, and not many men lived so long as to see four generations follow. Even so, today he felt sad that he would not know Cloud as a young woman, that by then, perhaps for a long time, he would be as dead as the flowers he was collecting in his hand. Did everyone, when they reached eighty, look at life that way? he wondered.

A benign Alex, infected by the atmosphere of excitement in the house, was teaching Shona how to use the computer. Not that she needed much instruction. 'You're a natural,' he said admiringly.

'I know,' Shona said, with a complacent grin. 'I'm going to be a genius when I grow up.'

Mary Murphy swung higher and higher on the rope suspended from the oak tree at the front, until she felt dizzy. Some of the happiest times of her life had been spent on this swing, thinking about the future, what it would bring. It had brought her a job she loved, and many friends in London. Today, though, Mary felt a touch out of things, slightly excluded from events. But it would pass. One day she, too, would get married and

Emily would make sure her daughter had a day like this for herself.

In the kitchen, Emily and Mae worked efficiently together. More and more food emerged from the oven, and was transferred to the fridge when it cooled. They opened a bottle of wine. Then another. They laughed quite a lot, and cried just a little. Emily hiccupped loudly at exactly the same time as Mae. They caught each other's eyes and giggled. Then Emily held out her arms and hugged Mae tightly. 'Oh, I *do* love you, Mae.'

'And I love you too, Em.'

It was not a day for watching television. Everyone in Thorntons on that exquisite day existed in their own little world. They didn't know, they didn't care, what might be happening in the unimportant world outside. When everything was done that could be done, by which time Mae was too inebriated to drive, a still unnaturally benign Alex offered to drive to Kirkby to collect Craig, Dicky and Cecil, the dog (who would pine if left alone too long). Oh, and Eddie if he was there.

Eddie had just arrived in Daffodil Close. He had never met Alex, but some sixth sense warned him of who it was, and he just had time to nip upstairs and change out of the pale blue linen suit with a 20 per cent silk content before its previous owner was let in.

Anyway, only Alex would have understood the significance of the announcement on Channel 4 news that the workers at one of the biggest car makers in Germany, Hauptmannwagen, had come out on strike.

'Work ground to a halt when copies of a plan to install an intrusive spying system in Hauptmannwagen's newly erected factories in Slovakia, Serbia and Latvia were revealed,' the announcer said gravely. '"If it can happen there, it can happen here," a spokesman for the workers claimed. Leaders of the various unions involved are meeting this weekend to discuss sympathy strikes in other German car plants next week. There is talk of the plan having been initiated in this country, though Otto Vogler, the man who exposed this monstrous invasion of civil liberties, refused to talk in detail to our reporter. "All will be revealed in good time," Mr Vogler said, somewhat enigmatically. We now go over to Frankfurt, where our reporter, Colin Templeman, is with the workers outside Hauptmannwagen's factory gates . . .'

CHAPTER FIFTEEN

His last week in Cambridge was a non-stop round of farewell dinners, goodbye parties, and one last drink with the new pals he had made. His health had been drunk so often that it had begun to suffer badly as he drifted from one blinding hangover to the next. He was leaving for Boston early on Monday morning, and tonight his host, Bill Pullman, was throwing another big party in his honour, but until then Taki Ariake had Saturday to himself. There was half a day left to find Mae. He woke up late and found himself on the floor of the lavatory, with the vague memory of falling asleep singing 'Somewhere Over The Rainbow' in the manner of the late Judy Garland. It was a rather ramshackle Professor of Biology who climbed into the borrowed sports car, and set off in the direction of Liverpool.

By that time, Rajendra Ali had negotiated the heavy traffic around Birmingham in his black Mercedes and had reached the M6. If he'd been asked, he would have been unable to describe his mood. This was to be a day unlike any other. By the end of it, a girl he did not know might have called him 'Father'. Yet he was still unable to rid himself of the anger he felt for his own father. As if he would divorce Vandana, as Mahesh had thought, because the gods had decreed she be born with a dry womb! She was his wife, he had married her in good faith, he loved her dutifully. Vandana would never know about today, where he was going, whom he was hoping to see. She might care. She might not. That was something Rajendra would never know.

He had almost forgotten about Mae until he was reminded. Then he remembered her well. She was fair-haired, sweet-faced, not very tall. They had fallen in love, and he had wanted her for his wife. He was eighteen, Mae a year younger. She was his first woman, but he was not her first man. She already had a child.

In those days Mahesh had not been so gentle. When

Rajendra informed him of his intentions, his reaction was terrifying. 'You are already promised to another,' he raged. 'Have you forgotten? If you break your word then I shall never be able to hold up my head in Delhi again.'

As his father spent little time in Delhi, Rajendra could not understand why this should matter. Nevertheless, he was a good son. With an aching heart, he saw that his duty lay with his faith, his father and the girl, Vandana. He was despatched forthwith to Delhi, like an unwanted parcel, not even given time to say goodbye to Mae.

'What happened, Father,' he had asked, the other day when he first heard the shattering news, 'when you discovered that Mae was with child?'

'I don't understand.'

'Then let me repeat the words,' Rajendra said coldly. He was as furious with Mahesh as Mahesh had been with him all those years ago, possibly more so. He could understand, just, his banishment back to India; after all, promises had been made, words had been given, vows taken, but the rest was unforgivable. How dare his father keep from him the existence of a child, as if he, Rajendra, was a child himself, not old enough to deal with the situation in a wise and proper manner? 'What happened when you learnt that Mae was expecting your grandchild?'

His father didn't answer. He turned to look out of the kitchen window.

'Did you make sure that she was properly taken care of, for example?' Rajendra pressed. 'That she went to a good hospital? Was money offered in support?'

Mahesh shook his head and mumbled something inaudible.

'I didn't quite catch that, Father.'

'I said, I sacked her. I let her go.'

'And you have had nothing to do with her since?' Rajendra's normally calm and temperate tones trembled with an anger he could scarcely contain. 'As you seem to have lost your voice, I take it the answer to that is "No", which means that for almost eighteen years I have had a daughter who could well have been in need of help, money, advice and, most importantly of all, the presence of her blood-father in times of trouble.'

'I'm sorry.' Mahesh couldn't bring himself to turn back and meet his son's eyes. He had expected the revelation to be greeted with pleasure, surprise, shock, even, but not to be made to feel hard and cruel, as if he had thrown his son's child to the baying wolves. He had believed it then, and believed it now, that Mae was a bad woman who had seduced an innocent boy. He wanted nothing to do with the fruit of such an unwholesome liaison, something he now realised was selfish in the extreme, particularly in view of Rajendra's barren marriage.

'There must have been some contact afterwards. How do you know Mae named her baby – *our* baby – Alice?' Alice! She used to call *him* Ali. Mae had named their daughter after him, Rajendra realised tenderly.

'Someone told me, a friend.'

'A friend from Liverpool, I assume. Does this friend still live there?'

His father seemed to have lost the power of speech. He nodded again.

'Then will you kindly contact this friend immediately and request that he discover the whereabouts of Mae? Her other name was McNulty. If she has married, there might well be other relatives of the same name. It can be done with a combination of a telephone directory and the electoral roll, so I have been led to believe. If necessary, hire a private detective, though make sure you have the bill sent to me. I would not want you to be out of pocket with regard to the only grandchild you will ever have.' Rajendra's lips twisted bitterly. 'Today is Thursday. On Saturday it is my intention to go to Liverpool to see my daughter.'

The package with the German postmark struggled through the letterbox and landed on the mat with a loud thud. Bessie Riddick, who had been waiting anxiously all week for it to arrive, gave a little shriek as she ran out into the narrow hall and picked it up. 'It's come,' she breathed.

'What's come? What is it?' her ninety-six-year-old mother squawked from upstairs, where she was sleeping off last night's Guinness.

'What the bleedin' hell d'you think it is, Mam? It's the post. It comes most days. I'd have thought you'd have noticed by now.'

'Is there a letter there from your dad?'

'You ask the same thing every bleedin' morning. It's fifty-five years since he left. He's not likely to write a letter at a hundred and two.'

'You just watch yourself, girl, else you'll get the back of me hand across your cheeky gob. No wonder you never caught a feller – you've got a tongue on you as sharp as a bee-sting.'

'It was knowing they had to take you on as well that put the fellers off, not me tongue,' Bessie replied, not loud enough for her mother to hear. There was no love lost between the pair but you had to be careful with a woman of ninety-six. 'Oh, shurrup, Mam,' she said aloud. 'I'll fetch you a cup of tea in a minute.'

Bessie opened the envelope, poured herself a cup of dark brown tea, added a dash of milk, and settled in a comfortable leatherette armchair that was as old as she was. She lit a fag, her third that morning, breathed in the smoke and blew it out again with the ferocity of a dragon in a tight corner. Her long, thin body twitched in anticipation as she began to read the thick file that Otto Vogler in Frankfurt had photocopied especially for her. The quick, clever eyes in the long, thin face skimmed rapidly over the pages, taking everything in. Several more fags and another cup of tea later, she threw down the file, finished.

She felt elated. She had been a shop steward in various factories for most of her working life, stirring up trouble whenever she could. But over the last two decades the title had become worthless. Surely, though, this would jerk those faint-hearted, shit-scared buggers in Hawkins & Son off their cowardly yellow arses and into industrial action for once.

'I'm going to work now, Mam,' she said, when she took the promised tea upstairs. She was already half an hour late through waiting for the post. 'Her next door will come and sit with you for a while later.'

Her mother's near-century-old face looked fretful. 'But it's Sat'day,' she whined.

'You know darn well I always work on Sat'day, Mam. If there's a rush on, old Hawkins only has to snap his fingers and we're in on Sundays, too.' Bessie knew she was lucky to have a job at sixty-two, but that didn't mean she had to be grateful. Work should be a right, not a favour, the same as a place to live, enough to eat and decent clothes on your back. She was fed up to the teeth with being part of a 'flexible workforce', which meant being available seven days a week and willing to be laid off at a moment's notice, even if it was only temporary. Why should the wealth of the country be dependent on those at the very bottom of the shit-heap being pissed around something rotten by those at the top? If a country was worth anything, it should look after all its people.

Bessie rode to work on her ancient scooter, her soul

boiling with rage. She clocked in, and entered the heat of the vile-smelling workshop with her crash helmet under her arm. There had been a time when she had brought people out when the temperature was a degree too high or too low, but nowadays there was no Health and Safety to speak of, no regard for workers' conditions. She stood inside the door and screamed, '*Down tools!*'

Oh, God, she'd missed those words so much!

No one took a blind bit of notice. They hadn't heard. Bessie picked up a spanner and banged it against a pipe on the wall until gradually the noise of machinery ground to a halt. '*Down tools!*' she screamed again, this time with a sense of exultation. 'We're walking out.'

'Eh?' demanded various voices. 'What's up, Bessie? Out where?' Bessie knew she was respected, though more often regarded as a figure of fun, a relic of the days when workers had rights, when they worked to live, not lived to work, when they preferred to die on their feet, rather than live on their knees. At least now she had their attention. She looked from one anxious, robotic face to the next. They were insecure, terrified of losing their jobs, of not being able to pay their bills and their mortgages, keep their cars on the road, buy bikes and designer training shoes for their kids, go on package holidays to Spain. She felt sorry for them because they were willing to abase themselves for possessions yet wouldn't lift a finger to support a principle.

'I'll not beat about the bush, comrades,' she shouted, 'but see those little contraptions in the roof, the ones that were put in last year which we were told were for the central heating?' Every head in the workshop turned to look at the small metal boxes, no bigger than a packet of ciggies, connected to each other by stout cable. 'Well, I wondered why it got no warmer last winter. Mind you, it's not surprising because they're nothing to do with the heating. They're cameras, miniature cameras, and they're filming everything that goes on in this workshop, every single bloody thing.'

'Who for? Hollywood?' someone quipped, and a few people laughed, though not many, Bessie noticed, pleased. Most faces were frowning, some with disbelief. Yet they wanted to know more.

'Did anybody see last night's news on Channel 4?' she demanded loudly.

'Yes.' More women replied than men. Bessie had great faith in the women. They had a sharper sense of injustice, a better awareness of what was right and what was wrong. Thatcher had cowed the men, but only got up the noses of the women. Now, more people had come into the workshop, from the spray shop, Assembly, the despatch bay, the canteen, curious to know why there was such an unusual silence.

'Then you'll know why our German comrades have come out on strike – because of a scabby plan to spy on the workers in factories in the old eastern bloc. And where was this plan first tried?' She paused for effect, as she felt the old power returning, the ability to bring an entire workforce to a halt, sometimes for the most trivial of reasons, but in Bessie's eyes the employers were the enemy, and she never wavered if there was the chance of a fight.

'It said on the news that there was a British connection,' a woman cried.

'Yes, and *that*'s the connection up there!' Bessie pointed a skinny finger dramatically to the roof. 'We've been guinea pigs, comrades.' She waved the file. 'If you don't believe me, I've got the proof here. You can read it, if you like. They tried the system out on us. They watched us scratch our arses and pick our noses while we worked. Remember those men who were sacked for nicking a few odds and sods that weren't worth anything? How did management know? Because we were being spied on, that's why, like we're likely being spied on now. Hawkins will be shitting his pants if he's got the monitor switched on in his posh house in Birkdale, wondering what's going on in his lousy factory. Any minute now, his piss-artist of a son will come in to try and find out. Well, let's tell him to fuck off if he does.'

The door that led to the offices opened, and Hawkins's son appeared, to be met by a united, threatening roar of 'Fuck off,' which he did, extremely fearfully, and went to phone his father.

'What do we do now, Bessie?'

Bessie shrugged. 'It's up to you. What do you want to do? Stay? That means sending a message to Hawkins to say he's broken us, we're not people any more, we're not employees, we're just things, without dignity, without feelings, no more important than a piece of bleedin' machinery.' Oh, if only she could be more eloquent, put into long, learned words what she felt in her soul, like the young Michael Foot or Tony Benn. Her heart was racing. If her audience let her down, she'd hand in her notice, live on her pension and never work again. 'Or we can send Hawkins a different message,' she went on, her voice hoarse with passion and disuse. 'We can tell him that we want to be treated like human beings, who don't like being spied on, being watched on a screen like we're figures in a computer game. He's already taken our leisure. We can't make arrangements to go anywhere at weekends in case he wants us to work, but we don't get paid double time on Sundays like we once did. He's taken our afternoon tea break, our subsidised meals in the canteen. He's knocked a week off our holidays. But he can't take our privacy an' all. We have a right to that, if nothing else. What do you say, comrades?'

There was silence. Bessie watched their puzzled faces, her heart beating even faster than before. The majority were young, under forty. All this was new to them. Most were skilled, essential workers, yet they did what they were told, conformed, never protested, except to each other, when Hawkins pissed them around. They didn't know they had the power to bring the company to its knees. A replacement workforce of the same calibre couldn't be acquired within a month of Sundays.

'I say Hawkins can go fuck himself,' a man shouted. 'I'm going home.'

'Hear, hear!' The response was tremendous. The little metal boxes under the roof shivered when the roar reached them.

Bessie smiled. She raised her arms and everyone fell

into a respectful silence. She felt like Nelson Mandela or Jesse Jackson. 'No one's going home, comrades,' she shouted. 'Instead, we're going on a little march along the road to a firm called Murphy Computers to have a few words with the jerk who invented this spying system. He's the one who experimented on us to make sure it worked. Monday, we come back and we form a picket to keep out the scabs. We'll need placards, badges, I'll get in touch with the press.' If only it were winter and they could stand round braziers, put together a little hut.

'What's the jerk's name, Bessie?' a woman called. Everyone was removing their overalls, collecting their coats.

'Alexander Murphy.'

'Then, Alexander Murphy, here we come.'

Rajendra Ali had twice knocked on the door of number six Daffodil Close without any response, when a woman appeared from a house opposite.

'You're too late, luv. They've gone.'

He approached her courteously. 'Gone where?' For a moment, he thought she meant Mae had moved elsewhere.

'To the wedding, o' course. Their Alice is getting married today. Didn't you know?'

'No,' he conceded, 'but I would very much like to be there.' His daughter was getting married! He *had* to be there. 'If you could give me directions to the church . . .'

'It's not a church, luv. It's the register office in Prescot. If you hurry, you might just get there in time.'

'Will you share my bed with me tonight, whoever you are?'

The words, his first ever to Emily, had come back to him, and they had been buzzing through his head ever since Alex had seen his wife dressed for the wedding that morning in the filmy lilac dress that swirled around her shapely calves. The sleeves were long and tight, the neck round and plain. The dress had no adornments, except for a row of tiny pearl buttons that went from the top right down to the extravagantly floating hem. She wore a picture hat in the same lilac shade, which partially concealed her eyes and cast the rest of her face in shadow, so that it seemed as if she was hiding from him, drawing away. He felt as if he was meeting her for the first time — not the chaste, fresh-faced teenager who didn't know much about anything, but a beautiful, sophisticated woman he wanted badly to know better.

'Will you share my bed with me tonight, my darling Emily?'

He longed to say the words out loud, tell her how much he loved her. Because Alex did. He always had. He knew that now, and the knowledge had arrived with a force that left him reeling. There had never been anyone else for him but Emily. He felt as if he had spent a long, unpleasant time walking on hot coals and had just reached the sanctuary of soft, damp grass. But did she love him?

In the packed register office, he was aware of her presence at his side, Mary on the other; her perfume, her tallness, her arm pressing against his. She turned and smiled; there was no animosity between them on the day of their son's wedding.

Alice looked so sweet, a perfect bride, despite the hopsack dress and rubber-soled boots. Her hair, not quite black, not quite brown, was combed loose for a change, and the daisy chain that encircled it made her look like a pagan saint. Gareth, in jeans and denim jacket, looked only slightly nervous. Shona, the bridesmaid, an Oriental cherub in wine-coloured silk, appeared rather bored, while Cloud, about to become Alex's sort-of granddaughter, sat on Mae's knee, sucking noisily on her dummy.

The registrar was proceeding quickly with the ceremony. The Murphy-McNulty nuptials were merely one of many that day.

'And who gives this woman in matrimony to this man?' he enquired brusquely.

Craig McNulty stepped forward to give his sister away, but before he could speak, a deep voice at the back of the room said firmly, 'I do. I am her father. I will give her away.'

There were gasps, and everyone twisted round in amazement to watch the distinguished figure of Rajendra Ali stride through the two rows of seats towards the bridal couple. He was a handsome man, clean-shaven, with thick dark brows above the brown eyes that were so similar to his daughter's. He wore an expensive, well-cut suit of charcoal grey wool and bore himself with an air of quiet confidence.

Mae gave a little scream. 'Ali!'

Alice went pale. 'My father!' She looked at Mae, who nodded in confirmation.

He had found her just in time to give her to another man, but Rajendra Ali felt nothing but joy as he stared into the face of the starry-eyed, breathtaking young woman who was his daughter.

The registrar was becoming impatient with the strange shenanigans, half expecting Jeremy Beadle to pop up from somewhere with his camera. Rajendra kissed Alice on both cheeks, sensing that the gesture would not be unwelcome.

'Hello, Father,' Alice whispered.

Outside the single-storey building that was Murphy Computers, Hawkins & Son's entire workforce was gathered, Bessie Riddick in the forefront, chanting, 'We want Murphy, Alexander Murphy. We want Murphy, Alexander Murphy.'

Gaynor had already locked the main door and phoned the police. Then she called Thorntons to tell Alex that he was wanted urgently, but there was no reply and she remembered it was the wedding that day.

Several of the white-collar staff had collected in her office. They looked nervous. Some of their own workers had gone out the back and were fraternising with the enemy, wanting to know what was going on.

'What shall we do till the police arrive?' the chief designer asked nervously.

'Nothing,' Gaynor said sensibly. It was the first major crisis she had ever had to face, and she was impressed with how calmly she was taking it. 'Alex is the person they want, not us.'

Fists pounded on the frosted-glass windows. 'We want Murphy, Alexander Murphy,' angry voices demanded. Any minute now they'd discover the back entrance, which Gaynor daren't lock for fear of antagonising their own workforce.

'Yes, but do they know what he looks like? How can I – how can any of us – convince them we're not him?'

'You won't need to. I'll tell them where Alex is.' Hell hath no fury like a woman scorned, Gaynor thought, as she patted her hair, adjusted her blouse, smoothed her skirt, and went outside to give the crowd careful directions to Thorntons.

'You know, Mae, I haven't a clue who some of these people are,' Emily remarked, staring out of the window during a lull in the kitchen. The guests had been served and were scattered around the house and the garden with their refreshments. Alex's collection of Beatles records must have been found, and 'Can't Buy Me Love' came drifting from somewhere within the house. Cecil barked agitatedly at the strange dog staring up at him from the pond.

Mae was scarcely listening. She was watching Ali in his shirt-sleeves giving Cloud a piggy-back. What a great-looking man he'd turned out to be, and he looked so proud today, so incredibly pleased with himself, as if all his dreams had been fulfilled. There hadn't been time to have a quiet word with him yet. Anyroad, he seemed far more interested in Alice than her. Perhaps later.

'What was that you just said, Em?'

'I mean, who's that woman by the well? She wasn't in the register office. Is she one of yours?'

'I've never seen her before.' Mae glanced across the garden. 'Maybe our Alice asked her, or your Gareth.'

'Hmm.' Emily saw that the woman didn't have food — she hadn't come into the kitchen. She was quite well dressed in a neat navy suit, and a white hat with a little veil. She was sitting clumsily, crossing her legs and uncrossing them, as if she felt uncomfortable, and she didn't seem to know quite what to do with her handbag. 'I'll take her something to eat in a minute, if I remember. And there's someone else, another woman. Where is she? She's talking to your grandad. Is she one of yours, Mae? I can't remember us being introduced.' The second woman looked old and was shabbily dressed in a too-short Crimplene frock and a hat quite unsuitable for today's lovely weather: a jersey turban with a brooch in the middle.

'I've never seen her before either,' Mae said.

'Who's that gorgeous young man who's just come in? He's giving something to Alice.'

'Jaysus, Mary and Joseph!' Mae gasped. 'If it isn't Patrick Watson.'

'Who?'

'Patrick Watson, me ex-husband.' Mae's face had flushed bright red with anger. 'He's giving Alice a present. If it weren't the wedding, Em, I'd tell him to get lost.'

'Actually, Mae,' Emily said thoughtfully, 'he looks quite nice. I'd always visualised someone very different, like a bullet-headed thug in a fluorescent shellsuit. And, you must admit, it's a rather kind gesture to come all this way with a gift. People can't be all bad. I'm sure I've heard you say the same thing more than once.'

'I suppose you could be right, Em,' Mae said grudgingly. 'I must admit, he looks different. But I'd still like to tell him to get lost.'

Just beyond the rear boundary wall of Thorntons, Detective Constable Michael Jones was perched half-way up a tree in an extremely painful position, clutching a pair of binoculars and watching his sergeant play the gentleman among the wedding guests. Nice work if you can get it, he thought spitefully.

He carefully surveyed the male guests to see if any bore the faintest resemblance to Sean Donovan, the wanted terrorist, there for an apparently innocent meeting with Alexander Murphy, son of another noted terrorist. That dark chap, for instance, the one giving the little kid a piggy-back, could he be Donovan in disguise? If so, what was Watson doing about it? Was he keeping his eye open for the missing Semtex?

Please, God, Michael Jones prayed fervently, if this case is brought to a satisfactory conclusion, let the person responsible for it be me, not Watson. His foot slipped and he nearly fell out of the tree, almost dropping the binoculars. He swore robustly and lengthily, entirely negating the briefly good impression his prayer had made on God, and unaware that while he watched the back of the house, there was quite a disturbance going on at the front.

The cars had come streaming into the narrow lane, more than a hundred of them, Bessie Riddick at their head on her scooter. She turned through the gate to Thorntons and raised her hand. The drive was already full. The car behind sounded its horn and stopped. She waited until all the cars had stopped, the occupants had alighted and formed into an orderly procession.

'Now!' she shouted.

'We want Murphy, Alexander Murphy,' they obediently began to chant, as they shuffled towards the house. 'We want Murphy, Alexander Murphy. We want Murphy . . .'

A police car containing two uniformed men raced down the lane on the wrong side, its blue light flashing and the siren on, screeching to a halt at the head of the procession. Having arrived at Murphy Computers, they had been told the protestors had left for Ince Blundell. The passenger, a sergeant, got out.

'What's going on?' he asked genially.

'Who do you think you are? Dixon of Dock Green?' an older man, unused to humour and good manners from a policeman, asked huffily. 'It's a peaceful protest, that's what it is.'

Alex had always regarded Emily's family as an ignorant shower and had treated them with appropriate disdain.

They were Cockneys, and he had nothing but contempt for Pearly Kings and Queens, and people who sang 'Boiled Beef And Carrots', and did the Lambeth Walk and shouted 'Oy' when they were in their cups. Today, though, he was tucked in a cosy corner with Mrs Paynter, Emily's mother, a formidable woman with iron grey hair and a steely face (only when it came to Alex), being thoroughly charming, so that she would say nice things about him when he tried to win back her daughter, when he heard the voices in his drive.

'We want Murphy, Alexander Murphy.'

He broke out into a sweat. There was something frighteningly sinister about hearing your name chanted so wrathfully by an apparently very large group of people. Why did they want him? What had he done?

The knocker thumped menacingly, and the bell rang loudly, both at the same time.

'Excuse me,' he said to Mrs Paynter, and was rather peeved to note she looked amused.

It was fortunate that there was so much noise inside the house that not many people had heard the noise outside. Only Mary and Craig were standing in the hall. 'What's going on, Dad?' Mary enquired anxiously.

'I'm not sure,' Alex replied, in a quivery voice.

He opened the door, to be met with catcalls, a chorus of abusive whistling, and an angry crowd headed by a policeman and a very tall, thin woman, wearing a crash helmet and a flowered frock.

'Are you Alexander Murphy?' the policeman asked chummily.

'I am,' Alex conceded, incurring more catcalls and whistles.

'In that case, these people would like a word with you.' The policeman coughed importantly. 'In this situation, you have two alternatives. You can either refuse to have anything to do with them, in which case I'll call for reinforcements and have them removed by force, or you can see a deputation and let them air their grievances in a civilised manner. If I were you, I'd go for the second option. It's less trouble, less violent, and less expensive on the tax-payers.'

Alex swallowed hard. 'I'll see a deputation in my study.'

The tall, thin woman detached herself from the crowd, called for two other protestors, a man and a woman, to come with her, and entered the house. There was something about her that reminded Alex of himself, he thought, as she removed the crash helmet, placed it on the floor with her large handbag and sat down. Her body could scarcely keep still, as if live electricity ran through her veins. Her nose twitched, her eyes gleamed, she kept snapping her long fingers, and he half expected to see sparks fly.

'Perhaps we should introduce ourselves, seeing as we're expected to be civilised, like,' she said, in a hoarse voice that throbbed with excitement. 'That's Sandra Bell, he's Joey O'Brien, and I'm Bessie Riddick, shop steward at Hawkins and Son. We're on strike, the whole workforce has just walked out. I expect you know the reason why.'

'Aaah!' Alex slumped into a chair as everything became clear. Hawkins & Son, where Peek-a-Boo had been installed to see if it worked. 'How did you find out?' he whispered.

Bessie rummaged in her capacious bag and produced a file with a tremendous flourish. As she turned the pages, he recognised it as a copy of his quotation. How the hell had she got hold of it? 'It's all down here,' she cried triumphantly. 'You were using us as guinea pigs, like we were animals, or something, not people.'

'You should be ashamed of yourself,' Joey O'Brien

said contemptuously. 'How would you like it if the same thing was done to you?'

In view of the crowd still mumbling threateningly outside, Alex decided the safest thing to do was grovel, admit to everything. 'I should hate it,' he said abjectly. 'I suppose I just thought I was being clever. I never considered the human consequences, the people involved. All I can say is that I'm most terribly sorry. By the way, would you like a drink and some wedding cake? My only son got married this morning to a really lovely girl. You came in the middle of the reception.'

'I wouldn't say no to a glass of wine,' Sandra Bell said eagerly. 'White, please.'

'Me neither,' concurred Joey O'Brien.

Bessie turned on the pair angrily. 'That's not why we're here, to stuff ourselves with food and drink. He's only trying to get round us.'

But Alex had already opened the door, to find his worried daughter still outside. He asked for four white wines and four large slices of cake. 'At least with me it wasn't personal,' he said humbly. 'In my own way I am a scientist, always looking for ways to further the boundaries of knowledge, but not always concerned about the outcome, I regret to say.' He hung his head in shame.

'Meeting you has brought me to my senses. I realise how very wrong I've been, one could even say unscrupulous.' His tone changed, became slightly firmer. 'Though with Hawkins, your boss, it was entirely different, extremely personal. He's the one your quarrel should be with. He wanted the system put in so that he could keep a close eye on his workers' movements. Did you know I fitted it free of charge? I made no profit.'

'Yes, but don't forget I've read this.' Bessie waved the file. 'Free or not, you tried it out on us only so you could make more profit in the end,' she sneered.

The crowd outside were becoming restless. 'What's going on in there, Bessie?' someone shouted.

Alex moistened his lips. What could he do to get rid of them? Mary came in with a tray, and Sandra and Joey helped themselves to wine and cake. Bessie refused, with pursed lips and a sour glance at her comrades. Alex took a glass of wine. 'If you like, I'll have the cameras removed.'

He saw Bessie's eyes glint with something like alarm, and realised he was being too amenable. She'd come spoiling for a fight and felt let down. He recalled having the same feeling when he had organised a protest at university, was looking forward to a few days of enjoyable chaos and the authorities had given in immediately to his demands. He had had a sense of anti-climax. He said, 'Even better, you could take them down yourselves, dump them in Hawkins's front garden. That would be a magnificently defiant gesture. He would really know you meant business.'

Bessie realised she was being manipulated. This Alexander Murphy was a clever chap altogether. Her eyes narrowed. 'You sound as if you've done this sort of thing before.'

'Indeed I have,' Alex assured her stoutly. 'Though it's many years since I marched alongside King Arthur.'

That was enough for Bessie. What more could the chap do? He'd apologised. He seemed genuinely sorry. She could go outside and announce a victory. She was quite taken with his suggestion that they dump the cameras on Hawkins. And they could still strike in protest at the monstrous invasion of their privacy. She got to her feet, for once stuck for words. Murphy might well be a bloody rotten capitalist but he'd been so pleasant and reasonable that she didn't like to be rude.

Alex was also standing. He handed her the fourth glass of wine. 'Let's drink to . . .' He paused.

'To what?' demanded Bessie.

'Well, to the workers. Who else?'

He watched from the study window as she spoke to the crowd. They looked puzzled at first, but after a while they nodded approvingly. He breathed a sigh of relief as they gradually returned to their cars. Bessie was the last to go, a proud figure, he thought, on her rusty scooter. He'd liked her. She was the firebrand he'd been himself, but three times as old. In those days, he'd never expected to change, become the sort of person he had loathed. He realised he was still shaking, but it wasn't just with fright. It had come as a considerable shock to Alex's already shocked system to find himself an object of hatred by people he had once regarded as the salt of the earth.

Emily came in. 'What's going on, Alex? You look upset. Mary said there was some sort of commotion going on out front.'

'Nothing,' Alex said carelessly. 'I'm not the least upset. It was all a misunderstanding. Go back to the wedding, Em. I'll be there in a minute.'

But Alex *was* upset. It was partly true what he'd said to Bessie, that he hadn't given much thought to the consequences of Peek-a-Boo. He had found the project, the skills involved, challenging and exciting. The scientists who had split the atom must have felt the same, concerned only with the means, not the end, but that hadn't stopped the youthful, idealistic Alex from joining CND. Even the older, wiser Alex knew that if he ever found himself subjected to the prying eyes of secret cameras in his place of work, he would milk the situation for all it was worth. He wouldn't just call a strike. No, he would take the matter all the way to the European Court of Human Rights and all points in between. After all the bad publicity, life would no longer be worth living for the bastard who was responsible for inventing and installing the damn things.

In other words, *him*!

Oh, my God!

Alex dropped his head into his hands, but was so distraught he missed. Until now he had merely faced ruin. Now he faced disgrace as well.

CHAPTER SIXTEEN

After half an hour, during which Alex remained completely immobile, he thought he had better call Heinrich Hauptmann to warn him there might be trouble if Peek-a-Boo was leaked in Germany.

'Where else would it be leaked, if not in Germany?' Heinrich said thinly. 'That's where you sent the damn thing to the wrong address. The fucking *Kommunist* shoemaker guy who got hold of it has leaked it to every fucking newspaper, and I'm sick to death of seeing his gloating face on my fucking TV screen. He's become quite the star. Hauptmannwagen is surrounded by demonstrators from all over the shitty world, and no one can get in, even if they wanted to, which might be the case with every other car maker in the country by next week. The matter is being raised in the *Bundestag* on

Monday. Chancellor Helmut Kohl himself has become involved. I would cross the Fatherland off my list of holiday destinations for the foreseeable future, if I were you, Alex. You're not welcome here. You've really landed us in deep shit. I tried to ring you this morning, put you in the picture, but there was no reply.'

'I was out. My son got married,' Alex stammered.

'Congratulate him from me. I hope he is going far away for the honeymoon because, very soon, the name Murphy will be mud in the British media. This Vogler chap is determined to wring all he can out of the situation. He's kept you out of it till now, I don't know why.'

Because he had wanted Bessie Riddick to know first, Alex realised, so she would have the element of surprise.

Heinrich continued, in a childish whinge, 'The thing is, the old man blames me for everything. You're my *Freund*, so he considers me responsible.'

'I'm so sorry, Heinrich.'

'And so you should be, *Freund*. I hope the reporters and TV crews don't land on your doorstep before the wedding is over, if only for your son's sake, certainly not yours.'

The receiver in Frankfurt was replaced with a thud

that hurt Alex's tender ear, and he stayed where he was, sinking further down into the murky Slough of Despond than he had ever been before.

When Taki Ariake called at number six Daffodil Close the same neighbour emerged to tell him everyone was out. 'Their Alice got married this morning. They'll have left the register office by now and be at the reception. Do you have a map, luv, because it's a bugger to find. I only know because me husband and I went for a drive the other night and we went that way just to see what the place looks like. Lovely house it is, little tiled roof an' all, though me, I prefer slates. I said to me hubby, "Who'd have thought Alice McNulty would get in with a family like that?" Mind you, it's only 'cos Mae was cleaning for them, otherwise never would the twain have met, if you know what I mean, luv.'

He knocked on the door of the impressively ancient cottage, and it was opened by a smiling woman who told him to go into the kitchen and help himself to food. Taki, who was starving, did. He took the plate into the sunny, crowded garden, where guests were lounging on the grass or standing in groups, talking. There seemed to be a great deal of laughter, and the sound of the Beatles

'Yellow Submarine' came from an open window. He hummed along happily as he looked around for Mae, but could see no sign of her. Now that they would shortly meet, he had butterflies in his stomach. Would she remember him, and if so, would it be with the same pleasure that he remembered her? Was she truly lovely? Would it matter if she wasn't, that he had seen her merely through a drunken haze? Whatever way, nothing could take away the kindness she had shown him. He had brought a present, not too expensive, a gold necklace and earrings set with garnets. Her ears were pierced, and on the night they'd made love she'd worn little pearl studs . . .

The other guests were very friendly, apart from a tall woman in a dark blue suit who walked away rudely when he spoke to her.

'Do you come from round here, luv?' or 'Are you a friend of the bride or the groom?' A dog licked his hand. The woman who had let him in turned out to have come from London. She was the sister of the bridegroom's mother. Taki had taken her address and promised to send the next Boston Red Sox programme for her grandson, when she was called inside. He was wondering whether to follow and search for Mae when he noticed the child, a little girl in a long red dress. She was sitting alone in a leafy arch, and there was something oddly familiar about her.

'Hallo.' He climbed the steps and sat beside her.

'Hi.' She looked at him with interest. 'We're almost the same colour, 'cept I'm paler.'

He put his hand beside hers, resting on the wooden seat. 'So we are. What's your name?'

'Shona McNulty. What's yours?'

'Takahashi Ariake, but you can call me Taki.' If her name was McNulty then in some way she must be related to Mae.

'Are you Chinese?'

'No, I'm American, but my parents come from Korea.'

Her next question astonished him, coming from one so young. She only looked five or six. 'North or South?' she asked.

'North. You're a smart kid,' he said, impressed.

She preened herself. 'What do you do in America?' she asked.

'I'm Professor of Biology at the University of Boston. Do you know what biology is?'

'Course I do. I saw this programme once on telly. It's

the science of life. I've got a biological clock, everyone has, but I'm not sure where it is. I suppose it just ticks away till the battery runs out. Then I'll die.' She looked up at him, her tawny eyes huge, and Taki was aware of his own tiny reflection in the black pupils. There seemed to be something heartstoppingly significant about this, as if he was part of this amazingly clever child, or she was part of him. He felt unaccountably bewildered. 'But that won't be for a long time yet, 'cept if I get killed in an accident or something.'

'Let's hope that doesn't happen.'

'Shona! Has anyone seen our Shona?'

He would have recognised the voice anywhere. Mae! He looked eagerly through the chattering guests towards the door. This was the moment he had been anticipating for so long. She had come out of the house accompanied by a majestic woman in a lilac dress. When she spied Shona in the arch, she came towards them. She wore blue, with a little matching hat, and she was as beautiful as he remembered, if not more so.

Shona groaned. 'I'll have to go, me mam wants me.' She took his hand. 'Will you talk to me again later? Tell me more about biology.'

Taki nodded, wild speculation racing through his brain. He glanced down at the small hand holding his, the flesh almost identical in tone. Could it possibly be . . .? She was about the right age.

Mae had reached them. 'C'mon, luv. We're going to take some photos indoors.' She smiled at Taki. 'Hallo, luv.' Then her eyes seemed to glaze, and she looked from Shona to Taki, from Taki to Shona, and back again.

'Oh, dear God!' she gulped. Then burst into tears.

'I'm not surprised you're upset,' Emily said, a few minutes later in the bedroom where she had taken Mae for privacy in her obvious distress. 'Three different fathers turning up out of the blue, all on the same day, would knock anyone for six.'

'It's not that, Em.' Mae sobbed, face down on the bed. 'It's Kevin I'm thinking of, Craig's dad. He can't turn up, can he, 'cos he's dead, and it seems awful unfair on our poor Craig.'

'Yes, but Craig did meet his dad when he was little, even if it was only for a short while,' Emily said soothingly. At least, she thought so. She still hadn't completely got the hang of Mae's affairs.

'And what will your family think, Em?' Mae lifted her

head, distraught, her tiny blue hat askew. 'I'm not ashamed or anything, not for a minute, but you all seem so straitlaced, so normal, compared to us. They'll think your Gareth's landed up with a right shower.'

'They only knew about Ali in the register office, and Mum thought that very dramatic and moving. He's such a nice person, and terribly good-looking. In fact, all three fathers are extremely dishy.'

Mae sat up and wiped her eyes. Her lips curved into a smile. 'They are, aren't they? And Patrick seems to have turned over a new leaf. He actually asked if I'd mind if he made himself known to Dicky, ever so courteous, like.'

'I don't believe you,' Dicky said. He was a come-day-go-day sort of lad, not easily ruffled. But it was a bit much for this geezer to sit on the grass beside him and claim he was his dad.

'I promise, on my honour, that I am.'

'I still don't believe you.'

'Ask your mam. We're a bit alike. You've got my nose.'

Dicky rubbed his nose hard with the palm of his hand, as if he'd like to alter it there and then. 'I've got me own nose, thanks very much,' he said tartly. 'Anyroad, I'd sooner not have a copper for a dad.'

'How did you know I was a copper?' Patrick Watson asked, surprised. Kirsty had told him not to expect too much too soon, so he wasn't too bothered by Dicky's refusal to accept him straight away.

'You were in the car that day when your mate tried to pull me ear off.' Dicky also recalled that he had knocked on the window to restrain his mate from further excesses.

'You have good powers of observation,' Patrick said admiringly. 'You'd make a grand copper yourself when you grow up.'

Dicky squirmed, unwilling to show he was flattered. 'I wouldn't mind being a detective,' he grudgingly conceded. 'Plainclothes.' He wouldn't be seen dead in a uniform.

'That's what I am, a detective sergeant.'

'Are you really?'

Patrick nodded, pleased that the ice appeared to have been broken, until Dicky said, with a sneer, 'It can't be all that great if you have to go chasing round after eight-year-old kids and trying to batter them.'

'I ticked my partner off for that. He was completely

out of line.' Patrick was unaware that the same partner was perched up a tree a few hundred feet away watching him through binoculars with grim dislike. 'Anyroad, we were after a pair of terrorists, not you. You just happened to get in the way.' He regarded Dicky curiously. He'd had no intention of bringing the matter up, but seeing as the lad had brought it up himself . . . 'Out of interest, what did you do with the Semtex? Who were you told to give it to, assuming it wasn't Rory Quinn?'

'The what?' Dicky asked, round-eyed. The cop who'd grabbed his ear had ranted on about something called Semtex, and Dicky assumed he'd been talking through the back of his thick neck.

'Semtex, son. It looks like blue Plasticine. A very dangerous substance, Semtex is. I'm no expert, but there must have been a couple of pounds in the package you were given; enough to blow up a house ten times the size of this one. Where are you going, Dicky?'

'To the lavvy. I need to pee.'

He'd played with the Semtex, moulded it, pulled it apart, thrown it at the wall, stuck things in it, given it eyes, a nose and a mouth. He'd even licked it. He'd made it into a ball for Cyril. He'd sat on it one day by mistake. It had been under his and Craig's beds for weeks. The whole of Kirkby might have been blown sky high because of him.

Dicky was frightened and badly needed his mam, but she'd looked very emotional last time he'd seen her, which wasn't surprising, what with Alice and Shona's dads turning up unexpectedly, as well as his own.

If he couldn't have his mam then his dad would have to do. Dicky had been quite taken with him, though he wasn't prepared to show it yet. Him being a copper, like, he'd know what to do. Presumably not even a copper would rat on his own son. He'd hand the Semtex over to his dad, and let him take it from there.

He flushed the lavatory, and returned to the garden. His dad was still sitting on the grass, looking rather forlorn, Dicky thought. He waved, and his dad waved back. In a way, it was the gear, just *thinking* the word 'dad'.

Dicky furtively made his way towards the lily-pond. He skirted it a few times followed by an interested Cecil, tail wagging, and beneath the murky water could just make out a corner of the Tesco bag which he'd covered with stones. He glanced left, then right. No one was looking. Dicky rolled up the right sleeve of his new white shirt, knelt down, reached for the bag and pulled it to the surface. Someone blew a whistle, very loud, and there was shouting, but Dicky had no idea it was anything to do with him.

Alex could never remember what he was doing when there was a frantic banging on the front door for the second time that day. Probably staring into space, in a trance, wishing he were somewhere else, or someone else, or even dead. He answered it, half expecting his own workforce to be outside demanding his head, in which case they could have it with pleasure.

'Alexander Murphy?' demanded a burly man with crew-cut hair and a broken nose, who could only be a policeman, particularly as he was flashing the appropriate badge. He was surrounded by three clones.

'Yes,' Alex said tiredly.

'I'm Detective Constable Michael Jones, and I'd like to ask you a few questions, if you don't mind, sir.'

'In connection with what?' Alex had no idea why he bothered to ask. Had they come to accuse him of the foulest of murders, it wouldn't have surprised him. Nothing could any more.

'In connection with two pounds of Semtex, which you may know something about.'

'Really!' Alex didn't bat an eyelid. 'You'd better come into the study.' He stood aside to let the men in. Mary was in the hall.

'What's happening now, Dad? Is everything all right?'

He looked vacantly at his daughter before closing the study door. Who was she?

'First of all, sir, I must warn you that anything you say . . .'

'Yeah, yeah.' Alex waved a limp hand as the man droned on. 'Sit down, why don't you?'

'We'd sooner stand, sir, if that's all right with you.'

'Stand, sit, I really don't care.'

'Firstly, sir, I would like to know if there is a Sean Donovan present anywhere on this property?'

'Never heard of him,' Alex said listlessly.

'How about Paddy Feenan?'

'Or him either.'

'Micky Rourke?'

'I've heard of Mickey Rourke, of course.'

The detective bared his teeth fiendishly. 'You don't say, sir!'

The fake courtesy grated on Alex's nerves because it was obvious the man would prefer to thump him. 'I saw

Mickey Rourke in *Angel Heart*, and several other pictures.'

'It won't help to play games with us, sir. How long have you known Sean Donovan?'

'I told you, I've never heard of him.' Alex ran his finger around his collar, suddenly nervous. This encounter seemed far more worrying than the one with Bessie Riddick.

The policeman's attitude had suddenly become threatening. He loomed over Alex and said in a hard voice, 'Did you have an assignation with him in this house today?'

'How could I have an assignation with someone I've never heard of?'

'Are you saying you knew nothing about the Semtex hidden in your lily-pond?'

Jesus Christ! 'Yes, I am.'

The man laughed sarcastically. 'Oh, really!'

'Yes, really.' Alex came to life and lost his temper. 'Look, what's this all about? Who the hell do you think you are, bursting into the house in the middle of a wedding?'

'You allowed us in quite willingly, if I remember right. Didn't he lads?' The clones grinned and nodded, like three bloody donkeys, Alex thought.

The questions continued until his head began to buzz and he thought about contacting his solicitor, but that would only lengthen the proceedings. He wanted the policemen gone. As far as he knew, he'd said nothing to incriminate himself, because none of the questions made sense. No, he'd never belonged to a terrorist organisation. He didn't believe in violence, he'd been a pacifist all his life. Yes, he'd organised protests at university (how did they know?) but that was a different thing altogether: there had been no violence involved. Yes, he'd heard of Dicky McNulty, the cleaner's son, but he'd never met him until today.

'You're using him as a go-between, aren't you?'

'A go-between between what?'

'Between you and Sean Donovan.'

Alex didn't answer. The door opened and a man entered holding a Tesco carrier-bag and leading Dicky McNulty by the hand. Alex vaguely recognised the man as a guest at the wedding. Had the police managed to infiltrate the guest list?

The man glared at Alex's questioner. 'What's going on, Jones? Who gave you permission to pull the plug? Who's in charge of this operation, you or me?'

Jones's attitude changed again. He shuffled his feet

and said, a touch defiantly, 'I was only acting on my initiative, Sarge. I saw this little scumbag take the Semtex out the pond, and that seemed proof enough to me.'

'Proof enough of what?' the newcomer demanded.

'That it was meant for Murphy here.'

'If you want the promotion you've been after for so long, Jones, you'll need more proof than that before you start interrogating suspects.' The sergeant turned to Dicky. 'Tell us what you told me before, son, about how and why you came by this lot.' He held up the Tesco bag and ruffled the lad's fair hair so that it stood up around his cherubic face like a halo.

Dicky coughed, clearly enjoying the limelight. 'I was on me way to school one day about two months ago,' he said, in a clear, sweet treble, 'and I stopped by a mate's house, Quentin Quinn, his name is. As I was leaving, these two fellas came up and asked if I'd do them a favour. They wanted me to look after something for them.' He nodded towards the bag. 'They said they were being followed by two hooligans in a car and felt dead frightened.' His face creased earnestly. 'I took it because it seemed a nice thing to do, and the teacher's always saying we should be nice to people. The men said they'd come back and collect it in a few days. Then Quentin's house got done over twice, and I realised the men, or the hooligans, must have thought I was him because I was coming out their house, and I felt scared. One day, when I came here with me mam, I hid it in the pond outside.'

'Did you look in the bag?' Jones asked, his dull face a mask of disbelief.

Dicky assumed the aspect of a childish saint, his blue eyes two pools of naked innocence. 'Oh, no. It wasn't mine, was it? If I'd known it was Semtex, I wouldn't have taken it for anything.' Which was the only thing that Dicky had said which wasn't a lie. He'd no intention of getting Quentin Quinn or his dad into trouble by telling the truth.

'You lying little ratbag!' Jones lunged at Dicky, and was only prevented from getting his big hands around the boy's throat by Alex sticking out his foot and bringing him crashing to the floor.

The clones smirked. The sergeant knelt beside the fallen man and hissed, 'He's not lying Jones, and he's not a ratbag, either. You got the whole thing wrong right from the beginning. Murphy here's not involved. Sean Donovan is, but he's not involved with Murphy. He's probably back in Ireland by now, laughing his head

447

off if he knows the time and money that's been wasted bugging this house and tapping the phone.'

Jones looked discomfited, but not beaten. He got clumsily to his feet. 'You've left something out, Sarge,' he said nastily. 'You left out the history. Sean Donovan *is* involved with Murphy, even if only indirectly. Liam O'Connell was a wanted terrorist and responsible for the death of Donovan's father, if I remember right.'

'Who is Liam O'Connell?' asked Alex. He had thought that nothing else could shock him, but it had. There had been Semtex in his lily-pond, his house had been watched, his phones had been tapped. Even worse, it would appear there might be some connection between him and a wanted terrorist called Liam O'Connell.

'He's your father,' said Michael Jones.

The woman in the jersey hat found the woman in the navy blue suit lurking within the dark shade of the trees that bordered the spacious garden. Here, the grass was sparse and damp, and the earth smelt of soot and rotting wood. 'Can I have a word with you for a wee minute?' she asked graciously.

The second woman appeared unwilling, but said curtly, 'Go ahead.'

Two children ran shrieking past in the middle of a game of hide-and-seek. 'Somewhere more private,' said Jersey Hat. She led the way through the trees to Eustace's shed, where the small window sparkled in the late-afternoon sunshine, the other woman following reluctantly. When they were inside, Jersey Hat closed the door. The interior was as hot as a furnace, and still reeked of the creosote recently applied by Jim McNulty.

'What's this all about?' the second woman asked.

Jersey Hat spread her arms so that she looked like a scraggy scarecrow in the middle of a field. Her already too-short skirt rode up exposing ugly, bony knees. 'Why don't you kill me?' she said dramatically. 'I'm fed up running, I'm fed up hiding. Why not kill me now and get it over with?'

The second woman who, like Alex, had thought that there was nothing left in life that would surprise her, appeared dumbfounded. 'Do I look like a murderer?' she asked.

'No, but you look like Sean Donovan, who I know to a murderer.' With a maniacal gesture, Jersey Hat removed her jersey hat and flung it to the floor, to reveal a pinkly bald head surrounded by a fringe of silver hair.

'Liam O'Connell!' Sean Donovan gasped.

'You're only here in the hope of finding me, and you only want to find me so you can kill me. So kill me now, for Christ's sake, before the cancer does, and get the bloody thing over and done with.' Liam O'Connell picked up a club hammer and tried to force it into Donovan's hand. He bent his head, so that the pink scalp was under the other man's nose. 'Go on,' he said encouragingly.

Sean ignored the hammer. He clicked open his handbag and took out a packet of cigarettes. He needed something to calm himself. He had been waiting his entire adult life to come face to face with this man, but the situation seemed farcical, what with O'Connell in such a ridiculous get-up and Sean himself in women's clothes. He'd only come to the wedding to establish if his enemy was still alive. Death would have come later, quietly and efficiently, when he was more suitably attired. 'I can't kill someone in cold blood,' he grunted.

'I suppose you'd prefer a gun. Well, I'm afraid I haven't got a gun, so a hammer will have to do. Or a spade. What about these shears? You could chop me head off in one go – I've only got a wee neck.'

'You've only got a wee brain an' all by the sound of it, Liam O'Connell. You've gone senile, I reckon.'

'No, Sean, it's that I'm quite demented. I've lost me senses altogether,' O'Connell said wildly. 'It's with running and hiding all this while, you see. I've scarcely stopped since fifteen years ago when I heard you'd found me. Then I saw the notice in the newspaper to say me only grandson was getting married, and I knew someone was sure to let you know. It meant the only way I could come was in disguise, otherwise you might shoot me to death on me son's lovely green grass lawn. When I saw you – you're the image of your ould ma, by the way – I thought to meself, why not get the whole thing over and done with, give Sean his revenge while there's still the time?'

'You've said that twice already.' He looked quite mad, Sean thought, with his desperate manner, pale, popping eyes and slack jaw. He was actually slobbering. This man was nothing like the man in the photograph his mam had given him, the man whose treachery had led to the death of his ould da. His mam's words came back to him over the years, 'Kill him for me, Sean. Kill him!'

Could he kill such an altogether pathetic creature? Certainly not with a hammer. Certainly not here, in this shed, in the middle of a wedding. He remembered he'd already killed one innocent old man thinking it was

O'Connell, but the snitch had told him the poor git had merely been the gardener. Sean had firm ideas about guilt and justice, and had felt terrible ever since.

'Have you ever been married, Sean?' O'Connell asked, in his desperate old-man's voice.

'Once, a long time ago.'

'And did she have a brother?'

'She had many, six, I think,' Sean muttered.

'And if you'd heard our crowd planned on killing one, would you not have tried to save him?'

Sean shrugged. 'I dunno.'

'Come off it, Sean. Sure you would. If you had loved your dear wife, you would. I sent a message back to your da, saying what I'd done, that I'd told on him and not to come, but he took no notice and came all the same. That was a very foolish thing to do, Sean, brave but foolish. He walked right into the trap with his eyes wide open.'

'Are you calling me ould da foolish?' Sean's dark eyes flashed.

'Yes, but I also called him brave. Could I have a ciggie, do you mind, Sean? I'm aching for a smoke.'

'Help yourself. What was that you said earlier about cancer?'

O'Connell sank down on to an upturned dustbin, and

lit a cigarette. He waved it in the air. 'It's these. What do they call them? Cylinders of death, I think it is. I must have smoked a million over the last fifteen years. It's in both lungs. I've got six months at the most. Christ, these tights are strangling me. How do women sit down?'

Sean was looking out of the window, at Emily, who looked regally lovely in a mauvish frock. She'd lost weight since they'd made love in that Liverpool hotel. 'Sometimes I think I'd like to settle down, Liam,' he said softly. 'Find meself another wife, have children. Before it's too late, that is.'

'That's a fine idea, Sean.' Liam coughed until his breath rasped and his face had turned as pink as his head. 'Shit, these things play havoc with me tattered lungs. What happened to the wife you had a long time ago?'

'She died. It was a bomb. One of ours. We'd been married less than a year.'

'That's a terrible waste, Sean. Looking back, it was all a terrible waste.'

Sean turned on him, 'Of course it wasn't a waste,' he said heatedly. 'Would this Blair chap be trying to force peace upon us if we hadn't started the war in the first place? And if there'd been a politician strong enough to put things right long before my lifetime, there would have been no need for a war and all the killing that went on.'

Liam sighed. 'You might be right. I just think that people like you and me are no longer what's needed on the island of Ireland.'

'Perhaps not.' Sean looked at Emily again. A wife like her, younger, able to bear him two or three children. 'I'll not be killing you, Liam O'Connell,' he said softly. How could he hate such a second-rate, ridiculous creature who had only six months to live? 'I'm too weary, and you're too old and feeble. It would be like killing a cat.' And he didn't have the stomach for it any more.

Sean Donovan had gone, Liam threw the ciggie down and stamped it out. He had never smoked, he didn't have cancer; in fact, he'd felt as fit as a racehorse since he'd cut down on the drink. That was a great act altogether he'd just put on. Sean had been taken in so easily that Liam felt a bit bad about it, but it meant that now he could get on with the remainder of his life in peace.

He turned over the dustbin and took out a large plastic bag. Inside, was a lightweight beige suit, a cream shirt still in its original wrapping, a tie, socks and shoes. With a feeling of relief, he removed the women's clothes he had bought from Oxfam. Every single piece had stuck into him somewhere that hurt.

Properly dressed, he smoothed down what was left of his hair, opened the shed and went out to find his son, Alex.

The sergeant had returned to the reception with Dicky, the clones had gone, and Michael Jones had been left to make a fulsome apology to Alexander Murphy in the hope that he wouldn't make a formal complaint, or sue.

Alex was wondering how much he would get if he did. Not much, he thought, and it would take years. The interrogation had only lasted a few minutes, and he hadn't suffered any harm. He fervently wished he had, that they'd beaten him up and he could sue their pants off. Then at least there'd have been several thou to look forward to, though it would be too late to help him now. As to making a formal complaint, it would mean writing a letter and he couldn't be bothered.

The oafish Jones was staring at him intently, and so far had made no hint of an apology, fulsome or otherwise. 'I know you from way back,' he said eventually. 'Didn't you go to St Luke's School?'

Alex stiffened and his aching head swam. He had

gone through several intensely terrible experiences that day, but this could possibly be the most terrible of all. 'No,' he said shortly.

'Yes, you did.' Jones slapped his knee. 'Of course, you did. We were in the same class. I remember now, you're Curtsy-Wurtsy.'

It was Prizegiving. Alex already knew he had passed the eleven-plus and was going to grammar school. He had won three prizes: Maths, History and Spelling. He had come top in every other subject except Art, but as Mr Barker, the head, had said to him, 'We've got to share the prizes round a bit, or we'll have the whole class thinking they're losers, which won't do their egos much good. The parents won't be pleased, either.'

Alex didn't say anything but he thought it most unfair. If he had won ten prizes, then he should get them. Why should he suffer because the rest of the class were losers?

The wife of the local MP had been there to present the prizes. It was a sunny day and the ceremony was held in the playground. The teachers were on a dais, three steps up from the parents, and children sitting in rows in front.

Three girls went up before Alex, one at a time. They wore their best frocks and curtsied prettily when presented with their prizes. He burned with resentment when he saw them return with the books that should have been his by rights.

Mr Barker called his name and he swaggered towards the dais. At least he was getting *three*, and everyone would be impressed. At least he *deserved* them, not like the others, except for Art, which was a useless subject, anyroad. He was conscious of what a fine, upstanding figure he made as he climbed the steps. He imagined the parents nudging each other and saying, 'He's ever such a clever lad, according to our Tom/Dick/Harry. He came top in virtually everything. I'd have thought he should have got more prizes than just three.'

The head beamed at his star pupil's approach. The MP's wife was smiling as she held out the books.

Then Alex did something that would haunt him till his dying day. He clutched the sides of the short grey trousers that his mam had pressed so carefully the night before, and *made a pretty little curtsy just like the girls*.

There was silence for a while, then a snigger, then another snigger, and another, and suddenly the entire school, the parents — even Alex's thought it cutely funny — the teachers and the wife of the MP were laughing. They laughed till tears ran down their cheeks, and the Art teacher nearly choked. The only two people who didn't laugh were Mr Barker, who was as mad as hell that his favourite day of the year had been turned into a joke, and Alex, who prayed that God would make him disappear altogether in a puff of smoke.

Perhaps the children wouldn't have laughed so hard had it been someone else, but Alexander Murphy was such a superior sod, who thought very highly of himself and extremely little of them.

This was Alex's Dark Secret. He had never told it to another soul, not even Emily. Since that day, he couldn't abide to be laughed at. Thirty-seven years later, the memory still made him squirm.

'I've got a photo of it at home,' said Michael Jones. 'I won the Art prize, so me mam took a camera — she thought the whole thing rather sweet, by the way.'

'Did she really?' Alex was sweating and badly wanted to go to the lavatory.

'Making a formal complaint, suing, it's the sort of thing that gets in the papers.' Jones chuckled. 'They may not be interested in an old photo like that, but the *Police Gazette* would. And *Private Eye*.'

'I had no intention of complaining or suing. I knew I'd done nothing wrong and it didn't bother me.'

'Ah, well, that's nice to know. Anyroad, I was only doing me job. I suppose I'd better be off. I'm on duty till midnight.'

'Do take care,' Alex said pleasantly. 'A policeman's lot is not a happy one, so I'm given to understand. All those dangerous eight-year-old boys to cope with.' He got to his feet. 'I'll see you out.'

A young man was standing outside, one hand poised ready to ring the bell, the other clutching a notebook. 'Is either of you Alexander Murphy?'

'He is,' Jones grunted. 'Otherwise known as Curtsy-Wurtsy.'

'I'm from the *Liverpool Echo*, Mr Wurtsy,' the young man said eagerly. 'I'd like to ask a few questions, if you don't mind. I understand you're the person ultimately responsible for the industrial unrest sweeping Germany, as well as the strike at Hawkins & Son in Skelmersdale. And is it true you're about to be charged with a serious act of terrorism?'

What else could he do but slam the door in the young

man's face and spreadeagle himself against it to keep the outside world at bay? There was a lunatic glint in the eyes that watched his wife come tripping into the hall, her face shining.

'Alex, what on earth have you been doing all day? We've hardly seen you. And why are you standing like that, darling? Is something wrong with the door? Anyway, dear, Gareth and Alice are leaving in a minute. There's wonderful news. Alice's father has managed to book a honeymoon for them in the Outer Hebrides. So much better than a tent in Bath. And, oh, Alex, best of all, the most incredible thing has happened. You'll be so pleased. Your father has arrived. Liam's here. Isn't that marvellous?'

Alex slid down the door until he was crouched on the floor, his arms clasped tightly around his knees. 'I want me da,' he bawled. 'I want me da.'

CHAPTER SEVENTEEN

The sun had gone, the darkening sky was daubed with slashes of brilliantly glowing colours that seemed to be melting into each other. The horizon was a shimmering line of gold. The Paynter and McNulty children darted in and out of the dusky shadows of the garden.

It had been the most unusual wedding anyone could remember. Apart from that dramatic incident at the ceremony, better than *Kilroy* any day, when the bride's father had turned up, knocking the bride's mother for six, they had a feeling that other, equally odd things had been happening just out of sight, or out of earshot, giving the occasion an extra piquancy. Mrs Paynter swore there had been hundreds of people outside shouting for Alex. Someone had seen the police arrive. And who was that sweet Japanese gentleman whose presence had knocked the bride's mother for six a second time? Finally, the icing on the cake as it were, had been the total collapse of the man of the house, from brilliant scientist to gibbering idiot in less than a minute. From then on, there had been non-stop phone calls from the media, as if news of Alex's sudden decline was of international importance. In the end, Emily had left all the receivers off their hooks.

The London clan had just finished an exhausting session of 'Knees Up, Mother Brown', when Eddie McNulty, gorgeous in pearl grey with a rose pink tie, his hair freshly tinted a delightful yellow only the day before, rose to sing every Irish song he knew in his fine, contralto voice. (Yes, contralto.) It was hard to believe, Emily thought, as she watched him, that for a short while he had been such an important person in her life. Now she looked upon him merely as a business partner, though she'd grown fond of him in a way. Since he had discovered his vocation, he had become a hard, dedicated worker (possibly *too* dedicated — she still worried about what he got up to behind the curtains of his cubicle). One of these days, very shortly in fact, everyone would have to be told about Cleopatra's. No one would laugh now that it had turned out to be a sound business venture, and Eddie had stopped claiming benefit for the first time in seventeen years.

She went upstairs again to check on Alex. Liam put a finger to his lips and whispered, 'He's asleep,' when she opened the bedroom door.

'Would you like something to eat?' she whispered back.

'Not just now, Em. I'll be down later.'

Alex wasn't asleep. His eyes were closed, he lay completely still, not exactly wide awake, just dreamily conscious. His in-laws were singing 'Boiled Beef And Carrots', and shouting 'Oy!' but it didn't bother him in the least. These people were his relatives. And the other people, the ones singing the lovely Irish songs, they were his relatives, too, since Gareth had married Alice. None of these people wished him any harm, not like the people outside who wished Alex very great harm indeed.

When he had had his breakdown, when he had slid down the door shouting for his da, those people downstairs had come leaping to his aid, picking him up, patting him, consoling him, slapping his face, pinching him and telling him nothing was as bad as it seemed. He was having a panic attack, they said, and they all knew at least a dozen others who suffered from the same thing, high achievers who worked too hard and strained their brains to breaking point. He needed a rest, a holiday, so that his brain could mend. Three of these kind people had produced tranquillising tablets, and Alex had swallowed them with a glass of red wine.

Since then, his flesh had become a giant, downy cushion, sheer heaven to move round in. He no longer walked, but floated from one foot to the other. He felt like the Michelin Man, with the same empty head.

Emily had insisted on calling the doctor, who gave Alex another tranquilliser and advised him to go to bed. Emily had sat with him for a while, but she had guests to see to so his dad had willingly taken over.

In a halting, airy, nothing sort of voice, Alex had told his dad everything that had happened that day, and the history preceding it.

'Never mind, son,' Liam soothed. 'Everything'll turn out all right in the end, you'll see. These things are only sent to try us. You must look on the bright side. Every cloud has a silver lining.'

There was something very comforting about clichés, Alex thought, like old socks that didn't pinch, or porridge for breakfast.

'Were you really Liam O'Connell once?' he asked.

His dad nodded gravely. 'Yes, son.' Then, just like in far-off days when Alex had been a little lad and his dad had sat on the bed, as he was doing now, holding Alex's hand and telling him quaint stories about old Ireland, about leprechauns and the Blarney Stone, and St Patrick's dad having been called Calpurnius, he told Alex about the men he had murdered, the bombs he had planted, the guns he had owned, the Black and Tans, the RUC, the betrayals, the treacheries, the hatred, and the love of country that was so great and so fierce that it ran through your body like fire, and you'd kill your own brother if he spoke up for the other side.

'But I never killed a civilian,' Liam said, 'not once in all those years. And I changed when I met your mam. I thought I loved Ireland more than life itself, but I found I loved a Protestant woman more.'

'Farewell, my dearest Mae,' Taki said emotionally, when he was leaving. He had forgotten about the party being thrown in his honour in Cambridge. 'I will come back to see you as soon as I can. I've already said goodbye to Shona. I promised to write every week.'

'You won't put big words will you, luv?' Mae said

anxiously. 'She's a lovely girl, but you'll have already noticed she's not exactly bright.'

Taki was indignant: his daughter, not bright! 'Why, Mae, she's a brilliant child, almost unnaturally clever, a prodigy.'

'Well, she's certainly kept *that* a secret, though I sometimes suspected she was having us all on. I'd better have a word with the teachers when she goes back to school.' Mae took his hands. 'Ta-ra, luv. It's been a pleasure meeting you again after all this time. Thank you for the necklace and earrings, they're really lovely. I'll treasure them as long as I live.'

'Goodbye, Mae.' Rajendra Ali kissed Mae gently on her forehead. 'Our daughter has grown to become a fine human being. You must be very proud. There hasn't been much time for us to talk, but one of these days I will tell you how much finding Alice meant to me.'

Mae smiled brilliantly. 'It's gone midnight. That wife of yours will be wondering where you are. What did you say her name was?'

'Vandana. I phoned hours ago to tell her I'd be late.' But not why, never why.

'Vandana! It's ever such a pretty name, Ali.'

Rajendra touched his first love's little round chin with his forefinger. 'Not so pretty as Mae. Not quite so nice, not nearly so loved.'

Mae flushed. 'Don't, Ali. It's too late for that.'

'I know, but I will see you again when I come to visit Alice?'

'Of course, luv. She's yours and mine, isn't she? We should be friends.'

'Then friends we shall be.'

'I don't suppose you think back on me exactly fondly, do you, Mae?'

'Not with any fondness at all, Patrick.'

'I've changed, Mae. I'm different. It happened the first time I clapped eyes on Dicky. I'm getting married again next year to a lovely girl called Kirsty.'

'I hope you'll both be very happy,' Mae said, trying to keep the stiffness out of her voice.

Patrick realised it was going to be a hard slog convincing her that he was no longer the lout who'd knocked her about, abused her. It was the way he'd been brought up, without any respect for women. He wasn't sure if she would trust him with his son. 'Me and Kirsty wondered if we could take Dicky to Disneyland next year.'

'We'll just have to see, Patrick. Perhaps you could come and visit him occasionally.' She had an idea. 'You could take him to the football. Me dad and grandad aren't interested, and he'd love to go.'

'I'd like nothing better, Mae. Well, I suppose I should be saying ta-ra. I'll just find Dicky and tell him I'm going.'

They shook hands formally. 'Ta-ra, Patrick.'

Mae went into the garden and sat in the arch where she used to sit with Eustace and had a good old cry. What a day!

It was almost four in the morning by the time the dancing had stopped and the singing was no more. All the drink had gone and, as Mrs Paynter remarked sarcastically, the Almighty Alex, being incapacitated, could not be called upon to turn the water into wine. The McNultys and their friends had returned to Kirkby. Mrs Paynter, Beryl, Katie and their husbands went to bed, and the younger members of the family settled down on chairs and sofas or wherever they could. The coach they had come on would be taking them back at midday.

Emily went into the kitchen and tidied up as best she

could. She loaded the dishwasher, wishing she had bought paper plates and cups as Mae had suggested. She scraped plates, washed glasses, put the best of the food away, wiped the table, the worktops, swept the floor. Then she crept through the silent house, stepping over the sleeping bodies, to collect more dirty dishes for when the machine had finished its cycle.

It was almost daylight by the time she had finished. She had been up exactly twenty-four hours, yet she wasn't tired. Her head merely felt thick and a bit sluggish — strangely enough, in the way it had until recently when she had slept like a log the whole night through.

She was wondering what else she could do, but realised she was merely putting off going upstairs to Alex. Liam had told her the whole sad story from beginning to end; that Alex was ruined, the house had to be sold, that he was about to be subjected to some very unfriendly attention from the world's media — Emily had already guessed as much from the phone calls the night before. It was as if she and Alex had been on a see-saw for many years, with her always at the bottom, but lately, as she had swung upwards, he had swung down.

'He's been a bloody eejit altogether,' Liam said. 'He always was hotheaded, too damn sure of his cocky self. I hope you don't mind me saying this, Em, but it'll do him good to be taken down a peg or two. Mind you, I'll not see me own son and his missus put out on the streets. I've got a few bob stashed away, and you're welcome to it, girl.'

'We'll be all right, thank you, Liam.' Emily kissed him. She was pleased he was back, she had always liked her father-in-law. Liam really had gone to Mexico all those years ago for a reason he promised to explain some other time. He had done well for himself, exporting Mexican artefacts all over the world. Last January, he had returned to Liverpool, but had been too nervous to approach Alex, worried what sort of welcome he would get.

'You couldn't have turned up at a better time,' Emily said. 'I doubt if I could have coped with Alex on my own. You've been a great help, Liam.'

She sighed, made two cups of tea and took them upstairs. Alex opened his eyes and smiled when she went in. He looked like a sleepy little boy, she thought, without his glasses and his dark hair tousled. The lines of strain had gone. He looked years younger.

'Hi, Em. I feel super, so relaxed it's unbelievable. I think I might take Valium for the rest of my life.'

'I'd prefer it if you didn't,' Emily said briskly. 'You'd no longer be you. You've never said "super" in your life before. It doesn't suit you.'

'Do you want me to be me?'

She sat on the bed and stared at him intently. 'I'd like you to be the Alex I married.' Conceited and unbearably arrogant, but madly in love with his wife.

'I'd quite like that too, Em. I changed, I became a louse. I didn't realise how much of a louse until yesterday. But deep down at heart, I've never stopped loving you – I only realised that yesterday, as well. It's just that I forgot for quite a while. I went into fifth gear when I should have stayed in fourth.' His voice was unnaturally gentle, and she knew it wouldn't last. Once the tablets had worn off, he'd be leaping around and yelling like a maniac all over again.

'Has Liam told you about, well, about everything? I asked him to.' Emily nodded. 'I'm sorry, Em. We're ruined. Do you think you can ever forgive me?'

She nodded again. 'I never wanted to be rich, Alex. I was happier before, and I've never particularly liked this house.' It wasn't the over-ambition, the lack of caution,

471

the desperate borrowing, the loss of Thorntons, the silly mistake with the quotation that she was absolving him from, but the way he had treated her over all those years, making her lose her self-respect, thinking she was invisible. Though that had been partly her own fault. Another woman with a bit more spunk would have picked herself up and made something of her life a long time ago. Another woman wouldn't have allowed the man she loved to ignore her.

'As soon as the fuss has died down,' Alex was saying, 'and we're living somewhere else, I'll start again. But not computers. I never want to see a computer again for as long as I live. If we buy somewhere small, there'll be enough to live on until I'm back on my feet.'

She patted his arm. 'We'll be all right for money, Alex. Don't worry.'

Even though he was drugged to the bones, he still managed to look faintly pompous. 'I don't want you working, Em, not at your age. I'd guessed you'd found yourself a little job, but I'd sooner you gave it up.'

'I haven't got a little job, Alex. I have my own business. It's a health and beauty salon in Bootle called Cleopatra's. We've only been going a few weeks but we're doing very well. We might open another in the new year.'

'We?' Alex said feebly. His mouth fell open.

'I started it with a friend, but it was me who put up the money.' She closed his mouth with slightly more force than was necessary. 'Would you like to sit up and drink this tea?'

'I'm not sure I can move, Em. I think I'm going to be stuck here for ever.'

She put her strong arms around his waist and hauled him to a sitting position, plumping up the pillows behind his back. He felt so light, looked so vulnerable, seemed so weak, like a sick little boy, like Gareth when he'd had chicken-pox and measles, she thought tenderly. She'd build him up again, make him nourishing stews with the dumplings he used to love. That's if he'd let her once he heard the other thing she had to tell, far more startling than the salon. She went over to the window with her own tea, drew back the curtains and watched the birds flutter their feathers in the trees.

'Forgiveness goes two ways, Alex,' she said.

'Of course it does, darling.' He looked at her, flushed with relief, thinking everything had been sorted when it hadn't. 'If you mean Cleopatra's, I forgive you totally for starting secretly, behind my back. I haven't been an exactly receptive or understanding sort of person in a long while.'

'I thought you'd laugh,' Emily murmured. 'No one likes being laughed at.' He more than most, as it happened. Liam had told her about the Curtsy-Wurtsy business. Only Alex, who had probably come strutting out of his mother's womb thinking he'd done the world a favour by condescending to be born, could let such a trivial incident dwell on his mind all this time. She twiddled with the curtains, took a deep breath, and prayed he'd be receptive and understanding now. 'I think I'm pregnant, Alex. In fact, I'm sure I am. I'm having a baby.'

Had she only forgiven him so easily because she had a far greater sin of her own to confess, Alex wanted to know, as angry as a man who was stoked to the gills on Valium could be. Who was the father? Just give him his name, and once he was himself again he'd knock his broody blains out. He'd beat him all the way to Timtucboo.

Emily was silent. How could she tell him she didn't *know* who the father was? It might be Eddie, or it might be Martin McCutcheon, the dark-haired, dark-eyed

Irishman with whom she'd spent one heady afternoon in a Liverpool hotel. She'd only slept with Eddie because she'd felt so desperately, achingly lonely, and wouldn't have dreamt of going off with the Irishman had things been going well with Alex.

But it seemed silly to allot blame, tell Alex it was all his fault. And it also seemed silly to say she'd had *two* affairs, make things doubly worse, when she need only admit to one. Certain secrets were best kept that way.

'You can ask till the cows come home,' she said eventually, 'but I won't ever tell you the man's name. It's someone you've never met, and never will.'

'How could you *do* it, Em?' Alex wailed, then remembered Gaynor, which had seemed to matter so little at the time. 'Why didn't you get rid of it, and I need never have known? Or are you just being totally honest with me, and getting rid of it anyway? Women don't have babies at your age.'

'That's the second time you've referred disparagingly to my age,' Emily said, annoyed, 'I'm forty-five, scarcely over the hill. Two years younger than you in fact. Lots of women have babies in their forties. I can quote a dozen only recently, if you like. And I've no intention of getting rid of it, as you so nicely put it.' She laid a hand on her stomach. 'I'm very much looking forward to having this baby, Alex.'

He looked puzzled. 'You don't seem particularly sorry about anything, Emily.'

'Oh, Alex!' She went over and sat beside him on the bed, but didn't touch him. 'I'm not sorry I'm pregnant, though more than anything in the world I wish it were by you. But you seemed to have forgotten I existed.' She was almost glad that they were starting again, *if* they started again, on equal terms, him with something to forgive as well as her, so that she wasn't the sad, neglected wife taking back an errant husband.

'Will we come through this, d'you think, Em?' He tried to lift a hand, but the effort was too much and it fell limply back on to the duvet.

'I'm not sure, Alex.' She had changed as well as him. If he threw himself into another business, she wasn't prepared to be sidelined again, made to feel second-rate. She envisaged flaming rows ahead. 'All we can do is try,' she said.

'Do you love me, Em?'

'I've never loved anyone else.'

Alex sighed. 'Then I think we should try. I need you

beside me over the next few days. I guess they're going to be really rough.'

She'd tell him about the phone calls later, when he was more up to it. 'Shall I go downstairs and see if there's anything about it on television? The seven o'clock news is about to start.'

'If you wouldn't mind. I'd go myself, but I'm stuck. You know,' he said thoughtfully, 'I always meant to buy a portable TV for in here. We could watch old movies late at night in bed, the way we used to do in our bedsit in Blundellsands. Remember those days, Em?'

'How could I forget them, darling? I won't be a minute.' She patted his shoulder. 'Don't go away.'

She was gone five whole minutes. When she came back, her face was serious and Alex thought that something terrible must have happened. It had, but it wasn't anything to do with him.

'I don't think you need worry about what's happening in Germany or Skelmersdale, Alex. Princess Diana is dead. Nobody will be interested in you, or anything else, for a long time.'

Mae came on Monday, the first day of September. 'I'm glad you're here, Em. I've got some news,' she said, as soon as she came in. 'It's good for me, but I'm afraid it's bad for you.'

'I only stayed at home because I've got good and bad news myself,' Emily said cheerfully. 'You go first.'

She already had coffee made. They sat facing each other across the big table. 'Well,' Mae began, 'the good part is me grandad's won a fortune on the lottery, sneaky bugger that he is. He only told me this morning, but he always swore blind he'd never buy a ticket. He won't say exactly how much, except that it's almost seven figures.'

'Oh, Mae, that's wonderful,' Emily said sincerely, from the bottom of her heart. 'I suppose the bad part is that you're leaving?'

'Well, if you don't mind, Em. Course, I'll work out me notice. I wouldn't dream of letting you down.'

'As if I'd allow you to lift another finger! As soon as we've had coffee, you must go home and start spending all your lovely money.'

'Grandad's buying us a house.' Mae rolled her eyes nervously. 'I can't imagine owning me own house, being a lady of leisure, like.'

They discussed the best areas to go. Mae didn't want anywhere dead posh where she'd feel out of place. After they had exhausted the subject, Mae asked, 'Anyroad, what's your news?'

'The best bit is that Alex and I are expecting a baby. The other bit no longer applies. It's just that we're putting Thorntons on the market and buying somewhere smaller. Once it's sold, I would have had to let you go.' Alex, half himself already, had tried to insist Mae go immediately, but Emily had refused. 'She's not going until the very last minute,' she had said adamantly, but that didn't matter now.

They held hands across the table. 'Congratulations, Em. Having a baby is just as good as winning nearly a million pounds,' Mae said.

'It is to me,' Emily agreed, though she doubted Alex would.

Mae watched through the driving mirror, smiling. Emily and Alex were standing outside the front door, hand in hand, waving goodbye. She saw them kiss, and they forgot her for the moment. She waved until she turned the car into the narrow, lonely lane, and headed home.

Since she had heard about the money, instead of being overjoyed she had felt strangely topsy-turvy, a bit scared, thinking about herself, which she had hardly ever done before. She almost wished Grandad had won just a few thousand, enough to clear the debts, buy a new three-piece, a few clothes, a slightly younger car, have a holiday.

If she told them people would think her mad, but she kept wondering what she would do without all her jobs and the non-stop worry over money. She had always looked upon life as a battle, and it was the fight to keep her head above water, her family fed and clothed, that kept her going. Would there be the same thrill of pleasure out of sailing into George Henry Lees for a winter coat for Shona as finding something nice that fitted in a car-boot sale? Mae wasn't sure. Of course, it would be great for a few months, lying late in bed, not feeling so tired all the time, but once she'd got used to it . . .

Money is the root of all evil. She remembered thinking that once. Money doesn't buy happiness. Sometimes the poorest people in the world seemed to be the richest. Money couldn't buy you love, the Beatles had sung. Look at poor Diana, in a position to buy anything she wanted yet so desperate in her search for love that it killed her in the end. Life was so tenuous, you only managed to hold on to it by the skin of your teeth.

When she turned on to the motorway, a car zoomed past, hooting angrily that she'd not been looking. See? She'd never done that before, not even when weighed down by problems that had seemed insurmountable at the time.

She arrived home to find one of her front gardens a hive of activity. Grandad had dug a hole in the middle, Cecil was half-way down it, Shona and Dicky were holding something green between them.

'We didn't expect you yet, luv,' Jim McNulty said. She looked peaked, he thought, which was surprising in view of their change in fortune. There had been two prizes due on Eustace's lottery tickets, and he had only just managed to claim the biggest within the deadline. 'We're planting rosebushes, a bit late in the day, I know, but these are the worst gardens in Daffodil Close. I thought I'd leave a bit of colour for whoever gets them after we're gone.'

'One's got red roses, and the other's yellow,' Shona said. 'Aren't they lovely, Mam?'

'Dead pretty, luv.' Mae breathed a sigh of relief at the sight of half her family so happily employed. She resolved to stop being so introspective and thank her lucky stars instead. After she'd made something to eat

481

they'd all go into town and she'd get Shona the computer she'd been promised, and one of those mountain bikes for Dicky. The kids were excited by the windfall, though they had no idea how much it was. Craig had gone to work as usual. He still wanted to learn about flowers and stuff.

She hugged Shona and Dicky, kissed her grandad. 'I'll just put the kettle on, I'm dying for a cuppa. I'll give you a shout in a minute.'

'Okay, luv.'

'Can we have a chocolate biccy, Mam?'

She'd bought a load of groceries that morning, the sort of things they could never have afforded before, not a single budget item among them. 'You can have a chocolate biccy every day for the rest of your life,' she cried gaily, as she went in.

Mae sang as she ran water in the battered kettle. Everything would be all right.

Wouldn't it?

ALMOST ONE YEAR LATER

GAYNOR joined the police force, became an expert in crowd control, and was quickly promoted to sergeant.

MICHAEL JONES resigned from the police force and started his own security business.

PATRICK WATSON married KIRSTY TURNER as soon as her divorce came through.

PADDY FEENAN and MICKY ROURKE are living in Kilburn where they earn a few bob in the black economy.

THE SNITCH is still a snitch.

TILLY QUINN bought more paint, and is still trying to persuade RORY to decorate the front room.

OTTO VOGLER's health improved considerably when his public onslaught on multinationals proved so successful. He is now a frequent guest on chat shows, and has his own weekly column in *Der Spiegel*, wherein he muses ironically on the state of politics in Germany and the rest of the world.

BESSIE RIDDICK gave in her notice when the strike at Hawkins & Son fizzled out after a few days, though it cost the company millions in lost production and an enforced change of name to counter the bad publicity that followed. Bessie and Otto Vogler are engaged, and will marry when her aged mother dies.

MRS RIDDICK recently celebrated her ninety-seventh birthday with a crate of Guinness.

STEVE WEATHERSPOON (HELGA) returned to Bolsover and his family when a scary encounter with a homophobic Norwegian nearly resulted in a change too far. He now works for £3.60 an hour making silk flowers in a factory specially set up with a government grant to provide employment for redundant miners. Steve anxiously awaits the Prime Minister (TONY BLAIR) bringing in the promised minimum wage, as he finds it impossible to keep a wife and two children (soon to be three) on such paltry pay.

HEINRICH HAUPTMANN found himself the scapegoat for all the troubles that engulfed Hauptmannwagen. During a snarling television interview, he was spotted by a film company and given a major part as a heavy in their next film. Heinrich is now in Hollywood and has become a minor celebrity, thanks entirely to his looks.

SEAN DONOVAN grew a beard, changed his name to AIDAN O'GALLAGHER and went to live in America. He is still looking for a suitable wife, preferably one who looks a wee bit like Emily.

RAJENDRA ALI persuaded his wife, VANDANA, to seek fertility treatment. She is expecting their first child at Christmas.

MARY MURPHY is engaged to be married.

TAKAHASHI ARIAKE communicates with his clever daughter every week by e-mail. So far, he has never found time to visit Mae. He is pleased to have found her, but rarely thinks about her nowadays.

EDDIE MCNULTY moved in with a woman of less than half his age who found herself with child after a full body massage turned out to be a bit too thorough. He recently became father to a baby girl, Demi, a half-sister for Mae, aunt to her four children, and great-aunt to Cloud.

It would not be precisely true to say that EMILY and ALEXANDER MURPHY lived happily ever after, but it would be close. A humbled Alex managed to escape the worst consequences of Peek-a-Boo-Gate, as it was called in the media, by simply moving house. After casting round for a business that would fully occupy his superlative brain, he finally settled on establishing his own Think Tank. With Emily's full approval, just after Christmas, the Murphys moved to the capital to be within reach of Westminster, where Alex could nurture contacts and decide what to Think. Emily is opening a branch of Cleopatra's in London's East End as soon as she recovers from the birth of Sean – the name just came to her from nowhere. She is pleased that Sean looks rather like Alex, and he regards the child as his own.

Emily sometimes feels like a person waking up from a dreadful nightmare, relieved to discover it had all been a dream, and finding Alex, the man she had married, had never changed.

LIAM O'CONNELL/MURPHY moved to London to be near his family.

MAE MCNULTY bought Thorntons fully furnished, the house she fell in love with at the moment she first set foot inside it, particularly the wonderful garden. For six months, she didn't think she had ever been so happy, with the place full of family and so much to do. Then Eddie left, and ALICE and GARETH understandably said they would like somewhere of their own with a little garden for CLOUD and the baby they were expecting in June. Mae bought them a pretty little cottage in Ormskirk, but was more than sad to see them go. The house seemed very quiet without them, and even quieter when her beloved grandad, JIM MCNULTY, died in his sleep one night, peacefully and painlessly, the way he would have wanted. DICKY thought his dad the gear. He saw him every weekend, and spent a lot of time in Kirkby with the mates he badly missed. SHONA wasn't much company, always stuck in the study with the computer, and now CRAIG had started courting and was hardly ever home. Even CECIL moped around the garden with his tail between his legs, miserable without other dogs to play with. Mae missed Emily badly – they had become such great friends. The house seemed different now that she was alone. The ghosts were no longer friendly: they hissed and whispered angrily when she went in and out of the silent rooms, and she realised the Thorntons' ghosts were only content if the people who lived in the house were happy. Mae was not prepared to go the same way as Em. When she found an old embroidered sampler in the desperately gloomy attic, saying, 'Money is muck, not good except it be spread around', she knew what she must do. She let Thorntons rent-free to a charity that provided holidays for sick children, settled large amounts on her own children, and bought a little pub in Waterloo with what was left. She is a very popular landlady. She works hard, life is a struggle, but that's the way Mae likes it for, as she quickly discovered, a too easy life can destroy the soul.

THE MET OFFICE continued to claim that the summer of 1997 had been the wettest for a century, but nobody believed them. Just as the days of childhood are fondly recalled as being a time when the sun always shone, so the months following the election of New Labour were looked upon as days of clear blue skies and glorious sunshine, a golden time during which people's hearts beat faster with the hope that their country was on the verge of a great renaissance. The rain fell even more heavily the following summer which the Met Office declared was the wettest since records began. This time they were believed. The New Labour government had been in for fourteen months, and some people even complained that it felt as if it had been raining for ever.